# VOYAGEUR CLASSICS

## BOOKS THAT EXPLORE CANADA

Michael Gnarowski — Series Editor

Dundurn Press presents the Voyageur Classics series, building on the tradition of exploration and rediscovery and bringing forward time-tested writing about the Canadian experience in all its varieties.

This series of original or translated works in the fields of literature, history, politics, and biography has been gathered to enrich and illuminate our understanding of a multi-faceted Canada. Through straightforward, knowledgeable, and reader-friendly introductions the Voyageur Classics series provides context and accessibility while breathing new life into these timeless Canadian masterpieces.

The Voyageur Classics series was designed with the widest possible readership in mind and sees a place for itself with the interested reader as well as in the classroom. Physically attractive and reset in a contemporary format, these books aim at an enlivened and updated sense of Canada's written heritage.

# OTHER VOYAGEUR CLASSICS TITLES

*The Blue Castle* by Lucy Maud Montgomery, introduced by Dr. Collett Tracey 978-1-55002-666-5

*Canadian Exploration Literature: An Anthology*,
edited and introduced by Germaine Warkentin 978-1-55002-661-0

*Combat Journal for Place d'Armes: A Personal Narrative* by Scott Symons,
introduced by Christopher Elson 978-1-55488-457-5

*The Donnellys* by James Reaney, introduced by Alan Filewod 978-1-55002-832-4

*Empire and Communications* by Harold A. Innis,
introduced by Alexander John Watson 978-1-55002-662-7

*The Firebrand: William Lyon Mackenzie and the Rebellion in Upper Canada* by William Kilbourn,
introduced by Ronald Stagg 978-1-55002-800-3

*In This Poem I Am: Selected Poetry of Robin Skelton*,
edited and introduced by Harold Rhenisch 978-1-55002-769-3

*The Letters and Journals of Simon Fraser 1806–1808*,
edited and introduced by W. Kaye Lamb, foreword by Michael Gnarowski 978-1-55002-713-6

*Maria Chapdelaine: A Tale of French Canada* by Louis Hémon, translated by W.H. Blake,
introduction and notes by Michael Gnarowski 978-1-55002-712-9

*The Men of the Last Frontier* by Grey Owl, introduced by James Polk 978-1-55488-804-7

*Mrs. Simcoe's Diary* by Elizabeth Posthuma Simcoe,
edited and introduced by Mary Quayle Innis, foreword by Michael Gnarowski 978-1-55002-768-6

*Pilgrims of the Wild*, edited and introduced by Michael Gnarowski 978-1-55488-734-7

*The Refugee: Narratives of Fugitive Slaves in Canada* by Benjamin Drew,
introduced by George Elliott Clarke 978-1-55002-801-0

*The Scalpel, the Sword: The Story of Doctor Norman Bethune* by Ted Allan and Sydney Ostrovsky,
introduced by Julie Allan, Dr. Norman Allan, and Susan Ostrovsky 978-1-55488-402-5

*Selected Writings* by A.J.M. Smith, edited and introduced by Michael Gnarowski 978-1-55002-665-8

*Self Condemned* by Wyndham Lewis, introduced by Allan Pero 978-1-55488-735-4

*The Silence on the Shore* by Hugh Garner, introduced by George Fetherling 978-1-55488-782-8

*Storm Below* by Hugh Garner, introduced by Paul Stuewe 978-1-55488-456-8

*A Tangled Web* by Lucy Maud Montgomery, introduced by Benjamin Lefebvre 978-1-55488-403-2

*The Yellow Briar: A Story of the Irish on the Canadian Countryside* by Patrick Slater,
introduced by Michael Gnarowski 978-1-55002-848-5

*The Town Below* by Roger Lemelin, introduced by Michael Gnarowski 978-1-55488-803-0

*Pauline Johnson: Selected Poetry and Prose* by Pauline Johnson,
selected and introduced by Michael Gnarowski 978-1-45970-428-2

*The Kindred of the Wild: A Book of Animal Life* by Charles G.D. Roberts,
introduced by James Polk 978-1-45970-147-2

*All Else Is Folly: A Tale of War and Passion* by Peregrine Acland, introduced by Brian Busby and
James Calhoun, and with a preface by Ford Madox Ford 978-1-45970-423-7

*In Flanders Fields and Other Poems* by John McCrae,
introduced by Michael Gnarowski 978-1-45972-864-6

*Ringing the Changes: An Autobiography* by Mazo de la Roche,
introduced by Heather Kirk 978-1-45973-037-3

*The Regiment* by Farley Mowat, introduced by Lee Windsor 978-1-45973-389-3

# VOYAGEUR CLASSICS

BOOKS THAT EXPLORE CANADA

# GOD'S SPARROWS

## PHILIP CHILD

INTRODUCTION BY JAMES R. CALHOUN

**DUNDURN**
TORONTO

Printer: Webcom

**Library and Archives Canada Cataloguing in Publication**

Child, Philip, 1898-1978, author
    God's sparrows / Philip Child ; introduction by James R. Calhoun.

(Voyageur classics)
Issued in print and electronic formats.
ISBN 978-1-4597-3643-6 (softcover).--ISBN 978-1-4597-3644-3 (PDF).--
ISBN 978-1-4597-3645-0 (EPUB)

    I. Title. II. Series: Voyageur classics

PS8505.H52G63 2017          C813'.52          C2016-907642-3
                                               C2016-907643-1

1  2  3  4  5    21  20  19  18  17

We acknowledge the support of the **Canada Council for the Arts** and the **Ontario Arts Council** for our publishing program. We also acknowledge the financial support of the **Government of Ontario**, through the **Ontario Book Publishing Tax Credit** and the **Ontario Media Development Corporation**, and the **Government of Canada**.

Care has been taken to trace the ownership of copyright material used in this book. The author and the publisher welcome any information enabling them to rectify any references or credits in subsequent editions.

— *J. Kirk Howard, President*

The publisher is not responsible for websites or their content unless they are owned by the publisher.

VISIT US AT

 dundurn.com | @dundurnpress | dundurnpress | dundurnpress

Dundurn
3 Church Street, Suite 500
Toronto, Ontario, Canada
M5E 1M2

# CONTENTS

# INTRODUCTION

When Philip Child's novel *God's Sparrows* was published in the spring of 1937 by the British publisher Thornton Butterworth, the realistic war novel was a more than decade-old phenomenon, familiar to readers in all the combatant nations of the Great War. What we now think of as the canonical texts of the First World War: Ford Madox Ford's *Parade's End* (1924–28), Siegfried Sassoon's *Memoirs of a Fox-Hunting Man* (1929), Ernest Hemingway's *A Farewell to Arms* (1929), and Erich Maria Remarque's *All Quiet on the Western Front* (1929), had established a pattern of gritty realism, detailing both the physical and psychological horrors of modern war. Any serious novel with literary ambitions that followed these was required to fall in step and deliver what readers and reviewers had come to see as an "authentic" portrait of war. Authors who failed to detail the innumerable horrors of combat were dismissed as writers of romance or worse, propaganda, and not to be taken seriously.

Canadian writers who had served during the war contributed to and mirrored the trend that favoured realism in war literature, while simultaneously addressing how the Canadian war experience, though similar, differed from that of our allies. Peregrine Acland's *All Else is Folly* (1929), republished by Dundurn in 2014, was the first of several realistic Canadian war novels published in Canada, the United States, and Great Britain that showed the war from a distinctly Canadian perspective. Several more significant novels would follow in quick succession: Leslie Roberts's *When the Gods Laughed*, George Godwin's *Why Stay We Here?*, W. Redvers Dent's *Show Me Death!*, and Charles Yale Harrison's *Generals Die in Bed* would all be published in 1930 in multiple editions throughout the English-speaking world, to varying levels of critical and commercial success.

As the effects of the Great Depression worsened, however, Canadian war novels written by veterans ceased to appear altogether.[1] Why this is so is not entirely clear: Canadian memoirs and histories continued to be published throughout the 1930s, while writers such as Will R. Bird, Harold Cruickshank, and Benge Atlee published dozens of short stories in the pulps and newspapers that dealt directly with the war. Despite the popularity of other forms of Canadian war writing, the Canadian war novel entered a dormant period after the boom of 1930. *God's Sparrows*, published in 1937, was the last Canadian novel of the war written by a combatant before the Second World War began.

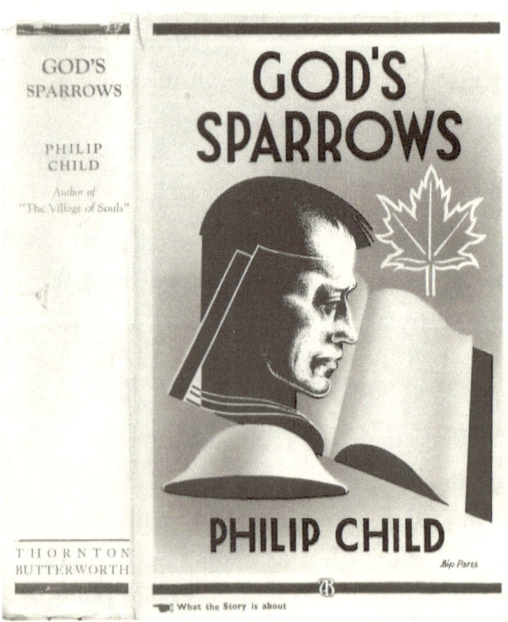

*This is the jacket of the rare first edition of* God's Sparrows, *published in 1937 by Thornton Butterworth.*

Despite its appearance at the tail end of the war book boom, *God's Sparrows* was "one of the most favourably reviewed books of 1937" in Canada.[2] Though many expressed minor reservations about the novel, the overall tone was glowing: the *Globe and Mail's* Saturday Review of Books section, edited by William Arthur Deacon, stated, "there are realistic descriptions of trench fighting that are second to none, and the minute-to-minute recording of mental states in the half-hour before zero is an impressive climax, calculated to move the indifferent."[3] The novel was hailed by Dr. J.R. MacGillivray in the *University of Toronto Quarterly*, while the *McMaster Quarterly* recommended the novel as "a distinguished work of Canadian literature."[4] The *Sarnia Observer's* reviewer wrote: Child's "description of the actual fighting in France is one of the most convincing, and therefore the most distressing that I have ever read." B.K. Sandwell, writing for *Saturday Night Magazine* stated: *God's Sparrows* "takes its place in the main body of sincere and valuable fiction of this decade ... and it is a place well towards the front." Child's hometown paper, the *Hamilton Spectator*, called the novel "a triumph" and "a thought-provoking and beautifully done piece of literature."[5]

The enthusiastic reception of *God's Sparrows* by Canadian critics came as a both a relief and a vindication for Philip Child. While it is undoubtedly true that the war had a profound effect on everyone whose life it touched, the First World War had an especially deep and lasting effect on Child. A quiet and scholarly man with a gentle disposition, he was the most unlikely of soldiers, and he spent a great deal of the post-war period wrestling with what the war had meant and how to faithfully write about the war. Child wrote poetry, short stories, and a novella about the war, all unpublished, working steadily towards the novel that would become *God's Sparrows*. It took him thirteen years.

★ ★ ★

Philip Child's father, William Addison Child, was born in 1862 in Mayville, Wisconsin. After completing a master's degree in history at Kenyon College in Ohio, William emigrated to Canada in 1883 and became a secretary of the Ontario Rolling Mills. The company would later amalgamate with the Hamilton Steel and Iron Company, and eventually become the Steel Company of Canada; from 1883 to when he retired just before the First World War, William Child would be a key player in the development of Hamilton's steel industry, and one of the city's more prominent citizens.

In 1892, William Child married Elizabeth Helen Harvey (b. 1857), of Hamilton; within a year they had a daughter, Helen Mary Child (b. 1893). Five years later, they would have a son: Philip Albert Gillet Child was born on January 19, 1898.

In 1902, the Childs purchased a new family home on 389 Hess Street South in Hamilton. Noted for its beautiful gardens, this stately Victorian home would later form the basis of Philip Child's 1951 collection of poetry, *The Victorian House and Other Poems*.

The Child household was affluent, scholarly, and civic-minded. William Child was a keen historian, a fellow of the Royal Anthropological Institute, an officer and honorary president of the Hamilton Scientific Association, as well as a member of the Hamilton Library Board and the Hamilton Health Association. Elizabeth Child hosted numerous society events in support of Hamilton's arts and culture institutions, as well as being active in the charitable programs of Hamilton's Anglican church.

Philip Child was soft-spoken and studious growing up, and distinguished himself academically at the Highfield School, the first private school for boys in Hamilton. His natural academic curiosity was encouraged at every turn by his parents: his mother fostered his love of music and painting, while his father indulged Philip's interest in botany, philately, and book collecting.

There was, however, a spectre hanging over the Child household: Philip's sister, Helen, was diagnosed with epilepsy as a young

*389 Hess Street South, Hamilton: The Victorian house that Child grew up in.*

girl, and she was prone to seizures and fainting spells throughout her childhood. Helen's health was a constant concern, and the medical wisdom of the period advised her to avoid any excitement, lest it cause a seizure. The Childs were quiet, thoughtful people by nature, but Helen's condition added an additional impetus for personal restraint to the household. For Philip, his sister's condition would elicit a sense of responsibility and protectiveness, a feeling that weighed heavily on the much younger Philip throughout his childhood.

Philip's childhood was not restricted to interactions with only his immediate family, however. Although William Child's family was scattered across the eastern United States and visited Hamilton infrequently, Elizabeth's family was a constant presence in Philip's upbringing. Philip grew particularly close to his uncle, William Harvey, who was boisterous and fun-loving in a way the Childs were not. Philip's dear "Unc" showed Philip a more lively side of life, and, by frequently taking his nephew to see the Hamilton Tigers play football, encouraged Philip to develop a more rough-and-tumble side through athletics. Philip Child would later play football in each of his years at Trinity College, University of Toronto, and would be president of the Athletic Association in his senior year.

Before that, however, tragedy struck the family. Helen died as a result of her epilepsy on September 6, 1912. Philip was fourteen at the time of her death, and would carry a tremendous sense of grief over the loss of his sister for the rest of his life. In many of his early unpublished poems, he alluded to her and how she shouldered her illness with grace.

In late 1913, the family travelled to Europe for an extensive tour of the continent, both to escape a home still shrouded in mourning and to further Philip's prodigious academic talents. He would spend "six or seven months" studying in Lausanne and Dresden, immersed in European culture and, ironically, improving his German. It would soon serve him well. The family ended their trip in Italy, returning to New York in early June of 1914. Within three weeks of the Childs having returned to Hamilton, Archduke Franz Ferdinand of the Austro-Hungarian Empire, and his wife, Sophie, were assassinated in Sarajevo, initiating a sequence of events that would lead the world to war.

In the fall of 1914, as the first Canadian Division was assembling at Valcartier, Quebec, preparing to embark for Europe, Philip Child, not yet seventeen, was finishing his final term at the Highfield School in Hamilton. Ostensibly to better prepare his son for admission to the University of Toronto, Philip's father sent him to the prestigious Ridley College for the spring term in 1915, but he had an alternative motive: Highfield functioned as a preparatory school for boys wishing to enter the Royal Military College of Canada. Ridley, though it had a cadet corps and military education courses, placed a greater emphasis on university preparation and Anglican religious instruction. William Child did not want his only son running away to war, and this wouldn't be the last time he attempted to steer Philip in a direction that delayed the inevitable for as long as possible.

Philip Child entered Trinity College, University of Toronto, in the fall of 1915, studying literature. At the end of his freshman year, he was officially old enough for military service, having turned eighteen in January. Many of Philip's peers had already enlisted, and his father was concerned that he would abandon his studies to join up.

In July 1916, as the staggering toll of the Battle of the Somme became widely known, William took Philip across the country by train. On reaching the West Coast, they set off for Ketchikan, Alaska, for a vacation far away from military recruiters and the peer pressure to enlist. But these delaying tactics of a concerned father could not hold the war at bay for long. As Philip Child would write years later in *The Wood of the Nightingale*, his 1965 epic poem of the war: "You cannot prod the loitering minutes round / To joy, nor hold them back from Zero Hour."[6]

When Philip returned to Trinity College in the fall of 1916, the time had come for him to join the war.

On June 24, 1916, the preparatory artillery bombardment for what would be known as the Battle of the Somme began. Along a fourteen-mile-long front, Allied field artillery began cutting the German barbed wire in no man's land. After two days of shelling, the heavy artillery commenced a planned three-day bombardment against more hardened German defensive positions. Poor weather delayed the infantry attack for two more days, and so the bombardment continued. In those seven days preceding the Battle of the Somme, the British Artillery fired more than 1.5 million shells; more than they had fired in all of 1914. A further 250,000 shells were fired on July 1, Dominion Day, the day the troops went "over the top."

Despite amassing nearly three times the number of field artillery and four times the number of heavy artillery as was used at the Battle of Loos in the fall of 1915, the combined artillery force at the Somme was insufficient to destroy the German defenses. The inability of the massed artillery to completely shatter the succeeding lines of German trenches and artillery left much of the advancing infantry exposed, and they were cut down in waves. From July 1 to November 18, 1916, the Somme would claim an astonishing toll: nearly 480,000 British and Commonwealth men were killed, and just shy of 800,000 were wounded.

One of the many costly lessons of the Somme was the realization that greater artillery effectiveness needed to be brought to bear against the German lines, and that better artillery tactics, particularly an emphasis on counter-battery fire, needed to be developed if the Allies were to win the war.

It was against this historical backdrop that Philip Child, then an eighteen-year-old student in his second year studying arts at the University of Toronto, decided to join the artillery.

*This photo of Philip Child was likely taken before he shipped out to England in 1917.*

Philip Child Fonds, Local History and Archives Department, Hamilton Public Library.

Like many university students in Canada during the war, Philip Child began his military career by joining the school's Officer Training Corps. The University of Toronto, under the guidance of its president, Robert Falconer, set up a military training program in which students would learn basic military and leadership skills while still enrolled in their regular academic programs. As the war progressed, so too did the involvement of Canada's universities; they provided technical courses for soldiers not otherwise affiliated with the university, covering topics such as engineering, ballistics, and mathematics in a program called the Overseas Training Company. Philip Child joined the OSTC in the fall of 1916, and spent the first two months of term refreshing the mathematical skills he would need to be an artillery officer.

In November of 1916, Child joined the 14th Battery of the Canadian Field Artillery (CFA) and was granted the rank of provisional lieutenant while he underwent training at the School of Artillery in Kingston. He qualified as a lieutenant in artillery in March 1917, but unfortunately for Child, the 14th Battery CFA had been absorbed into two other artillery units and disbanded as a result of losses sustained in France. So, when Child signed his attestation papers on April 23, 1917, officially making him a member of the Canadian Expeditionary Force, he was caught in administrative limbo, waiting for the military bureaucracy to send him to a Canadian artillery battery with an opening for a junior officer. None were immediately available with the Canadian Expeditionary Force (CEF), but there were opportunities in the Imperial Army. As British subjects, Canadians could serve in the British military, and Philip Child jumped at the chance. He was discharged from the CEF and was accepted as a candidate for a commission in the British Army.

When he arrived in England at the end of June 1917, Philip Child joined the 28th Battalion, the London Regiment, 2nd Artists Rifles as a private, but this was merely for administrative purposes. Within three days, he was transferred to the 2nd

*Philip Child in the uniform of the Royal Garrison Artillery, taken in London, circa 1917–18. It was taken either on leave during 1918 (which is most likely) or before he was sent to France.*

reserve brigade of the Royal Garrison Artillery Territorial Force as a gunner (the artillery equivalent of a private) and sent to the Royal Artillery Officer Cadet School at Trowbridge, Wiltshire. On December 2, 1917, his training was complete, and he was commissioned as an officer. He was now Second Lieutenant Philip Child, Royal Garrison Artillery (RGA).

The Royal Garrison Artillery was officially created in 1899 as a branch of the Royal Artillery; armed with heavy guns, they were tasked with coastal and fort defence throughout the British Empire. Typically firing from fixed positions, the RGA was the artillery branch that brought overwhelming firepower to the battle, while the other branches, the Royal Horse Artillery and Royal Field Artillery, stressed mobility and were armed with smaller artillery pieces.

Philip Child arrived in France on January 13, 1918, and joined the 262nd Siege Battery of the RGA. Siege batteries were deployed well behind the front line trenches, equipped with heavy howitzers firing 6", 8", or 9.2" shells, and their mission was to destroy enemy artillery emplacements, supply routes, railway lines, strong points, and ammunition stores. The 262nd was equipped with six 8" howitzers. These artillery pieces weighed between 8.74 to 13.5 tons (depending on the model) and would fire a two-hundred-pound, high-explosive shell in a high trajectory to a range of between ten and eleven kilometres. A siege battery would have five officers and one hundred and seventy-seven men, along with a hundred or so horses for transport. The guns themselves would be moved with a combination of Holt tractors and horsepower. Four of these siege batteries would make up a heavy artillery brigade; during Child's service in 1918 the 262nd Siege Battery was part of the 54th Heavy Artillery Brigade (HAB).

As a "subaltern," or junior officer, Philip Child was the officer in charge of a section of two of the battery's six guns. His epic poem of the Great War, *The Wood of the Nightingale* (1965), contains a first person account of him issuing orders for the battery to fire:

*8" howitzers of 135th Siege Battery at La Houssoye on the Somme, August 25, 1916.*

I hear my voice. I hear it giving orders:
Deflection from the zero line, the range,
The fuse – worked out before the dance began.
And – *Fire when ready, number one.* My voice
Sounds calm and matter of fact … and facts are facts.[7]

The early months of 1918 were relatively quiet for the 54th HAB, as they were moved in and around the Arras and Amiens sectors in northeast France. That sense of calm would be shattered on the morning of March 21, 1918, when the German Army began their spring campaign, the *Kaiserschlacht* or Ludendorff Offensive.

When the Russians negotiated an exit from the war on their Eastern Front, the Germans were able to transfer resources to the west, and consequently held a temporary numerical advantage over the Allies. Eager to attack before the Americans could effectively deploy their military might, the Germans threw everything they had at the Allies, hoping to drive the British back to the Channel ports and then force the French to surrender. The attack drove deep into Allied territory, and the German advance captured more ground than at any point since 1914.

Philip Child and the 262nd Siege Battery were then deployed in Vaulx-Vraucourt, up the Noreuil valley, which had been christened "Death Valley" by the troops. The Germans opened up with a tremendous artillery barrage just after 04:30, and within minutes Child and his men were responding to SOS flares from troops in the front trenches. Communications were cut between the forward observation officers, the battery's guns, and the officer commanding the battery, Major du Neufville. At 05:15, the left and right sections of the battery were pounded by German artillery fire and each section took heavy casualties; German 5.9" shells were raining in at a rate of about three a minute, but the battery somehow maintained their rate of fire, their shelling being the lifeline for the overwhelmed infantry.

Just before about 09:00, Philip Child was hit by shrapnel, and though his wounds were light he was momentarily knocked unconscious and evacuated to a first aid post for treatment. Shortly after, the intensity of the German artillery fire increased, and the battery command post had to be abandoned. His wounds bandaged, Child returned to the fight shortly before the Germans overwhelmed the British trenches in front of them. The gunners reported German machine gun fire was coming over, and there was hand-to-hand fighting in a trench on their right flank a thousand yards away. By 12:30, RGA Lewis gunners were defending the battery's guns from direct German infantry assault.

The major went forward to assess the situation, and seeing no British infantry in front of him, with vast numbers of the enemy pouring down the valley, he gave the order to scupper their four forward guns and retire. Major De Neufville visited every dugout and gun emplacement to make sure all his men were safely away; on his way out, he was caught by German machine guns sweeping the road. He was hit in the head and killed instantly.

Major Eustace Charles De Neufville was awarded the Distinguished Service Order as well as the Belgian Croix de Guerre, and he is commemorated on the Arras Memorial. His grave was never found. Philip Child would pay homage to his fallen commanding officer years later in *God's Sparrows*; Child gave his character Uncle Charles the major's courage, character and name.

Over the course of the next weeks, the German advance would falter in the face of overstretched supply lines and the British and Commonwealth reinforcements who were rushed into defensive positions. The Germans had captured much ground, but they could not hold it, nor could they take the key Allied positions of Arras and Amiens. It was their last, desperate chance of winning the war, and the gamble failed.

The 262nd Siege Battery was knocked out of the war in the short term. Having lost four of its 8" howitzers in the initial German advance, another was damaged in the withdrawal on the evening of March 21. The battery's last gun was damaged the following day by German shell fire. Without armaments, the unit was pulled out of the line, rested and refitted. It would be operational again by June.

One of Philip Child's fellow officers in the 262nd, Captain Philip Russell Knightly, wrote long letters home throughout the war, and they provide the only accurate record of the battery's movements throughout the spring and summer of 1918.[8] In June and July he complains of boredom: "We are back again to the old, old round of stationary warfare — observation post shoots, shells, and shelling. Once more these have come to seem part of our everyday life, which is now almost monotonous. There are now no heroic stunts or strategic movements. We are once again a dull, lifeless crowd, but with one burning topic — leave."[9] Philip Child was granted leave to Paris for ten days from July 7 to 16, and to the U.K. from September 9 to 23.

They would need the rest. The Hundred Days Offensive, a series of attacks against the Germans across the Western Front, began with the Battle of Amiens on August 8, and would continue until the Germans were driven from France and Belgium, forced to retreat behind the Hindenburg Line and, finally, agree to an Armistice on November 11. The pace of the Allied advance was staggering; it was the breakout they had been hoping for since 1914.

In *The War Memorial Volume of Trinity College*, published in Toronto in 1922, Philip Child states that he saw service "in actions of August 28, Sept 2 [Croisilles], Sept 27–29 [Hermies and Etricourt along the Fins-Gouzeaucort Road], Oct 11 [Montigny], Oct 21 [the Le Fayt Audencourt Road], and Nov 6, 1918 [Ovillers]."

The war diary of the 54th Heavy Artillery Brigade states where the 262nd Siege Battery was located, and when they moved to a new location, but does not contain details of when the guns were firing, what the objective was, or which guns were held in reserve. The record of September 27, 1918 in the official war diary is a representative example: "Hermies 27/08/18 5:20 am. Zero Hour. Infantry attacked covered by H.A. [heavy artillery]." In each of these attacks, Philip Child and the 262nd Siege Battery would have been well back of the advancing troops of General Julian Byng's British Third Army, providing fire support as needed. But the details that exist for engagements earlier in the war have been lost for this final phase.

Two weeks after the Armistice, Philip Child fell ill. Exhausted from the frenetic pace of the Hundred Days Offensive and the cumulative effects of a year in France, he was admitted to hospital on November 28, 1918. Child had contracted the Spanish Flu and would be in hospital recovering for nearly a month. Throughout his illness, he was plagued by fevered dreams of all he had witnessed in his time at the front. He returned to his battery on December 22 in time for their final Christmas dinner in France, but, still weak, he was overcome both with the realization that the war was finally over and at the absence of so many comrades who had perished.

*This photograph of Philip Child was most likely taken post war (he's in the uniform of the RGA, and he couldn't have had that shot taken before he returned home).*

In mid-January, he was en route back to England and would be demobilized on January 25, 1919. But nightmares of the war would continue to haunt him for months after he'd left the artillery.[10]

Philip Child returned to Canada in 1919, and resumed his studies at Trinity College, University of Toronto, graduating with a B.A. in 1921, and winning the Moss Scholarship for the best all-round student. He would study at Christ College, Cambridge, in the fall of 1921, completing an affiliated Bachelor's degree before earning a Master's degree at Harvard in 1923. In the fall of 1923, he was hired as a lecturer in English at Trinity College, University of Toronto, a post he would hold until 1926.

It was in this period that Child began working on the poems that would end each section of *God's Sparrows*. The poems "The Apple" and "Brother Newt to Brother Fly," which follow the first and third sections of the novel respectively, were written in the summer of 1924. An early version of the latter poem was briefly entitled "Brother Rat to Brother Fly," but rats had become an all-too-common device in war poetry, and, thus, one that Child wanted to avoid. He also began playing with the couplet "Beyond my sight the cloudless sky / Is troubled with artillery" in his notebooks; it would become the final couplet of his poem "Macrocosm," published years later in *The Victorian House and Other Poems* (1951). There are a handful of unpublished war poems from this period as well amongst Child's papers: "An Eight-Inch Howitzer," and "Battle Scene" both date from 1924, while Child began to draft a much longer poem at about this time called "Thompson's Death," in which a soldier explains to a grieving father how his son really died.

On August 5, 1925, Philip Child married Gertrude Helen Potts (b. July 30, 1900) in Saint Thomas Anglican Church in Toronto. They'd met at Trinity College when Child returned from the war, where she was doing honours work in English and history. They were ideally suited: as bookish as Philip, Gertrude was the head of the college library and editor of the school's literary magazine, *Chronicle*. At the time Child proposed, she was working as a college instructor at the University of Toronto.

Philip and Gertrude Child went to Harvard in the fall of 1926, where Philip began his Ph.D. They would have their first child, John Philip Child, on April 10, 1927. Later that year, Philip managed to return home with his expanding family to Hamilton for Christmas. Philip presented his parents with a handwritten collection of eighteen of his poems, titled *Heaven in Hell's Despite: Verses by Philip Child*. Among other poems, the collection contains "Brother Newt to Brother Fly," "Battle Scene," and "The Apple."

The next year, Philip's mother Elizabeth would die, passing away as a result of arteriosclerosis on March 25, 1928, shortly before he finished his doctorate. She was seventy-one. The Child's second child, born October 13, 1931, would be named after both her and Philip's late sister: Elizabeth Helen Child.

In the fall of 1928, the Childs moved to Vancouver, where Philip began a two-year appointment as assistant professor of English at the University of British Columbia. It was here that Philip began his first attempts at writing war fiction. An unpublished short story from 1928, "The Phantom Battery," is essentially an "Angel of Mons" story set during the German Spring Offensive. In it, a battery of the fallen followed by a column of ghostly infantry rush into the fight, "rolling on a cloud of light" to cover their comrades' retreat. It is in this story that Child begins wrestling with the problem of presenting the war to the reading public, and he immediately addresses the central problem of war fiction: "You may think you can imagine the horror of battle never having taken part; you do not, you cannot."[11] So, how then to faithfully render the war for readers who would never be able to grasp its horrors? For the time being, Child would err on the side of conservatism:

I will not dilate on the things we went through. Everyone who has fought knows something of how it is. Not the wounds, nor the terror, nor the death, but the cumulative effect of them on those spared, and the persistent apprehension of them, the feeling of war as a vivid denial of all order and wisdom in things; in a word, we were in danger of becoming sick souls, that could see only slimy things.[12]

As Child read the war novels that began appearing in 1920s, he was struck by how frequently the authors seemed mired in just such an existential crisis, and in response he drafted an outline for his own war novel, one that he hoped would act as a counterweight to the overwhelming pessimism of the recent novels of the war. He began writing it while still at UBC, and by early 1932, having returned to Harvard to teach, he had a hundred-page novella titled *A Toast to the Victor*, which he sent to the major American publishers. None of them were interested.

*A Toast to the Victor* is *God's Sparrows* in utero. Told in the first person, it's about a Canadian named Hill who joins the fictional 701st Siege Battery of the Royal Garrison Artillery. While serving in the regiment, he encounters a hard drinking mystic of an officer named Vance, and after meeting the rest of the officers, he is initiated into the battery by helping the men dig a gun emplacement. The battle scene, which begins midway through the novella, is a depiction of the German Spring Offensive of March 21, 1918; the climax occurs when a character named Cayley sacrifices himself by blowing a bridge to slow the German advance. The second half of *A Toast to the Victor* deals with the Hundred Days Offensive, and Hill's befriending of French locals; several of the scenes in the second half of *A Toast to the Victor* reappear in two of Child's later war works: an unpublished 1953 short story titled *We Set Out For Rossignol Wood*, and the 1965 epic poem *The Wood of the Nightingale*.

*The jacket of Child's 1965 book of poems,* The Wood of the Nightingale. *Daniel and Alastair Thatcher make a cameo appearance in the book (on page 9).*

Unable to interest any publishers in *A Toast to the Victor*, Child turned to another novel he had been working on since returning to Harvard. Based on the historical document the *Jesuit Relations, The Village of Souls* was published in Britain in 1933 by Thornton Butterworth. A story of voyageurs in seventeenth-century Quebec, it met with modest success in the U.K. after receiving a glowing review in the *Times Literary Supplement*. Canadian distribution was to be handled by the publishers Thomas Nelson and Sons of Toronto, but the ship carrying copies for the Canadian market sank in the North Atlantic, and the publishers declined to print another edition. The only copies that made it to North America were those Child sent to friends and family, and a handful of review copies, which were understandably ignored by book reviewers who were uninterested in reviewing a novel that would be unobtainable in Canada.[13]

This was an inauspicious beginning for a Canadian writer who would later go on to win the Governor General's award for fiction and two Ryerson Fiction Awards, but, critically, Philip Child now had a publisher, one interested in a First World War novel similar in size and scope to *The Village of Souls*. Child tore apart all of his previous war writing, lifting the scenes and characters with the most potential, and, most critically, decided to include two of his strongest poems of the post-war period: "The Apple" and "Brother Newt to Brother Fly." By the summer of 1933, he had an outline for an "epic war novel," and by Christmas he had a title: *God's Sparrows*. Child spent the next three years writing *God's Sparrows* from Harvard. It was published in the spring of 1937 by Thornton Butterworth in the United Kingdom, and distributed by Thomas Nelson and Sons of Toronto in Canada. There was only one printing.

*God's Sparrows* opens in the final years of the nineteenth century in Wellington, Ontario (a fictional town modeled on Child's hometown of Hamilton), and in the initial chapters the reader is introduced to the extended family surrounding the young Daniel Thatcher. His father, Penuel, is both biologically and temperamentally Puritan, while his mother, Maud, and uncle, Charles Burnet, possess more cheerful, playful dispositions, befitting their Cavalier ancestry. Daniel's younger brother, Alastair, is handsome, charming, and irresponsible, taking after the Burnet side of the family, while Daniel is often sullen and willful: a Thatcher to the bone. Joanna, the youngest Thatcher child is "not well"; like Philip Child's real-life sister, Helen, Joanna suffers from fits and her care and well-being is both a constant concern and a source of guilt for Dan.

As Dan gets older, a cousin named Quentin joins the Thatcher boys at the St. Horatius school after his parents are lost aboard the *Titanic*. Quentin quickly forms an intense and often strained friendship with Dan, who, most days, would rather be courting his neighbour Cynthia Elton than discussing philosophy with Quentin.

The pre-war world of Wellington is on the whole bucolic; however, there are numerous tensions exerting themselves, particularly upon Dan, in the opening chapters of the novel: the differing natures of the Thatchers and Burnets, traditional versus progressive attitudes, the struggle between duty to oneself and others, the line between guilt and innocence.

When the war arrives, this world is blown apart and these tensions are amplified. Uncle Charles becomes a captain in the Wellington Artillery Battery and several of Dan's university classmates, as well as Quentin, rush to sign up, but Dan feels bound to stay home and look after his sister. Conflicted, and under tremendous pressure to "do his bit," Dan receives a white feather for cowardice from Beatrice Elton, Cynthia's elder sister, whose husband was killed at the battle of St. Julien. Alastair, unfettered by the same sense of familial responsibility as his brother, joins up, and having taken advantage of the deterioration of Dan and Cynthia's relationship, surreptitiously marries Cynthia on the eve of being shipped overseas.

Adding to Dan's sense of humiliation, Quentin writes him from France, telling of the butchery of killing prisoners, and mistakenly applauds what he believes is Dan's principled decision to stay out of the war. That Quentin assumes Dan is a pacifist is the last straw; after attending a no-nonsense recruiting speech delivered by a Victoria Cross recipient, Joanna, understanding her brother's turmoil at being left behind, gives Dan her blessing to go to war, making her own sacrifice for the war effort. "Why should men be the only ones to sacrifice anything for their country?" she asks.

Meanwhile, Pen Thatcher, dismayed by a civilization destroying itself, decides to cease paying taxes to support the war. After receiving a bureaucratic response from the government, he writes to the local newspapers. His opposition to the war attracts more than criticism from his neighbours; he will eventually face a mob of drunken soldiers for daring to question the righteousness of the war. Pen confronts the mob with courage and dignity; shamed, most of them lose heart, but one soldier lashes out, knocking Pen unconscious — a blow that ultimately kills him. In Philip Child's portrait of war, casualties are not confined to the front.

The large cast of characters in *God's Sparrows* permits Philip Child to examine the war from multiple perspectives in a way that no other Canadian novel of the war is able to do. None portray the struggle of those left at home quite as vividly or as sympathetically as Child does: Pen Thatcher's pacifist beliefs are not invalidated merely because he is a civilian, and the sacrifices Joanna and Beatrice have made are not minimized because they aren't in the trenches. The war consumed everything and everyone, and Child is at pains to stress that sacrifice and suffering were not confined to those in uniform.

Moving from Canada to the Western Front, Dan Thatcher joins his Uncle Charles and brother Alastair in the Wellington Battery in the spring of 1917, a full year before Philip Child was himself deployed to France. This deviation from his own war experience exists so that Child can depict the Battle of Passchendaele, or the Third Battle of Ypres (July 31–November 10, 1917), during which the Canadian Corps continued to distinguish itself, despite heavy casualties and impossible terrain, capturing the town of Passchendaele in early November. "Somehow," Child writes, "many of them existed and survived; but they were not the same men afterwards, for they had seen more than death, they had faced corruption of the soul, and despair."

One of the casualties of this battle in *God's Sparrows* is an officer "with the expression of an imperturbable owl," a "stolid" man "who died without making a fuss, on the duckboards outside the battery." Introduced as "Currie" initially, the spelling inexplicably changes to "Curry" at his death. Child certainly wished to pay homage to the most famous Canadian gunner of the war, General Arthur Currie, commander of the Canadian Corps. Like

Official CEF Photo, Seaforth Highlanders of Canada Museum and Archives.

*Canadian troops man a Vickers gun in the mud and shell holes near the front line at Passchendaele.*

Peregrine Acland, who named a character for Robert Borden in his novel *All Else is Folly* (1929), Child continues the curious and distinctly Canadian war novel convention of naming noble, but minor, characters after major national personalities.

While the Battle of Passchendaele is raging, Quentin becomes a conscientious objector, and is arrested and charged for refusing a lawful order. Quentin eventually concludes that he must return to the war, but, significantly, this the only instance of a character in Canadian war fiction of the period who chooses conscientious objection.

The final battle scenes in *God's Sparrows* closely adhere to Philip Child's own experience as a subaltern in the 262nd Siege Battery of the Royal Garrison Artillery during the German Spring Offensive of 1918 and the subsequent Hundred Days Offensive. Dolughoff's descent into madness and his eventual suicide, as well as Charles Burnet's heroic sacrifice to blow the bridge and slow the German advance, are both fictional, though

Dan's progressive shell shock and fever dreams are very much rooted in Child's war experience.

The elaborate and allegorical dream sequence toward the end of the novel is not only unique in Canadian war fiction, it is also a fitting climax for a novel that is so concerned with what motivates the characters, how they think, and how their thinking progresses throughout the course of the war. Philip Child does not rely on graphic description of the horrors of war to move his readers; he doesn't linger on the grim details, as a writer like Charles Yale Harrison did in the infamous bayoneting scene in *Generals Die in Bed* (1930). Rather, he describes the effect of these innumerable horrors on the psyches of the characters in *God's Sparrows*, shows how they persevere, falter, succumb to, or overcome what they have experienced. This is why *God's Sparrows* concludes not with the image of Jobey's corpse, or Dan broken on a stretcher, but with Quentin's poem and its appeal to our shared humanity.

Since 1937, there have been two brief revivals of interest in *God's Sparrows*. In November of 1970, a battle scene from the novel was adapted by Philip Child for the CBC television program *Theatre Canada: Canadian Short Stories*. Directed by David Peddie and starring Donnelly Rhodes and Tim Henry, this half-hour drama was broadcast only once, aired to tie in with the network's Remembrance Day programming. Eight years later, following Philip Child's death on February 6, 1978, McClelland & Stewart published *God's Sparrows* as part of its New Canadian Library series. It was dropped from the series after a single printing.

Nearly eight decades after it was first published, and having been out of print for thirty-eight years, *God's Sparrows* is now being republished as part of Dundurn Press's Voyageur Classics series. It deserves a permanent place in Canada's literary canon. It is a great Canadian war novel, with a large cast of characters and an epic scope that addresses Canada's war experience in a way few Canadian war novels can match. At the same time, *God's Sparrows* has the courage to challenge many of the prevailing tropes of the anti-war novels of the 1920s and '30s, where senior officers were treated as if they were the enemy (or died in bed), those on the home front were hopelessly naïve, and where soldiers were frequently portrayed as either innocent victims or savage killers. As Child would write, in the most frequently cited passage from the novel:

> The thousands went into battle not ignobly, not as driven sheep or hired murderers — in many moods, doubtless — but as free men with a corporate if vague feeling of brotherhood because of a tradition they shared and an honest belief that they were doing their duty in a necessary task. He who says otherwise lies, or has forgotten.

Philip Child could not forget. He was haunted by the First World War for his entire adult life, and would write about it continually for nearly fifty years in both poetry and prose. His best work, and one of the finest Canadian novels to emerge from the war, was *God's Sparrows*.

## NOTES

1.  Humphrey Cobb, an American who served in the 14th Battalion (The Royal Montreal Regiment) published *Paths to Glory* in 1935, but the novel, about French mutinies and subsequent arbitrary military justice, can only tangentially be considered "Canadian" in light of both his service and a later novella about a Canadian soldier serialized in *Collier's Magazine*, *None But the Brave* (1938).

2.  Jonathan Vance, *Death So Noble: Memory, Meaning, and the First World War* (Vancouver: UBC Press, 1997), 3.

3.  *Globe and Mail*, March 20, 1937, 12.

4.  *McMaster Quarterly*, April 1937.

5.  *Hamilton Spectator*, April 10, 1937.

6.  Philip Child, *The Wood of the Nightingale* (Toronto: Ryerson, 1965), 104.

7.  Ibid., 47.

8.  Many official war diaries were lost or destroyed during the bombing of the Second World War.

9.  Captain Philip Russell Knightly, letter, July 26, 1918. *Among the Guns: Intimate Letters from Ypres and the Somme* (self published, no date).

10. Dennis Duffy, "Memory=Pain: The Haunted World of Philip Child's Fiction," *Canadian Literature* No.84, (Spring 1980): 54.

11. Philip Child, *The Phantom Battery*, 1928 (unpublished), 2.

12. Ibid, 3.

13. *The Village of Souls* would be republished by Ryerson in 1948, with illustrations by Roloff Beny, after Child won the 1948 Governor General's Award for fiction for *Mr. Ames Against Time*.

# PART I

# THE SEED AND THE SOIL

# CHAPTER I

In the beginning the wizened, cone-headed, shrimp-coloured little bundle of flesh tied with a diaper and known as Daniel Burnet Thatcher reposed like a vegetable in the midst of the family that was so much more aware of him than he of them. First he felt the fear of noise and the fear of falling, never entirely to be lost until Daniel Thatcher should lose hold and fall out of the body. Then came sight and smell. Then walking.... Pen, taking the baby by the hand walked on the snowy sidewalk and began to step high and stamp the snow off his feet; Daniel did likewise. Then came speech, and with it the binding sense of time. "Tomorrow is Christmas, Daniel, and you will see a wonderful tree, all lighted with candles." "When is tomorrow? Is today tomorrow?" He was taken in to see the tree and his little tummy tight as a soccer football was distended with ice cream. "Do you think he will remember this, Pen?" Maud Thatcher asked her husband. "At two years? Hardly, Maud. He might remember seeing dim faces about a tree, but without recalling how he felt...."

Dan with his brother and sister lived in Ardentinny, a square house of trimmed stone with tall stone chimneys, built on a hill so that it could overlook the town of Wellington in Ontario without too vulgarly congregating with more plebian houses.

Maud Thatcher's grandfather, Sir Cyprian Burnet, had built it early in Queen Victoria's reign to resemble an old country manor house. It was solid and feudal looking and the very devil to heat in winter.

The children's room on the top floor was large and full of angles and shadows caused by the slope of the gabled roof. Dan, as the oldest, slept in a four-poster with a network of cord instead of springs, sagging in the centre like a fallen cake. It stood so high that he could look down through the window upon Galinée Street leading to Wellington's "downtown" and upon the roofs and chimneys of Wellington itself. He always went to sleep to the tinkling of a music box which faithfully repeated "Take a pair of ruby lips" over and over without having to be rewound. When the leaves fell, he used to long for the first snow, and often, going to the window at night and seeing a sheet of moonlight on the lawn, he would think snow had come. When at last it did come by stealth, always taking him by surprise, then it was glorious. He would wake up, perhaps on a Sunday morning, to find the snow clinging in dazzling white clouds to the branches and covering the roofs of the town, and the air coming in at the open window made his cheeks tingle as he lay listening to the *spitter-spangle* of church bells playing "Hark the Herald!" …

It was Pen's custom to pronounce a special sort of grace at breakfast: "Children, may we all use this day well. Amen." This gave one a sense of dedication to the day, though as a doubter he conscientiously refrained from associating Deity with his wish. To himself he always added: "May I not lose my temper with Daniel. If I have to punish him, may I punish him dispassionately. Amen."

He had made up his mind to launch his children into the twentieth century unchristened, "with no millstones from the past about their necks." This decision Maud had bowed to — for the time being; in fact, she never opposed him directly in anything. But she could never understand why Pen had to torture himself by thinking differently from other people. It only made one unhappy. When there was a thing to do, something that people *did* — like christening, why could one not simply do it without *worrying*?

"The children are growing older, Pen," said Maud one Sunday at breakfast. "I have been thinking over what you said about their being 'undisciplined little barbarians,' and I think you may be right … wouldn't it be wise to take them to church — a little?" Once, a year before, during Pen's absence, Maud had taken Dan and Alastair, but the experiment had not been exactly a success and Maud's nerves, though strong, had only held out until the second hymn.

After a moment's hesitation, Pen agreed. After all, what harm could it do? He groaned. "I'll have to put on my 'Sunday-go-to-meeting' clothes." This homely joke belonged to Pen's father and had its roots in the past; for Pen, the meeting house had long since changed to "the church."

The news was broken to the children.

Alastair was frankly overcome by a sudden illness, which he did very well, and upon being ruthlessly put to bed, resigned himself, merely asking for the mechanical windmill and the box of British grenadiers. But the other children, never knowing their own minds as well as Alastair, fortified besides by the knowledge that going to church was a grown-up thing to do, submitted to being dressed in their best. Presently, they set forth in the victoria, behind the coachman wearing in his silk hat the Burnet colours.

They were late. All the rear pews were occupied, so they had to sit under the pulpit. "Now be quiet children and listen," whispered Maud. It was all right while the choir marched in singing "Onward Christian Soldiers," which gave Joanna a glorious thumpy feeling like watching the circus parade that time. But after a short time nature began to assert itself. Dan's mouth dropped open and he began to twist and turn and invent things for his fingers to do. Joanna, with a woman's social sense, twisted less, but she stood up when others sat down, and when others sat down, she stood up and sat down, and finally, during a lull in matins, she whispered sibilantly, "Mother, why am I here?" Dan began to punch his father gently, and at last folded himself jack-knife fashion over the back of the pew in front.

"*Ssh*, dear," whispered Maud fearfully.

Why did you have to whisper in church? The clergyman boomed down at you from the high platform that was like a turret in a castle. "Repent ye; for the kingdom of heaven is at hand."

"Father, I'm *tired*. Can't we go now?"

"In a minute, Daniel; have patience."

"I *can't*, father."

"Think of something nice, Dan," said Maud.

The clergyman was reading the first lesson from the Book of Job. *Wherefore is light given to him that is in misery, and life unto the bitter in soul?* "I am Job," thought Pen. "On me is put the curse of unbelief."

A canticle filled the church with thundering squadrons of praise. Praise him and magnify him forever. Maud was thinking of that poet (she never could remember the names of authors) who said the *Benedicite* was like a wave turning over? Kipling was it? "Must tell Joanna that." Dan was pulling in turn each of the buttons of his father's coat. It was rhythmical to do that; it helped when you turned being bored into rhythm. Pen, unconscious of his nervous habit, fidgeted and muttered under his breath, "Damn fool! Damn fool!" The *Benedicite* rolled on with its inexorable praise. First the natural phenomena, then the creatures of the earth from the whales to children of men, then "O let Israel bless the Lord," with a change of tune that gave one a new lease of life. Asiatic imagery for Anglo-Saxons, thought Pen. They had got to the beasts and cattle, and after another quarter of a page they could sit down and Dan's patience might revive. A woman with a tinny soprano lifted up her praise with immolating vigour just behind Pen's ear, dominating everyone else in church, imposing her ego. These little egotisms of people bothered Pen, he could never see beyond them. Maud's voice, "Dan, dear, don't *wriggle!" Praise him and magnify him forever.* A part of Pen's mind not under control, thinking of Dan, said fervently, "Not *forever!"* It was like those moments, he thought, when you are in a cab on the way to the station. You will miss the train. The coachman flicks his horse and it giddaps into a shambling trot while mentally you push the cab to its destination.

At last the third hymn, the one before the sermon. You could go out. Hats and coats. Dan's hat mysteriously missing, to be finally retrieved from under the next pew but one.... They are out in the frosty air in the carriage going home. The children at last are quiet, for there is always something fresh to look at when you go for a ride. "The choir sings beautifully, don't you think?" remarked Maud. "The children behaved very well considering —"

Pen felt worn out and church always made him morose. "It's nice," he said, a sense of duty reasserting itself, "to get the children into the habit of going to church." In his own ears his voice sounded thin, not from the depths of his convictions. It can do no harm to "expose" them, he thought; it might take. And any help a man can get — *The end of life, sudden darkness, oblivion.*

"Oh, it is, dear!" agreed Maud warmly.

Dan's mouth was open, and he was engrossed in the mysterious thoughts of his age. "Father," he said unexpectedly, "What is the kingdom of heaven?"

One never knew what would catch a child's attention. Pen answered carefully, for he believed in talking to children as though they were grown up.

"It is the agreement of the heart with the will. But you are too young to understand that yet."

"The poor little monkey!" interposed Maud.

"Is everyone in it?"

"No, Daniel."

"Why isn't everyone in it? Are you in it, Father?"

Maud said quickly: "Children! What do you think we are going to have for dinner?"

On Sunday evenings after church, all Maud's family came to Ardentinny for high tea. The sound of talk and music floated up to the children, and often Dan and Alastair would creep out of bed and tiptoe to the edge of the stairs to listen with faces pressed to the banister, but Joanna, who was the baby of the family, was always too tired to stay awake for the singing, though she tried valiantly.... It was fun to hear their mother singing

> "*Ma mère, hélas, mariez-moi,*
> *Puisque le temps est à plaisir ...*"

when you did not know what the words meant and could not see Mother. It made her seem like a different person and yet the same. "It would be perfect," Dan thought, "if only I could stay downstairs in the dining room with Mother and Father and listen. Grown-ups can go where they like."

Little knows the gosling what the gander thinks.

At such times Pen Thatcher, sitting with Maud's family in the dining room, felt himself an alien. The Burnets, who regarded Ardentinny as a Burnet stronghold, always outnumbered the Thatchers, most of whom lived in the States. Pen sometimes wondered whether, in marrying Maud Burnet (whom he loved), he had not really married Ardentinny. The house had been left to him because Maud's father believed that "a man should be master in his own household." But the Burnets still regarded it as their castle, and not even marriage had been allowed to make any difference in their family solidarity.

The room surrounded the Burnets and Pen with an atmosphere of dignity and tradition which did not belong to the new world. It was unmistakably a room in which one dined rather than "had dinner." In these years no modern chandelier of gas jets illumined too garishly the dark reticence of wainscoted corners; candles gleamed mellowly upon silver and upon oak panelling brought from Scotland years ago by Maud's grandfather. Two ancestral

Burnets in oils occupied panels on the west side of the room. They were Sir Murdo Burnet of Ardentinny Castle in Scotland, in the scarlet uniform and be-demned-careful-what-you-say-sir expression of a British general, and his wife, a dark, wild beauty in Gainsborough silks, bareheaded, with her hand touching the poised head of a greyhound nobly alive at her side. There could be no doubt that Sir Murdo felt at home in the eighteenth-century world upon which he stared with cold eyes. "I am a Burnet of Ardentinny," he seemed to say, "and pray, sir, who may you be?"

Since the general's time, the Burnets had run true to form. They were all sure of themselves and of their place in society. They were cavaliers by instinct, even Maud who was one of the good rather than brilliant Burnets, and they loved dash, colour, tradition, in fact all those things which Pen in his private mind called "swank."

The Burnet ancestor irked Pen. He sometimes fancied that the general's intolerant question was directed at none other than himself. "*Pray, sir, who may you be? A demned puritan in my household, sir!*"

Pen was by temperament and inheritance a New England puritan and by conviction a doubter. He was a puritan who had strayed from his own heritage into this tory background. Murdo Burnet, Pen's brother-in-law, who was a medical missionary in Japan, called him a zealot in search of a conviction. At forty-five he was slightly bald, with marked furrows on his forehead, and he had the prematurely middle-aged look of a man who already eats and drinks failure for his daily fare and wakes to it in the small hours of the morning.

One day Dan stared into the mirror over the mantelpiece at the dark little boy's face — it might have been a stranger's — and the thought suddenly flashed upon him: "Isn't it queer that I'm me?"

Dan had his times of fancy, but he was practical, too. He spent hours trying to find out how the piano worked. Aunt Euphemia Burnet, unable to explain, told him that the sounds were made by little fairies who stood on the wires and sang.

"Shucks! Why do fairies have to have wires in order to sing?" asked Dan reasonably.

He recognized vaguely that Aunt Euphemia was silly, but of course, as one of the family you "loved" her. The best thing about her was her parrot, which had once belonged to a spellbinding revivalist. When there were visitors, Aunt Euphemia had to cover the cage with a cloth because the sight of "two or three gathered together" always made the parrot cry: "*Prrt. Prrt.* Down on your knees, sinners!"

The family were always in the background somewhere, so on the whole you took them for granted, though some of them you avoided as much as you could. For instance, you avoided Aunt Fanny because "she has a lot of common sense about making children behave!" Uncle Daniel Thatcher, who taught at Toronto University, did not count, though he was Father's brother and Father always wanted you to talk to him; he was not an uncle like Uncle Charles. He lived in Toronto, and besides, he was old. Dan did not avoid Uncle Charles because he never seemed exactly like a grown-up. Uncle Charles took him to his first football game. "Now," said Uncle Charles, "the object of the game is to batter the other side until they lie down and let you put the ball behind the goal post. We are cheering for the Tigers. They have yellow and black stockings; and mind you make a lot of noise. Enjoy yourself and, well — don't ask me too many questions." Uncle Charles cocked his hat at a jauntier angle and sucked in his breath with excitement; it was impossible to be with him and not have fun.

The children did not go to school yet because Joanna was "not very well" and Pen thought it unkind to let the boys go without her. Instead they had a tutor, an old Austrian gentleman who taught them languages and the three *R*'s. Sometimes they played with the Elton children who lived next to Ardentinny.

"Do you think it is wise to encourage the Elton children?" said Fanny, the practical Burnet, to Maud. "It looks — well, people might think —"

"Why, they're *nice* children, and I feel sorry for the poor little things — no real mother."

The Eltons were queer. Mr. Elton's first wife had divorced him for the most obvious of all reasons, and he had married a divorcée for his second wife. He was a successful man but his morals — everyone knew what "morals" meant — were not impeccable. Wellington was not used to divorce.... Beatrice was the clever Elton, Cynthia the pretty one, and Eustace was the general nuisance whom Joanna in particular disliked. When the boys quarrelled, as they frequently did, Joanna, who could not bear arguing, would dissolve into tears.

"You must be careful with Joanna," said Pen to Dan, "you must be very careful not to excite her."

"Why, Father?" asked Dan, and saw his father wince.... Pen said with irritation:

"Doesn't it matter to you that your sister is not well?"

Dan was what was called a difficult child. His father could never understand where Dan got his temper and his dour obstinacy, for like many irritable people, Pen thought of himself as a patient man. Dan could not bear to see suffering. Once, while he was still a baby, Maud fell and broke her arm, and Dan, shocked at the sight of his mother suffering and not knowing what to do, began to punch her. He was not a handsome, winning boy like Alastair, who made the hearts of maiden ladies melt when he was called in to shake hands at Maud's afternoon teas. Alastair was a Burnet, and he had the faculty of never appearing in the wrong.

"That boy has a vicious streak," said Fanny of Dan.

"Fanny!" exclaimed Maud, up in arms in an instant. "How can you say such a thing?"

"Well, if it had not been for Dan's temper, Joanna's sickness —" began Fanny, but Maud would not let her go on.

"That was an accident! Don't ever think it anything else."

Once, when Dan was six, his parents overheard him calling Alastair a liar and locked him into his room until he should repent.

He upset all the furniture, broke all the glass in the pictures, and would not come to a state of grace. "Alastair *is* a liar!" he screamed over and over again so loudly that the nearest neighbours down Galinée Street could have heard him. "Alastair may not have told the truth," shouted Maud to the accompaniment of thumps from the other side of the door, "and if so, he will be punished. But you are being punished because it isn't nice, it is not brotherly to say that about Alastair." "He did lie. He *did!*" It always made Joanna sick at her stomach when Dan was unhappy. Presently, she came to the door and whispered through the keyhole:

"Dan, I have a piece of cake for you. Please tell Mother you're sorry."

"No! Go away, Joanna," thundered Dan, so she went away and was sick. In the end it was the parents who had to give in hours afterward and invent a pretext for unlocking the door.

"You're a passionate child. A passionate child!" Pen would exclaim, and Maud would say: "Do you think there is something *worrying* the child? Sometimes when children have something on their minds that they don't know how to tell you about ..."

Pen believed in discipline, and these tantrums somehow seemed always to develop into a personal issue between him and the boy. He was more stern with Dan than with Alastair because he had made up his mind that Dan, unlike Alastair, could be moulded into a Thatcher.

The victoria had given place to a motorcar as the family conveyance. Going out in the "devil-wagon," as Pen called it, was always an adventure; the wheels never quite fitted the ruts in the narrow clay roads, and sometimes they would have to crawl along for miles behind a farmer in a gig who, pretending not to hear their honking, refused to turn out for the city folks and their newfangled contraption. Sometimes they went through the park, past the quarry where workmen had found the mammoth's tusks, and out to Cholera Point, where years ago during a cholera plague, people had been buried five or six at a time in a great pit. Every August a gipsy caravan bivouacked on the point, now grassy and treeless.

One Sunday in August they drove there, Joanna sitting beside her mother, Pen on the seat between the two boys to keep them from fighting.

"Mother, why do gipsies live in carts?"

"Gipsies are like that, Dan. They live on *kekkeno mush's poov*; that means no man's land. They are queer people, dears. They come when they like and go when they like."

"It must be fun not to live in a house and go where you like. Mother, do they like it?"

"I expect they do."

"And do they *do* what they like, Mother?"

"Well, not exactly. No one does. But they do what they like more than most people. They have the sun and stars over them, and they don't care much what people think of them."

"I wish I were a gipsy. Could I be a gipsy when I grow up, do you think?"

Maud gave Pen a queer look.

"My dear boy," said Pen. "You can get away from most people, but there is one person you can't get away from. Do you know whom I mean?"

"No, Father, who?"

"You can't get away from yourself. Don't try."

"Why aren't we all gipsies?" asked Dan.

"A man maun dree his weird," said Maud. This proverb was one of several she had inherited from her ancestors; these sayings were her only obvious link with Scotland.

Dan could not tell when he had first realized that his father was not happy like Mother or Uncle Charles or Aunt Fanny. Father talked to you as if you were a grown-up. This was flattering, but you never felt quite as much at ease as you did with Uncle Charles. You could never be with Father without knowing you were being taught. But Dan admired his father tremendously and was a little afraid of him. His father knew everything. And he kept on pounding at people — and they listened! He was never unfair. Never! But sometimes Dan felt dimly that he was not angry at anything Dan had done but at Dan himself.

"Well, laddie, dreaming as usual?" asked Maud with a smile in her voice.

"I hope I don't have to grow up," said Dan, suddenly listless.

"Why ever not?"

"I don't want to. I might have to do things I don't want to."

## ii

Peace reigned at the breakfast table. The children had passed the age when their attention had, figuratively speaking, to be caught and rubbed into the porridge, and they ate with silent fervour, thinking of what they would do with the summer day. The gipsies were at Cholera Point again, Uncle Charles said, and there was going to be a gipsy wedding.... Pen, whose vitality was low in the morning, had shut himself off from the world behind a newspaper. Civilized people, he believed, ought not to speak to one another until after breakfast. Maud was reading her letters.

The psychic sense possessed by experienced husbands told Pen that Maud had ceased reading and was waiting for him to look up. With a sigh he put down the paper and asked: "What is it, Maud?"

"Oh, nothing, Pen."

That sounded dangerous to his peace of mind. With apprehension he asked: "Whom is the letter from?"

"Murdo."

"What does he say?"

Maud scanned Murdo's letter again hurriedly. It was written in his bold, impatient hand with two ink splotches from a too vigorously dotted i.... "The children must be getting past the puppy stage," Murdo had written. "Do bring them up, Maud, with some regard for the past; anything but this grovelling mediocrity of mind, this cheap scepticism without style or quality. A man ought to believe what his parents teach him to believe. Tell my Ishmaelitish brother-in-law that I'll christen your children yet, in spite of him!" Maud passed the raw material of this letter through the sieve of her sex, the mesh of which is tact, and began:

"Murdo is to go to China from Japan. He thinks trouble is brewing in China." She gave Pen a smile and a little shrug, in which Murdo's wish to be in the thick of trouble was delicately transformed into a woman's humorous comment on the sex in general. "Murdo says his hair is turning grey." Maud smiled uneasily under the special quality of his look, and uttered the unspoken thought between them.

"We are, too," she said.

Pen dwelt on the picture of Murdo facing the little death of middle age. "So he goes off to China to find trouble," he thought.

"Murdo mailed the letter at Shanghai just before sailing. He's staying with us just long enough to do his business — less than a week. He says the West upsets him. Then he is going back by way of England."

"I see," said Pen.... Out of the corner of his eye he observed that Daniel was kicking Alastair under the table — or was it Alastair kicking Daniel? "Boys!" he said sharply. Joanna winced at her father's tone and came behind his chair, smoothing out the frown from his forehead; she could not bear to see anyone frown. "Daddy, are you good?" she asked anxiously. He could not help smiling.

The children clattered out of the room.

"It will be pleasant to see Murdo again," said Pen generously.

"Pen, the children will be in their teens before we know it, and we're not getting younger ourselves. Couldn't we have them christened? Murdo could do it." He put his hand over hers, but she stiffened it slightly against him.

"You want it very much, Maud, don't you?"

"It's right to. After all, we're Christians."

"Do you think Joanna is well enough? ... The excitement — you know what the doctor said —"

"We could have it in Ardentinny."

"Well, since you want it so much.... But mind you, my dear, I'll have no one for godfather but myself. That's my responsibility!"

Maud's eyes glistened with tears. "You're so *just*, Pen. You have such *true* ideas for the children, and yet you always make me feel that you want my beliefs — though I dare say they are often only women's ideas — to count, too. And I can't tell you how much ... I think almost everyday of my life how lucky the children are to have you to give them a broader view — to give them intellectual breadth, Pen."

Pen smiled a little ruefully. No one knew how to make him hug his fetters like Maud, he thought.... "You know, Maud, I often think I've spent my life ploughing the sky. What seems important to me — loyalty to reason — other people simply do not think about. It seems to me that a zealot who isn't ruthless enough to stay a zealot is nature's most abhorred vacuum."

"Pen?"

"Yes, Maud?"

She hesitated. "We have been fortunate — in each other, I mean."

Pen squeezed her hand and said: "*You* ought to know."

"My father used to say 'the sweetest fruit comes after frost.'"

"Well — perhaps. That is, if things only happened to one and not in one.... I shouldn't care what happened if only Joanna —"

But Maud, forcing herself to smile, shook her head at him.

# CHAPTER II

i

The christening was to be held on the afternoon of Murdo's arrival.

Summer stole into the gloomy drawing room, bringing to those inside the hum of insects and the fanning of a light breeze. An open French window framed a picture of ladies in muslin dresses "looking at the garden" and of the two boys skylarking on the lawn.

The room in which three of the last children of the nineteenth century were to be made children of God embodied the dim gentility of the Victorian age. Here the more Victorian members of the family had by now assembled. The Burnets were contriving to be subtly at home to the Thatchers from New England, whom for the first time they beheld as a clan within a clan in their own territory. No one versed in the delicate antagonisms of "in-laws" could have failed to observe that this was a family gathering.

About the Thatchers there was a bred-in-the-bone stiffness; they were too much in earnest, too desirous to "do what's right" to thread their way with finesse through the iridescent web of the social relations. To a Burnet — to Charles Burnet, for instance, who moved carelessly in flannels and blazer through a phalanx of formal cutaways — there was a locked-up look about the expressions of the Thatchers. The faces of the Thatcher women were all that women's faces should be, gentle and solicitous; and yet always with a shade of obstinacy, of reserved opinion. Studiously affable, they mingled warily with the Burnets, evincing an interest, more than usually proprietary, in Pen's children, as if subtly to underline the fact that the children were, after all, Thatchers. Their talk was of the family, the never stale epic of Thatcher births, marriages, and deaths.

Several of them were clustered near the fireplace, drawing, perhaps unconsciously, a feeling of family solidarity from the photographs of Thatchers past and present who gazed uncompromisingly from the mantelpiece upon this Burnet room. There Pen was talking to his eldest brother Diodate who had come from Ohio for the christening. Diodate sat in silence, making his presence felt, though he uttered no word, by the decisive severity of his attention. In him the inherited puritan earnestness, informing a more robust nature than Pen's, had settled solidly into an upright practicality. He began to speak in a deep voice that boomed sepulchrally upon an instantly attentive circle, patting his knee at each point made. "They have — too many — missionaries (pat) — seem to think — they can't get along without more (pat) — so I don't help them — when they come to me (decisive pat) — I say let them get together and fight the devil at home (pat) — if that's what they really want to do" (hands folded, knees crossed: full stop). The ladies confronted with indubitable male logic, fluttered and hastened to agree.... Something very likeable about Diodate: ability, honesty, kindliness.

His son Quentin, too shy to join his cousins on the lawn, stood near his father, swaying backward and forward on his heels and pretending that the Thatchers on the mantelpiece (especially the whiskered ones in the daguerreotypes) were a jury — no, better than that, were congress, whom he was swaying by a speech of great eloquence. There was a war — it was like the

Civil War. The land was torn with strife and no one knew what to do. Then he, Quentin Thatcher.... Then after the war, the plaudits of his grateful countrymen surrounding him whenever he stirred abroad in his state carriage, preceded by a glittering escort of cavalry, brought tears to his eyes. It was tremendous.... Diodate exclaimed: "Quentin, stop mooning! ... He's a strange boy, Penuel. Half the time he does not seem to hear what you say." The boy was like his mother, Diodate thought, lovable but not well-balanced. Emotional, not solid.... He had the Thatcher conscience, though.

But the very pith of the Thatchers was the old lady who sat on a horsehair sofa beside the pianola. There might be fewer Thatchers than Burnets present, but at no assemblage attended by Great-Aunt Joanna could the family be held inadequately represented. The repository of Thatcher lore, no baptism, marriage, or funeral could have taken place without her cognizance. She sat stiffly with her hands folded like talons over her ear trumpet, which she was holding in the lap of a formless dress of some black stuff that made little Joanna, who could not take her eyes from her godmother-to-be, think of "my Jewish gaberdine." It was because of little Joanna that she had stirred from the old Thatcher house on the Connecticut river where, the last of her generation, she passed her days alone, utterly determined to die as she had lived without being "looked after" by a companion or even a servant.

Euphemia Burnet, thinking that the old lady, because of her tranquil attitude, would be a suitable subject for her own histrionics, set sail for the pianola and dropped anchor with the air of having at last reached port after a long voyage. Composing her features to an air of mysticism, she addressed Great-Aunt Joanna in the brassy voice of one summoning spirits from the vasty deep or addressing the very deaf.

"I am *so* glad to speak with one of the same generation as my dear father, Sir Rae Burnet," she announced, carefully articulating each syllable. "I am strongly of the opinion, dear Miss Thatcher," she went on, "that we do not have time really to live nowadays. No time to 'loaf and invite the soul' as your great poet Walt Whitman puts it. I think that is *so* important. Do you not agree? Now baptism, for example. I have vainly urged my brother-in-law to hold the service in the open air where the great words of the ritual could come to one reinforced by the beauty of nature and where one could linger over those magnificent phrases and savour them. Children's little minds are so open to nature's beauty, don't you think?" With a studied wave of her hand Euphemia indicated Dan and Alastair who were lingering on the lawn till the last possible moment because of a conviction that the Thatcher aunts and uncles were hearty kissers.

No longer hearing a buzzing in her ear, Great-Aunt Joanna perceived that she had been asked a question and smiled blandly. Sensitive of her deafness, she had a disconcerting habit of not using her ear trumpet when she thought the conversation would not interest her.

But a smile was all Euphemia needed and she plunged into her latest religiosity (she was always titillating her imagination with new cults). The children, she said, ought to be christened amid nature's foison and under heaven's sun — an influence so favourable to young and impressionable spirits. Within an old house like this, haunted by who knew what malign effluences of people who formerly dwelt there.

"Whutt?" asked the old lady. "Whutt did you say?"

"*Malign effluences*," shouted Euphemia. "*I am referring, Miss Thatcher, to the malign animal magnetism of an old house!* In an old house who knows what malign effluences —"

Great-Aunt Joanna had caught the single word "animal," and fixing Euphemia with a look of uncomprehending benevolence, she began to tell of an experience she had had downtown in Wellington. For several moments both spoke together, but the old lady had the placid self-sufficiency of a natural phenomenon, of a river or a waterfall, whereas Euphemia, an artist, needed an audience. Charles and Murdo Burnet, attracted by Euphemia's struggle to be heard, came up in time to witness her discomfiture. One of those horseless wagons — those *contraptions!* said the old lady, had spattered her with mud. She had marched out into the traffic and seized a policeman by the sleeve and made him blow his whistle.

Charles seized the ear trumpet, and putting it to Aunt Joanna's ear, shouted: "What did you tell him, Miss Thatcher?"

"Whutt? I said to him, 'Young man, in *my* country we respect old folks!'"

"Good for you!" said Charles.

"Don't shout!" rebuked Aunt Joanna, "the trumpet isn't deaf."

"My sister Euphemia," said Charles mischievously, "thinks christenings should be held out of doors. That's how the Druids did it. Euphemia is a piercer of the veil. It's her latest religion. What do *you* think, Miss Thatcher?"

"Hold your tongue, Charles!" exclaimed Euphemia. But Murdo interposed irritably:

"Euphemia, you've been talking nonsense. Charles, you're a scatterbrain."

"On the contrary," said Charles, "I think Euphemia has hit on a charming idea — really, Euphemia, I must look into the Druids. *I say I like beauty, Miss Thatcher. Yes — beauty.* Beauty in nature, you know. Fauns and satyrs and so on. Pan ready to twitch the nymph's last garment off, you know. I quote from Browning, of course, Miss Thatcher.... Don't you?"

"Whutt? You're a mischievous young man! And you're trying to tease an old lady. But you can't. I understand young folks. Like 'em, too!"

"I bet you do!" said Charles enthusiastically.

"Nobody," asserted Murdo crisply, "pays the slightest attention to Charles. He is a rattle."

"Charming to have you home again, my dear Murdo," said Charles.

Murdo turned his back on Charles and stumped away. Piercers of the veil. Bosh! Nymphs and satyrs. Rubbish! That made him think of the children. Little pagans! he thought. Bound to be.... "I suppose I'd better see them."

He spoke to Maud and she called the children into the room.

Joanna came first and curtsyed to him. Murdo humphed — "Sort of thing Maud would teach a child!" — but he was pleased; the girl was graceful, a Burnet.

"Well, goddaughter?" he said. He did not smile, but the grimness melted from his face.

Alastair marched up with a confident grin, his hand out-stretched, looking the image of Charles; he was followed by Dan, hanging back unwillingly. "This is the mischievous one," said Maud smiling at Alastair, "very annoying sometimes, and very lovable." The high spirits shining in the boy's face moved her so that she could not help hugging him. Who could resist Alastair when he smiled at you? She turned to Daniel who was standing awkwardly, waiting to be noticed: he did not go out to people like Alastair. Maud put her arm about him, too, and gave him a special hug because she had noticed Alastair first. "My *two* dear boys!" she said. Dan was undemonstrative and often he gave her such a queer feeling: as if she were a stranger to her own son. Even now he was stiff and resisting beneath her arm. "Dan is the silent one," she said, "he runs deep. Alastair is like his mother, Dan like his father."

Murdo looked at Dan. The boy was hostile to him. "Are you afraid of me, my boy?" he said.

"No, sir!" said Dan promptly.

"I see. Well, sullen he may be, hangdog he is not!" Nothing ever prevented Murdo from saying what he thought; he believed that character, like water, should find its own level, especially within a family. He addressed Maud over Dan.

"Is this the one who —" But Maud stopped him with a warning glance and whispered: "*Prends garde!* We don't speak of it. It's to be forgotten."

Murdo muttered thoughtfully. "It may be a mistake to ignore it with the boy. Um, yes. I shouldn't be surprised if he thinks of it more than you imagine. He's sullen, that boy."

Pen's other brother, Daniel Thatcher, was peering nearsightedly across the room at his young wife. Tessa was a butterfly. She flitted about the room chattering to anybody and everybody about anything or nothing; though, once she came lightly to rest beside her husband, putting her hand on his sleeve and smiling up at him confidentially without saying anything. He was still a little afraid of her, wondering what a sober old stick such as he should say to a young girl who happened to be his wife; and he watched her coming into her careless youth not without a pang.

Daniel was not the only one who watched Tessa Thatcher. Like Maud, she was really a Burnet, the children's second cousin. Two months before on her eighteenth birthday, she had been married to Daniel ("a birthday present that won't wear out, my dear Tessa," said the irrepressible Charles), and she epitomized in her small self Burnet fire and Burnet recklessness. Secretly, the Burnets wondered how the marriage would turn out. "Such a charming, high-spirited girl," said Fanny to Maud. "It would be a pity if — Do you think it will do, Maud? Daniel's a splendid man. Tessa needs ballast."

"Perhaps. But a Burnet and a New England puritan?"

"*I* married one."

"Yes, but you two are of an age. And besides, you have poise.... Well, we'll see." Fanny, who was forty and unmarried, was sceptical of most marriages.

Tessa was pretty and vivacious, therefore Charles came to talk to her. He liked to pronounce her name; it made him think of a peal of bells or of curls flung upward from a nymph's forehead.

Eyes dancing, Tessa seized his arm and swung him round to face her. "Good afternoon *Uncle* Charles. I hear you don't like me!"

Charles's age was near enough to hers to make the "uncle" piquant. Joyously, he adjusted his mind to a skirmish. "Now who could have told you that! I only said it in the family."

"Then it is true? You did say it.... Charles, what *did* you say, really?"

Charles liked to say outrageous things with a charming smile. "I told your mother," said he, "that you were a graceful brat; 'unspanked but graceful' was the phrase I used. I was annoyed because you were flirting with green youths — with my junior at the bank, if you want to know. It interferes with his bookkeeping and makes a lot of trouble for me."

"But I didn't."

"You have all the stability of a kitten. You can't help it: champagne bubbles and you flirt.... Like you? You're my dearest enemy.... Heard anything else about me, Mrs. Thatcher?"

"Yes," said Tessa spitefully, "I heard you lost a lot of money buying stocks on margin — do they call it?"

"And claws, too," murmured Charles. "Oh, *that*? Unlucky in money — you know the rest of it, Tessa."

"Are you lucky in love, Charles?"

"It is a family characteristic, Tessa," said Charles bowing with mock gallantry.

The children, according to their different natures, considered this thing that was presently to be done to them. Dan was rebellious. Alastair, always willing to take a new experience in his stride, felt rather important. But Joanna was so excited that she could not wait another minute for the ceremony to begin. She stood beside her mother, who was talking to Fanny, and tugged at her sleeve.

"In a minute, dear," said her mother and went on talking. Joanna was an imaginative and believing little girl, and she wondered what it would feel like when you were made into a Christian. Would it be like a miracle? Like the devils coming out of the sick man and going into the herd of swine? She felt queer and tickly in the pit of her stomach.

"When will it start, Mother? Mother, when will it start?" she whispered urgently, and sidling up to her mother, she took her arm and put it round her own shoulders.

"Presently, dear. Now, Joanna, I want you to talk to your Great-Aunt Joanna. She's your godmother. Remember to curtsy and to speak into her trumpet. And if she asks you questions, dear, answer her truthfully and politely."

Great-Aunt Joanna, perhaps dozing a little, perhaps fallen into a reverie, did not at first notice her great-niece, so Joanna took the ear trumpet and breathed into it the word "godmother." She thought her great-aunt looked fearfully like the picture of the witch in *Rapunzel, Rapunzel, let down your hair.*

The old lady turned her head as quickly as a bird, and saw that the child was frightened. "You need not curtsy to me, little Joanna," she said kindly. "I like little girls. When I was young, people used to frighten me, too, but you must not be afraid of me. Come here, goddaughter." She made Joanna sit on a leather hassock and smiled down at her.... "She is a beautiful child," the old lady thought, "but such an odd, elfin, little face."

She said to Joanna:

"Do you know, Joanna, that I was once a little girl rather like you?"

"Yes," said Joanna, but it was a child's answer, for she had no real sense of time passing and of herself growing old like Great-Aunt Joanna.

"Joanna, bring me that small photograph from the mantelpiece."

Joanna brought her a daguerreotype of a child in a velvet crinoline. She had to tilt it to just the right angle to make the small, stiff figure appear from the background.

"Do you see that she has brown curls to her shoulders just like you?"

"Oh, Great-Aunt Joanna, is that really you?"

"It was, Joanna.... Now let me see what sort of a child my goddaughter is. Do you love your brothers?"

"Oh, yes! 'Specially Dan. I love him awfully." She went on with a rush of confidence: "Sometimes when I don't feel very well I am cross."

"So are we all.... Do you go to church? Did you go this morning, Joanna?"

"Yes," said Joanna, pleased.

"Tell me about the sermon."

"All of it?"

"Why, yes, whatever you can remember."

"The text, too? Everything he said?"

Surprised at the girl's eagerness, Aunt Joanna nodded with a smile. Joanna settled herself comfortably on the hassock and a faraway look came into her eyes.

"The third chapter of the Book of Job, and the third verse," she announced in a low, intense voice; then with a slight altera- tion of tone: "The *third* chapter of the Book of Job, and the *third* verse. Let the day perish wherein I was born, and the night in which it was said, There is a man child conceived."

Aunt Joanna moved uneasily and put down her trumpet for a moment. The note of human despair on a child's lips sounded eerie and dreadful.... But how perfectly and how unconsciously the child mimicked with her thin voice the intonations of a theatrical preacher. The old lady began to think: "I ought not to have —"

"My dear friends," said Joanna, raising both her palms with the gesture of a preacher compelling the attention of his congre- gation. "These terrible words of the man of Uz, spoken from the tomb of the past, bring us face to face with the age old problem of evil. Sickness? Suffering? Why must they be? Who among us, seeing his dear ones, his parents and children bearing the mysteri- ous cross of suffering, has not asked that question...."

Great-Aunt Joanna Thatcher gazed at the rapt face of her goddaughter. Did the child know what she was saying? One by one the Thatchers and the Burnets in the room stopped talk- ing and listened in tense silence to a child's voice uttering the thoughts of a rather unctuous man.

"Oh-h, my dear friends" — the thin little voice swelled with the studied emotion of a preacher whose voice reaches out and gathers his audience into an embrace — "The suffering of those we love, is it not a challenge to us who are whole? How ap-applicable to us of the twentieth century is this Bible of ours! Sickness! Social injustice! Bereavement! War, bringing suffering to the innocent with the guilty! All the ills of human life! Have we not all had our pride humbled into the dust through seeing those whom we deemed part of ourselves — our own children, perhaps — suffering, and we powerless to help them...?"

Word for word Joanna repeated what she had heard that morning, with the same gestures, the same florid fluctuations of emotion. Unmindful of herself and of her audience of grown-ups, and unconscious that she, a child of six about to be baptized, was a figure of irony, she pierced the heart of more than one person in the room: of Pen, who thought how a man spends his youth trying to make a secure inner life for himself, only to see it vanish like a puff of smoke when he finds himself living his own bitter troubles over again in his children's lives; of Maud, who always managed her moods and was cheerful except when unexpected chance brought her face to face with a hidden fear; of the old lady sitting on the sofa, in whom age had long since dulled the pain of life so terribly uttered by a young voice.

She put her hand on her godchild's shoulder and her voice shook a little. "Thank you, Joanna. You are a dear little girl. But now I think you should stop before you become too excited."

Murdo in surplice and stole came into the room and the service began. Joanna was excited, and all at once she felt that the pain which she knew so well was not far away. That would be dreadful! ... The words of the service moved her to the depth of her soul.... *And being steadfast in faith, may so pass the waves of this troublesome world....* The waves rolled in like surf beating on the shore. She trembled.... Great-Aunt Joanna lifted her trumpet and gave response in a firm voice: *All this I steadfastly believe.* Presently, everyone knelt and there was a rustle of silk like a breeze passing through leaves. The scene and the spoken words became dulled to Joanna, for pain had surrounded her like a mist. She whispered: "Father, please take me upstairs. I feel ill."

Pen gathered her in his arms and took her upstairs, and Maud followed.

Burnets and Thatchers, drawn for a moment into one family by the too-bigness of life, watched them go in silence.

Dan stood by himself, awkward and self-conscious, though no one was looking at him. Murdo noticed him and said in a voice which he meant to be kind, but which sounded stern to Dan: "Well, my boy. You must take care of your sister. Someday it may be your responsibility. We don't choose our responsibilities, you know; they choose us."

Dan did not answer. He looked at the ground with the confused, troubled expression of a child who has been scolded; he was not quite sure why.

ii

Most of the relations had left Ardentinny after the christening. Dan mooned about watching his mother and Aunt Fanny. His mother was ironing a flannel nightgown for Joanna. *Tamp-tamp-tamp* with the iron in short jabs on the collar and sleeves; then she lifted the garment carefully to fold it. Looking up, she smiled at him with her calm smile; it made him feel better.

Aunt Fanny was talking in an undertone, but he heard a little. "The doctor ... Maud, it's a terrible thing...."

Mother put down the iron carefully on the mat and her look went inside as if she were thinking to herself. "It's devilish," she said softly.

He went up to his room and undressed by candlelight, dawdling in order to put off being put in bed with the light out. Alastair was asleep, and Joanna now slept in another room. He heard his mother's murmur from Joanna's room telling Joanna about the Princess Perdita and the fairy toadstools. "Ten good fairies sat on a circle of toadstools, and on another magic circle sat ten bad fairies; the good fairies liked people and wanted to help them, but the bad fairies wanted to harm them. One day Perdita went for a walk and all the fairies, both the good fairies and the bad fairies, beckoned to her...." The wax melted and ran down the candle, making a glistening pool at the bottom. Idly, Dan picked up the lump of hot wax and pressed it into a pellet. "If I flip this so that it hits the doorknob, Joanna will get well," he thought. But he was afraid to throw it. He blew out the candle, and presently, he went to sleep.

He awoke with a voice ringing in his ears and knew instantly whose it was. It was still nighttime, but moonlight lightened the room with cold brightness. The boy listened with taut muscles for the cry that had awakened him, and almost at once it came again. "Mother! Where are you? Come quickly!" Then the sound of his parents, hurrying up the stairs, their footfalls as they moved about the room, their voices talking low so that he and Alastair should not hear. Alastair was still asleep — of course.

Dan got out of bed, and barefoot, tiptoed down the hall until he stood outside the room. He listened, his heart thumping in his breast like a clock in an empty room.

He heard his father's voice. "We must never let him feel it was his fault, Maud. It would do him harm to grow up with a thought like that."

"We must not think it ourselves, Pen. You can't blame a child for an accident.... Do you think he remembers?"

"No! No, of course not, thank heaven. A child doesn't look backward or forward."

The little boy standing outside the door did not know that he was shivering from cold. He was not conscious of himself standing there with the moonlight cleaving the dark, still hall to his feet like a spear. He did not even think, with the detachment of grown people, that he felt miserable, but a terrible dart pierced him, as when in a dream you fall suddenly before you can brace yourself. He felt a sickening dread, but he felt it as a child feels it, with no remembered pattern of dismay and panic to teach him that even despair heals, leaving a scar to be sure, but smoothed out to a recollection.

The picture that flashed in his memory was of Joanna crumpled on the floor of the barn with her head gashed ... the other children stricken suddenly into silence ... his father carrying Joanna in his arms and giving Dan, as he passed him, an unforgettable look of horror. "Come into the house, all of you," he had said. Hours later, it seemed, his father had come out to them and asked sternly: "How did this happen?"

They had all answered at once, except Dan, who could not have spoken. "We were playing theatre — Dan was going to juggle with croquet balls and —"

"Alastair, you tell me," said Pen.

"Dan had on a dress suit, Father, and when he started to juggle, he fell and lost his temper and —"

"Mr. Thatcher," exclaimed Beatrice Elton indignantly (she always took Dan's side), "it wasn't like that at all. Alastair tripped Dan on purpose and Dan fell and was hit by a ball and ripped his dress suit. Then Dan lost his temper and he threw a ball at Alastair and Alastair ducked and it hit Joanna and it knocked her off the stage and she hit a shovel and Alastair is a sneak and Dan didn't do it on purpose, truly he didn't."

His father had said: "My boy, you have done a terrible thing."

Joanna's voice, calling in panic out of the night's vacancy, froze his heart. He was too young to bear the knowledge of man's insecurity in life, and yet the urgency of the cry sank down to that dark fear born with the child, only later to be understood completely by the man.... Beyond the door he could still hear his parents' voices whispering so that he should not hear. He could not bear it.

There was only one thing for a child to do, and he did it instinctively. He had to run away. He was fleeing from himself, not from persons or places.

He crept back to his room and sat down on the bed, dangling his legs in the path of the moonbeam. Silence now in the house except for the footsteps pacing up and down, up and down in Joanna's room.... You wished to march out into the wide world — there it lay, outside the window, you had only to step into it.

He put on old clothes, quietly, so as not to wake Alastair. Then he took his twenty-two rifle out of the bureau drawer; for a gipsy often had to shoot rabbits for the pot. Gipsies lived by their good right arm; here today and gone tomorrow, they roamed over the wide world with never a care as long as they had horses and tents and their guns to get food with. He dropped the rifle from the window, climbed out, walked along a ledge to the upper veranda, and swarmed down a post onto the lawn. The grass was wet with dew and shone like silver.

At the gate he turned and looked back at Ardentinny. It stood rambling, ivy-clad, its incongruities mellowed as age mellows the visible marks of conflict in a man; dark, though, and a little grim, like the visage of a puritan. But to the boy it was simply his home. He said goodbye to it.

He turned his face down Galinée Street and began to walk fast. The gipsies! *Kekkeno mush's poov.* There was not a single foot-fall but his own in the deserted streets. Presently, he had passed the limits of the city and was walking down a dusty country road toward Cholera Point. He began to feel tired, but he was still elated. Beside the road there was a neglected garden; he climbed the fence and lay down in the long grass under a snowball bush in blossom, and stared up through the leaves into the moon-white sky. Behind the bush a Lombardy poplar pointed its spear to the sky, standing guard over the blossoming shrub like a pikeman over dreaming beauty. But Dan did not think of that; no words came to him to express the poetry of the night. Uncorrupted by the need of maturity to voice the beauty that eluded us, he could drink it in, not with coldly analyzing reason, but with his whole soul. *This is to be free! No moment before or after — only this!*

He got up and walked on and on.

A dog barked and Dan, rounding a turn in the road, spied the gaudy gipsy wagons with their empty shafts nuzzling the grass and the horses tethered to their carved sides. A man was sitting beside the embers of a fire in front of the wagons, mending a harness. He was the colour of an Indian, Dan thought, only with sharper features. He went on working at the harness without looking up. Dan was very tired, and all at once he felt frightened. His boy's dream of himself living a glorious life among gipsies changed to reality. These were strangers; what would they say?

He marched forward over his fear, and the gipsy looked up and surveyed with sharp eyes the small apparition shouldering a twenty-two rifle. He showed no surprise, and Dan suddenly realized that he had been observed for some time.

He planted himself in front of the man and said, "Good morning," in a faltering voice.

"Is it?" said the gipsy impassively.... "Now who may you be?"

"I'm Daniel Thatcher."

"Thatcher? And where do you live?"

"I live in Ardentinny. That's the big house under the hill, near the asylum.... Only I don't anymore."

"Oho! So you don't anymore?"

"No.... I'd like to be a gipsy."

The man did not seem in the least surprised. He turned his head a little, without taking his eyes from Dan, and called: "Lil, *auvacoi!*" A woman glided out from the caravan door and stood beside him. The man spoke to her quietly and so low that Dan could not hear what they said. Gipsy talk? he wondered. Then the man raised his voice. "He wants to be a Romany *chal*, Lil."

The woman stared at Dan, then she and the man looked at each other. Dan thought they smiled.

"He looks like a —" began the woman, but the man said imperiously, "*Jal* a bit!" Then to Dan, "So you want to be a gipsy, boy?"

"Yes," said Dan.

"What does your father do?"

"He is a maner — manufacturer of steel."

"Of steel, eh? Why did you run away?"

"Because — because I wanted to."

"To see the world, eh?"

"Yes."

"And what will your father and mother say?"

Dan hung his head.

"Don't they want you at home?"

"Oh, yes!" exclaimed Dan, "but — but you see my sister —"
But he could not tell strangers about Joanna.

"What can you do, boy? Could you go without food for three
days? Could you lie all night under a hedgerow when it's raining?
Could you walk all day and watch the horses at night? Could you?"

"Yes," said Dan stoutly.

"Do you know how to steal chickens?" asked the man with a
twinkle. "Do you know how to lie? Can you *bakkarder* a horse —
tell fortunes — read a *patteran*? What can you do?"

"I can shoot rabbits," asserted Dan.

"He can shoot rabbits!" repeated the gipsy drolly to Lil,
and they both burst into laughter that was so contagious and so
friendly that he began to like them.

"Now look you, boy. You have to be born free to be a gipsy....
Now you lie down here and put this blanket over you."

"But I don't want to sleep," said Dan suspiciously.

"Then look at the stars. Which is the Pole Star?"

"I don't know," said Dan sheepishly.

"And you want to be a gipsy!"

Dan settled into the blanket which the gipsy woman tucked
around his shoulders. From the caravan came a procession of dark
sprites younger than Dan, without so much as a rag of clothing
over their little pot bellies; they formed a ring around Dan and
stared at him solemnly. They began to whisper to their mother.

"Hush!" said the woman sternly. "Don't you know enough not to *rakker* Romany before a *gorgio*?"

"But he's dark like us."

"He's not a Romany *chal*, he's a *gorgio*."

Dan watched the gipsy unhitch a horse, mount him bareback and set off into the night toward Wellington.

He slept and dreamed that he and the little gipsies were playing together. He was one of them; they talked gipsy and he could understand them. Joanna was there, too, but she was not one of them. They all began to tease her because she could not understand what they said. He was teasing her, too. She burst out weeping and began to cry for her mother, but no one came.... In his sleep Dan tossed off his blanket and called shrilly for his mother. Then he awoke. Dazed with sleep, he saw his mother and father bending over him. He clung to his mother as if he would never let her go.

Behind his parents stood Uncle Murdo and Uncle Charles. Murdo looked grim as if he had been prepared for the worst all along. Uncle Charles winked at him and grinned. A bill changed hands between Pen and the gipsy.

"It's worth more than a ten spot, ain't it boss, me being honest and riding miles into the city?"

"And mind you," said Pen, but with a humorous twinkle to take the edge off his words, "the house has police protection and burglar alarms."

"Right you are, sir," said the gipsy with a gracious wave of the hand. "Nothing in it for me in them old houses. Give me the noovoo rich every time."

"Goodbye, my little *chal*," called the woman, "you come back to me when you're a grown man!" and the gipsy woman and the gipsy man and Uncle Charles and even the gipsy dogs laughed; Dan could not see why. But his father and Uncle Murdo looked angry.

They were in the carriage going back to Ardentinny. Dan sat hunched up between his father and Uncle Murdo; his mother and Uncle Charles were on the seat facing him. "Well, Daniel?" said Pen. "Do you think it was kind to your mother to run away without a word?" Dan hung his head.

"One would suppose," put in Murdo, talking across Dan, "that his mother and father had troubles enough without his adding to them." He gave the boy a penetrating look. "You hadn't thought of that, had you?"

Dan began to weep.

"What you seem to need is stiffening. Stop snivelling, my boy! You've got to learn to be a man. You mustn't shirk your responsibilities."

Charles exclaimed indignantly: "Fiddlesticks, Murdo! He's only a boy. And I'm glad he had the — the guts to run away! Much better than getting sullen and curdled inside. It's a promising sign — action, no brooding." Dan sobbed uncontrollably.

"I will say only this," said Pen, "and then we won't speak of it again. Never again run away from your troubles, my dear boy. Face them. Fight them out. Do you understand? And will you promise?"

"Y-yes."

Maud put her hand on his knee and whispered: "Tell me, dear, why did you?" The boy stiffened; at last, under her coaxing, he stammered: "I thought you didn't love me because I hurt Jo." Appalled, she stared mistily over his head. "How could you think such a thing!" she choked.

"It's damned odd," said Charles hastily, "that he should run to a gipsy camp. Damned odd!"

No one answered him.

"Well, in that boy New England meets the cavaliers, Pen — and we'll see."

"Pen," said Maud, "I think Dan needs to get away from home more. Why not send him to school? There's St. Horatius. He and Alastair could go in the autumn."

Pen considered. "He does need discipline."

"Yes. To iron out that sullen temper of his," agreed Murdo.

"There's temper on *both* sides of the family, Murdo," said Maud quickly.

Pen said doubtfully: "It's a poor school, though. They don't teach them anything much."

"It is not bad in some ways, Pen. They make gentlemen of them and the boys have a happy time there. And, Pen, they do have good discipline."

The carriage stopped before Ardentinny and they got out. Walking up from the front gate, Charles put one arm in Dan's and thumped him in the ribs. "You poor little shrimp!... Listen to me Dan. I'll tell you a secret. Things don't matter as much as you think they do, laddie. Now you enjoy life, keep your own counsel and your private thoughts, and think how amusing people are. Most likely you'll take it hard, though — you're a Thatcher, I expect.... Chin up, now! You're only a boy, but you'll make a man someday."

Dan liked his tone, though he did not understand him.

# CHAPTER III

St. Horatius School was a thick-walled stone house built as a residence during the Crimean War; it was as square, as angular, as bleakly severe as the Scot who had planned it. Built before the days of central heating, it still lacked a furnace. Each classroom had an open fireplace during winter; but in the cold, wet, autumn weather the stone walls of the classrooms sweated clammily. "Boys should become used to *res augustae*," said Mr. Mandover, the headmaster. "No better training in the world. I allow of no pampering in my school!"

The cornerstones of Mr. Mandover's theory of education were cricket and Latin. Cricket, he believed, taught one to play games like a gentleman, while the study of a dead language, he maintained, built character by forcing a boy to do regularly what he did not want to do. "*Justum et tenacem propositi vir.* Tenacem propositi — 'tenacious of,' Thatcher? That makes neither English nor Latin nor common sense! Remember, Thatcher, that in translating Latin — called by egregious oafs a dead language! — you are dealing not with a bludgeon but a rapier. Translate with that subtlety you would use in cutting a fast ball through the slips. Horace is giving us a picture of the ideal man. 'Tenacious of,' indeed!"

Mr. Mandover began the day at St. Horatius with a chapter from the Bible followed by other religious exercises, such as the proper intoning of "when two or three are gathered together." Religion attended to for the day, justice followed. "Tripp!" Mr. Mandover would expel the name in a voice that cut through the torpid atmosphere of schoolboy devotion like a whiplash. No further explanation was needed. Knowing the ceremonial of punishment, Tripp would stand up slowly and march to the centre of the room.

"How many hours, Tripp?"

"Five, sir."

If a tongue-lashing followed, the class relaxed, for Mr. Mandover considered it unjust to mingle exhortation and punishment. Usually, however, Mandover would send the culprit to his study for the stick.

Silence while Tripp went for the cane. Mr. Mandover rustled papers, and the class held its breath wondering whether Tripp would whimper. Tripp returned and handed the cane handle foremost to Mr. Mandover. The cane descended *whish-h* — *whack* and the victim, practised in the art of taking a licking, lowered his hand with the swing of the stick to minimize the impact.

"Now, Tripp. Don't let me see you here again for at least a month."

"Yes, sir. No, sir."

In all this there was nothing degrading. It was felt that one was not properly blooded, one had not really smelt powder, until one had taken a caning without a whimper. At ten years and under, the chastisement was light and private, administered on a part of the anatomy specially padded by nature for the contingency. Over ten and up to adolescence, the culprit, having reached years of dignity if not of discretion, received a swipe for each hour of detention on alternate palms — in public. The occasion satisfied all the canons of Greek tragedy. There was dignity, ceremonial, a chorus, and a sense of the ineluctable justice of the gods (shared even by the protagonist). On the part of the onlookers there was an enjoyable feeling of awe and terror, if not of pity, which might have been expressed by the phrase, "There but for the grace of God go I, Smith Minor."

Spring brought long, lazy afternoons of cricket on green grass under the clear sky, before time had any particular meaning. Sometimes when there was a match with another school, there would be a short report in the paper. "For St. Horatius, Thatcher Minor scored forty-two runs. Thatcher Major also did well." The chink of a ball well hit, the stately march of flannelled figures after an over, the thrill of seeing the bails fly after a well-pitched ball, the fearful delight of stalking out from the pavilion under all eyes to take the first ball; these things one remembered after years when one told oneself, "Anyway, I had a jolly happy childhood."

Once Dan learnt his new world, he took it pretty much for granted. He learnt the different sizes and sorts of human nature. There were amiable scamps, like Geoffrey Tripp. There were boys who were clever and unpopular, like Flint, and boys who were both clever and popular, like Alastair; there were boys who got bullied and boys who bullied; there were those masters you could rag and those you couldn't. These were not matters for specula-tion, they were simply facts.

Alastair, easily the leader in all he attempted, was sought by everyone. But with one exception, Dan chose his friends rather than they him. The exception was his cousin Quentin Thatcher.

One day Jiffy Tripp greeted him in the hall with the news that there was a new boy in the school, a boarder.

"I know him," said Dan, "he's my cousin."

"Well, if you ask me, he's a bit of an ass. Last night dur-ing study Mandover asked him if he could translate. He said he could and — listen Granny! — he spouted the whole passage, quantities and all. Then he told Mandover he'd been taught to pronounce Latin as the Romans pronounced it, not the English."

Dan grinned. "And what did Cut-to-slips say?"

"Stared at him for a minute — you know, as if he were a laboratory specimen not well pickled, and said that German methods of scholarship were rapidly making it impossible for a gentleman to quote Latin at all.... Come on! The fellows are going to rag him."

One of the doors in the great hall led into a corridor opening into what had once been a scullery. Now it was lined with handwash basins, and it was a polite fiction that the boys washed their hands and faces before going home from school. This room was sometimes put to more clandestine uses, and at the present moment it and the corridor leading to it were crammed with boys, their backs turned to Dan and Tripp.

A tall, dark boy with a fiery, contemptuous expression faced the jeering ring of boys.

"What's your name?"

"What do you want to know for?"

"Well, you don't want us to call you Grubby or Hatpin or Stinkfish, do you?"

"My name's Thatcher."

"An honourable name! Alastair, Granny, where are you? Here's your long lost uncle from Patagonia. I bet you're a nigger, Thatcher, aren't you? What's your full name?"

"George Pilgrim Thatcher."

"Is your name Pilgrim!"

"Yes, it is — if it's any of your business!"

It seemed too good to be true. Several boys embraced one another in convulsive merriment.

"Well, Pill, what have you come here for? Come on, Pill, speak up. You had enough to say for yourself last night!"

"To go to school."

"To go to school! Now isn't that nice for us. Pill's going to school with us, and maybe if we're nice he'll teach us how to read our Latin properly. Well, Pill, so you'll feel at home, we're going to initiate you into the Order of the Bath."

Dan pushed through the circle and said briefly: "No, you're not!"

"Hello, Granny! Look here, is he really your cousin?"

"Yes, he is. And if you want to know what he's here for, I'll tell you. His parents were drowned on the *Titanic*, and Pill was in a lifeboat for forty-eight hours."

Mockery gave place to curiosity and even respect in the faces of his tormentors.

"Say, Pill, were your parents really drowned?"

"Yes."

"*Both* of them?"

"Yes."

"Holy smoke!"

"Come on, Pill," said Dan, "we'll go and get some ginger beer."

They went down the path to the tuck shop. "You're snivelling, you mug!" exclaimed Dan. "You don't need to bother about them. You should have seen what they did to me when I was a new boy.... Besides, they think you're a stout fellow. Your parents were drowned on the *Titanic* — see?"

Quentin stamped his foot — just like a girl! thought Dan — and said furiously: "I'm not snivelling. I'm angry! And 'I loathe the vulgar mob and avoid them' *arceo valgum profanum*, you know." Dan gaped at him. "I'm going to be a great writer, and great writers are always misunderstood by the mob.... I'm not snivelling! I'll punch you if you say I am. It's because you're so darned decent.... Look here, Dan, let's swear friendship forever and ever."

Dan stared at him curiously, not unkindly, but as at a strange animal. "You're a queer fish, Pill. You're like my sister. She always wants to cry when she's happy or sad. She cries when I remember to give her a birthday present, and she cries when I don't. If she doesn't give *me* one, I get mad as blazes, but I don't cry!"

Quentin paid not the least attention to this. He went on ardently. "And you'll see what a good friend I'll be. I bet you there'll be a war someday and I'll save your life.... Will you?"

"Will I what?"

"Be brothers-in-arms."

"Not yet. I'll see.… There's no war now. Let's forget it, Pill, and get that ginger beer."

"I'll never forget it," said Quentin.… "All right, I'll buy the beer and we'll drink a toast to our friendship. And will you kindly remember not to call me 'Pill'? I'll poke you one if you do."

Quentin boarded at St. Horatius, and being a year older than Dan, he became Thatcher Maximus. The boys let him alone because of his sharp tongue, but he never won popularity, for he was nearsighted and had to peer at people and he was no good at games; try how he would — and he tried again and again — he could not catch a ball to save his life. Moreover, he was too proud to accept the role of the clever ass who is a mug at games. He and Dan were opposites. Dan was steady, except when he lost his temper; Quentin was changeable and moody. He was both timid and reckless and, plagued by too vivid an imagination, he was afraid of a thousand things — and dared not give in to a single fear.

The boys were growing up. Growing outward, they burst the chrysalis and began to show the kind of insect they were going to become; growing inward, they became aware of other boys as different persons from themselves. Coming back from the holidays, one found one's best friend turned into an alien creature in long trousers with an uncertain command over his voice.

Mr. Mandover annually delivered a lecture to those boys who had newly assumed the *toga virilis*. Tilting his chair back and twisting his moustache, he talked with complacency and gusto.

"For tomorrow," he began, "you will write an essay on the 'Awkward Age.' The Awkward Age is when a boy first realizes that he is grubby without and unkempt within. Plastered with mud, he comes running into the house screaming at the top of his voice. Having been told to clean his boots lest worse befall him and because there are guests in the house, he wipes them off on the guest towel, stumbles down the stairs, and rushing into the room where his mother is giving tea to some ladies, he trips over a chair and measures his length on the floor. Recovering himself, he has eyes for nothing but the cake plate, whence he seizes a cake in each hand, and cramming his mouth, full rushes from the room without having uttered a single civilized word. He has an awkward body and a clumsy little soul. If by instinct and nurture he is a gentleman, he will content himself with sticking hatpins into his fellows and perpetrating strange odours in the classroom; if, however, he is a cad, he will pull the wings off flies and bully smaller boys — and worse. Though he tells the truth manfully, he is still a savage. Nonetheless, he is beginning to realize dimly that he is no longer a child. To be sure, he has not yet looked at himself and seen himself for the shameless little ruffian he is, nor has he looked below the surface of his fellows. In his folly he is still inclined to say of Shrimp Minor, 'Shrimp Minor is a worm,' simply because Shrimp Minor is no good at games and cries if you look at him — not realizing that Shrimp is handicapped by bad eyesight and can't fight and knows it…. Mark my words, boys, your comings and your goings are observed by your elders. Not a day passes in which I do not have to write a letter of recommendation for some old boy whose virtues and failings — whose *failings and virtues* I know even better than my own. Most of you, by an incredible miracle of nature will eventually turn into men. One or two of you — I name no names, but I know the ones I speak of, and *let them beware!* — will, I am convinced, end their days hanging higher than Haman…. Three pages on the 'Awkward Age' — not less than ten words to the line — for tomorrow at nine o'clock."

## ii

Pen remarked in the noncommittal voice he always used when speaking of his brother-in-law: "Murdo thinks Europe is drifting toward war. He thinks he ought to come back to the West."

"Sounds like Murdo," said Charles; "he left Japan because he thought there would be trouble in China, now he wants to leave China because he hopes there will be trouble at home."

"'Hopes,' Charles?" exclaimed Euphemia severely.

"Oh, he doesn't call it hope. But make no mistake about Murdo. It's meat and drink to him to be in the centre of a row! I know my brother; he's a restless soul."

It was "after church" in the evening and, as usual, the family had gathered together for high tea. On Sunday evenings no servants were present and the family relaxed and expanded, each member talking of his own interests to whomever would listen, so that before long, by a process of social selection, there was always a cleavage of sexes. The men (and Euphemia) discussed the affairs of the universe, the women were soon engrossed in their practical world within a world. Everyone was talking except Joanna, who was quiet as a mouse, liking best to listen, and Tessa Thatcher, who ate scarcely anything and who hoped that, presently, her husband would feel the quality of her silence.

Alastair, to stir up mischief, began to talk of the Thatcher family motto. Balancing a fork on his finger to attract attention, he said: "I came across the Thatcher motto today. It's pretty loathsome." Pen looked up quickly and exclaimed: "Indeed! What's wrong with it?" — "It's so stuffy, Father. *Virtute*. So obvious, so trite. They might as well hurl the Bible in your face.... What's the Burnet motto?" Three voices answered in unison. "*Curre ad astras.*" — "That means, 'curry favour with the big wigs,' doesn't it?" asked Alastair innocently. Fanny who had not much humour cried indignantly: "No! It means, roughly, 'hitch your wagon to a star.' Does that mean anything to you, young sir? It ought to, it's four hundred years old!"

"As a matter of fact," put in Charles, "the first Burnet who could steal enough money to buy a coat of arms, proved the motto by running away at the battle of Flodden. But everybody ran at Flodden and you'll find that the Burnets are never left behind." "Well," said Alastair, "I think everyone ought to make their own motto, so I've thought of one in French because French is the language of chivalry." — "What is it," asked Euphemia incautiously. "*Toujours les entrailles*," said Alastair. After a pause, during which the family translated this effort, Maud said severely: "Alastair, children should be seen but not heard!"

The conversation divided into streams, each stream isolated by the general din. Charles turned to Tessa Thatcher. "You're very quiet tonight, Tessa, *mia*. It isn't like you." Because he was talking to a pretty woman, his voice curled up into an ingratiating laugh at the end of his sentence.

"Don't you ever feel, Charles, that you want to go inside and shut the door after you?"

"Not often. I'd rather be outside. I like noise and chatter and gaiety."

"But aren't you *ever* serious?"

"As little as possible. You know what the sundial says?"

"What does it say?"

"It says, *horas non numero nisi serenas*. I'll translate it for you. 'I record only the sunny times' .... That's me, Tessa. But I should have thought that you, too —"

"Much you know about me, Charles Burnet.... Sometimes I could almost scream at people's lack of sensibility. People say the same things over and over simply because they're used to saying them and without ever thinking what they mean!"

"Who, for instance?"

"Well ... Pen and my husband. They're talking about war and the institution of marriage and stoicism — whatever that is. Words, Charles! Who cares about war in the Balkans? I don't! But Daniel says we all think too much about ourselves. He says we should all get along better if we only took life quietly and were a little stoical.... Do you know, sometimes I could almost *hate* men!"

This was more than Charles had bargained for, and instinct warned him of something wrong. He was afraid of women when they were like this. He liked to feel gay and frivolous and he did not like to look too closely at things.... Better turn it off lightly, he thought, then she would see that he didn't want to —

"Well, Charles, what *do* you think of me? You think I'm always empty headed?"

"No, not empty headed."

"Empty hearted, then. That's what you really think of me! ... What are you thinking of, Charles? Now! Right this minute!"

Something to say popped into Charles's head, and being Charles, he said it without thinking first. "I was thinking of Aurora and Tithonus — but you wouldn't understand."

"Aren't we literary? ... As a matter of fact, I do understand. You mean the myth about Aurora asking every good gift for her lover except one — youth, so that, though Tithonus is immortal, he is old?"

"I swear to heaven, Tessa —" began Charles, horrified. "What a God-forgotten fool I am!"

But Tessa said recklessly: "Why not say it, Charles ... only, you see, it isn't true. Daniel's sun doesn't rise by me. And he isn't immortal — not even old.... And I do love him. It isn't as simple as that!"

"Tessa, will you believe me when I say —"

Tessa leaned forward, laying her hand on his sleeve, and lowered her voice. "We're good friends, aren't we, Charles?"

"Always have been. Always will be!"

"Then keep it to yourself, dear Charles.... You see, it's not Daniel's fault. I'm just a restless person, that's all."

At one end of the table Maud was reflecting how odd it was that men could get so very excited over *ideas.* "And why do they love to talk about war?" The word always chilled her heart and made her unreasonably angry. "But they like to. In their hearts they think of it as adventure and change: boys to the end of their days, every one of them."

She relaxed and took in the family with an affectionate look, feeling at the very centre of it. She thought, if only Daniel could go out to people; so formal, so humourless. Not even to Tessa, so much younger than he. And she is so quiet it frightens one. I'd rather see her flighty and gay as she was before she lost her baby — If only she were well enough to have another child —

Maud's thoughts were interrupted by a piercing yell from Dan. "You hound! My shin! You wait!"

"He was asleep," explained Alastair coolly, "so I just woke him up."

"I wasn't, I was thinking.... Mother, why do people always speak of Uncle Murdo as restless?"

Everyone felt that this was an awkward question.... But really, why did people? Each one there had his own private opinion of the matter. Pen secretly suspected that Murdo's faith had been undermined; Fanny believed that Murdo honestly enjoyed being in the thick of trouble, while Maud merely included Murdo's restlessness in the eternal restlessness of all males. Euphemia said sentimentally: "I suppose the children are old enough to be told, Maud? Your uncle, children, was unfortunate in his marriage. I think it has preyed on his mind a good deal."

"Bosh, Euphemia!" cried Fanny.

But Alastair, who had reached the brash age of adolescence, was not satisfied. "I suppose you mean about his wife running away with someone better looking? Why didn't he divorce her and marry someone else, like the Eltons?"

Euphemia gasped, and Maud exclaimed, "Alastair!"

"Well, why didn't he? I would have."

"Nice people don't talk —" began Maud.

"Let's hear no more of it, Alastair!" said Pen sternly. "One would think you'd no breeding at all."

Dan, who thought slowly, was struggling with an idea. "But *I* think —" he began.

"Children! You may all leave the table," ordered Pen.

"You see, you juggins?" commented Alastair very unfairly. "You never know when to stop."

Sulkily the children trooped from the room. Alastair and Joanna went upstairs to get some sheet music.

It seemed to Dan that he had got hold of an important idea, and he wanted to be by himself to wrestle with it. He went into the drawing room where there was a fine fire blazing away; moving a sofa in front of the hearth, he lay down and watched the flames.

In the dining room, with the constraint of the children removed, the grown-ups were talking more freely. With her infallible instinct for saying the wrong thing, Euphemia was discussing divorce. "Divorce is much commoner nowadays because people lack the spiritual resources they used to have." Secretly it pleased Euphemia a little when marriages were unsuccessful.

Placing the tips of his fingers together with precision, Daniel Thatcher ventured to disagree with his sister-in-law. "I believe the usual cause of divorce is that one partner demands too much of the other. 'There is always one who loves and one who is loved' is a French proverb containing much shrewd truth. Yes. No one should place his whole life utterly in the hands of his partner, keeping nothing back for his private life. No. A man should always possess his own soul away from even those closest to him. How else can he be secure? He should guard his reserve against all importunings. Indeed, yes!"

To Tessa, her husband's dry, precise voice had suddenly become intolerable. She could not reach him at all. No matter what happened he would regard it judicially as an intellectual problem. He would put his finger tips carefully together, look at her mildly from that inner place you could not reach, and say: "Let us consider it calmly, my dear." ... If only she could really shake his self-sufficiency just once and make him suffer!

She burst out: "Oh, Daniel! Daniel! That's just selfish! I think people ought to spend themselves on others even if it destroys them!"

All around the table, chairs creaked from the slight, startled movements of those sitting on them. Daniel blinked and changed colour. Called back to the domestic relations from the pure intellectual pleasure of expressing an idea with precision, he remembered that Tessa always had the faculty of making him feel uneasy. She made one feel that one's ideas always had some personal application.

Maud tried to change the subject, but Tessa would not let her. Flushed and panting, she released a reckless torrent of words: "Why shouldn't Murdo have got a divorce, and why shouldn't his wife? You have only one life to live, and after a woman's forty, she might as well be dead! ... I'm sorry! I know I'm making a scene.... I didn't mean to.... I don't want to! I'm so ashamed!" She bit her lip and shook her head to keep the tears back.

Daniel said: "Tessa!" and coming round, tried clumsily to take her hands. She pushed him away with an inarticulate cry and rushed from the room with her hands over her face. Complete silence ensued for a moment. Maud gathered her wits together and quietly accepted the situation.

"Tessa hasn't been herself since the baby died," she said. "Go to her, Daniel. And, Daniel — coax her to talk to you." Daniel went, looking bewildered.

Charles said tentatively: "A good bust-up once in a while is the very best thing for a family. Clears the air." And Euphemia whispered to Fanny: "I've been thinking for some time that the child has been going through a religious crisis of some sort." Fanny exclaimed: "Rubbish!" And Pen snorted derisively.

Tessa had flung herself on a chesterfield in the drawing room. Dan's tousled head peered over the back of the sofa before the fire like a startled deer from a covert, and he saw a woman with her face buried in the cushions — crying. What ought he to do? If he stole away she might see him, and dimly he felt that that would never do. Then Uncle Daniel came into the room. Too late to go now.

Daniel sat on the couch beside her. For a long time she would neither answer him nor move, except to shake his hand from her shoulder.

Daniel said miserably: "When I said that, I didn't mean *us*. I wasn't thinking of us."

Tessa sat up at last. "Oh, Daniel. This is a miserable life we lead!"

There was fear in his eyes. "I'm sorry, Tessa."

"Why are we like this together?"

Daniel gave a mirthless laugh. "I am old, Tessa; you are young."

"No! It isn't that. But you are so stiff and cold and unnatural with me. It freezes me."

Daniel began to stride up and down. Several times he began to speak, but each time he stopped, defeated. "If —" he said at last "— if you want — I mean, if I don't — if I can't make you happy, you could — sometimes I think the devil is between us, Tessa!"

"I don't want a divorce, Daniel. But I want to feel alive. Life's passing, and I feel as if I'd never truly lived it.... Make me feel alive, Daniel!"

He came to her, put his hand awkwardly on her shoulder, then removed it, feeling her muscles tense against him. "Tessa, why must we? You know the sort of torment this leads us to."

"Put your hands on my shoulders again, Daniel. Please."

He did as she asked. She was trembling.

"Now say you love me, Daniel."

He tried to utter the simple sentence, but he could not. What he felt he could not utter — no, not if his life were to depend upon it.... And at times like these, the tension rising, like a sudden demon out of nothing, would unfurl to their minds and nerves a mortal hell divided between them.

"If only —" began Daniel, but he did not finish the phrase. But both of them knew what he meant: if only, while she was with child, Tessa had been quiet and hadn't gadded about and played games. Daniel said heavily: "The doctor says there must never be another. It might mean —"

"I'm willing! I don't care!"

She fingered the lapel of his coat and dropped her eyes. "Daniel. Other people —" She stopped.

"I know, my dear. But it wouldn't be right. It isn't right. We've talked about that before, over and over again. It wouldn't be right."

Presently, they went slowly out of the room together, and a sorely perplexed and abashed boy stood up. His mind was in a turmoil. He did not completely understand what he had heard, but he understood enough to be frightened. Was this what it was like to be grown up? he wondered. He felt obscurely that he was looking for the first time into a fearful world…. He began to jingle some loose cartridges in his coat pocket. He did not want to think of it. "Tomorrow I'll get up at dawn and set up a target against the escarpment. Two bulls and four inners last time; not bad!"

### iii

On the way to the garden Dan stopped, as usual, to stare at the portrait of Great-Great-Grandmother Burnet which stood in a panel of the dining room beside that of her husband, General Sir Murdo Burnet. Sir Murdo had a hooked nose, a smoky look, and a face that always reminded Dan of the graven image in Joanna's coloured Bible. Uncle Charles always called him Sir Tradition Gruff, and he might have been Dan's own Uncle Murdo.

But it was Sir Rae's lady that teased the boy's imagination. She was dressed in flowing Gainsborough silks, as befitted a general's lady of the eighteenth century, but the artist — perhaps with intentional irony — had left out of the picture the usual picture hat and shepherdess crook; instead, he had painted her with uncovered head, and in her blue-black hair above one ear was thrust a flower — not an English rose but some vivid flower of the south. She was dark and beautiful and strange, and out of her frame she stared not at her descendants, the most British Burnets, but beyond them — at what?

Charles Burnet came into the dining room and followed the boy's glance. "The mysterious Lady Burnet," thought Charles. "And worth looking at, too. Fifty devils in her eyes, and in her body the sway of an angel — no peace there…. But let the boy find out all that for himself."

"Well, Dan, what do you think of your great-grandmother?"

"She has a strange look in her eyes, hasn't she?"

"Spells and incantations, my lad. Haven't they told you about her?"

"Not much."

"Want to know?"

"Yes. I bet there's a lot to know."

"Very discerning of you. I dare say there is, too, and I wish I knew it…. Would you say she was an aristocrat?"

"No-o — I see what you mean. She looks as if she didn't care a hang for people."

"Not much for people and less for their *things*, Dan. Her name was Faa and she belonged to a very special sort of aristocracy, the aristocracy of poverty and freedom."

"Faa is Mother's second name."

"Quite. The Burnets have always been proud of her. She was a gipsy, Dan, a full-blooded Romany rawnie. What d'you think of that?"

Dan stared at his gipsy ancestor.

"It's a fact. It's the family skeleton — though we're secretly proud of it — that her grandfather was hanged for theft in the seventeen-thirties at the Tolbooth in Edinburgh."

"It must have been strange to be married to a gipsy. I wonder what she was like. Did she have children and was she happy, I wonder?"

"Children? Scads of them. Happy? I don't know. Somehow — perhaps after her marriage — she learned to read and write. She could play the violin and sing like a bird. They say she met Robert Burns and Mr. Hume and the rest of them; she'd only have to be herself to be distinguished — look at her portrait! She left her husband twice, and twice she came back."

"Went back to the tribe?"

Charles grinned impishly. "Oh, I dare say she had a gipsy husband, too. Shocks you? Lord bless you, she was a gipsy. I think she paid the Burnets a great compliment, loving my great-great-grandfather enough to come back to him twice."

"I wonder what she's looking at, Uncle Charles?"

"Strange look, isn't it. As if she saw through things. I always think she is looking at things as they really are, and people, too. I should think that might be a terrifying experience even for a gipsy. You know the pagans believed that anyone who saw Pan — that is, nature — died. Why should *she* be bound by our conventional prejudices?"

"She wasn't, was she?"

"Not if the stories about her are true."

"Did she always do what she wanted to?"

"How can we tell? … I think there was always something she was afraid of."

"How do you know?"

"It's just a guess. Don't forget I've a little of her blood in me…. When she was an old woman, she became bedridden, and one day she suddenly fell silent, not because she was stricken dumb, but through sheer determination not to speak to a soul, not even to her husband. No one thought she could walk a step, but one night, without a word to anyone, she walked out into the dark, and when they found her next day, she was miles away, lying in the middle of a meadow looking up at the stars."

"And was she dead?"

"Yes."

"Why did she do that, Uncle Charles?"

"Who knows? They say a cat goes in and a gipsy goes out, to die. Escape from walls and a roof — or from the body, it's all the same, very likely."

"Escape?"

"It must be strange, Dan, to be born free of all the restrictions — moral codes and that sort of thing — we're born into and can never escape from. If we could escape, I wonder whether we should really find it was an escape. Perhaps she found herself even more bound than we; perhaps that's what her look means.... But you probably don't know what I'm talking about."

"Yes, I do, I think. For instance, last week at the dance — I wouldn't tell this to anyone but you — Mother told us beforehand to try and see that Joanna had a good time. Well, Alastair promised easily without a moment's hesitation, you know what Alastair is like. But me it made quite irritable for a minute, not because she asked it but because she looked — well, wistful in a way, you know. That's something you can't get over, do you see what I mean? Then, of course, I promised and I meant it a lot more than Alastair did. Well, at the dance, I wanted to take Cynthia Elton in to supper. I wanted to badly because I knew if I didn't, Alastair would. She's the sort of girl I'd like to marry someday.... Are you laughing at me?"

"No, laddie. Not I."

"Just before supper Joanna became ill, and of course, I had to bring her home. And the strange thing was that I forgot all about Cynthia."

"And Alastair took her in to supper?"

"Yes, as a matter of fact, he did."

Charles grinned at his favourite nephew. "I see you're thinking of becoming a man these days."

"Why didn't you get married, Uncle Charles?"

"Several reasons. I wasn't caught young enough, for one. Spoiled, for another; too popular with women, you know. But mainly it was because I could never make up my mind to be satisfied with the many in one; it always seemed more exciting to discover the one in many ... as usual I'm talking too much. I'm rightly considered a bad influence on the young."

"Do you know I've thought of that a lot, too. Answer me a question honestly, Uncle Charles. Does the gipsy blood ever bother us?"

"Oho! Well, maybe. It breaks out every so often; the upfling of the satyr's heels, you know. A scandal here, an elopement there, and the production of a number of irresponsible scamps — brilliant and likable, usually — like yours truly."

"What about Uncle Murdo?"

"No. The trouble with Murdo is his pride, though he doesn't know it. You see, plenty of Burnets have deserted their wives, but he's the first Burnet whose wife deserted him. That's why he became a medical missionary and went to the East."

Sudden compunction overtook Charles. One oughtn't to talk thus to the young. "It won't bother you," he said. "You're a Thatcher. You're a steady sort of chap."

"I don't know.... Am I?"


iv


To Dan, the freedom of college was a heady draught. There seemed nothing in the world ahead of him that threatened to baffle his growing sense of power. Dan and Alastair viewed failure, sickness, old age, and all the other evils of life with confident superciliousness.

Dan roomed with Quentin Thatcher, partly because Quentin wished it and partly because he did not want to room with Alastair. Quentin he found a prickly person to live with, morose often, serious minded, and very exacting in friendship.

The sight of Quentin poring grimly over a book as if his life depended on it made Dan feel uneasily that perhaps Quentin's life *did* depend on it. It wasn't normal. Sometimes the way Quentin breathed bothered Dan; he almost panted after knowledge.... Why do I like him, anyway? I suppose because he likes me. And besides, well — hang it! He's Quentin. He's always been my friend.... If only he had a sense of humour. But Quentin was always harping on their friendship. If only he wouldn't talk so much about it. It wasn't normal for a person to be so dependent on one friend. It was womanish of Quentin! Besides, there were so many things and people that he himself was interested in that he had no intention of giving himself to the Damon and Pythias business. He didn't want to be pinned down!

"Tell you what, Quentin," he said one day, "I'm taking Cynthia Elton to the Lotus Club dance. Why don't you go stag?"

"Do *you* want me to, Dan?"

"What on earth has that got to do with it?" exclaimed Dan irritably.

"All right. I'm sorry. I'll go, if you like."

Dan had no time for Quentin mainly because his interest was focused on Cynthia Elton.

Beatrice, the cleverest of the sisters, had gone to college with a scholarship. Cynthia wanted to go, too, but Mr. Elton, who had not gone to college himself, felt that a higher education unfitted women for the role of man's inferior, which he firmly held to be their true destiny. So he sent her instead to a "finishing school" in Toronto where she was taught, by way of compensation, the polite art of social superiority. Cynthia did not have it in her to become a snob, but being young and conventional she accepted the *finish* superficially and studied poise, manner, the correct thing to say in the usual social crises, small talk about the arts, and even cookery and the managing of servants. In short, she prepared herself to occupy in matrimony "the position to which she had been accustomed." In spite of her education, Cynthia was a charming and natural girl.

Charles Burnet, watching them together, said to Maud: "Why is it that each batch of youngsters coming along thinks it is going to make so much more of a success in marriage than its elders did?"

"Puppy love!" said Maud tartly. She did not like the idea of the boys marrying. "Most people in our class," she took occasion to say to Dan, "don't marry until they are thirty or so."

v

The orchestra twittered tentative notes over the empty ballroom, inviting the ladies, already present in their partners' minds, to finish powdering quickly and to descend in their amethyst, turquoise, and pastel silks and satins to be carried off over the forgetful sea of rhythm. Dan stood with Quentin Thatcher, waiting for Cynthia. "When she comes," thought Dan, "she won't look like just any girl you are going to dance with. It will be as if we stood apart from other people, and together. I don't know why she makes me feel that way, but she does." Thus to feel, made him happy and triumphant; it made everything so simple.

At this moment he frankly resented the presence of Quentin, an earth-bound spirit willing to drag one to his own ironic level.

"Whom are you dancing with, Quentin?"

"Oh, Tessa, I suppose, and Cynthia if she'll spare me one, and Beatrice, I dare say."

"Isn't there anyone you really want to dance with?"

"No! I loathe women, if you want to know. They exist for the sole purpose of getting you into nature's trap and making you toe the line for the rest of your life. That's all they think of, really; it's what they call romance! It's all so darned biological! A man might as well be an amoeba…. This" — he waved his cigarette — "is all just part of the game."

"That sounds pretty silly to me! After all, people have to get married — and that means courting, doesn't it?"

"Most people do. I don't. If I have to make any changes in my plan of life, I'll superintend them myself. I shan't have my life arranged for me by someone else."

"I bet you make a mess of it, then, old man."

Quentin crushed out his cigarette and turned to Dan seriously. "Listen, Dan. I'd let a friend interfere, perhaps. Yes, I would. There would be some sense to that. A friend likes you for what you are — for what's in your mind, I mean — not simply for the purpose of tying you up so you'll raise a family of brats exactly like a million other brats —"

He might just as well not have spoken, for Cynthia had appeared, and Dan had neither eyes nor ears for him. In her ball dress, with her hair done up, she looked taller. Her eyes were shining with joy, her lips were parted in laughter, and she stood swaying gracefully to the music, young, triumphant, and completely mistress of herself. She smiled to him and he saw her with the unspoilt eyes of youth, not noticing the mould of her features or the colour of her hair, but seeing beauty itself.

"It will always be like this," thought Cynthia. The music stopped, and for no clear reason at all, she curled her fingers about his hand and gripped convulsively.

"What is it, Cynthia? Is anything the matter!"

"Nothing. Just foolishness. The music stopped and all at once I felt as if you had gone far off from me."

"I shan't go far," said Dan with a laugh, "and you can have me back whenever you want me."

He looked at his program. He had a dance with Tessa, of course, and the next with Beatrice. Most of the program was marked with crosses. "Whom are you dancing with, Cynthia?"

"Alastair."

"Don't let him fascinate you, Cynthia. My brother's good at that! You're my girl, you know."

"Am I, Dan? Who is your partner?"

"Beatrice."

"Well, she's safe. She's engaged, or I mightn't trust you."

Dan exclaimed at this with whimsical incredulity: "Beatrice!" But Cynthia was serious.

"She's clever, Dan. Like you."

"So are you, Cynthia."

"No, I'm not. I can't talk except just the things everyone says."

"But we do talk. As much as we want to."

"I wish I hadn't said that, you mightn't have noticed. Never mind, Dan. Go and dance with Beatrice. I'm glad you like her. She's worth it."

With Beatrice he wanted to talk. It was extraordinary how well their ideas fitted, he reflected. It was odd, too, that that hadn't occurred to him before — particularly.... It was not at all like being with Cynthia, of course. That always seemed — well, inevitable. One didn't need to talk to Cynthia.

"Dan, this is the first time we've danced together since my engagement. Am I different?"

"Do you know, you are somehow. Your expression, I mean. Being engaged becomes you, Beatrice. I've never seen you look so pretty."

She blushed. "I wouldn't have blushed if anyone else had said that, Dan. But it's the first compliment you ever paid me.... I used to be awfully fond of you."

"And still are, I hope?"

"Of course. But —"

"But now you're in love. And that automatically divides the world into two hemispheres. You and Matthew Wilmot in one hemisphere, *people* in the other."

She laughed. "Well, yes, in a way. You'll find out."

"Is it very difficult to live marooned in a whole hemisphere with only one other person?"

Beatrice smiled absently. "Will you answer a question, Dan? I'm serious.... Are you in love with Cynthia?"

Dan adopted an air of whimsical caution. "Why do you ask?"

"A good reason. I like you and, naturally, I like my sister."

"I don't know, Beatrice. I think so. I'm young and so is Cynthia. You see, I've got to finish college and learn a profession. That's a long time. I don't want to let myself go yet."

"Because if you are, you ought to understand her better. I don't think you do."

"Well, what ought I to understand, lady?"

"That Cynthia's spoilt, Dan."

"Cynthia!"

"Oh, not in the way you think. She's sweet and unselfish — I don't mean that. But she is spoilt just the same. And so am I, Dan. You see, she and I are both afraid — oh, of life, let's say. It's true. You can't understand that, can you? … You've always been so safe and secure … in your home, while we —" Beatrice would not meet his enquiring look and the phrase died on her lips.

"You mean —"

She nodded. "There hasn't been much in our home to give us confidence, Dan. That seems such a rotten thing to say. But you ought to know. Cynthia's very conventional because she isn't sure of herself. She may marry you, but she will never trust you completely unless — You'll have to change a bit, Dan. You'll have to sweep her off her feet, if you really want to win her."

"But you, Beatrice — how did you put it? — *you've* given your trust completely."

"Yes, I have. Once and for all. If Matthew asked me to go anywhere or do anything for him, I'd do it." She gave a little, shaky laugh. "That's how I know. I'm not like Cynthia. I'm more impulsive and reckless. You see, Dan, it makes me feel so marvellously settled and secure. It brings everything to life. Ideas, yes, and principles, too, I'd believed in just with my mind before, I believe in with my heart and that's the important thing…. If anything should happen to us, to Matthew and me, I'd — I couldn't stand it!"

"Why should anything happen? There's a clear sea and a fair wind, Beatrice."

She said nothing for a minute, then — "If you were really in love, you'd be afraid."

"I don't believe in fear," said Dan confidently.

When he got back from the dance he found Quentin sitting before the fire poking it idly, still dressed. Dan was tired and wanted to sleep, but Quentin wanted to talk. "It's odd," thought Dan, "that a person as sensitive to his own feelings as Quentin is, should be so insensitive to other people's moods. Are poets all like that, I wonder." Before long Quentin's talk had slid into the inevitable groove — himself, his feelings. For once Dan's irritation broke loose.

"For goodness' sake, Quentin! Why do you talk about your feelings all the time? It isn't wholesome. It's not normal."

Quentin flared up. "All right, I'm not normal and wholesome, if you like! Never have been, very likely. Probably never will be. It's a hell of a world, Dan, and people are rotten!"

"That's a rotten thing to believe!"

"Do you think I want to believe it? I just see clearly, that's all. Why, Dan, when my mother was ill — but that's none of your business! Oh, why don't you let me alone!" He threw down the paper in a rage and began to pace about. "Now I won't sleep. Why don't you let me be the way I am?" He sat down and sank his head in his hands.

Dan gazed at him, startled and a little frightened. "I think if you don't look out, Quentin, you'll have a nervous breakdown."

"Very likely you're right — I've been working too hard." He began to writhe his head between his hands. "Damn! Damn! Damn! I'm not like other people because I *can't* be like other people. Can't you understand that?"

"But I'd no idea, Quentin — I never thought —"

"You never do. You understand nothing! … Do you remember when I jumped off the thirty-foot bridge over the canal and broke a rib? Do you know why I jumped?"

"Because the rest of us had jumped."

"No! Because I knew you would despise me if I didn't."

"According to you, Quentin, friendship is a kind of tyranny. You can never accept a friend for what he is — though you want me to accept you that way — you must always be exacting something from him that he hasn't got to give. There's no comfortable give and take about that."

"I don't want there to be."

"*You* don't." Dan became angry. He now saw clearly what he hadn't quite realized before. Quentin was an egotist.

"I'm not talking about what usually passes for friendship between people who choose their friends because they think they'll be of use in business! I'm talking of what every mother's son of us needs and has got to have in order to get out of himself. If you can make a friend it's proof that you've got some grandeur of spirit. But you don't see it. You probably never will. You're so damned mediocre. You're a philistine. You're one of the *sheep*. You think you have got to feel and do what every Tom, Dick, and Harry feels —"

"Oh, Lord, Quentin! Do change the needle. Let's have a new record."

"Don't you *see*? When someone chooses you for a friend, you're saddled with a responsibility. You can't help yourself, you're simply chosen. And a friend has a right to demand of you all you have to give and more!"

"That's beyond me, Quentin. I'm just an ordinary clod. Anyway, it seems to me you've a right to choose to be chosen, or not, just as you please. And what's more *I* think one shouldn't talk about one's — one's sentiments. It's womanish, and when you put them into words, they lose their power. And, anyway, by jingo, it *bores* me!"

"Probably," said Quentin bitterly, "you'll fall for that — girl!"

"You mind your business about Cynthia!" said Dan hotly.

"Perhaps," Quentin suggested, "you would like to room with someone else."

"Perhaps I should...."

At seventeen, with at least three more years of college ahead of him, it had certainly never occurred to Dan to become engaged to Cynthia. Time passed so pleasantly and so slowly.... The great world peace had yet a few months to run.

## The Apple

Yonder withered apple
Clings to its tree,
But the winter wind is sweeping
And the snow swings free.

Gnarled and ugly covering
And brittle stem,
Live seeds — and the shrivelled flesh
To cover them.

Fifty knife-cut wrinkles
In a haggard skin.
There was once a blossom
When Spring came in.

Blow the stem asunder
You death-keen wind.
None can read the seed beneath
The wrinkled rind.

(From Quentin's Notebook)

# PART II

# THE WHEAT

# CHAPTER IV

### i

In the summer of 1914 the Thatchers took a cottage on Georgian Bay because the quiet of that northern country was good for Joanna's health.

One August night Dan and his father walked to the railway station for news of peace or war. The platform was deserted. The station agent stooped over the telegraph key, coat off, perspiration streaming down his face. Presently, they heard the whistle of the approaching train.

"Supposing —" began Dan.

"Supposing what?" interrupted his father quickly.

"Oh, nothing. I was just thinking — you know father, I'm seventeen."

Pen said nothing, but neither of them thought the remark irrelevant.

The train swung round the bend into sight.

Pen seized Dan's arm with a sudden tight clutch. Scrawled on the coaches in large letters of chalk was the single word *WAR!*

Dan drew in his breath sharply, but his father said nothing, simply stared like a man in a dream.

Soon the train gathered itself together, grunted, and chugged into motion. The songs and the shouting advanced into the darkness and grew faint. The crickets renewed their triumph over the still night.

"Well, Dan?" said Pen.

"Uncle Charles will go!"

"This isn't romance, Dan! It is not a page out of the *Iliad*. It's the devil let loose in the world. You must use your brains and your conscience, my dear boy. You mustn't swing in behind the devil with the rest of the sheep."

ii

Outwardly, "a state of war" caused little immediate change in the Thatcher family. They still went their ways in civilian clothes, thinking civilian thoughts, but with an uneasy feeling that a thread was attached to each one of them, drawing them to a strange web.

Sunday evening supper was still an institution at Ardentinny, but Charles brought his fellow subalterns, and with khaki in the ascendant, there was much talk of the humours of camp life, while Pen Thatcher, who had his own good reason for loathing war, held his peace. A veteran of Mons came and told of a major with a glorious sense of humour, rallying stragglers, and marching them back to the "British Grenadiers," played on a penny whistle and a child's toy drum, when nothing else would have budged them. In a sentimental voice, Euphemia asked this hero about the angels at Mons. "Have you heard, Captain, of how the ghosts of our longbowmen who fell at Crécy and Agincourt helped our men at Mons?"

"The angels at Mons? Ah, yes, indeed. The fact is we had a subaltern who could never do anything right, Miss Burnet. He was wounded in the — ah — forgive me, dear Miss Burnet — he was shot from behind in the most curious and painful way. The doctors could scarcely believe their eyes, but I give you my word that what they finally wrote on his wound tag was bowshot wound in the — er — posterior anatomy."

In October Charles Burnet left Wellington with his battery on the first stage of a well-trodden road.

"Are you glad you are going, Uncle?" asked Dan, for he really wanted to know.

And Charles answered, "It's my chance, laddie." But why it was his chance, and what for, he did not explain.

When the taxi came to take him to the station, Joanna burst into tears, but Charles exclaimed gaily, "No trumpets — by request."

"Whatever happens to him," thought Maud, "let him not be changed!"

He would not let them go to the train with him, and the last they saw of him was a hand wave from the taxi before it whisked him round the corner to France.

Dan and Alastair went back to college at the end of September. At first there were the usual number of undergraduates, but as the term wore on, first one by one and then in greater numbers, the older men exchanged the gown for a uniform.

Just before Christmas the St. Horatius old boys at college met in Alastair's rooms.

"I wonder," mused Flint, "how many of us will be back next term."

Down the corridor the incoming freshmen were being drilled by seniors, as the custom was, in the college song, which says in Greek "after the dust and heat of conflict comes the laurel wreath." Through the window opening upon the campus could be seen members of the Second Canadian Overseas Contingent performing their early and clumsy evolutions under the cynical eyes of NCOs who had been in the Regular Army; soon to go to Valcartier, then to England, then to France.

"Anyone eighteen yet?"

"Granny, your uncle's a captain in the Wellington Battery, isn't he? I suppose he'll get you and Alastair commissions.... Any chance for me, I wonder?" Dan did not answer.

"I wonder who will go first. I know a fellow who was accepted at sixteen —"

"I bet on old Pill. He's such a military looking chap!"

Everyone laughed; the thought of Quentin Thatcher in a uniform was vaguely funny, though no one was quite certain why.

"As a matter of fact," said Quentin flicking his cigarette, "I enlisted today. Report for duty tomorrow."

"Good man! How old are you, Quentin?"

"Eighteen."

Dan with Quentin and Alastair came out of the room together and went downstairs to the entrance hall of the college. There they happened to meet Beatrice Elton who had come across the campus from the women's college to post a letter.

"'Life is real, life is earnest,' Beatrice," quoted Alastair flippantly. "We've just decided that there's a war on, and — you never know, you know."

Beatrice was unexpectedly serious. "It's real enough. What are you so excited and — and *pleased* about? You're such children!"

"Why, Beatrice! Where is that exquisite poise I've always admired in you, that sophisticated diablerie, that —"

"Shut up, Alastair," Dan interrupted; "Beatrice is really upset."

"I am upset. Matthew went to Valcartier yesterday. Of course, I didn't let him see it, but I'm just *afraid* all the time. If anything happened, I'd be done for. It's all or nothing with me.... Other people seem so much braver than I. Am I soft, Dan?"

Dan tried to soothe her. "You're not taking it right, Beatrice. It's an adventure. Everyone takes the same risk and has the same chance. Only about one in twenty got hurt in the Boer War. Matthew won't be hurt."

"I think he will," said Beatrice soberly. "I feel it, I *know* it, somehow."

She smiled ironically at their shocked expressions. "When I woke up this morning I suddenly realized what it might mean.... How do people manage to be brave, Dan?" she burst out wildly,

"And why should they be! What do we care about Belgium! What business is it of ours?"

"Our own people are in it, Beatrice."

"Oh, I know. And I'm ashamed to be talking like this. I suppose I shall get used to it — though I don't believe I ever shall. I shan't let Matthew know, though. He was always brave about things — about everything, and I was always a coward."

"*Is* brave," corrected Dan, but Beatrice simply stared at him strickenly without answering. Presently, she said in a low voice, "I'm sorry to be such a little beast. People say now that private lives don't count anymore because the thing is more important than we are. But I don't feel that way. What's more important than my life and Matthew's and yours and every other single person's? … How do you keep from being afraid?"

Alastair answered seriously for once. "Listen, Beatrice, you work it like this. If you're afraid, you fight. When you fight, you hate! When you hate, you forget about fear."

"Sweet world!" murmured Quentin Thatcher.

She left them and Quentin whispered to Dan: "Come up to my room, Dan." They went to Quentin's room and sported the oak.

"You're the first, Quentin."

"Yes."

They smoked in silence for several minutes. As usual, a book lay open on Quentin's table.

Dan picked up the book. It was the *Iliad*. *My goddess Mother, silver-footed Thetis*, Dan read, *warns me that fate lays two paths to bear me deathward. If I abide and fight before the walls of Troy, my return to Hellas is undone, but fame imperishable remains for me. If I return to my dear country then my good glory dies, but long life awaits me, nor will the term of death be hastened.*

Quentin watched Dan read, and blew rings of smoke the while. "Odd sort of Achilles, I'd make?" said he with a wry smile. "The doom of Quentin Thatcher will bring no fame imperishable, eh?"

"Doom?"

"There's only one way to go into this scrap, Dan, and that's expecting to be killed: any other way would be obscene."

Dan shook his head. "That's beyond me, Quentin."

"And mind you, I'm glad I've decided to. If you give up life beforehand then you're strong as hell, *I* think; then they can't hurt anything but your body.... Funny send off they give you in the army, Dan. You know Thetis gave Achilles a good send off by grabbing his heel and dipping him in the Styx to make him invulnerable. Instead of that they grabbed *me* — somewhere else and said, 'cough and say ninety-nine.' Not very heroic. And they thumped me and bumped me all over, and made me squat and jump up. I'm not absolutely fit in some ways, Dan. But it was easy to fool them. They were willing to be fooled. Then they mumbled the Oath of Allegiance — I suppose they'd probably said it so often that it had become a rigmarole to them — and I held the Bible and repeated it.... Strange beginning, somehow."

In 1915 the first long casualty lists appeared in the papers, and people ceased to live the war in their minds and began to live it in their nerves. "*Killed at St. Julien.* Lieutenant Matthew Wilmot was the son of Dr. and Mrs. W.E. Wilmot of Wellington. He attended school at St. Horatius and was well-known in this city...."

Pen Thatcher took the war hard. In place of a religious belief, he had always clung to a desperate faith in the good will of man whom he regarded as the sole inventor and upholder of right and wrong in a mechanical universe. This creative fiat of mankind which he had believed in — where was it? Yet him, too, the war had made illogical. He believed that this catastrophe had come of the false values of a mechanical civilization, and yet in the same angry breath, he lamented bitterly that war had made a scrapheap of that civilization.... So, austerely and tragically, justified to himself by a fatal pride of intellect, he moved sternly toward his own destruction.

Dan felt unhappy and restless at college. He was still under the enlisting age, but already several of his friends younger than he had sworn to a false age and been accepted. During the Christmas holidays, he stood with his father and watched the passing of a military funeral for a returned veteran. The troops marched with arms reversed to the surging anguish of Chopin's "Funeral March," and to each slow step, a brazen note beat the air like a nail hammered into a coffin. The dead officer's charger passed with empty saddle and boots reversed. A lump came into Dan's throat, and he shook his head to master his emotion....

Dan thought with a conviction deeper than reason, "There, someday, I shall march." Pen watched the play of expression on his boy's face and read it too clearly. As for himself, he knew he was in for an attack of angina, emotion sometimes brought it on, so he turned his face from Dan and stared into a shop window. As yet the family did not know of his ailment.

When he could speak, he said bitterly: "One needs an old head to resist this sort of thing."

"We didn't start it, Father. If a man hits you, you have to fight."

"This isn't a fist fight. All the marching and music, Dan, the bands swinging down the street, mean just one thing — killing people you've never seen before and whom you don't even see die, killing them at three miles distance."

"But, Father, a man has to be loyal to his country. You can't sit back and let your friends fight for you."

Pen was silent for a moment, then he said in a tone of absolute conviction: "You have other loyalties, Dan. Don't you know that?"

The question flattened Dan's elation instantly and left him angry and rebellious but bound. He knew what his father meant. It was not merely that Grandfather Thatcher had been a pacifist years ago before the word was invented, even — that Dan did not regard as his own affair at all. But — Joanna. Neither of his parents was in good health and soon, perhaps, someone would have to take care of her. To leave her for the rest of her life to the care of strangers was unthinkable. And there was no blinking the hard fact that he, Dan, was in a way responsible for her illness. That was not a fact that he was ever likely to forget.

Dan's wounded pride spoilt everything between him and Cynthia. When he went for a walk with her and they passed soldiers of about his own age, his heart sank for shame and he wanted to turn his eyes away from them; but instead, he would stare at them aggressively, and sometimes stealing a look at them after they had passed, it seemed to him they, too, were looking back and jeering at him amongst themselves. He hated them, he hated himself, and the times were out of joint — but what could he do?

"What *is* the matter, Dan?" Cynthia protested. "You're so *strange*. I felt as if I couldn't reach you anymore."

"Nothing!" said Dan in a gruff tone that warned her from dangerous ground.

One day Alastair said to Dan, "What would Father say if we went?"

"What about Joanna?"

"I'm going, Dan. I can get a commission in the battery. Of course, I understand how you feel about Jo. But that seems somehow more your job than mine. I mean, you've always looked out for her. Anyway, I've got to go! … Look here, Dan, tell Father for me, will you?"

Pen took this news well. He felt that Alastair was Maud's boy — a Burnet, while Dan was his. "After all, everyone over seventeen is a man these days, and he must do as he thinks right." And now, he wanted the Allies to win. The whole business was wicked! But the Allies must win. In this desire he was pure parent, it was inconsistent with his conscientious conviction that the enemy to be fought was not Germany but war itself.

Pen suspected that he was a man of tragedy. Too fast bound by duty; no time to sit down and simply live without feeling the past or fearing the future. In the last year he had retired from business, and he viewed the sterility of his life against the background of approaching old age with a kind of quiet despair. The prison of the fifties. Most people became reconciled to their futility, but he couldn't.... Less resilience, habits harder to change, no *soar* to the mind. And failure shrinks your personality, steals your virtue, and makes you less of a man. For instance, the talents he had once had — unused they festered. "Thatcher's an honest man," people said, "but he doesn't like his job." ... Must swallow my own smoke, though. I hate a man who is sorry for himself.

His own name always seemed to Pen the ultimate irony: Penuel, the mountain whence Moses caught a glimpse of the promised land. What promised land? What glimpse? If only life would make use of you to the top of your bent, not merely as a vessel for stale habits and baffled emotions.

# CHAPTER V

i

*O for a man who is a man, and, as my neighbor says,
has a bone in his back which you cannot pass your
hand through....*
— Henry David Thoreau, *Civil Disobedience*

Pen was reading Thoreau and he put the book down in great
excitement. Thoreau did not believe in supporting a government
that permitted slavery, that waged war. What, then, did he do? He
refused to pay his taxes and they imprisoned him.

Pen began to pace the study in great excitement. It seemed
so simple, after all, that he wondered it had never occurred to
him. He searched feverishly for pen and notepaper. He must act
before the old habit of futile doubt got hold of him.

> Sir,
> I have the honour to inform you that I firmly
> refuse to pay taxes to the state for the pur-
> pose of waging war. Permit me to assert that
> I take this stand as the only effective means of
> opposing war at the disposal of a citizen at the
> present time.

I beg that you will bring this letter to the attention of the proper authorities that they may take whatever action they may deem appropriate.

I am, sir, yours faithfully,

Penuel Thatcher

ii

After the Easter holiday Dan refused to go back to college. "I can't do any work. It's too unreal. I want a navvy's job. The harder the work, the better." So Pen got him a job at the steel company loading freight cars. The hard labour made him too tired to think much. This was a puritan's first compromise with his conscience, and it did not satisfy him. It was merely the first stage of his journey to France, though he did not yet realize that fact.

He met Mr. Mandover on the street one day. The headmaster twisted his moustache and flourished his stick; remembered gesture! "How d'ye do, Thatcher? Glad to hear that your cousin Thatcher Maximus has won the Military Medal. I am glad to say, my dear boy, that every St. Horatius old boy with whom I have kept in touch is doing his bit; except, of course, those who are not physically fit."

Dan neglected Cynthia and she was hurt. She wanted to be gay and have a good time, and Dan's seriousness sometimes frightened her. If only Dan was more enthusiastic and winning — like Alastair, she thought.

"Your Cynthia is a flirt," Alastair remarked casually to Dan, "but she's good fun. Mind if I take her to a dance at the barracks, old man? She'd enjoy seeing them, I think."

She went to a good many dances with that pleasant fellow, hiding from herself her reasons for doing so. One didn't have to worry with Alastair, of course, or take him seriously. He was Dan's brother.... And besides, if it made Dan a little jealous, all the better!

Alastair was never consciously a cad, but he was handsome and attractive and was possessed of what used to be called "air and countenance" in Jane Austen's day, and he knew it too well for his own good. He was not deliberately selfish, but he took good care never to let an unpleasant sense of reality tarnish his illusions. "Cynthia ought to have some fun," he said to himself, "and Dan's such a stick-in-the-mud. And besides, a month from now, I'll probably be in England." He made a point of praising Dan to Cynthia, telling her how, at school, Dan had been the best shot with a Ross rifle.

One day, coming home from work, Dan met them on their way to a tea dance. Alastair saluted him gaily. "Hello, Granny. I'm taking your girl to meet some of the fellows. You don't mind, do you? Lynch is coming and Jiffy Tripp will be there, too. Join us? You look all right, and you can clean up at the hotel. Do you good!" Cynthia put her hand on his sleeve and urged him: "Please come."

To go in civvies among a crowd of officers with whom he had gone to school was, for Dan, an impossibility. It was a weakness to feel thus, he knew, but he simply could not bring himself to do it. He said gruffly: "Thanks awfully, but I can't. I've been humping eighteen-pounder shells and I look like the devil."

That evening Cynthia telephoned him, "Dan, I want to talk to you."

Dan's old fault of moroseness often got the better of him these days. He said: "I'm sorry, Cynthia. I've got to go on night shift at the mill."

"Miss it for once. Please. They won't care.... You didn't mind my going with Alastair, did you? After all, he's your brother."

"It's all right, Cynthia.... Why mention it?"

After a moment her voice came in a different tone. "Dan, why are you so *beastly* to me? I can't understand you a bit!"

### iii

Having sent his letter of defiance to his majesty's government, Pen waited on tenterhooks for a reply. Every morning he sorted the letters impatiently, looking for an envelope with the government's frank on it.

But the sky took a long time to fall, for the mills of the gods, being enmeshed in red tape, ground slowly. At last he found himself staring at the official envelope he had been waiting for. He tore it open impatiently and, with trembling fingers, read the enclosure. It was a mimeographed notice, signed with an initial.

> Dear Sir,
> We beg to acknowledge your petition for an adjustment of your taxes. We wish to inform you that your claim has been forwarded to the proper authorities and will be acted upon in due course.
>
> I have the honour to be, sir, your obedient servant,
>
> J
> (For the Division of Taxes & Income)

If a man had hit Pen a blow in the face, he could not have been more affronted. Irony of ironies! This was the final insult delivered by the great impersonal machine whose official indifference could not even be ruffled into the anger of a personal reply. He realized for the first time that his true enemy was not men or their ideas but giant indifference.

The Thatcher temper, which for years he had suppressed to the level of a chronic irritability, flared up at last. He was completely, furiously, chaotically angry. So angry that he tore the letter into fragments and cast them from him, as though the printed slip of paper were his majesty's government and could be seized and torn and thrown in the gutter and stamped on!

He went to his study and, snatching a pen, composed a letter to be sent to all the newspapers he could think of.

> Sir,
>
> I wish to make a public announcement through the columns of your journal of the fact that I have refused to pay any taxes whatsoever in support of a war, the waging of which I consider an unspeakable folly, a threat to civilization, and an affront to all the decent impulses painfully fostered through two thousand years of Christianity.
>
> Whatever may be the justice of our cause — and I firmly believe that the right is on our side — the resort to arms is unchristian and can lead to nothing but destruction for *all* the combatants. Let men of good will, wherever they may be, take the only step in their power to end this war, by refusing to pay taxes until peace without victory or defeat has been honourably concluded.
>
> Yours faithfully,
> Penuel Thatcher

It was the ill-considered letter of an angry man. "And now I must tell Maud before sending it," he reflected. "It is only fair to her." He knew she would disapprove with the whole force and direction of her nature, and she had such a gentle, inexorable power to get her way. He went to the door and called her.

"Don't send it," she pleaded. "It would mean the end of our happy, quiet life here, and life's hard enough for Joanna, dear.... It isn't as if it would do any good. You've no idea of the blind, brute force you'll be struggling against."

Pen stood with his back to her, staring out of the window.

"And you're not physically fit for such a struggle, Pen. It would kill you."

"What does that matter?"

"And perhaps me, too.... Pen — I must say it — if you were yourself, if you were in good health, you wouldn't want to do this."

She waited in vain for him to speak. Coming beside him she murmured: "Pen?" ... For a long interval he still could not look at her, and he made a curious rhythmic hunching of his shoulders, as if his thoughts were physically scourging him. He straightened up at length and whispered in a parched voice: "I must."

And in that moment he felt that he had outraged some subtle, natural link between them, and that their relation could never again be quite the same.

That night he mailed his letters and once more waited for the skies to fall. But the firmament remained disconcertingly stable for many days. All but one of the newspaper editors threw his letter into the "crank" basket. These editors had known and respected him for many years. "Thatcher must be losing his grip. Pity.... Of course, he's getting on in years." But one paper, a flap-filthy of the yellowest variety, read his letter with avidity, and filed it against some day in the future when there should be a drought of sensational news. Such days were not common in 1916.


iv


On Dominion Day, a holiday, the family lingered over breakfast. Alastair had leave for the weekend, so of course, he had slept late and had not yet come downstairs. Pen lowered his paper to remark: "Our neighbour, the little Elton girl, the eldest — what's her name?"

"Beatrice."

"Yes. I always liked her. She has more in her than Cynthia. Well, she seems to have lost her balance completely. She has been sending white feathers to young men —"

Maud, with a quick sidelong glance at Dan, put down her cup. Dan asserted deliberately: "I don't blame her, in a way. Her fiancé was killed at St. Julien. I'd go and see her if I didn't think she might give me one." He began to open his mail.

Maud searched Pen's expression, asking him a mute question he did not want to answer. Pen cleared his throat.

Dan, hunched over the table with a white face, stared incredulously at the slit envelope in his hand. Shielding it from the others with his body, he spread the sides with his fingers and looked inside again.

Maud was saying: "One ought to make allowances for Beatrice, I think.… It is not surprising that the girl should be unbalanced. Fanny told me confidentially that, since the war, Mr. Elton has sometimes brought his *women* to the house." Maud touched the word with delicate disdain. Pen made a noncommittal sound. "Those girls haven't had a decent chance. The brother, Eustace, is a cad like his father. Why doesn't she give *him* a white feather?"

Pen looked at his wife in surprise; it was not like her to condemn people. And why was she angry? "Elton," he remarked judicially, "is the sort of man who thinks he can live like Punch without anyone minding as long as he takes care to be a 'good fellow.' Blessed are the cynics, Maud, for they shall believe that no one is any better than themselves."

Dan held up a white feather, clipped by scissors along its edges, for his parents to see. "What do I do with this?" he asked grimly. "Am I supposed to wear it in my hatband?"

Before anyone could answer, Alastair sauntered in. Instantly, Dan hid the feather. "Hullo, everyone. What's in the communiqué this morning? May I, for a moment, Father? Usual tripe, I see. 'All quiet in the West except for artillery duels.' And Hilaire Belloc swears the war can't last a year longer. German reserves all used up by the war of attrition. Trouble is, the fellow has been swearing that ever since November 1914, and here we still are."

"So damned sure of himself!" thought Dan. He stood up.

"I'm going to see Cynthia. That is, if you can spare me a morning with her, Alastair?"

"Of course, Granny. Is she still your girl, then? I rather thought you'd lost interest.... She thinks you have."

Boiling with rage, Dan stalked to the Eltons. He meant to find out whether Cynthia had had a hand in sending that feather. Had she? But that would be unlike her.

He decided to ask for Beatrice and have it out with her.

He rang the doorbell so violently that the maid peered through the glass to see whether the police had at last come about Mr. Elton's "goings-on."

"Will you kindly tell Miss Beatrice that a former friend would like to see her?"

"What name shall I say, sir?"

"Never mind the name. Just give her the message."

Beatrice came into the room, saw Dan, and recoiled.

"Yes," said Dan, "it's your former friend Daniel Thatcher. I've come to thank you for the white feather. Very considerate of you to send it, Beatrice. You did send it, didn't you?"

She looked at him defiantly. "Supposing I did. I'm not ashamed of sending it."

"Then why didn't you sign your name? Didn't you want me to know?"

She did not answer.

"I just wanted to tell you, Beatrice, that you're a true friend. You stick to a person through thick and thin!"

Beatrice wilted suddenly. She sank into a chair and began to weep. "I know it was beastly. I knew it when I sent it. I'm not myself. I don't know what I am anymore. Sometimes I think I'm nothing — just empty except for the ache. I want to *hurt* people, Dan. What right have other people to be safe when Matthew —"
She broke down.

"All right, Beatrice. I understand. I'm touchy as all get-out, too.... Did Cynthia know about the feather?"

Beatrice flared up again. "What do you care! You've made her so unhappy. I can't forgive you for that, Dan Thatcher."

Then she probably did know, thought Dan, gloomily, or Beatrice would have denied it. Shall I ask Cynthia point blank? He said in a surly voice: "Well, Cynthia promised to go for a walk."

"She is ready, Dan. Be nice to her. She isn't very happy these days.... I'm sorry I did — what I did."

Presently, Cynthia came out, and they climbed up the Wellington escarpment to the path along the crest, where you could look down through the tops of trees and catch glimpses of city roofs and the blue lake beyond.

They were not at ease with each other, and he felt that Cynthia was holding him at arm's length with chatter about trivialities. She was amiable, as impersonally amiable as one is to a friend with whom one has been out of touch for a long time. Did she know about the feather? He was too proud to ask her. Had she really become indifferent to him, or was she trying to make him jealous? He decided to start a quarrel in order to find out where he stood. "Decided" was too calm a word: he started a quarrel because he could not help himself.

"Cynthia, what about Alastair?"

"Why, Dan! What about him?" She added resentfully: "I like him. He's gay and good fun; and he's considerate, too. He's never sulky, and he likes me well enough to want to see me often. That's more than you do, Dan!"

"Not want to see you! Can't you understand why I haven't seen you much? That's why I want to talk seriously to you. Sometimes I think you'll drive me crazy! And you don't care a rap how you make a man feel. You are so beautiful.... All you think of is 'enjoying life.' You insist on talking about trivial things. You won't talk about us!"

She wondered fleetingly why men always wanted to say over and over again, "You're so beautiful," (though she liked being told). She did not want to make them suffer — or did she? She wanted to make Dan suffer! She thought of the wretched trouble about her father. Was that why Dan avoided her?

"It seems to me that you haven't made much effort to talk to me."

"I — you — we —" stammered Dan…. "Cynthia, I think you know very well why I haven't seen you."

"Well, why? If you liked me, you'd want to see me."

"Perhaps I've been a bit cowardly. Yes! I have been. I've been considering too much what people think of me. That was cowardly; I see that now. It's a sore spot — the whole wretched business…. I ought to be sturdier and not care what people think … but I'm not…. I simply can't talk about it. Can't you understand how a man feels about a thing like this?"

She looked at him with grave eyes. "Then there is something else the matter? It isn't just about Alastair?"

"You know there is! I have been furious with you — and myself, about Alastair. I could kick myself. I've been such a fool! … And being angry with you hasn't done me a bit of good. I'm in love with you, Cynthia."

This declaration both thrilled and troubled her.

"Alastair —" she began.

"Damn Alastair! Look here, has he been making love to you? Because if he has, I'll break his neck."

"Why shouldn't he make love to me? Perhaps he has. He does it simply to prove to himself how good he is at it … and he is good at it," she added spitefully. "You know, Dan, I wouldn't marry a man unless I knew that the thought of losing me made him desperate."

"It does me. That's why I am asking you to marry me. Will you, Cynthia?"

She would not meet his look. "I don't know, Dan. Why should I? Do you realize that this is the first time you have spoken to me like a human being since —"

"Since the war." Dan finished the sentence. The fatal curtain of misunderstanding dropped between them again. Dan thought she was ashamed of him and despised him for a slacker. Cynthia thought that Dan was ashamed of her father's ways but could not tell her so. She was abnormally sensitive about her father, and every misunderstanding she had with people she put down to their contempt for Mr. Elton, whom she knew they privately called "Punch." "It *is* about father," she thought miserably. "If only he would talk about it. How can *I?* ... How beastly it all is."

She was angry with Dan for not loving her well enough to forget about her father, but she loved him and she made a desperate attempt to rise above anger.

She swallowed her pride and plunged in, speaking breathlessly: "I think I know what is troubling you, though you can't talk about it. I — I oughtn't to say this, but I must tell you — it's so important! — that I, too, like people to be, oh, normal and honest and dependable and to do the usual things other people do —"

He stiffened. "So I see," he said in a voice of cold rage.

His surprising fury bewildered her. Why should he be angry? Why? It was not anything she had done or could help. She, too, gave way to her anger. Who was Dan Thatcher to criticize her father? — after all, if Dan were like other men, like Alastair, for instance, he'd be — "No. I *won't* think that," she vowed; and she banished the unhappy thought, as she had had to banish so many other painful thoughts lately. For several minutes, though they both wanted to speak, neither of them could. They walked side by side without looking at each other, and tension coiled and uncoiled and coiled again between them. Then, at the same instant, by a common impulse they turned to each other, each speaking the other's name.

"Cynthia, it's miserable to have it end like this —"

She interrupted him gently. "Dan, dear, let's not talk of it anymore. It's all so puzzling and wretched, and there seems no way out. I don't *want* to quarrel with you. Why do we make each other so unhappy? Let's not think of it anymore, let's just enjoy today and not think of the future at all.... We haven't been together for nearly a month, let's be happy today." She put her hand in his and felt him relax.

With the strange power women seem to have of putting trouble aside for a time, she began to chatter and laugh gaily. All at once, though there was no real reason for his change of mood, everything seemed to Dan bright and hopeful again.

They had come down from the woods and had reached the first houses of Wellington, the town lay before them, waiting to absorb them and steal them from each other. They looked at each other bleakly. It seemed impossible that they should be saying goodbye to each other. It seemed unnatural and impossible, but that was what it had come to.

She gave him her hand, and before they knew what had happened, she was in his arms. He kissed her again and again, murmuring how beautiful she was. She gasped and threw back her head. He kissed her throat. She felt strange and excited and afraid — afraid because she had meant him to kiss her, though she did not know why she had meant him to. She thought chaotically of a number of things all at once. That she loved Dan. That he did not love her enough. That he was ashamed of her father. That she was afraid of marriage and having babies and of love, that terrible force that made a man cruel and beastly. "My father ..." she thought. She stiffened in his arms and Dan let her go.

"You see, Cynthia, you and I love each other so much that nothing else matters."

"Doesn't it, Dan?" breathed Cynthia. "Are you sure? Do you love me enough to — to — oh, it's so hard to say it and you won't help me. Our families...."

Dan dropped his eyes from hers and thrust forth his chin doggedly.

"Can't you understand how I feel about that?" he murmured, "I want to marry you and I mean to marry you whatever you may say.... But there are some things I can't forget. A man can't always do what he wants to — just the way he wants to. Why can't you simply believe in me?" Why couldn't she understand about Joanna?

Cynthia turned away from him. "Then it's goodbye.... Goodbye, Dan."

"It isn't goodbye. We're both so upset that we can't think clearly now. We'll talk about it tomorrow."

"I'm going to Toronto to a wedding, Dan. After I come back, we'd better not see each other. It only makes us unhappy."

"I shall see you when you come back," said Dan, confidently.

"You must forget about me," murmured Cynthia, "and Dan, I want you to have a happy life. You'll meet someone you will really fall in love with, then you won't be bothered by any of these fears that trouble you."

That evening, when Dan got back to Ardentinny, he found the family much upset. Pen had received a letter and a telegram from Beulah, Connecticut, where Great-Aunt Joanna Thatcher lived.

My dear nephew Penuel,

I don't know that I agree with you about this terrible war. It must have been sent by God to punish men for their *sins* in forgetting him. I thank him daily that your boys are *too young* to bear such burdens. If your dear father was alive he would say this better than a *useless old woman* like me. He was a *good* man, Penuel, and he died for his belief. It seems strange and sad that I should see all this twice in my lifetime.

I go on about's usual and I am ashamed to be so comfortable and easy in my mind when there is so much *misery* in the world. Not but that I have my petty afflictions. Some boys of the village go in swimming in the river in front of my

piazza *without clothes.* I've gone to Judge Perkins
about it, but he don't know if he can do much.

     Your affectionate aunt,
     Joanna Thatcher

The telegram was from Mrs. Gustavson, the Swedish woman
who lived next door to Great-Aunt Joanna Thatcher and "tidied"
for her. Coming in one morning, she had found the old lady sitting
in her chair by the window; she had fallen into a doze and died in
her sleep.

"The last link with my father's generation," said Pen sadly. "I
shall have to sell the house, I suppose. My great-grandfather built it
almost a century and a half ago. Now, Dan, I should like you to come
with me. It will do you good to see the roots you've grown from."

Dan agreed to go. Cynthia would be in Toronto and he
thought, quite wrongly, that it would be a good thing to give her
time to think over what they had said to each other.

They went to Beulah. Pen had meant to stay a few days after
the funeral but a telegram from Maud called them back abruptly.
*Come back at once. Alastair leaving for overseas.*

v

Taking the earliest train from Beulah, they arrived in Wellington
early next morning. Maud was waiting for them on the station
platform in great excitement.

"Thank goodness you got here in time. Alastair's over there
with his men. They may go any moment." If Maud was overwrought, it was revealed only in the fact that she had put on her
hat without looking in the mirror so that it hung over her face at
a rakish angle. She was excited but completely mistress of herself.
She tucked her arm in Pen's. "Oh, let's hurry, Pen. Never mind
the baggage. Let it go on to Toronto! Let's hurry!"

Dan looked up toward the station. One could be in no uncertainty concerning the whereabouts of the troops. A long parade of coaches had been backed onto a siding, and from the windows, a lusty song came rolling down on the morning air.

> K-K-K-Katy, beautiful Katy,
> You're the only g-g-g-girl that I adore;
> When the m-m-m-moon shines,
> Over the cow shed,
> I'll be waiting at the k-k-k-kitchen door.

A great crowd of civilians, mothers, fathers, sisters, friends, and relatives were crowding about the coaches, cracking last minute jokes with a too-vociferous cheerfulness. Dan picked out the familiar figures of Cynthia and Joanna standing together beneath a window. Leaving his parents to hurry after him, he broke into a run.

Cynthia's head was tilted upward toward the car window from which the faces of Alastair and two other subalterns projected. As he ran, she turned her profile to him, and he caught a fleeting impression of her face. She looked white and wild-eyed, and her hair was dishevelled. Why? He came behind her, and waving at Alastair, spoke her name. She started and dropped her purse, then turned and faced him with an expression of sheer fright, without speaking and without meeting his eyes.

"Am I a ghost?" asked Dan, laughing.

"You startled me so, Dan."

He put his arm about Joanna and said, making his voice sound hearty: "Hullo, Alastair."

"Hullo, old man," responded Alastair.

Dan exclaimed: "What's the matter with you two? Am I improperly dressed? Coat, trousers, tie, hat?"

A secret glance passed between Alastair and Cynthia. Alastair nodded his head.

"Dan, dear," whispered Cynthia. "Please come over here. I want to tell you something."

Puzzled, he followed her to a bench by the station wall. She made him sit beside her.

"What's it all about, Cynthia?"

"You mustn't let this hurt you.... You see, Alastair only knew yesterday that he was going. He needs me more than you do, Dan. Truly, he does."

"But I don't understand."

"And," said Cynthia wildly, "now he'll have — this to remember at the front. He'll — he can think of — Oh, Dan!" Her words came rushing out and ended in a sob.

"You and Alastair —"

"Yes, Dan. We were married yesterday."

In a bewildered way he strove to comprehend the situation. Here was he, Dan Thatcher, come to say goodbye to his brother who was going overseas. And here was Cynthia — Oh my God! he thought, his heart turning over. *She belongs to Alastair....* "K-K-K-Katy" from the troops in the train hammered in the background of his mind.... "It isn't possible.... Must get hold of myself."

Cynthia was saying: "And we are still friends? You don't hate me?"

"One question, Cynthia. You love him, of course?"

She stared straight in front of her and a tear rolled down her cheek. "Yes, I do," she said defiantly.

"Well," said he in a hard voice: "that's that!"

Her hands were clenched into white fists. "Dan, will you be friends with Alastair ... for old time's sake?"

"Alastair can go to the dev — No, I certainly won't!"

She flared into sudden anger. "Why are you always so sure you're in the right! ... Haven't you a little bit of a mean streak in you, Dan?"

"Expect so," he muttered. "Anyway, I won't shake hands with him. Not yet." To quarrel certainly made it easier.

"I think you'll regret it if you don't. You may not have another chance."

"Alastair get killed? Not likely! You don't know my brother. He always falls on his feet."

"He's not a coward, if that's what you mean."

"And I am?"

"Oh, Dan, why do you twist everything I say into something I didn't mean!"

It suddenly struck him that besides being childish and a fool, he was being a perfect beast to her. He said: "I know he's not a coward. I didn't mean that.... I'll go and talk to him anyway."

He made his way through the crowd. Alastair, who had been watching him covertly, met him in the vestibule of the car.

"Well, Dan, do we shake hands?" said he jauntily.

"You let Cynthia think I was a slacker, Alastair."

"I know you're not a slacker.... Why didn't you tell her so yourself? She thought you shied off because of the old man, because of Punch Elton."

"Good God! And you let her think that?"

Alastair smiled uneasily. "How did I know it wasn't true? Look here, Dan. It was you who gave her up. If you'd really wanted her she wouldn't have fallen in love with me. Faint heart never won fair l — in love, I mean."

"You're my brother, but you'd better take that back!"

Alastair went white. "I didn't mean that!" he exclaimed, in consternation.

They looked at each other. *After all, Alastair is my brother; going to France.*

"I hope you come through safely, Alastair. But I won't shake hands with you."

Alastair fumbled for a cigarette and lit it, his hands trembling. "All right. If that's how you feel about it.... You always were a self-righteous devil."

"Did you tell Mother?"

Alastair blew a cloud of smoke. "No, I didn't want to upset them; they've enough to worry about."

"They'll be hurt if you don't."

"Oh, they'll understand," said Alastair easily. "*You* tell them."

Dan thought: "Lord, that's Alastair all over!" He said: "Goodbye, Alastair. And — good luck!"

His brother waved his cigarette gracefully, without replying.

Dan joined the family beneath Alastair's window. None of them seemed to find much to say, though whenever Alastair caught his mother's eye, she forced a smile as if to say: "We'll be all right. You needn't bother about us."

Military police, with swagger sticks and an official air, began to move up the platform from the rear coach, marshalling the crowd. "Please move back! Move back, please!" The crowd surged in for the farewell. Pen stretched up his arm to shake hands with his son. He cleared his throat. "Well, my dear boy. Well...." He could think of nothing to say and pressed Alastair's hand hard. All this time Maud had been forming a secret plan of her own. She had something to say to Alastair, but it must be at the last minute so that he would remember it.

He leaned over to kiss her and she took his hand and held it long enough to whisper, "Alastair. Be a good boy, my dear."

Alastair had the grace to flush.

A shudder ran through the length of the train; car after car was jerked forward against the couplings; the puffing engine began to pull slowly. Instantly, the crowd became quiet as death. White faces, upturned, watched their flesh and blood moving away from their ken — a long journey. The engine picked up the cars and made them at one with its motion. The finality of the slow start and the gathering speed smote Dan's imagination like a bolt of lightning. He thought: "God! I'm a swine to let Al go like that." He started to run. A soldier wearing a red brassard tried to stop him; Dan pushed the man aside and ran on, hand outstretched. Alastair leaned out toward him, but the train had given in to the pull of the locomotive and was sliding into smooth speed; they could not touch hands. Alastair waved, grinning — a derisive, debonair grin.

"'Ere!" said the military policeman, confronting Dan. "'Oo do you think yer knockin' arand? You have that for them Fritzes, chum. You ought to join up, that you ought."

Dan took a deep breath and surveyed the soldier levelly. "Will you please take a good long run and jump in the lake!" he said politely.

# CHAPTER VI

## i

The English language had changed. New phrases and words ate into the mind of a people and burrowed there like moles, throwing behind them aching glories and despairs: *going West, napoo, overseas, sector, over the top, no man's land, somewhere in France.* Battle names, weird and uncouth, echoed through the vast halls of the imagination: Mława, Przymyśl, Verdun — and Ypres, soon to emerge less a name than the symbol of a generation's Calvary. To have set up one's puny ego against the atmosphere of excitement, of desperate sacrifice, of bravely supported fear, of stoic grief, of fearful hope — to have pinnacled oneself, for instance, as a "conscientious objector" (that new sort of martyr, or of coward, or of crank, view it how you would) would have seemed an insufferable presumption to the battalions of eager and earnest young men of twenty, who were not at all presumptuous for all their swagger, but conventionally and rather humbly anxious to "do the right thing" even as their fathers and elder brothers were doing it.

Letter from Quentin Thatcher to Dan:

> My dear Dan,
> As you can see by the postmark on this letter,
> I am, at present, in cadet school in England. I

distinguished myself on the Somme and have been sent here to train for a commission. Yesterday I was paraded and decorated for "bravery and presence of mind in the face of the enemy." The irony of this lies in the fact that I was rewarded for doing a deed which has filled my waking and sleeping hours with horror ever since.

It happened during a raid into the German trenches. We had to throw smoke bombs into a dugout to ferret out the Germans who were cowering down there, hysterical after a long bombardment. The first who comes up is taken prisoner for questioning; the rest are bayoneted or shot as they file out into the sunlight; we can spare no men to look after prisoners, so this is a military necessity.

They come lurching up the steps of the dugout, and Quentin Thatcher, a soldier, is stationed at the entrance to receive them.

I find I make an unwilling butcher. One or two of the poor devils showed fight when they saw what had happened to their comrades who had tried to surrender, and I had to chase one little rabbit down the trench — no, I'll keep that to myself.

Most chaps get hardened to this sort of thing, but I find I can't. My God! I dream of them every night. What am I to do, Dan? I'm not physically afraid a bit and never was. But I haven't it in me to do a butchery like that again. Simply couldn't make myself do it. You know me, Dan; I never was the normal sort of lad who can pull wings off flies out of sheer curiosity. Shall I become a conscientious objector and fight this whole dirty business? Shall I stand up against the impersonal *machine* even if I get shot by a firing squad for it? What do *you* advise? If I had one friend who approved, I could do it. The reason I've written so frankly is that I am certain you, too, must be a pacifist at heart. It must have taken great courage to stay out of the war when all your friends and even your own brother —

Dan slammed down the letter and swore. To be called a pacifist by Quentin — even approvingly — made him furiously angry. "God! If I could go I wouldn't let myself bother about things like that. A man's got to fight. It's the way we are made. Well, then, all you need to worry about is whether you are fighting for what's right. And hang it! A man ought to stick to his job. That's what I am doing.... And all that womanish talk about friendship. A chap ought to stand on his own feet. Quentin's a weakling!"

Dan was in a quarrelsome mood these days. Nothing had gone right. He had to sit back in a passive role when the whole world was rushing to action, and yet without the privilege of feeling bitter toward Joanna on that account. And on top of that Alastair had snapped up his girl under his eyes, and since that was partly his own fault, he hadn't the privilege, either, of hating his brother or of feeling bitter toward Cynthia.

"I'm treed," he thought bitterly, "there is not one blasted thing I can do except go and get tight."

ii

Dan walked up Galinée Street in the rain, going home. A compact, swarthy man in a battered felt hat leaned against the brick wall that surrounded Ardentinny: his hands were in his pockets, his feet were crossed, and he was whistling.

"You're pretty cheerful," said Dan; "do you always stand in the rain and whistle?"

The man pushed up his hat and surveyed Dan quizzically. Dark eyes, but with a gleam in them. Mocking. Friendly, too. The look made him feel inexperienced. "It's worth a quarter to whistle in the rain."

"I see. Broke?" Dan handed over the coin.

The man took it and tossed it high in the air; it fell neatly into his coat pocket. He grinned at Dan; the small trick and the grin turned the alms into a fee. "Not broke as long as there's a fool to panhandle," he said.

Dan started to go through the gate, but a thought stopped him. Queer sort of a beggar, no whine, no abashment. He walked back to the man.

"You're a gipsy, aren't you?"

The man denied it vehemently.

"No offence," said Dan.

"Then don't say gipsy, say Romany. And you should say 'my *rye*' when you're talking to a traveller. '*Rye*' means 'gentleman.'"

They both laughed.

"You asked me for a quarter, but you still think you're as good a man as I am, don't you?"

"Sure. *Wafri bak in a boro ker, sin's adree a bitti ker!*"

"What's that mean?"

"You don't *rakker romanys*? It means 'bad luck in a big house as well as a small.'"

"I see, all brothers, eh? I thought gip— thought travellers never would rakker romanys except among themselves."

"That's right, pal. But you've got the Romany blood. You're *push-ratt* — a half blood."

"How'd you know!"

"A Romany knows things. You have the look. And you ain't exactly blond, now. An' you're restless. Yes, you've got a Romany look."

"I've seen you before."

"Sure."

"Now I know who you are. I've seen you twice. You used to come to Cholera Point every August. You've changed. Do you remember me?"

The gipsy gave a grin and a wink. "Sure. You're the little *chavo* who wanted to run away with the gipsies. Do you still want to run away?"

"Yes, in a way. But your caravan isn't on Cholera Point this year."

"Hard times like I told you. Too many motors. Horses no good now. No *prastering grayas* anymore — running horses."

"But you still whistle in the rain?"

"I was conceived under a hedge on a rainy November night, see?"— again the wink. "That's why I have hot blood in me even when it's cold."

"Oh. Where do you live now?"

"You know the boathouses on the bay by the railroad?"

"Yes."

"Third one from the city.… You come and see me and I'll tell you something."

"What will you tell me?"

"About yourself, what you're like. Maybe you don't know yet. You ain't happy like me."

"What's your name, my *rye*?"

"Jobey Loversedge — to you.… Now give me a dollar and I'll mark the house for you."

"Mark it?"

"So you won't be pestered by thieving, begging gipsies."

He decided that he would see Jobey Loversedge again.


"You're restless, pal," said Jobey Loversedge to Dan. "Ain't you found out what to do when you're restless? Come on, drink some more."

They drank, looking at each other curiously.

"Now," said Jobey, "you feel warm, eh? You don't give a damn, eh?"

"I still give a damn," said Dan grinning, "but not such a big one."

"Now Zillah will tell your future. Have you got any money? Zillah, tell his fortune."

"Is she your wife?"

Jobey laughed. "No. I wash my own shirts."

Zillah was a woman, neither old nor young. Her black hair was done up in many tiny plaits, and she had gold earrings in the pattern, though she did not know it, of the trident of Shiva. She looked at Dan suspiciously, not liking to hear the Romany spoken before a *gorgio*. Dan said:

"You told my future before. You said I'd be unlucky in love the first time. You were right."

"Well, there's a second time, maybe," said Jobey.

"Wait," Dan exclaimed, "never mind my future. You might see a coffin, perhaps. Or a little white cross. I'd sooner think about now."

"All right, brother. Drink some more, then! Do you know about women? Much — much trouble for you there, my *rye*. You ain't one of the tame ones and yet you ain't free, neither. You'll never be free like me.... You want to make something and do something, brother?"

"And *know* something."

"*Avali!*" Jobey nodded politely, a little drunk. "Drink, brother, drink."

"Somebody played me a dirty trick, Jobey, but I don't care now."

"Stole your girl?"

"I didn't say that!"

"No offence, pal."

"Jobey, should a man go to the war?"

"You're a thinkin' of these here little white crosses."

But Dan stiffened. "No, no. Mustn't talk about that. Settled. Can't talk about going.... Would *you* go, Jobey?"

"Why should I go? I ain't got nothing to run away from, pal. I got all I want, an' I'm free. Why should I want to go?"

"I know. You whistle in the rain. But supposing you see other men go, supposing you see people you know going?"

"This here war has nothing to do with the affairs of Egypt, pal. The good die young. Know why? 'Cos you don't find many of 'em about. S'up me duvel, that's true.... Maybe someday, when I'm drunk, I'll go — for fun."

"Think I'm afraid to go, Jobey?"

"No, you ain't afraid. But you'll never be free, pal. You'll be good maybe, and maybe you'll be happy sometimes, but you won't have joy like me."

"Sad, very sad! Whatsha meaning-of-it-all, Jobey?"

"It's what's in you, pal. Some folks is born with joy and not carin' a damn, and some folks is meant to be good. It ain't much use fightin' agin yourself. For every man there's sweet sleep at the end of a long road — that's what we say."

Dan, more than a little drunk, murmured solemnly: "'S God's truth." And for the moment he thought it was.


### iii


Occasionally, Dan took Joanna to a tea dance at the Royal Wellington Hotel. She could not dance, but it was characteristic of her to enjoy watching others do the things she was not well enough to do herself. Dan went for her sake. Looking at men in uniform of his own years, who were insouciant and feverishly gay, he had always a numbing feeling that he belonged to no generation. His own had cast him out without relieving him of its mistakes; he knew he lacked the quiet balance of older men.

He took Joanna one Saturday afternoon and unexpectedly discovered a throng of people within the hotel. They managed, with difficulty, to make their way to the tea room, only to find that not a single table was unoccupied. Dan said to his sister: "Wait here, Joanna. I'll see whether they've put extra tables in the ballroom."

But Joanna had an invalid's fear of being alone in a crowd, so they left the tea room together and turned down a corridor toward the ballroom. No sooner had they entered this corridor, however, when they found themselves caught in such a crowd going toward the ballroom that Dan gave up hope of getting a table there. When they tried to turn back, Joanna, because of her crutches, was unable to go against the tide of hurrying people. Forced in the same direction as the others, they came at last to the door of the great ballroom.

Dan stood stock-still in dismay. Entering, he found himself in a narrow aisle kept clear by soldiers. On one side of this aisle stood a platform on which he mistily discerned a group of seated figures, many of them in khaki. On the other side stood a tightly packed mass of human beings with their eyes fixed upon the platform.

It was the reception for the vice-chancellor which, until that moment, he had entirely forgotten. People behind him were impatiently urging him forward; there was nothing for it but to go in. The air was stifling, and once inside, the clatter of many voices confused Joanna and made her gasp, and she whispered urgently: "Can't we get out, somehow?"

At the end of the narrow lane made by the military was a door, in front of which stood a group of soldiers with swagger sticks tucked under their arms. Followed by Joanna, he made for this door and became a target for the impersonal gaze of four hundred people packed in like sardines. "This way please," said an NCO, taking Dan's arm, "You can't stay in the lane, here." Dan forged ahead.

The knot of soldiers stood between them and the door. "Will you let us pass, please?" Dan said. A pair of stupid eyes set in a beef-coloured face stared at him, took in his civvies and his young face and refused stolidly to budge an inch. A hatred of human beings in the mass flared up in the boy's mind. Stupidly, inertly cruel like this fellow, crassly judging a man by appearances.

"Will you let this lady pass!" he said savagely.

The man started to say something, thought better of it, and moved aside unwillingly. Dan shouldered past him and put his hand on the doorknob.

It was locked.

He turned to meet a mocking grin from the soldier. "What's the matter? 'Fraid you'll hear something you don't like? You stay and listen. It won't do you no harm."

People had sifted in behind them, they were wedged in. "Lean against the door, Joanna."

"I'm all right," murmured Joanna.

The chairman was addressing the crowd. "And now," said he, "we are to hear a message from one of Wellington's best-known and most respected — *most respected*" — he repeated the phrase a trifle belligerently — "citizens. Perhaps, ladies and gentlemen — our next mayor. Mr. James Elton...."

That prominent citizen rose slowly and impressively to his feet. Practised speaker though he was, it made him a little uneasy to discover that he felt no particular emotion. As he walked to the front of the platform, he looked curiously at the faces before him; some were antagonistic, the faces of the younger men were tense, a few were rapt. He did not really care very much what happened to these strangers; whether they stayed at home or went to France and were killed was a matter little likely to affect his digestion. On the whole he disliked young men in the mass: their raw enthusiasm contradicted a seasoned man's view of things as they really are. Sentimental young donkeys! Still, one had to make a good showing. Fortunately, the absence of strong feeling was rather an advantage to a good speaker. A government bureau had sent material for recruiting speeches. *Heavy toll — what man afraid to chance fate — all years of their life held in higher esteem — a firm clasp of the hand at meeting, a brighter smile at parting — if wounded, loving hands will nurse you — if fall, name always spoken with reverence as one who did duty for king and country — Be frank, earnest, hopeful — End on a cheering note.* Something from Shakespeare to wind up with. He always relied on Shakespeare for the right emotional touch and he had looked up *honour — death — England* in a Shakespeare concordance…. He reeled off his speech easily, then delivered his peroration — a trifle too ringingly.

> "'Come the three corners of the world in arms,
> And we shall shock them: Nought shall make
> us rue,
> If *England* to itself do rest but true.'

And I will add — *Canada!*"

A spatter of hand clapping rewarded Mr. Elton and he had started back to his seat when a young soldier with a wound stripe on his sleeve suddenly bobbed up at the foot of the platform.

"Lemme alone," said this veteran in a drunken voice, "I wanna speak to prospic — prospictive mayor of this city. Elton, you old bitch, what did *you* do in the Great War?

"And what about your own son, *Mister* Elton, hey? … Why ain't he serving his king and country? What about the loving hands to chuck him into a pit of quick lime same as the rest of us? What about that, hey?"

The chairman was on his feet shouting at the top of his voice. Several military policemen pounced on the disturber and began to frogmarch him toward the door. He clutched wildly with his hands and pushed over a woman, who screamed.

"Yuh mingy barstud!" he shouted. "What the hell does he care for England?"

The storm quieted, and many older men, ashamed of their emotion, clapped Elton. The drunken soldier disappeared from the scene, *spurlos versenkt.* The chairman turned to the vice-chancellor, "Now's your chance. Tell 'em the truth, old man; and make it simple."

The vice-chancellor held the young men in his hand from the first moment; they could tell he believed what he said: he had been in France; he had a right to speak. "Men, they need soldiers in France to take the place of men like me, and of better men than me who have fallen. I won't tell you a lot of bunk that you know isn't true. I once heard a man say on a recruiting platform that the uniform is attractive and will undoubtedly fetch the ladies. Maybe he was right, but I knew at once he was trying to fool young fellows with dirty, lying half-truths. I'll tell you what you're in for if you take the uniform. You're in for mud and lice and foul stenches and disgust and fear till you wonder if you're going mad. You're in for killing men you've never seen before, and wounds maybe, and maybe death hanging out on the barbed wire till you're blue in the face and the flies and the rats get you. Don't let the death and glory boys fool you — that's what you're in for. But in your hearts you know that. Remembered with reverence if you fall? — I don't know whether you will be; four or five million corpses will be a lot of people to remember.... And I won't tell you why you ought to go — you know that. But I will tell you this" — the vice-chancellor straightened up and took every face in the room squarely into his eyes — "if you don't go, *that's* something you'll remember all the days of your life. There isn't one man of you here at this moment who isn't asking himself a question — I know, I've asked myself that question, too; deep in your hearts you are all wondering, 'Would I be man enough to take that step over the top into no man's land when the barrage comes down and I've got nothing between me and death but my naked soul?' Men, there's only one way to answer that question. *Are you afraid to go and find out?*"

Were they afraid? The question touched a hidden truth in them and it froze the great room to the stillness of a heartbeat. The bugler stood at attention and blew one of the bugle calls of the British Army that men heard everywhere in those days. In barracks, on troopships, in bell tents or Flanders plains, or borne on the still air from a distance.

> *Fall in A,*
> *Fall in B,*
> *Fall in every company.*

Emotion, large and unreasoning, took them by the throats and drew them together with invisible bonds. The flag beckoned — to what? To wounds, perhaps, to death. Terrible and beautiful. Desire to throw oneself on the spear of fate and try its smart seized them. Could one remain inert and spiritless when other men marched, one's friends, one's nearest of kin and best admired? *Dare I enlist?*

Dan gasped and sweat stood on his forehead. Joanna swayed toward him. Her face was drawn and she looked ill. "Come on, Jo," he said harshly. He forced a way for her through the crowd.

Outside it was cool and the setting sun flaunted an oriflamme on the horizon, but Dan could not look up. They took a streetcar to Galinée Street and walked slowly up it toward Ardentinny. Joanna had not dared to break into his thoughts, but at last she caught his eye and he muttered:

"And now Eustace Elton —"

"But, Dan, how do you know —"

"Oh, his father will make him go.... We used to think him a milksop."

After that she was silent for so long that he glanced sideways and saw that her face was puckered like a child's. She caught his glance and began to weep, tossing her head helplessly at her inability to stop.

"What is it, Jo?"

"Nothing," she choked. "It's just — I want to do something and I'm such a coward."

"Do what?"

She wiped her eyes and smiled at him. "I'm all right now. Sometimes the meaning of things suddenly comes home to you. There's something we've got to talk about, Dan. It's something that has come between us. We've both felt it for a long time."

Dan was puzzled and alarmed. What could she mean?

"Dan, if it weren't for me you'd be at the front now." She was looking at him with luminous intensity. "No. Don't answer. I know. I could see your expression at the meeting while — while that man was speaking."

He pulled himself together and stammered: "No. Why, no! Of course not! ... Why, that's absurd. You know what Father thinks, Joanna. I am backing him up to the hilt."

Tranquilly, she ignored his protestation. "I've always known why you didn't go. I love you too much not to.... I've been selfish, Dan. I didn't want you to go. You don't agree with Father's opinion. And neither do I."

He gazed at her in amazement, suddenly discovering in her a stranger. This from Joanna! She had a private life of her own, with a vengeance.

"You must go, Dan. I'm sending you. I believe you should go."

A wild hope made his heart leap. Freedom to go honourably and with a clear conscience after all these miserable months! He muttered hoarsely:

"Can't be done, Joanna.... I'm all right as long as they fight me. It makes me stubborn."

"I know. It's when you have to fight yourself. I've had to fight myself, too, but that's all over now."

"I couldn't, Jo. I shouldn't respect myself if I did. Who would look after you if Mother and Father —"

She hushed him with the pressure of her hand on his arm. "Hasn't it ever occurred to you, Dan, that I've got a soul to save, too. Why should men be the only ones to sacrifice anything for their country? If I want to risk my security — and that's the only thing I can risk — why haven't I the right to? People have always done things for me. I couldn't live if I didn't think I could make my sacrifices, too. I'm not afraid."

"It would break Father's heart. I simply couldn't tell him."

"No, it won't, Dan. You see, I told him you wanted to go; I think he'd known it for a long time. He'll let you make your own choice, Dan; that is what *he* is doing.... Don't walk so fast, dear. I can't keep up."

"Sorry, Jo! Let's sit here for a minute." Then was an old stone horse trough at the curb. Joanna sat on the edge dabbling her fingers in the water. "Do you know what I'm thinking? That I'm happy! Do you love me, Dan?" Not for years had she asked him that in the old, childish way.

"I love you, Joanna! And you're the best, the most understanding sister a man's ever had."

A sudden sinking of her heart oppressed her and she almost sighed.... It was easy enough to deceive Daniel. The phrase "sacrifice for one's country" had little meaning for her. Martyred Belgium, embattled Britain, were merely ideas; her family was her country — an invalid's world. But men, she knew, had feelings and loyalties that were different from her own, and you had to help your menfolk and make them happy somehow. *You can't live only for yourself....* "I'll send you parcels, Dan. I know what you like to eat, don't I!"

"If I can manage it, I'll get into the battery with Uncle Charles."

"And with Alastair."

"Yes."

"It will be nice being with Uncle Charles."

Joanna shivered and stood up. "Let's go in now. It's cold."

Dan said absently: "You know, Joanna, Quentin wrote me a letter congratulating me on being a pacifist! I've never had the heart to answer it until now."

In the glow of his new determination, he began mentally to draft a reply to Quentin. To do that was a symbol of his own singlemindedness at last.... First tell Quentin that the way is clear for me to go honourably. And tell him I think he's wrong. Tell him I think he ought to stick to it. A man ought to hold his hand to the plough. And tell him for God's sake not to do it — that he'd hate himself if he did, as I hated myself.

## Pictures

I would paint a picture
Ere I die;
I would tint at shifting clouds
Upon the sky.

The clouds are vanishing, to form
Some other way.
But it was thus I painted
In my day.

Weaving clouds upon the sky
Who rack and swirl and rend,
You dissolve — and I must die,
In the end.

(From Quentin's Notebook)

# PART III

# THE SICKLE

# CHAPTER VII

i

For a night and a day the train carrying reinforcement drafts had been crawling toward the front at the average rate of one and a half miles an hour. For Dan Thatcher, a romantic youth untarnished by battle, even the third-class coach, whose upholstery had long since given up the unequal struggle with thousands of khaki breeches, dramatized the war; to him and to seven other raw subalterns, the coach whispered in excited black letters under the windows: "*Taisez-vous! Méfiez-vous! Les oreilles ennemies vous écoutent.*"

The train meandered through the outskirts of Amiens and turned north. Presently, they came to a mound of bricks on the bluff overlooking a splintered copse and a marsh, pockmarked and full of scummy water, sown with rusty, unkempt barbed wire. A subaltern with a jolly, round, mocking face, glanced at Dan quizzically. "That, my lad, is Thiepval. I was there in 1916."

"The Somme battlefield!"

"Ah, callow youth! Before the battle it was a village of ninety houses. My division lost five thousand men there on a single summer's day. You think it's romantic, what? 'God for Harry, England, and Saint George!' what?"

Less than a year ago, but already it was as if one said, "The windy plains of Troy."

At last at dusk, a staff captain came into Dan's compartment and read a list of names, and Dan got down from the train onto a barren stretch of road, about a mile from a "town" somewhere in the hinterland of the Canadian Corps.

"Get your kit," said the staff officer. "If you go to the Church Army hut, they'll look after you tonight."

"Right. How shall I get my bag — luggage there?"

"Don't know, I'm sure." The staff officer signified by a frigid look that a subaltern with a uniform just out of the bandbox and no active service experience might just as well stay where he was and fill up a shell hole in the road. Dan shouldered his Wolseley valise and strode out through the rain for the hut.

At the hut he found himself a section of floor that no one seemed to be occupying and crawled into his Kapok sleeping bag. Rain drummed on the metal roof of the hut, and when the door opened, he could see mules, GS wagons, and lorries sloshing past in the mud, the drivers' faces buried deep in the collars of their coats — all going to some known destination to do something definite. Belonging. Dan's mind was in a state of levitation, suspended between his past life and the different life which had not yet begun for him. He was longing for the war to begin so that he could slip into some sort of relation with it. About him, recumbent figures breathed stertorously, muttering and twitching in sleep that was troubled with premonitions. It was a lonely war. He went to sleep with unfamiliar sounds ringing in his ears: of dumb beasts and men trudging by on the muddy road; of trains puffing, grunting with mysterious shuntings, puffing off again full of *hommes 40, chevaux 8* or bearing, for all he knew, a more sinister freight.... *What will it be like?*

## ii

Next morning the director of the hut accosted Dan. "Did you say you were posted to the Wellington Siege Battery?"

Dan nodded.

"Well, I suppose they'll send for you when they get round to it. Meantime there's an officer of your battery here. Perhaps you could go up with him."

"Where is he?"

"In my room. Go in and make yourself known, if you like. His name is Dolughoff. Some sort of a Russian, I believe." The director gave Dan an amused, sidelong look. "Tell me what he says. I warn you, he's a prickly person."

The director's room was not really a room at all, simply an enclosure curtained off from the rest of the hut, containing a hand basin, a stove, and an army cot. One could not very well knock at a curtain, so Dan pushed it aside and went in.

A man with his back to Dan was kneeling before a stove, tending it, Dan supposed: a slender, gracefully built man, not young.

Dan ventured: "Are you Dolughoff?"

The figure, curiously still for a man making a fire, did not stir. Thinking Dolughoff might be deaf (a good many artillerymen were), Dan repeated in a loud voice: "Are you Dolughoff? I'm Thatcher. I'm joining the battery and I thought —"

The figure stood up, turned slowly, and gave Dan the benefit of a cool stare which started at Dan's chin and came to rest at the bridge of his nose — hostile. Confused, Dan gathered impressions of Dolughoff to be sorted out later. Two ribbons above his tunic pocket, MC and DCM — served in the ranks, then. Thin, straight lips, sensitive, and at the same time cruel; too ready to curve into sarcasm. A curiously delicate skin, like an alabaster statue. Eyes cold and proud; lids drooping but watchful; a stern pucker between the brows. A combative tilt to the head.... A face feline and dangerous.

"I am Dolughoff."

His voice was defiant and yet oddly eager. But having taken Dan's measure, disappointment swept over his face, as if he had been expecting not a stranger but someone important to him. "And who may you be?" he asked, and this time his sarcastic tone exactly matched his features.

"Whom did you expect to see?" countered Dan, annoyed. "You looked at me as if you expected to see someone important to you like the devil or the angel Gabriel!" He went through the rigmarole of introducing himself, and Dolughoff listened to him with that disconcerting stare. It suddenly struck Dan that he might be talking to a man a little drunk.

"You can't be twenty!" said Dolughoff contemptuously. "Yes, a child! ... Well, sit down. Sit down. Since you are here. Thatcher, hm? Your brother's in the battery, eh? You are the pacifist, aren't you?"

"No!"

"More fool you, then."

Dan sat down on the camp stool indicated by Dolughoff with the casual flick of a single outstretched finger from an unmoving hand, arm, and body. The irritation Dan felt at this unfriendly reception vented itself in a frown of dislike.

Dolughoff pounced on this revelation of personality; instantly, a rictus of fury contorted his face. "You didn't come here to spy on me, did you? You're not one of those hell-begotten political soldiers, are you? The general's nephew, eh? Something like that?"

"Wh — what do you mean?" stammered Dan.

"The politicians are against me. They hate me and fear me — that's all."

"I don't know what in the devil you're talking about," asserted Dan, raising his voice. Tight or sober, this was a formidable chap. A prickly person, true enough, and one not easy to read, especially for a callow youth who rather expected all subalterns to be like Harry Lorrequer and Charles O'Malley.

Dolughoff passed his hand over his eyes. "Never mind. One doesn't expect you to understand. You are a mere child. Here, smoke a cigar. It's a man's smoke. Usually I don't like people and they don't like me, but I feel like talking…. You think I am tight, eh? So I am a little, that's why I want to talk. But I'm probably the sanest officer in the British Army. People don't like me because I always say outright what everyone *thinks*. The British race hasn't the slightest respect for originality or even genius, all they care about is 'good form' (his voice trampled on the phrase contemptuously) and what they call a 'sound man,' by which they mean an obstinate, stupid sheep. Thank God I'm not British…. You see, I don't like people much."

"So I see."

"You don't really. You only think you do."

To light his cigar, Dolughoff came away from the stove, from which he had not previously budged. Then Dan saw something that gave him a shock. Spread open on top of the stove was a book. This book was the Bible. No sight could have struck him as more at variance with his first impression of Dolughoff. No wonder that Dolughoff had been irritated when he clumsily barged in and bawled his name at the top of his voice. He muttered:

"I'm awfully sorry for intruding. I didn't realize …"

Dolughoff followed Dan's glance to the Bible; then for the first time he laughed. "God bless you, I don't mind that. I rather like being caught by an Anglo-Saxon reading the Bible. They look so stupidly ashamed and self-conscious. It is no disgrace to read the Bible, is it?"

In order to put himself at ease — it wasn't a question of putting Dolughoff at ease — Dan blurted: "What book were you reading? My father used to read the book of Job once a month. He said it was the greatest piece of literature in the English language."

Removing his cigar, Dolughoff stared at him as at a queer animal.

"Literature? ... Well, so it is, I suppose. And I ought to know.... But my good chap, one doesn't think of it as *literature!* It's holy writ. One is humble before the Creator. Take the voice in the whirlwind, that shows one where one stands in God's universe: 'What is man, that thou art mindful of him,' eh? And what, indeed? Mind you, I don't hate men. I simply despise them."

"My God!" thought Dan. "I'm going to simply loathe this chap."

Dolughoff blew a cloud of smoke and watched it rise. "I am talking too much," he remarked, though not in the least apologetically, "because I am a little tight. One can't expect a child like you to understand these things. Trouble with me is I am a very sane person, a realist. I am what I am. I like what I like. Why not? God never made beauty to be gawked at from behind a stone wall with barred windows.... But you're a virgin, aren't you? One can always tell."

"Will you please go to the devil!" said Dan, getting up angrily.

Dolughoff frowned at his cigar end. "Very likely," said he. "As a matter of fact," he added, as though it were the most natural statement in the world, "I wasn't reading any particular part of the Bible. I opened it for a message ... then *you* came. And I imagined for a moment — what can't one imagine when one is hoping? ... What did you want to see me for?"

"I thought you might take me to the battery, but I'm damned if —"

"Sorry, I can't. They'll send for you. Why are you in such a hurry? You see, I want to walk there by myself. There is something I want to think over. I think perhaps — if you don't mind? — you'd better go now."

Thus summarily dismissed, Dan reflected on the most extraordinary conversation in which he had ever taken part. A man who upon the very first acquaintance talked about himself without the least reserve or shame ... like a page from Dostoyevsky! ... "Of course he was tight.... But was he? Hope there aren't anymore like Mister Dolughoff in the battery."

### iii

Charles arrived in the battery light car and shouted to him as if he had seen him only yesterday. "Shake a leg, Dan! Throw your kit in beside Smith and sit here beside the skipper. Well, how are you? I came by myself so we could have a talk."

"Hullo, sir. Is it a nuisance getting me?"

"Devil a bit! Good excuse for a joy ride to Amiens. I've had a splendid dinner at Godbert's. Left early this morning and got some stuff for the mess. I give you my word, I'll go after a sub any day!"

Charles Burnet had not changed — much. He had the same gleam in the eye, Dan thought. But — well, he was forty and looked it. Face sterner and sharper as if — what was the phrase? — as if three years had passed a sponge of hyssop over his features. He was amused to see his uncle wearing riding breeches of purplish-grey Bedford cord, what were called in the army "passionate breeches."

"Yes," said Charles complacently, "there's life in the old dog yet."

"You look fit, sir."

"Fair to middling, thanks.... You don't 'sir' me, of course, as you damned well know, except on parade. And if you 'uncle' me, I'll break your neck."

"Naturally."

"'Burnet' is what you call me on ordinary occasions."

"I shan't forget.... I met Dolughoff at the Church Army hut."

Charles Burnet's expression became quizzical. "Did you, by George! Then you met one of the oddest specimens of human frailty in the British Army, or anywhere else for that matter. He's back from a Lewis gun course."

Dan told Charles about his conversation with Dolughoff.

"Sounds like Dolughoff when he's a little tight and quarrelsome. When he's tight he can be downright offensive. The religion, by the way, is apparently quite sincere; so is his smut. He's not a gentleman, of course. He's a bundle of contradictions. I can't get to the bottom of him. No one can. If you could, I expect you'd find a mortal struggle of some sort going on, though it doesn't show on the surface. He goes his own way like a cat; he's a solitary, suspicious, quarrelsome, clever chap with artistic instincts and the worst possible taste in all human relations and no sense of shame whatsoever.... Odd thing, his religion — it's almost an obsession with him, and yet God knows he isn't what's called a decent man. Quite unscrupulous. I wouldn't play cards with him."

"What does the mess think of him?"

"They don't know what to think. Contempt for him in one way because he's a dirty-minded bounder — not clean bawdiness either, if you know what I mean. No one minds that much out here. But in another way they tolerate him and respect him because he's a daredevil and the best subaltern in the battery. Afraid of him, too. He's a dangerous friend and a worse enemy. Lone wolf, you know, with a chip on his shoulder. He's at daggers drawn with Lynch. There's another chap with a sharp tongue. Irishman. They can sling words. Some of Dolughoff's sayings are so odd that they got round to the colonel and the old boy, who is a dear old fire-eating dug-out, had Dolly's antecedents investigated. Foreign name and so on — thought he might be a spy. Well, he wasn't a spy, but they certainly uncovered an unsavoury background.... Now Dolughoff is obsessed with the idea that the colonel is persecuting him."

"I thought him a swine of the first water."

"Takes all kinds to make up this civilian army; you'll find some queer ducks in it that were never in the books of Charles Lever or G.A. Henty."

"All right. But I'll punch his head if he talks to me again the way he did at the hut."

"By the way, Dan," — Charles, as his custom was, had leapt sideways into an irrelevant thought — "why did you make me wangle you into this battery?"

"How's Alastair?" said Dan through his teeth.

"Why, you young snake-in-the-grass! So that's it.... Still rankles?"

"Yes.... I bet he's a good officer."

"He is."

"I'm glad."

"Now mind you, Dan, no nonsense between you two. This is a civilized battery fighting a civilized war."

"And Tripp's here?"

"Jiffy is very much with us, the mad young devil. I never saw a chap take life with so much gusto."

They went up the road with netting on high poles along one side and the sign: *Under enemy observation*. But still not a single gun spoke. The war seemed to have gone to sleep. A ramshackle ghost of a house inhabited by the last civilian in these parts said: *Here one makes the washing*. They passed a large gun on a railway mounting, snout erected, ready to bay the moon. An anti-aircraft battery was drawn up at the side of the road. A sausage balloon waved lazily in the upper aether. And Charles Burnet, heedless of mortality, chanted poetry about the splendour of the night-ingales, though only the splendour of his passionate breeches sprawled out against the front seat, and of his really melodious voice, defied the devastation.

"O mistress mine, where are you roaming —" sang Charles and suspired through his teeth in a sort of ecstasy. "By Phoebus Apollo there's beauty for you!" ... It astonished Dan to find his uncle, though now a soldier, so very much himself. He wondered whether Uncle Charles had really noticed the war. The Burnets never took themselves too seriously in their environment. That was the secret of their freedom. Not like the Thatchers who never took a holiday from their seriousness.

"We are nearly there now, Dan."

Ten minutes more, thought Dan, and I shall step into an absolutely different life. "How many officers are there?" he asked, hoping Charles would tell him about them.

"Let's see — nine. Major D'Arcy is a prewar regular. He is constantly amazed at us amateurs, at our inability to take a matter-of-fact view of the war as a strictly professional affair; he's a good fellow, though, and we amuse rather than annoy him. Then there is Kinney. He was some sort of a professor; he likes to lecture the mess as if they were a more than usually stupid class of freshmen. Imbrie. I call him the battery barometer because he is so abnormally average. If you want to know the opinion of the average subaltern on any subject whatsoever, you can get it from Imbrie. Currie. He's the stolid one. Lynch. Look out for Lynch. He doesn't care what he says. Celtic excitability. Clever chap; not 'sound' enough for the Anglo-Saxons. And, of course, Dolughoff. The Lord only knows where he came from. As a whole, the mess manages to be more or less normal members of the human race in spite of the war. They're neither heroes nor hellions, but good, sound in-betweens; they have guts, they're likable, some of them are gentlemen in *any* sense of the word and most are in the best sense."

Charles began to whistle under his breath.

"Do you still say *horas non numero nisi serenas*, Uncle Ch— sir?"

"Between you and me, I still talk through my hat, Dan, and always shall. Nowadays I talk through a shrapnel helmet — through a tin hat — a ridiculous headgear; it's always falling down and hitting you on the nose.... But never dully, I hope?"

iv

"Lynch," said Charles Burnet, "This is Don Beer Thatcher, Alastair's brother, you know.... Lynch is our mess president. See you later, Thatcher. I've got to go to the forward section."

Lynch, a gangling individual with a dangerously solemn face, took Dan in hand. "Cheeroh. Glad you've come, Thatcher. Imbrie, this is Thatcher ... Alastair's brother, you know. A spot of whisky? Bombardier! Bring my bottle. Here's mud in your eye! ... Major, this is Thatcher, Alastair's brother. Bound to be a good chap! ... What's that about conscientious objectors, Imbrie? What do you know about conchies; just hold on to that remark for a minute, I want to argue with you.... Everybody's here, Thatcher, but Jiffy Tripp and the Skipper, who is relieving Jiffy at the forward section. That lanky individual with the expression of an imperturbable owl sitting across from me is Currie. He appears to be thinking of something, but as a matter of fact, he is merely waiting for the next event to happen to him. And that reminds me — Bombardier! Buck up with dinner, will you? ... And the little squirt at the end of the table with the glasses is Brains Kinney. He's an Egyptologist in civil life; he regards the present battlefield as an archaeological stratum in the making. And Dolughoff. Have you met Dolly? Or rather, has he met you? If he isn't tight he might condescend to shake hands with you. Very exclusive bird, our Mr. Dolly — even with his friends.... All right, Dolly. Don't get shirty! It's only that crazy Irishman, Lynch.... Make yourself at home, Thatcher.... What were we saying about conchies, Imbrie?"

"Well, I mean to say they're rather dirty dogs after all, don't you know. I mean to say —"

"Then say it, man!"

"What I mean to say is — shooting our fellows in the back, I mean to say."

"On the contrary, my good fellow, they are simply guilty of the military crime of stirring up mutual forbearance between enemies."

"What," remarked the major, somewhat obscurely, "can you expect of a government led by a whippersnapper who ditched the House of Lords, and wanted to give over England to any Tom, Dick, or Harry without a public school education? If we only had a sound conservative government —"

At this moment a stooping figure entered the door of the mess — it seemed to Dan that, in France, one always entered places in a stooping position. This was none other than Jiffy Tripp, looking very much as he had always looked, Dan thought. He came into the mess like a sudden draught of air.

"Hello, Granny! I'm glad to see you, you old hound."

"Hello, Jiffy. And I'm glad to see you, too."

"Chr-r-r-istmas, what's for dinner?" said Jiffy, rubbing his hands and beaming. "I'm as hungry as an elephant."

"You always are," said Lynch, "Thatcher, just hand me over my bottle of whisky where Tripp can't get hold of it, will you?"

They were sitting about what had once been the counter of an estaminet, a twentieth century "round table" (which, however, happened to be rectangular, with a wine-stained marble top), the major in the role of King Arthur at one end. The estaminet, which had been ventilated by only one window, had recently been improved for the British Army by a German five-point-nine shell. This extra window was covered by a copy of the Paris *Daily Mail*. In the corner of the room was a stove made out of an oil drum. They dined: soup in which the meat had been boiled, the meat, tinned vegetables, *apricots en casserole de tin can mâitre d'estaminet*, something called a *canapé* made of sardines on toast, bread, margarine, and coffee. Just like the Ritz-Carlton.

After dinner inevitably everyone talked shop, though that was taboo in a peacetime mess. They talked about a broken buffer spring in Number Two gun, about laying a new Vickers platform in Number One's gun pit, about Ypres which was beginning to warm up, about the war in general.

At one end of the table, Lynch, who liked to stir people up by taking the unpopular view, asserted that the war was as good as lost — and was jumped on. "It's simply incredible," said Lynch, "that we should go on pouring men uselessly into that cesspool. The Canadian Corps will go next, mark my words. In England they still think we are winning a great victory in Ypres."

From the other end of the table, the major remarked in a calm voice: "So we are. Wearing 'em out, what?"

Brains Kinney explained the situation for the benefit of the mess at large. He said ponderously that the British Army had to keep on stonewalling in the salient because the Russians had thrown in their hand, the Americans weren't ready yet, and the French, owing to a slight misunderstanding with the Germans at the Chemin des Dames, were not fighting this year. They had had a belly full, said Kinney, and it was rumoured that a French division had actually about-turned to march on Paris and end the war. It had something to do with Mata Hari, who, though over forty, was still sufficiently *ravissante* to go to bed with important French staff officers and worm secrets from them.

"Perhaps," suggested Lynch, eyeing Dolughoff, "Mr. Bloody Dolughoff would address us on the defection of the Russian armies."

Dan glanced quickly at Dolughoff. Evidently he and Lynch were old enemies, for he did not appear surprised. Nor did he seem in the least daunted. More than ever it struck Dan that there was something catlike about the Russian — if he was a Russian. Formidable, heedless of other people, simply going his own way — then springing suddenly with a fierce pounce.... Dolughoff eyed Lynch askance through languidly dropped lids. "The Russians," he said, "are going to teach people to forget boundaries.... But you wouldn't understand that. I'll tell you why they have been beaten in terms even you can understand. They were beaten because they aped the absurd bourgeois virtues of England. They were beaten, my good Lynch, because they were too chivalrous. Twice they attacked — once at Tannenburg and once in 1916 — before they were ready, fighting with pitchforks and bare hands many of them, in order to save their allies.... Put that in your pipe and choke on it!"

Currie intervened with stolid urbanity: "Why make a fuss, Lynch? My good Dolly, must you?"

"Let 'em go!" said Tripp, beaming. "They enjoy it. Slip the leash. At him, Lynch! At him, Dolly!"

At the major's end of the table, Kinney had embarked on his favourite topic and was talking about Egypt in a mumbling class-room drone. "The Egyptians," he said, "pictured the soul as a little birdman with a human head and arms extending to its nostrils, in one hand the figure of a swelling sail, the hieroglyph for wind or breath, and in the other the *crux ansata* as the symbol of life. This little birdman-soul they called the *ba*. A man also had a *ka*, a sort of guardian spirit who aided him in the difficult and untried business of living after death."

"A sort of spiritual gas helmet, no doubt," said Lynch.

Tripp said: "Let not your *ka* know what your *ba* is doing."

But even Lynch's satirical efforts to stop Kinney were in vain; he was an enthusiast, a virtuoso; the war was a mere incident, something that happened to his external body, but the Egyptians were important, they were reality. "The fact is the notion of life after death was much more vital to the Egyptian of six thousand years ago than it is to modern, civilized man...."

An instrument known as a Don H., which was in fact a field telephone, had uttered a sort of buzz. "Well," thought Dan, "I suppose I am the junior sub. I might as well start my job now." He lifted the receiver. A rumbling, which he eventually recognized as a human voice, said: "Ascot speaking. What about those coils of wire?" — "Coils of wire?" repeated Dan, bewildered. — "Coils of wire! What's that! Give me the phone," exclaimed the major, pouncing on the receiver. "That you, Jeepers? ... Oh, you want our coils of wire, do you? You would! Damn it, you're taking a low advantage of us, Jeepers. You know damned well we've got them because you scrounged them for us yourself. I didn't think it of you. It's low, that's what it is. Next time you visit the mess bring your own whisky, Jeepers.... And by the way, old man, do come and see us soon." The major explained to Dan: "That's Jeepers. He used to be battery signals officer, and a jolly good one. He scrounged those coils of wire for us. Now he's signals officer at group and he's going to take them away from us, the hound!"

"In that soil," droned Kinney, "bodies will remain for an indefinite time without corruption. Brooding, no doubt, on this fact, the Egyptians came to the conclusion that life continued after death as long as the body remained inviolate. Hence the elaborate mummification, the vast pyramids to protect the body, all the material equipment to insure life after death. They are the most imposing manifestation of man's ancient struggle to conquer purely physical forces."

"They should have known Ypres," said Lynch; "it would have given them a jolt."

Dolughoff said in a bored voice: "I wish they'd send us to Ypres. Life is so dull here."

"*Dull*," repeated Lynch in a soft voice, staring with jutting chin at Dolughoff. "Dolly thinks it's dull.... What he really means," Lynch explained to Dan, "is that he hasn't slept with a woman since his last Paris leave. He's an awful bastard, is Dolughoff. The fact is, Thatcher, Dolughoff is one of the seven hundred sons of Abdul Hamid, by a Circassian dancing girl. His mother and father didn't get on. As a matter of fact, his mother only saw Abdul once in her life. Dolly has been a pimp in civil life and also a missionary of Beelzebub, and he can't make up his mind whether he is to be a priest or a pimp; he rather thinks he can have it both ways. He's quite proud of it, aren't you, Dolly? He is very religious. Greek orthodox á la Rasputin. Black masses, mystic orgies, the Satanic element in beauty — that sort of tripe. He prefers the authorized version of the Bible, however, and quotes it to us hot, to make us uncomfortable. He's quite sincere in all of his two hundred different personalities. He thinks all men are brothers, though he isn't a family man himself, and he intends to be a writer and made a life work of preaching the evangel of lust to unenlightened puritans. He's a blasphemous lecher.... How the hell did you ever get a commission in the British army, Dolughoff?"

"Have you quite finished, Lynch?"

"Quite, thank you. Your turn."

Dolughoff lit his cigarette and blew out the match with a reflective frown. "I pass over the more obvious aspects of your character, Lynch: that you are an acrimonious, mordacious, and envenomed male virago of an Irishman who, in his adolescence, kissed the backside of the Blarney Stone, possessing an all-embracing hypocrisy fit to make Ananias puke. Everyone knows that. For the moment I'll content myself with pointing out that as a renegade Catholic, whom I happened to observe one day stealing the crucifix from a gutted church near Vimy for a souvenir, you are obviously unfitted to criticize the religion of an original and serious-minded person like myself."

Lynch's face twisted. His fingers curled about the neck of a bottle and he hurled it at the loathed face of Dolughoff who always remained so hatefully calm. The bottle smashed on the wall above the Russian's head and showered him with fragments of glass. Dolughoff remained completely impassive. He raised his cigarette to his lips with a contemptuous expression and blew a cloud of smoke in Lynch's direction.

"Lynch!" ordered the major in a voice that crackled. "Go to your quarters. You, too, Dolughoff! Another word of this sort of thing from either of you and I'll place you under arrest."

"Right, sir. I'll go," stuttered Lynch excitedly, "but he told a dirty lie. He made it up on the spur of the moment."

Dolughoff stood up languidly and crushed out his cigarette. "Oh, well, one good lie deserves another. Lynch talking about religion — to *me!* ... You needn't be afraid, sir. Lynch won't start it again. He's afraid of me now."

Lynch opened his mouth to retort, saw the major's expression and held his peace. He and Dolughoff went to their quarters. "If they weren't such damned good officers ..." said the major. Tripp winked at Dan.

After a while the major stood up. "I think I shall turn in." Leaving the mess, he passed Dan. "You'll soon find your feet, Thatcher."

Dan found an old acquaintance in the battery; this was none other than Jobey Loversedge, the gipsy. With a full pack on his shoulders, Jobey was doing field punishment drill — twenty yards up and twenty yards back he marched, over and over, to the order of a bored corporal.

"Halt! What the devil are you doing here, Loversedge?" said Dan.

"Well, sir, you see, I did get drunk and enlist for fun."

"Are you getting it?"

The same irrepressible grin. "In between pack drills, sir."

"How would you like to be my servant, Loversedge?"

"Did they tell you I'd steal the shirt off your back, sir?"

"You'll steal for me, not from me. That's what a good batman does, isn't it?"

"Gipsies ain't much good as servants, sir."

"Oh, damn it. I like you — so be cheerful about it."

"Well, sir, I've tried about everything else so — is it an order, sir?"

"Yes. Mind you look after me well."

v

The impertinent features of Gunner Loversedge appeared in the doorway. "Mr. Thatcher, sir, your brother has come back to the battery and he says he is going up to the forward section with you."

Dan took his time going out. "I'm hanged if I'll hurry for Alastair."

Alastair had his shrapnel helmet tilted on one side of his head with the strap under his chin. He was tapping his stick on his boots. He grinned and half put out his hand and drew it back as Dan half put out his. They both laughed and shook hands.

"How's Cynthia, Alastair?"

"All right. Why didn't you call on her in London?"

Dan hated himself for flushing. "Charles says you're a hell of a good officer."

"I'm all right," admitted Alastair and added gracefully, "but you'll get the MC before I shall." *Confound his self-possession!*

"You'll smell powder tonight, Dan," said Alastair, grinning.

"Well, there has to be a first time," said Dan coolly, but his heart beat more quickly.

"Yes … are we friends, Dan?"

"Sort of," conceded Dan, but his expression was obstinate.

In pitch darkness they walked for a long time up a paved road toward the flares that flowered wanly over the trenches. All at once vague heaps of rubble, which had once been the houses of a village, rose up at the side of the road.

"There are the guns," said Alastair. "They'll be working all night putting down a Vickers platform. I'm going back now to get some sleep. You'll find Charles in the gun pits."

There was a faint odour of gas — like onions, but tasting sweet, too. By the carefully shaded light of a lantern, twenty gnomes, stooped and intent, clinked pickaxe and spade against the mixed earth and foundation material; their leather jerkins glistened with wetness. Silently, in the rain, with the dim light that left their faces swathed in dark shadow, they worked with an air of tenseness and stealth, as if their nocturnal task was somehow sinister. Charles loomed in the watery half-light, taller than the rest, in gumboots and a gunner's leather jerkin, his gas mask strapped across his chest "at the alert."

"Hello, Dan. You're just in time to do a spot of work. We laid the platforms last night on a centre line bearing of 90 degrees grid; it took us all night. No sooner had we got it done, than orders came through to the major that it should have been 125 degrees grid. You should have heard what the men said! They were not undemonstrative." He and the sergeant went into a discussion about bolts, arcs, side beams, and wheel plates. It was

technically remote to Dan as yet but interesting; especially when
you saw the huge bulks weighing each of them, a ton perhaps,
which had to be manhandled with levers and dragropes an inch
or two at a time into pits dug for them, to make a snug platform
for the howies.

The two howitzers projected their ugly, piebald snouts over
the edges of what had once been the cellars of houses, waiting to
be escorted into their new dens. About midnight the Caterpillar
tractors came to Croisilles to pull the guns into position, but they
arrived too soon and they also stood waiting like patient mythological creatures — gryphons or something of that sort. It began
to rain heavily and Charles grumbled that it always poured when
they shifted the guns. In a few minutes they were soaked to the
skin and the ground became slippery glue, making them slither as
they walked and sticking in heavy gobs to their boots.

"Can you handle a shovel, Dan?" asked Charles.

"Yes."

"Then dig — here."

Glad of even a gunner's job, Dan dug till his muscles ached.
At midnight the digging was finished, and they began to heave
the balks slowly forward, inch by inch, toward the gun pit.
Presently, they heard an aeroplane high above them: it sounded
like the uneven drone of a mosquito, and it seemed directly over
their heads. "Gotha. Put out the light," snapped Charles, and they
squatted down in silence, waiting for the first bomb to drop. It
dropped with a dull boom miles away down the valley; then a
sharper *boom-boom* — coming nearer; then *sh-ssh-crash* into the
village by the church; then *boom-boom* — receding down the valley into the distance. The work went on in sober silence.

But that was only the overture to the concert. All at once a
high velocity shell erupted from the dark. No warning this time.
Simply a sharp, vicious crack, like a bursting tire, on the heap
of stones at the edge of the gun pit (close this time!) followed
immediately by the rushing sound of the shell's coming and, last

of all, by the crack of its firing miles away behind the German line; this was one that had travelled faster than sound. No one was hit. But the sudden unheralded explosion had startled the men on the pit side of the balk so that they had let go their grip on the levers and dragropes with which they had been easing it into place, and the huge timber began to slither slowly, then faster, down the slope of the pit like an unwieldy hippopotamus taking the water, and landed with a sickening *whumpf* athwart the wet floor of the pit. Someone uttered a scalding shriek and went on shrieking. And in the midst of that horrible outcry, another shell arrived *crack — whish — sh — boom*. Not quite so close, but they could hear the splinters whining over their heads and striking the earth above the pit with a thud. "Quick — the lever here!" shouted Charles, and they saw that one of the men had slipped and been pinned by the falling balk. They placed a fulcrum and heaved all together at the balk while the man below them looked up past them with eyeballs starting and with shrieks streaming from his lips. They could not budge the huge timber. Coolly, Charles rearranged the fulcrum and they heaved again, and as they heaved, two more shells burst, one on each side of the pit. This time they got the man out. Charles took a quick look and shook his head. Then they brought a stretcher and Charles said: "You go with him, Dan. There's a field dressing station in the village. Down the road to the right." They went out into the darkness with the poor devil who tried to writhe and twist himself off the stretcher and had to be held down. Into a dugout in the ruins where sleepy, pale faces peered at them and where a sergeant took charge, grumbling a little, but very gentle. Routine for him.... Then back to the pit to weary hours of work at the fallen timber.

# CHAPTER VIII

### i

Coming back to the battery from the trenches late one night, Dan found that the guns had mysteriously disappeared. Lorries were being loaded, batmen appeared from huts and dugouts carrying Wolseley valises, torches flashed and lit up the figures of men in marching equipment. The battery was being torn from the little patch of ground that had grown familiar and was now landless and rootless as any gipsy caravan.

He asked Lynch whom he found, flashlight in hand, checking stores: "Where are we off to?"

Lynch flashed the torch onto Dan's face, thereby obscuring his own; from obscurity his disembodied voice uttered a single word with prophetic distinctness. "The salient...." There were many bulges in the thin red line, but only one that all men called *the* salient.

A whole army corps on the march and in a hurry cluttered every highway and byway, a caterpillar with seventy thousand legs slowly creeping toward Ypres. The plans had been made, the fates of the marching myriad signed and sealed: a slow journey of days to end at a given moment of time in a single sharp leap of thousands, all at once, into the unknown. And during that slow progress, minds and spirits gathered and tensed themselves for that leap.

Officers and men of the battery travelled in lorries except for a handful who marched with the guns. They were a mighty caravan: caterpillar tractors and guns, Commer lorries, battery light cars, motorcycles and sidecars. The lorries kept together like a mechanical dragon with each of its vertebrae clanking and weaving in a separate, yet connected, curve. The tractors and guns followed in a column of their own at about three miles an hour.

The uncertainty and mystery of the nocturnal rendezvous had a charm for Dan which he never forgot. You were homeless wanderers travelling from infinity to infinity. Sent on an errand, you left your brother subalterns at daybreak and met them again at night at some crossroad that had reality only because it was marked on the map. You slept in haylofts or on the muddy floors of barns which rose like magic out of the darkness, never again to be seen and recognized afterwards.

They passed famous British regiments coming out of the line. Major D'Arcy knew all about them. He knew why one regiment was called the Pompadours and another the Moonrakers and another the Bloody Eleventh. Why one wore the Tudor dragon on their caps and another the paschal lamb of Charles II's Portuguese wife and another the castle and keys of Gibraltar. He knew their battle honours, their nicknames, their marching tunes, the peculiarities of their uniforms, and why those peculiarities existed in honour of some forgotten heroism. "There go the 'Dirty Half-Hundred.' The Duke of Wellington said to them after Vimeiro, 'Not a good looking regiment, but devilish steady.' They had black facings then, cheap dyed, and when they dragged the cuffs across their sweating faces, the dye came off.... Those are the Greys — they've worn the eagle of France on their caps since Waterloo." They passed the Sherwood Foresters marching to "The Young May Moon," the tune they marched to when they arrived at the breach at Badajoz after a long, forced march.... It was not the first time most of these regiments had fought in Flanders.

Who could have said that they were marching to a battle that might break the heart of England? The thousands went into battle not ignobly, not as driven sheep or hired murderers — in many moods, doubtless — but as free men with a corporate, if vague, feeling of brotherhood because of a tradition they shared and an honest belief that they were doing their duty in a necessary task. He who says otherwise lies or has forgotten.

Ypres still had a skyline. You could not altogether wipe out seven hundred years of history with three years of even the modern spirit. Approaching the town, talk ceased and there was a kind of mental girding of the loins, for all ranks felt, each in its way, that this was the valley of the shadow of death. Not that there was quiet over Ypres. For a month and more the guns had been in full cry without once being called home, and since the Battle of Messines, men had swarmed and slithered and crawled and struggled in the quivering mud like maggots in a neglected wound.

In the city, the streets had lost sharpness of contour and had become passages cleared through heaps of fallen brick. In the *place d'armes*, where the Cloth Hall lay like a beheaded torso, a river of traffic streamed toward the Menin Gate and the one "road" to the front. For it was night, the time when the army came out of its many graves and walked. High velocity shells of large calibre fell at steady intervals onto the road as they had fallen for months and months. Men scattered, other men picked up the wounded, if they were to be found; only the military police, forbidden to leave their posts, hunched their shoulders momentarily and continued to direct the traffic. The human stream flowed together again and flowed on.

They passed the moat where swans still swam hard by a sixty pounder battery in the ramparts near the Menin Gate, and followed the caterpillars and guns down the Zonnebeke Road toward Hellfire Corner. Mist and drizzle, salient weather, soaked them to the skin, getting beneath the neck and armholes of leather jerkins, compressing the night into a drumming opaqueness that enclosed and isolated their little section of the artery that carried life blood to the front. The pavement petered out and was replaced by a plank road of beechwood laid over the liquid mud; the planks squelched and tip-tilted under them. The debris of caissons, of horses, of GS wagons, of rusted tanks with their treads twisted up and out like a wounded man flinging up his arms, of what had once been men, lined the road like sea wrack. Several times they had to halt when, up ahead, some shell of the ever-searching stream had found the exact line of the road, flinging upward men, planks, guns, or transport wagons indiscriminately.

At last they reached the battery position and laid a ribbon of planks on brushwood and chicken netting to get to it from the road, with a tank to pull them close to the emplacements. The tank officer said: "You're lucky. You've got a bit of dry ground here." Dry ground it may have been, but the term seemed merely relative to the festering slough that surrounded them. Exhausted and wet to the skin, they laboured all night, laying platforms and manhandling the guns. A squall of shells swept over them: seventy-sevens and four-point-twos searching and sweeping, certain of hitting something in an area where three thousand guns and more were sitting in mud without cover. They picked up the wounded and went on with the work, and the squall passed on to other areas of decompression. The guns went in and sat like awkward boys at a tea party, and before daybreak, they fired their first shells. "That's the stuff to give 'em!"

But with the grey daylight they found themselves in a morass utterly devoid of any homely landmarks. The shell-pocked terrain had been chewed and spat forth by a cyclops. The landscape lacked relevance to humanity or to anything growing. It was simply *empty*. True, a captured pillbox and a few rotting tanks were visible; on the crest of the ridge ahead, paleolithic rubble marked what had been a village, and here and there splintered tree trunks cut off short, bristled like the beard on a corpse. But all these things had long since died; men had gone to earth there, earth to mud, and trees to splintered stumps. The only living things visible were the guns scattered everywhere, barely discernible in the conquering monotony, and inhabiting the waste like lost spirits in hell. The landscape was significant of nothing, and the significance of mere emptiness was appalling. To see so vast a tract of fruitful earth pulped into a cancerous girdle made one feel uneasy in that part of one deep down that never feels secure because it belongs to the earth and fears to be reduced to the primitive element of mud into which human clay and man's machines have been absorbed. It was a landscape. It was a raped landscape, naked, raw, and expiring.... A cockney dispatch rider came chugging up the road (almost deserted in daytime) whistling cheerfully. His appearance in that place and in that mood was ridiculous and inappropriate — and reassuringly human.

On the 7th of June, 1917, the British Army took Messines and began the Third Battle of Ypres; on November 6th they took Passchendaele, and looking down for the first time since 1914 on the plain of Flanders, ended the battle having advanced through 14,300 yards of hell at a cost of 300,000 casualties. Pilckem Ridge, Langemarck, Menin Road, Polygon Wood, Brookseinde, Poelcappelle, Passchendaele, and again Passchendaele — these are the battles of 1917 fought in the salient, and in these battles, at some time or another, the majority of the divisions of the British Army in France went through the bloodbath — often twice or thrice; grim names for Britain to remember and sacred.

Men advanced through porridge-like mud in which they sometimes sank to their waists, wearing sandbags about their boots to keep them from sinking deeper, using a sandbag filled with mud for a pillow when they infrequently slept; slipping, stumbling, gliddering, struggling, pulling one another out of that slough. In broad daylight flights of wasps with black crosses on their wings flew low and stung them with machine guns as if they were crawling grubs. At night the roads and duckboards were continuously swinged with steel, yet over them men, mules, and ammunition had to go. Blazing shell dumps lit their purgatorial passage. They fought incessantly, gaining a rod here, often pushed back in a counterattack there, struggling in gas masks, holding rifles in numbed hands. Frequently, they suffered many barrages in a single day. The stretcher bearers — eight men to a stretcher in that mud — wandered in no man's land; sometimes their bullets found them and they fell and, sinking into the mud, were not. Often men sat down and cursed and sobbed and then got up and stumbled on. Rarely, they hummed a song or whistled, *Instead of hugging a saucy wench, I cuddle a sandbag in a trench* — only there were few sandbags and fewer trenches. Somehow many of them existed and survived; but they were not the same men afterwards, for they had seen more than death, they had faced corruption of the soul and despair.

There was a saying about Ypres which, for a time, was proverbial and which, repeated now out of its time, seems feverish and unreticent: "Men saw one another's souls at Ypres." Perhaps they did, but if so, the seeing was a matter of reading hints, for Anglo-Saxon reserve, which foreigners sometimes mistake for stolidity, never had a more severe test and never emerged more triumphantly. At Ypres each member of the mess still seemed to be himself, only more essentially so. Lynch, the Irishman, was more excitable, alternately gay and savage. Dolughoff, who shared a waterlogged bivvy with Dan, became more and more quarrelsome; he did his job as an officer well, but he asked for no man's friendship. Alastair, that exasperating brother of Dan's, remained unruffled, and contrived somehow, even in that muck, always to have his boots polished. Charles Burnet was as erratic and gay in talk as ever (the men wrote home: "We've got a skipper that's one of the best"), but drank more than usual. Major D'Arcy was his cool and ironic self, faintly amused at the crude efforts of shells to disturb his aplomb — *quare fremuerunt gentes!* Tripp came into the mess grinning, always grinning, and rubbing his hands, ready for dinner; his favourite saying was "Cheer up, cully, you'll soon be dead. A short life and a gay one!" Brains Kinney was wounded and sent to England, which on the whole pleased him since Ypres had begun to interfere with his historical perspective. But Curry, stolid Curry, did not change because he was dead. He was mortally wounded and died without making a fuss on the duckboards outside the battery.

## ii

Dan lay asleep on two boards raised a few inches above the water which covered the muddy floor of his foxhole. Opposite him, similarly raised above the water, lay Dolughoff. The smell of fecal decomposition and the fact that the entrance faced the wrong way meant that, a few weeks ago, it had been lived in by Germans. An hour or two earlier when they had been lying waiting for sleep, gas shells, the most civilized of all the sounds of war, had been sighing through the night and announcing their arrival with a subdued *plop* that was almost apologetic. It was difficult to sleep in a gas helmet, though when you were very tired you could sometimes manage it.

A sharp cry cut into the troubled texture of Dan's dreams: *Oh God! Oh God!* followed by a gabbled recitative in some foreign language, rhythmical even though hurried by panic; it might have been a prayer.

He sat bolt upright on the side of the planks, his booted feet dipping into foul water. He put out his hand to find a wall and touched wet mud. Then he knew where he was. The cry? Dolughoff, of course … or was it simply his own dream? He was shivering, and the wet drizzle, sifting into their home, had misted the eye pieces of his gas helmet and made his blankets dripping wet. He fumbled in the pocket of his trench coat for a flashlight, turned it on, and swept the beam in a circle about the mud sides of the bivvy. The beam came to rest on the figure of Dolughoff sitting hunched on his plank bed. His shoulders heaved as if he were panting for breath, and in his gas mask, with his hands gripping the edge of the planks, he made Dan think of an evil spirit suddenly rising from his coffin.

Dan scrambled down from his bed and splashed over to Dolughoff. "Are you gassed, man?"

The Russian shook his head and waved his hand in wordless denial. For several instants the goggled eyes stared at Dan, then Dolughoff relaxed and swung his legs over the edge of the planks.

"God! What a dream." The clip of the gas mask, sitting over his nose, made the words come with a nasal boom. He tossed his head to rid his mind of the fumes of sleep. "Is there still gas, Thatcher?"

Dan climbed out of the bivvy and tested for gas. The shelling had stopped during their sleep and the air was clean and rain washed. He called back to Dolughoff. "No gas.... I'll nip into the BC post and get us a tot of rum."

The guns were at work on a routine harassing program, and the momentary gun flashes lit the familiar plank road crossing a sea of mud, on which flowed the stream of men, mules, and guns going up the line. Dan lifted the gas curtains and went into the concrete pillbox, the battery commander's post, which was the brain and nerve centre of the battery. Lynch, who was orderly officer, silently handed him a message from group headquarters. Dan stretched it out close to the candle and read:

> *The Wellington Battery will provide a working party of two officers, two full ranks, and twelve other ranks, to go to (see appended sketch map and note co-ordinates of route and destination). On arrival at the destination, the officer in charge of the party will report to the RE officer in charge of —*

"Who is to go, Imbrie?"

"Alastair and Dolughoff tomorrow. You relieve them the day after. You are supposed to put up an OP. Crazy idea! You'll have to take iron rations and live on 'em for God knows how long. Going up you'll have to rope the men together. I've told the BSM to tick off a party from the roster."

Dan studied the sketch map. "That's in the front line."

"It was today. It may not be tomorrow."

Dan went back to the bivvy and found that Dolughoff had lit a candle and was sitting up in his bunk with his blankets drawn tight about his shoulders. He paid no attention to Dan.

"You and Alastair are taking a working party up the line tomorrow."

"All right," said Dolughoff in a flat tone.

Dan saw that he was shivering. "Got the wind up, Dolly? Here, drink some of this."

"Wind up, you bloody fool?" exclaimed Dolughoff vehemently. "No! I've never been afraid of a shell in my life. No bullet, bomb, or shell has got *my* name on it. They won't touch me till I've delivered my message. I've been put into this blasted war to do a special job. And I'll do it. You'll see."

"A message? What is this message you are always talking about, Dolly?"

"Why should I tell you? You don't like me and I am indifferent to you. As a matter of fact, I heartily dislike practically all human beings. 'Specially women."

"And yet if a quarter of what you tell me is true, there isn't a more lecherous, prancing old goat than you in this world, Dolly."

Dolughoff was not in the least offended. "All right, granted. That doesn't keep me from despising the darlings. I've never surrendered my integrity by *loving* a woman and I never shall. They want only to turn a man from himself and make him weak."

"You certainly are a work of art, Dolly! Can't you see that a woman is a person — not *just* a woman."

"Not to me," said Dolughoff succinctly.

Dolughoff got a tin mug and poured a tot of rum into it; the rim of the mug clattered against the neck of the rum jar. "I am a deeply unhappy man, Thatcher. Do you suppose I enjoy despising people and loathing them? Do you think I like being what I am? I tell you, I have been made that way for a purpose. I *cannot* like people."

Completely nonplussed and in his heart ashamed for Dolughoff, Dan mumbled: "I don't know what to say."

"Don't say anything! Do you think *you* can help me? Just listen to me, that's all I want of you…. I want to tell you about the dream I had…. You know the plank road out there?" Dolughoff gestured with outstretched finger.

"Of course."

"I thought I was standing in the mud near that road. Beside me was a shadowy figure, very tall, very imposing, though I couldn't see his face. In front of him was a machine gun. The gun's muzzle was pointed toward the road and over it was stretched a black cloth. Up the planks marched the usual column of men, mules, then more men, just as they are marching at this minute. The odd thing was they didn't make a sound, no footfalls or clank of accoutrement. Then I heard myself saying to him — to it (and my voice sounded like some other person's): 'It is strange, sir, that they don't make any sound. You'd think they were going to heaven.'

"The figure laughed. The laugh made me jump, it was so unexpected and I give you my word, Thatcher, it was an ugly sound! Then he said:

"'To heaven! That is an odd idea. Do they think so?'

"I said: 'I don't believe so, sir. They've given up thinking much about it. They just go on, I suppose.' He was silent for a minute, then he said:

"'There is a lot of power let loose in this world. Do they know that?'

"'Yes, sir,' I answered.... 'Why is it let loose?'

"The figure shook his head slowly. 'Power is an end in itself. It is enough simply to see it unleashed — if you only look at it in the right way. Beauty, the unleashing of power — they are the same thing. In the spring of a panther, the coiling of a python about its prey, in all nature, if you'd only look at it dispassionately.... Now watch.' He tapped the barrel of the machine gun with his foot, then pointed at the head of a battalion in the marching river of men. 'From there'— he swept his finger in an arc to the tail of the battalion — 'to there.'"

"What did you do?" asked Dan.

"I was horrified. I cried something like: 'Wait! Christ, you can't do that. Those are our men.'

"'Ours?' inquired the figure in an icy voice.

"Then I tried to reach him to throw myself on him, but my feet caught in the sucking mud. The machine gun spoke briefly and precisely. The plodding column fell to earth symmetrically like a row of toy figures.

"'Power!' said the calm, cold voice.... '*Barrage!*' When he gave that curt order, a hurricane of shells came down on the plank road and tossed planks and bodies into the air amid gouts of mud and geysers of smoke.... When the smoke cleared, Thatcher, there wasn't a trace of that section of the plank road or of the dead men lying upon it. They were obliterated, simply buried in the sea of mud, gone as though they had never been."

"Did the figure say anything after that?" Dan asked.

"Yes, he did. I can't remember his exact words. He said something about your having to put yourself into the mind of a god possessing power. Looking from without. From without! ... And even as he spoke, the next battalion was ploughing ahead through the gap in the plank road, heads down, feet dragging, eyes vacant.... What I do remember is that his words, whatever they were, filled me with horror so that I awoke in a cold sweat, screaming."

"You certainly did! You scared the wits out of me."

"You see, Thatcher, it wasn't that *I* minded about those men being wiped out, but I wanted Deity — if it was Deity — to mind."

"You mean, you thought the figure in your dream was — Deity? "

Dolughoff denied this vehemently. "No! It was the devil.... But for a moment I thought.... I was tempted to think —"The strange Russian, the madman (if he was mad) buried his face in his hands and groaned.

"What did you think for a moment?" persisted Dan.

"That it might be Deity. That that dream might be my message.... How could I make you understand? That figure was like me, Thatcher. I'm cruel — I like it. I like to feel that I have unlimited power ... to give pain. But then again, I don't want to be like that. We're strange creatures, Thatcher. God is love. Why can't I love my fellow men?"

"Don't ask me, Dolughoff," said Dan fervently.

"I'm not asking you. I've been made that way for a purpose. Nobody who cared a fig for other people could do what I am to be privileged to do. I must be completely detached from human beings in order that I may have courage to do my task. When the war began, I understood at once for the first time why I had been made as I was made. The things I suffered before then. But never mind that!" he broke off in a voice suddenly angry. "What I have suffered is my own affair, but what I *am* is going to be the concern of the whole world!"

"My God!" breathed Dan. "You don't say! And what *is* this task, Dolly?"

"In some way, which will be revealed to me in due course, I am to stop the war."

"And how will you know, Dolly? If a mere human being may presume to ask you that question. How will it be revealed?"

"Perhaps in the Bible. Perhaps in a dream. When the message comes, I shall recognize it.... Look here, Thatcher, twice I have disbelieved. Twice, under bombardments, I have said, 'There is no God!' Those are the only sins I have ever committed; all the other things — what I am — were put upon me for a purpose. I've known despair, Thatcher. Once — one of those times under a bombardment — I thought of killing myself. And it wasn't because I was afraid. It was because, for an instant, I believed there was no God."

"Dolly," said Dan with sudden insight, "the trouble with you is that you *are* afraid. You are afraid of the truth about yourself."

The fury in Dolughoff's face was not pleasant to look upon. "Never say that again! As God is my master, if you do, I shall kill you, Thatcher!"

# CHAPTER IX

By 1917 the transition from peace to war was complete. Not merely had the war changed the landscape and sown it with encampments, barracks, practice trenches, aeroplane hangars, and marching troops; it had also played a strange trick with time. The years of war were as unnatural as those hours when Joshua bade the sun to stand still; they were shut off from the orderly flux of past into present of peace times. People spoke of "before the war" as they might have spoken of the nineteenth century, as a time remembered but already remote and almost unreal.

Returning late in the evening to Ardentinny from the bulletin board of the *Wellington Register,* Pen found the family occupied in exactly the ways he had expected to find them occupied. Maud was writing to the boys, Joanna was writing to Dan. Fanny and Euphemia, who now lived at Ardentinny, were having an argument. Tessa Thatcher, who was staying at Ardentinny, had gone up to her room.

All the Burnets had to have some escape from the sordid task, the trivial round. Fanny found hers in managing people. Her real feelings she kept to herself, and being conventional in the social relations, her opinions about matters like the war were always those of society. Consequently, on the rare occasions when she could not avoid generalizing about it, she always referred to it as a matter of tragic heroism. The actual truth of the matter was that it really touched her very little, except that it made life interesting by giving her a great deal to do — committees, boards, auxiliaries, bazaars, and still more committees. She was not a woman of imagination or of strong feelings.

For Euphemia, however, the war had entailed several changes of religion. It was characteristic of her that, at a time when casualty lists were convincing most people that human life was worth about as much as the life of a stray dog in Constantinople, she should suddenly have become convinced of life's sanctity. She had discovered that lover of the human form divine, Lavater. Ah, *he* had a feminine nature, a nature most profoundly religious. At this moment she was reading from the master to Fanny who, instead of listening, was busy drawing up agenda for a meeting.

"Listen to what Lavater says about the mouth. 'This part of our body is so sacred to me that I scarcely dare to speak of it. What a subject of admiration! What a sublime marvel in the midst of so many other marvels of which my being consists.'" Here she came to a passage referring to the functions which the human mouth shares with those of animals. This she adroitly skipped. "'It serves to form speech; it speaks, and will still speak, when it can never open again.'"

"Well, Euphemia," said Pen savagely, "there was another battle today at Passchendaele, and as a result, I suppose there are thirty or forty thousand mouths that will never speak again."

This remark struck the room to silence and the pen ceased scratching on notepaper. Euphemia came back unwillingly from her fairyland and sighed. Maud crushed her handkerchief into a hard little ball and stared at what she had written without seeing it. Pen said:

"I'm sorry. I ought not to have said that. The whole business gets on my nerves and sometimes I lash out without thinking."

Fanny got up and went upstairs to her room. She wanted to be alone. It was one of the rare moments when she felt like meeting and talking to that hidden person, the real Frances Burnet, of whose existence she was almost unaware. Who was she? She was a sensible, practical, solid woman who prided herself on that fact. She did not like men very much and often said so in such a way that shrewd observers ventured to believe she obtained a thrill of vicarious romance by rejecting the sex *in toto*. The world, she believed, is on the whole a pleasant place if one keeps a calm mind, does one's duty, and seldom worries. Nevertheless, her room revealed a secret strain of sentiment. There were lace pillow slips on the bed and a picture of the Christ Child above it. And here and there in the room, among the intimate knickknacks of a bedroom, there were couches of feminine fastidiousness. It was a woman's room. She took a sheet of notepaper and wrote at the top. *Dear Charles* — Then she lifted her pen and mused. Why was it hard to write to Charles today? Usually it was not. Resolutely, she attacked the unwritten sheets and filled two pages with her crisp, vigorous handwriting, retailing the ploys of the family and the small talk of the town. This she signed, *Your affec^ate sister, Frances*, and reached for an envelope. But in the act of bidding the sheets she hesitated again, smoothing the crease. Then without giving herself time to weigh words, with the feeling that she was revealing herself almost immodestly, she seized the pen and dashed off these words below her signature: "That God may bless and keep you safe, dear Charles, is the constant thought and prayer of your loving sister." Without looking at what she had written, she sealed the envelope and leaned back in the chair. It was strange to feel so moved. She was trembling and she wanted to weep.

At that moment in another bedroom, Tessa Thatcher sat at a dressing table reading a letter from her husband. Daniel, still an American citizen, was in the city of Washington writing a book on civilian morale for the government which believed that spiritual setting-up exercises might well be applied to civilians as well as to the military. The government paid Daniel a dollar a year to argue that the man who applied the morale of a good soldier to the affairs of civilian life was leading "the disciplined life" which was also "the good life." His letter to Tessa indirectly concerned "the disciplined life." Not without alarm, he was opposing her desire to go to England and serve as an amateur nurse. The brutal fact was that he was both alarmed and jealous. But this the psychologist did not admit to himself. One of the advantages of being a professional psychologist is that you can always use a convincing terminology to prove that what you would like to believe about human nature, particularly women's human nature, is a scientific fact. In his letter to Tessa, he pointed out with sweet reasonableness that what women in their hearts desired, though often they did not recognize their real wish, was security. They needed it for biological reasons because they were weak and wanted safety to bring up.... But this last clause Daniel had erased, for the phrase "bring up a family" aroused a train of thought which was unpleasant to him.

Tessa, that member of the sex desiring security, put down the letter and studied her face in the mirror. Faint lines were visible, which spoke too eloquently not to any calm system of philosophy but straight to a primitive emotion which she was too much of a woman and too little of a philosopher to disregard. She was thirty, still good looking, youthful looking even, certainly youthful in her manner. She was beginning to feel passé, she was not free, she felt that she never had been. "This life, this feeling alive in every bit of you which is what we all want, is it *never* to come for me?" Sometimes, as at present, this question was frantically insistent, and then for months, even years, you could keep it safely in the bottom of your mind.

Downstairs, Maud having schooled herself to calmness, was once more writing. Pen watched her over the covers of a book. Supposing, he thought for the thousandth time, they did take me seriously, could they seize Ardentinny for taxes, simply because I am the nominal owner? ... He thought of himself and Maud. In the old days, though Pen, making a point of rebellion, had never said prayers, Maud had always knelt at the bed holding his hand. Since they had differed about the war — since the tax business, she always went to the window and said them to the stars; it was the sole symbol of a difference between them. This hurt Pen, though he had only once referred to it. He had asked her: "What do you say when you pray, Maud?" And she had answered: "For those we love — to keep them safe. And for you too, dear. Just as always."

Maud was writing: "Your father and I feel sure — we do not doubt it for an instant! — that whatever ordeals you may have to go through, things we at home know nothing about and could not even imagine perhaps, you will always remain fine, honourable men —"

Suddenly, she dropped her pen with a queer, urgent cry. Pen ran to her and put his arm about her. She was dazed and white as death.

"What is it, dear? Tell me!"

When she could speak, she gasped brokenly: "Alastair is wounded.... He called me.... I looked and he was here in this room."

"Maud! My dear! That's — why that isn't reasonable! ... You are overwrought."


The editor of *Tell 'Em the Truth*, a weekly of versatile veracity with a large circulation in saloons and barber shops, was glancing with distaste at the galley of an article on the Battle of Passchendaele. His practised eye lingered only over the verbs and adjectives which were the pothooks and hangers of *Tell 'Em the Truth*'s style. In a war write-up, people expected certain adjectives — *glorious, intrepid, lion-hearted*, etc. — but as to the verbs, an editor could shoot the ink pot. No doubt about it, the article was lousy. He rang a bell for the Smart Young Man who as cub, detective, and re-write man was his principal lieutenant. He himself was a specialist on the laws relating to libel.

The Smart Young Man strolled in and sat on the editor's desk. Under his arm was a folded copy of their bread and butter.

"Smith," said the editor, punching the galley with his fist, "this article is lousy! It's nothing but a rehash of the dailies. Got to get a human angle. Just a battle — that's too big to go home to people; got to narrow it down and tie it up with Tom, Dick, and Harry. See? Got to think of the prim'ry emotions. Now get this, Smith. There are only three ways to work up a story for *Tell 'Em the Truth*. Only three. A kiss on the forehead, a sly poke in the ribs, or a kick in the pants. Kiss on the forehead is out here — all the daily papers are playing it that way, and a poke in the ribs is out — there's no sex angle to a battle. Now, how are we going to play this?"

"Kick in the pants, obviously," said the Smart Young Man and added hopefully, "How about soaking the generals?"

"Time you learnt a little common sense, young man! This country's at war, you can't print stuff like that — and get away with it. Besides, it's unpatriotic. Besides, it's stale. Besides, as far as *Tell 'Em* is concerned, the army — all of it — from general to drummer boy (do they have drummers nowadays?) is just swell. You can't blow up the army without blowing up the whole country and ourselves with it — this is a national war, see?"

"Sure, a nation in arms," said Smith glibly.

"Yeh. All heroes. And so help me, they are heroes, at that! … That gives me an idea. Get me that letter of Penuel Thatcher's out of the morgue, and bring the write-up on it."

Beatrice and Cynthia Elton, though they worked as VADs at different hospitals, roomed together in the West End of London. The work they were given to do — sweeping, scrubbing, emptying bedpans, bandaging wounds that stank — absorbed their physical and nervous endurance during the day and sent them home in the evening tired out physically, but not too exhausted to wake up, again, the uneasy burden of their private lives.

On the evening of the Battle of Passchendaele, Beatrice got home first and, throwing her hat on a chair, stood looking out the window, pressing the tips of her fingers over her forehead. The roar of traffic came up to her from the street. Newsboys were shouting about another victory at Ypres. Passersby dug into their lockets for a penny, handed it over, took the paper with mechanical movement and inscrutable faces. Sometimes the voice of the great machine, its never-ending low — roaring just like this before you were born, roaring on after you died, forever — frightened her because its impersonality, its heedlessness, was so brutal. It told you that the world was a terrible rushing river on which you floated — or which flowed past you or against you and over you no matter who you were or what you did.... Sometimes she wanted to be dominated by some passion so strong that it would make her forget herself, insignificant atom of wreckage that she was, tossed hither and thither on this mindless stream.

She got tea things and laid them on the table. Then she tried to think of something safe to talk to Cynthia about so that there would not be constraint between them. But her mind was too tired and slid back obstinately into the same groove.... *Why can't I forget?* and then, almost in the same instant, *Why can't I remember?*

Cynthia came in carrying an evening paper which she spread out on the tea table over the cups. They read together, without speaking, *Another Battle at Passchendaele.* "Ypres," thought Cynthia.... I wonder what it's really like there. Do they think of *us*? If I had known it would be like this: waiting, waiting, waiting.... Cynthia wanted to share her thoughts with her sister, but Beatrice said bitter things about the war that stole your courage.

"Have some cake, Cynthia. It's good. There's a little real butter in it."

"No. Just tea."

She took the cup and dropped in a saccharine pellet.

In a way it's easier for Beatrice. Everything is finished for her; completely ended. She knows where she stands and she can face it.... What a little fool I was with Alastair, wanting to hold on to what I was and not able to let go. I wasn't ready.... But he was not tender, he didn't understand....

She shuddered.

Beatrice said: "Why not have a glass of sherry if you won't drink the tea? It would do you good. I had a hard day.... Had you?"

"Yes, but I don't mind now."

"Neither do I. I never did. It's what I want, Cynthia. To work so hard I can't think."

Cynthia did not answer.

They *are* brutes, partly, thought Cynthia.... For instance, they like killing, really. The part of them that's a brute. They like it — and they hate it. Yes, and they come back to us hungry and don't want to talk. Just to sink down deep and forget it and themselves utterly. Alastair's letters.... Why can't I, too? At Shorncliffe when he was training and I was in the hospital and we only saw each other twice a week when we were both tired. Why am I like that? Somehow I never imagined him, then, in France. Why don't I ever imagine things beforehand? If I had it over again, I'd make him happy. I'd hold him closer and closer and wouldn't think of myself even for an instant. I'd just think of him and making him happy.... I wish I was going to have a child, then I'd forget everything, and think only of the child.... Oh, dear God, there's got to be *something*! Isn't there something to cling to!

"Cynthia, it's been a long time since we went to a show."

"I suppose it is."

"Like to go tonight?"

"Well ... oh, I don't think so.... All right. Something light. Let's see *Chu Chin Chow* again."

Beatrice removed the cups and washed them carefully. Surely, there ought to be something else to do. I must make something to do, to put off what lies in wait for you always just round the corner. She tidied the mantelpiece and looked over her civilian clothes. Old and getting shabby. I ought to get a new evening dress. But what for? … The old emotion swept over her but fixed with a new subtle anguish that lately had come often — a kind of treachery to that singleness of emotion which she wanted to cherish. Why did I think that about the dress? … She stabbed this treacherous thought viciously and slew it. She thought of Cynthia. I ought to help her but I can't. There's a barrier between us you can't pass; and we don't help each other. Being together only makes it worse. It's because she thinks of the living and I think of the dead.

But do I? It's so wretched to think and think, and pass people day after day without ever really seeing them or being seen. And when you've known what it is to be loved — only not really.… Everything he said and did was right just because he said it and did it. He could be tender and he knew when to be. And playful. Sometimes he was rough and almost cruel as if I was no one at all, and yet everything, and made me think … and, oh, I wish.… To want life is an obscenity. Beatrice Elton killed forever and ever on April the twenty-fourth, 1915, when her fiancé fell in the battle of St. Julien, and now she wants to be resurrected to life. *I … will … not!* … But I gave everything to him — all my soul. I gave it in thought before I ever knew he loved me. I couldn't do that again. It's gone, all the best part of it. All except being afraid and lonely and wanting.…

On October the twelfth, 1917, Quentin Thatcher, in the company of twelve others clad like himself in private's uniform and shackled with handcuffs, waited on the station platform at Rouen for the train to take them and their escort to Boulogne. The station was crowded with military details coming "up the line" from schools and reinforcement camps, coming out of the line to schools, or passing through to some other part of the front. Trains consisting of goods vans pulled into the station, the doors burst open like corks from bottles, and the troops foamed out and flowed instantly to stalls where coffee was being dished from buckets. Not until they had eaten and drunk did they notice the thirteen shackled privates sitting back in the dark shadows ("Jeeze, do you see them prisoners? Deserters?" — "Naw, too many of them. They're on their way to the glasshouse.") The thirteen stared straight in front of them with a fixed expression, but none of the little group suffered more keenly than Quentin under the lively and impersonal scrutiny of many pairs of eyes looking at them as if they were strange animals. Once he had been at one with these troops, now he was not; nor was he at one with the twelve Quakers who sat beside him. His fellow prisoners he knew well by this time; too well considering that he had not the least desire to know them at all. He felt he knew them far better than they could know him. He had been at the front; they had not. Every man of them, he knew, was sincere and honest according to his light. They were really "conscientious objectors"; if they had been merely slackers they would have compromised and accepted some sort of military duty in England. "Absolutists" they called themselves.

One of these Quakers, a man called Perrott, spoke to Quentin. "These poor devils" — he pointed to the tired troops on the platform — "do you think they've come from Passchendaele?"

"Quite likely," murmured Quentin, "they look beaten to the wide."

"I don't know how they stick it. In a way, it's harder for them than it is for us. We know we're right, while they know they're being driven to commit mass murder."

"Nonsense!" exclaimed Quentin sharply.

"Well, aren't they?"

"You don't understand a soldier's psychology."

"I think I do. What is it, then?"

"It's quite simple. You believe it is your duty to defend your country. Therefore, you deliver your will and conscience into the hands of your superior officer, and you are willing to pay for your belief by giving up the dearest thing you possess: your life. *We* don't have to give up our lives."

"I should have said the dearest thing you could give up would be your sense of doing what you know is right. You haven't a right to give up that!"

"That," said Quentin grimly, "is why I am sitting here with you now. And let me tell you, Perrott, it hasn't brought me peace of mind."

Quentin's tragedy was that, in taking on a new set of loyalties, even if they seemed higher, he had had to discard other loyalties which had become a part of him. He could not forget that he had been a soldier. Every evening these honest Quakers prayed for strength to carry them through their ordeals, but Quentin had been through ordeals at the front more severe physically than the most brutal prison. "These chaps," thought Quentin, "don't understand us — that is," he corrected himself bitterly, "they don't understand soldiers." … And yet, in his heart, Quentin believed that the conchies were in the right.

One day in England Quentin had written to the adjutant of the battalion simply refusing to rejoin the army or to accept any form of alternative service, stating that he would rather be shot than do so, and leaving his name and address for the adjutant's "information and necessary action."

This letter had delivered him into the hands of a natural force, of whose existence decent men doing their duty at the front were not permitted to be aware. There was a code, a gentleman's understanding, concerning the ordinary affairs of war, but when a man simply refused to fight, there was nothing to do but deliver him to society's brutes and close your eyes while the brutes did the army's necessary dirty work. Quentin's descent into hell was in three stages. First he was given a military command which he refused to obey. He then automatically became a soldier who has refused duty and, as such, is subject to the penalties of the Army Act, liable to imprisonment if in England, liable to be shot if in France. He was taken before authorities who asked him whether he refused duty. He said he did. The authorities stared at him as at an obscene animal. "Afraid to go, eh?" — "No, sir!" — "Do you refuse duty even as a non-combatant?" — "I do, sir." — "God help you, you blackguard. A man like you — (authority spluttered). Do you wash?" He was paraded and stripped of his medal. Then he was sent with twelve others to France, where a soldier refusing an order could be shot.

In France, a systematic effort was made to break their spirits. "Men, you have come to the worst prison in France. We can break a man's heart here." They were put in cells made of corrugated iron, so cold that frost rimed the walls; when they sat down they got so cold and stiff that they could not get up without using their hands. They were fed on army biscuit and water, and sometimes they were ironed with their faces to the wall. They still refused duty. They were knocked about by soldiers wearing boxing gloves for two or three hours, revived with cold water and kicks, knocked about again. (The brutes who battered them had a dim idea that these men were stabbing the boys in the trenches in the back.) They refused duty. They were given shot drill to "limber them up." One of the absolutists who refused even to march was frogmarched out of his cell and laid on his back with cable wire around his chest and dragged up a footpath of battened planks. (The three men responsible for this "discipline" were counted out by their mates and threatened with hand grenades.) Finally, they were marched into a hollow square of soldiers, had a list of their "crimes" read aloud to them, and were sentenced to suffer death by being shot. But here humanity stepped in, at last. Questions had been asked in parliament, and in the end, their sentence was commuted to imprisonment in England. (Though a number of conscientious objectors died in prison as a result of ill-treatment, and though still others lost their reason, none were actually shot during the war.) They were on their way to England now....

Another train came into the station, and a swarm of soldiers descended and rushed for the coffee stall. These were men not long away from the battle; little signs revealed this in an instant to one who, like Quentin, had been a soldier. Looking at them, his heart sank. They were wearing Canadian divisional patches — but that was not the cause of his agitation. *He knew these men.* None of them had seen him yet, but a group of officers strolled along the platform, and one of them caught sight of him and stopped stock still, the colour drained from his face. For a moment the officer hesitated, then he came uncertainly toward Quentin.

"You, Thatcher? What are you doing here?"

The two men stared at each other in an electric silence in which it seemed to Quentin he had lost his sense of personality. His answer, uttered from a dry throat, sounded in his ears as if it came from a long distance.

"I am a conscientious objector, sir."

The officer looked at him with a kind of stupefied owlishness and opened his lips to speak twice before he could think what to say. Then he said, "Oh!" and walked away.

The troops fell in and stood easy beside the train. Then they spied the shackled prisoners sitting in the shadow. "Hi! That's Pill Thatcher! — It isn't! — It is.... Hi, Thatcher! What are you doing there? I thought you were a bloody officer. — What did they crime you for? I bet you committed a rape, Pill. — Shut up, leave the poor beggar alone!"

*Battalion! Fall in.... Battalion! ... Battalion! Shun!*

The wavering, murmuring line of men turned into a stone wall.

*About — turn.*

"Now, men, if I catch anyone talking to a bloody, yellow-bellied deserter, I'll crime him! *Stand at ease. Stand easy.*"

Quentin and his fellows waited on the station platform for a long time. A Red Cross train slid quietly through the station without stopping, streaking against death for the coast. "I wonder," thought Quentin miserably, "whether Dan is up there at this minute?"

# CHAPTER X

"Time to go, sir. Sir, time to go!"

"Eh? ... All right. Cigarette, Loversedge."

"Here, sir."

"Are the men ready? "

"At the cookhouse, sir."

Dan looked at Jobey whose beaked brown face and sharp eyes peered back at him under a shrapnel helmet and who was weighted down like Santa Claus with equipment and two sandbags. "And where do *you* think you're going, Jobey?"

"Up the line, sir, with you. *Kekkeno mush's poov*," Jobey winked. "My place ain't in the home. Look, sir, I scrounged some Mills bombs. You never know up in them shell holes. Mr. Ack Emma Thatcher is a deadshot with a Webley, but he can't throw as straight as you, sir!" Jobey gave another wink and a grin.

"You're a discerning devil, Jobey. Come on, then."

Jobey inspected his sandbags. One of them was slotted like a string of sausages. At the bottom was tea — a knot, then sugar — a knot, butter — a knot, then bread and jam and tinned stuff. The knots were solid. You didn't want the butter muckin' in with the tea and sugar.

Presently, they were on the Zonnebeke Road, the one road to the front, their faces turned toward the flares which rose and flowered over those in shell holes, regular as breathings. The men carried picks, shovels, and rifles. "I hope my gunners know how to use them." They ploughed stoically after the officer, not knowing where they were going: that was the officer's job. Responsibility closed round Dan and shut him off from them as completely as the darkness walled off that crowded road from the rest of humanity. There were few landmarks visible even in the daytime — farmhouses, paths, copses, and even crossroads so bravely marked in the ordnance maps simply did not exist any longer. Shading his flashlight, he took a last glance at the map, memorizing it. The thing to do was to find the right duckboard path fingering off from the road. A phosphorous shell exploded ahead of them and lit the rubbish of the battlefield: capsized wagons and limbers with mules and drivers buried in the wreckage. They went on, the beech planks squidging and tipping under foot. They marched with ears cocked for the swelling phut of that heaving drone which meant that a howitzer shell would pitch close to them with a final swoop and whinnying of splinters that would make them cringe inwardly.

Sergeant Watts, an old policeman with a grizzled head, walked beside Dan. The sergeant was struggling with an idea. What he didn't like about this bloody war was the obscene sense of humour displayed by blind steel. The way he put it was: "Them shells play tricks on you, sir. Like a cat with a mouse. You know that a shell could kill you with a stroke of the paw, like, if it wanted to. But that it won't do — not yet." He explained with melancholy moroseness that his teeth had been destroyed by shell fire three days ago during the show. "I put them down for a minute, sir, meaning to clean them, and when I got back they simply wasn't there. A pipsqueak did it, sir. Of course, I've indented for a new set, but what with the red tape — I can't chew hard tack on my gums and the bully beef gives me indigestion. Makes you feel melancholy-like all the time. It does seem hard, sir, when a man can't eat." It filled the sergeant with bitterness. He seemed to feel that there was something indecently sadistic about destroying a man's teeth; it mucked up a man digestion, and so, interfered with his settled and intimate habits of thought.

Sergeant Watts began to tell him about the mutiny at Étaples. He said it wasn't a real mutiny, not like with them Russians walking out of the trenches and shooting their officers. It was just that the old timers thought there was too much bloody slaughter at Ypres. And getting nowhere. Going in seven hundred, coming out one hundred, filling up with fresh drafts of recruits, going in again. "Don't seem no sense to it, sir. The men sometimes wonder at them as send us up the line know what it's all about, sir."

"That's your teeth talking, sergeant. Not you." And Watts grinned a trifle sheepishly.

The trouble was, Dan reflected, that except for a few zealots like Quentin, who were liable to be shot for their pains, no one felt responsible for the war. The men thought the officers knew the rights of the matter but wondered; the officers put the responsibility of Ypres on the generals and cursed; the generals, no doubt, blamed the politicians; and the politicians talked about a war to save civilization, tacitly putting the latter up to God in whose interests civilization was supposed to be preserved. One might almost say that this progressive moral incompetence was feudal. Charles said that they usually chucked out the top men after a war and Dan, thinking of his talk with Dolughoff, wondered for a moment whether God would survive the war. It looked as if the politicians might do for him.

Dan began to think it almost certain that he had overshot the line, and he had a prickling sensation in the groin where he most disliked the idea of being hit. The pillbox loomed up before them suddenly, and at the same time, a voice from a shell hole in a little mound called his name hoarsely. It was Alastair. A dirty stubble of beard disguised him, and his eyes were haggard with fatigue and yet burning with excitement.

"Where is Dolughoff?" Dan asked.

"That man is clean off his rocker. We had a bit of a stink, you know, trench mortars mostly, and Dolly wanted to climb up on the parapet and take off his clothes to show them how little he thought of them, I've never before seen him go into a tailspin with rage.... Usually when he gets mad, you know he is simply putting on an act."

"Is he tight?"

"I guess so.... I had to put him under open arrest."

"Where is he now?"

"Oh, he's all right again for the time being — quite rational. He's round somewhere.... Did you hear them strafing us? I bet you had a sticky time getting up here."

"It was all right," said Dan briefly. "Let's get on with it, Al."

"The OP is a crazy idea. The fellow that chose this place, for one, ought to be shot!"

"Where are the Germans?"

Alastair waved his hand. "Here and there, in camouflaged shell holes mostly, like us. They are 'in depth,' of course. They won't let you stand up to look round. Yesterday a man started back to battalion headquarters, and the first thing he knew, he was challenged by the Buffs. He'd been through the German lines without knowing it."

A knee-high ditch had been cut from the shell hole to the concrete pillbox. Stooping, they scuttled to the pillbox, from the far side of which stretched another makeshift trench, somewhat deeper. Here an infantry subaltern stood talking to Alastair's sergeant. When Dan and his brother appeared, Alastair's men shouldered their picks and shovels with alacrity and looked meaningfully toward "home," which twelve hours had made desirable.

Dolughoff appeared from the pillbox, carrying the OP logbook. "Here's the book, Thatcher. Then aren't any distinguishing marks in the terrain, if you can call this damned rhinoceros wallow a terrain. Over there's the famous ridge. There's the promised land, eight degrees to the right of that bitched grove of trees.

That's Passchendaele village. And that's about all there is to see. Just mud and filthy skyline. Come on Ack Emma Thatcher, let's go."

"Eyes front!" exclaimed the infantry officer suddenly, and added in a resigned tone: "Now we won't go home until morning! ... Spread your men out, Thatcher, will you?"

A spray of multi-coloured lights had soared from the section of shell holes and pillboxes marked red in the trench maps, bursting into a shivering cluster. This beautiful firework, worthy of its task, had slipped the leash from a straining pack of upthrust, sleek steel muzzles and the barrage charged down upon them. It swooped down the air on steel wings. It gored the earth with self-destroying roars, blasting it and tossing it upward in great fistfuls.... Dan looked behind him: spouts of smoke and mud were dancing a hornpipe there, too, and to their flanks, and in front of them.... It was what gunners called a box barrage; its purpose was to isolate them within walls of steel and sound. You had the illusion that the earth was slipping about you, and it was no mere illusion. Beside Dan, a boy threw himself flat, then jumped up — to go where? A gout of wet mud plastered him across the shoulders and sent him squattering into the unsumped scum at the bottom of the enlarged shell hole. Officers and men had tensed themselves instantly, adopting to their sudden need their several tried soul-attitudes with the speed of habit, as one braces oneself to physical pain after a short surcease. One felt like a cork in a hurricane. What terrified was the rhythm of the sound to which one's nerves danced a jangled accompaniment. Each shell swinged the distant air, increased to a full-throated roar that promised completion this time, and burst its sides in triumphant self-immolation.... Time ceased to have meaning.... A long time. A long time. A long time.

Dan's mind was working queerly — shakily; it was abnormally lucid, but alarmingly separated from his body; it had suddenly become an instrument you were not quite sure of. He attempted to put it in its place by mocking it with a phrase of pedantic precision. "This," he informed himself, "is a barrage of no ordinary magnitude. (The infantry officer would not have agreed.) This is a — an experience!" It was an experience. One learnt things. *This is to be hunted.* He restrained an absurd impulse to shout, "Hi! Stop a minute. Wait till I get my breath."

He was astonished to find that two of his men had quietly crumpled up at his feet — when had they been hit? — and a portion of the abbreviated trench had lost its contour like a cake that someone had stepped on. Stooped figures scurried by and someone was yelling — you could hear a human voice, then — someone was yelling: "Give me that bloody, muckin' field dressing, quick! … Dusty, you're done for! They've got you…. Stretcher here…. Where did it hit you, chum?"

He realized that the infantry officer was watching him with a kind of secret malice. His look said: "How do you like it, you bleeding gunner? See what it's like when the artillery make war by pounding each other's infantry line!" He said in Dan's ear: "Pretty gusty, this is. I shouldn't wonder if they really came over this time."

Well, if they did, it would be a relief.

The thing to do was to unite oneself to Mother Earth with a clinging fondness till there wasn't room for a matchstick between one's belly and the mud — and wait. *Ashes to ashes — dust to dust, if the worms don't get you, the devil must.* Though, to be accurate, one ought to say mud, not dust…. Mud, mud, and a damned big thud, thur-ud, thur-ud, thurud-dud-dud. Rhythm…. A man maun dree his weird. Who used to say that? Mother. No wound in the groin, anyhow, if you lie on your belly. A yellow ticket that said, "gunshot wound in the groin." Umpteen units of anti-tetanus and a shot of morphine and you pass out and find yourself in the casualty clearing station.

Dan did the only thing a man could do when natural phenomena were asserting themselves — lit a cigarette, and waited. It surprised him to find that his hand was steady. He felt better. Anyhow, it couldn't go on forever. Either — or —

He was astonished to find that he was actually becoming adjusted to a world of noise and violence. For instance, he felt sure that he could manage himself. And he became aware of the other human beings beside him and round him — an immense comfort. Two infantry privates were carrying on a cozy chat by shouting at the tops of their voices. "What did you enlist for, chum?" — "Well, there was a poster of a girl. Very good looking, see? And she was saying: 'I wish I was a man; I'd join the infantry.' I wish she'd got her wish!"

He could distinguish the different noises. High explosive — a jealous roar; shrapnel bursting with a staccato *ping! let me in too!* Minnies, making a kind of satisfied crunching noise. To be familiar with the intimate hunting habits of the powers that destroyed, bred almost a contempt for their efficiency.... At any rate, so far none of them had considered him worth obliterating.

"Where's this Passiondale I've heard so much about, sir?"

"Up ahead. Mind you don't stand up."

"Doesn't seem much of a place to sweat your guts out for, sir."

"What were you, Timmis?"

"Bank clerk, sir."

"Going back to the bank, afterwards?"

"Lock myself into the teller's cage, sir, and never come out for anyone!"

Alastair's voice: "Well, Granny, you old philosopher, what are you thinking of?"

The question surprised Dan. It hadn't occurred to him that Alastair might have an affection for him. It struck him that Alastair was really hard to know because he had the Burnet trait of play-acting to people. Always the *beau geste* with Alastair.

Dan decided to make the rounds.... It was disquieting, on getting up and looking back over your shoulder, to find that the spot where you had been lying was turning over like a wave.... The shell holes about the pillbox had been enlarged and connected with shallow ditches to make a strong point. In one of the ditches next to Dan's shell hole, Sergeant Watts lay with his rifle pointing over what should have been the parapet. Dan crawled up to him. "See anything?" — "Not yet, sir." The sergeant gave him a mournful smile. "If only I had my teeth, sir, I wouldn't care." ... In the next shell hole the men were playing Kitty Nap with greasy franc notes. No. 00459, Gunner Loversedge put out his hand and gathered in a pile of notes. "You're unco lucky wi' the carrds, Jobey," said a gunner. "Dootless ye'll have your lights put out the day...." A man with a wound stripe on his sleeve was sitting with his head in his hands, moaning. "No, he ain't hurt, sir," explained the sentry apologetically, "he's always like that when the crumps come to set a while. Ever since he copped one. He'll be all right when they come over.... Will they come, sir?"

"Seems likely.... Keep your rifles out of the mud, men." Most of them were gunners to whom such precautions were not second nature. They grinned. The sentry actually winked. The strafe drew them together on a human plane, so that for the moment they forgot class consciousness.

He went back to his own shell hole.

The infantry officer had come back and was bending over a sprawling figure: "Conked, by God! And look, the wound's no bigger than a pinprick." A thin needle of steel through the heart.

"Where are you from?" the infantry officer was saying to Dan. "Oh, Wellington.... Me? I'm from Wiarton. Do you know the Bruce Peninsula? It's a sweet country. You can't make much of a living farming there, but it's a good land to remember. Lots of wild woods there, and fishing.... If they come before dark, we'll get them from the blockhouse. Unless they get in on the flank. Wish we had more bombs."

"I've got some," said Dan.

"Up the Royal Eight-Inch Rifle Brigade! We'll make pukka infantry out of you yet.... What I like to do is start out before dawn with a rod and haversack and try a stream at random. You don't have to buy the right to fish there at five dollars a dozen fish. By God, in Canada there's room to stretch your arms and breathe!"

One of his own men was saying something and pointing. The OP they had sweated blood over had been knocked into a memory. The gunner was angry; he said something about "bloody sods ... work all night ... bleeding waste." What got under the men's skins wasn't so much the straightforward destruction, it was the practical jokes played by mindless forces, destroying one's teeth and blotting out a night's work with a single metal bellow of laughter.

Dan was talking to Alastair when, suddenly, he was surprised to notice that they were shouting to each other. The barrage had stumbled down into silence, and its cessation called for a new adjustment of the nerves.

"Are they coming over?"

The infantry subaltern pointed in front of them. "See the control lights? They're redirecting their artillery. I'd like to know what in blazes has happened to our own guns."

"That's so like the infantry!" said Alastair. "As soon as there's the slightest bit of a stink, they howl for artillery support like a spanked child for its mother."

At this moment a strange figure, covered with mud, crawled over the broken rim of the trench, slumped head first into the muddy water at the bottom and sat up, wiping the muck from its eyes and cursing in a steady monotone. This figure was Dolughoff, and his eyes stared at them with insane excitement.

"And where in the name of old Satan have *you* been?" enquired Alastair levelly.

The Russian raised his finger impressively and pointed toward no man's land. "Out there. And there is one — person who will never, never trouble me again."

"Well," said Alastair, "as long as you don't want to take off your clothes again — God, man, but you must have been tight!"

Anger flashed in Dolughoff's eyes — for a moment he looked really dangerous. "Tight! I tell you there is no soberer, saner man in the salient than me.... I tell you I had had enough! They can't do that to *me* with impunity."

"Do what, Dolly?"

"Just before the first strafe started, I was doing a rear in a shell hole — if you laugh, Thatcher, I'll — I'll kill you! *He* must have seen me, for he let fly at me with his machine gun and I had to run for dear life — with my pants down. Every time I tripped and fell *he* would let me get up, then he would fire just behind me or just in front of me as I ran. Chased me round, do you see? Then, finally, let me go. Deliberately."

Alastair was laughing. "I'm sorry, Dolly. But I wish I had seen it!"

"Shut up!" said the Russian furiously. "You don't understand. Do you know who was shooting at me? It was the devil — Satan himself. He wanted to kill my dignity ... break my spirit. It's easy to kill a man's body, but he was after my soul, I tell you! *I* know.... Then, when he let me go — that was too much. I wouldn't have minded if he had killed me outright."

"I bet you wouldn't," agreed Alastair.

A cunning look came into Dolughoff's eyes. "But I fooled him. I showed him I could take off *all* my clothes and still be dignified.... And what is more, every time the devil pops off at me, I'll crawl into no man's land and cut his heart out. Look!"

Dolughoff opened his haversack, which was soaked with blood, and took out an object.... The three subalterns had been roaring with laughter at the thought of Dolughoff chased in circles with his breeches down, they could not help themselves (and besides, after the bombardment, anything that relieved their nervous tension was a godsend). But at the sight of the Russian holding that bloodstained object, their laughter ceased abruptly.

"My God!" breathed the infantry subaltern, his face colourless. "He's off his chump."

"Damn you!" screamed Dolughoff, in sudden fury. "You philistines with your nice, well-tubbed, little Anglo-Saxon souls understand nothing! But I've got a life inside me you know nothing about. You can't touch me. I'm above all of you, and you don't know what I think of you. I always do exactly what I want to, that's why I'm a great man. People don't want me. Well, let them go! What do I care? They are sticks and stones to me. There is nobody but me. Do you see? That is why nobody — *nobody* can touch me."

"And what about your message, Dolly? All that about the brotherhood of man and so on."

Dan nudged his brother and whispered: "Hold your tongue, Alastair, for God's sake!"

Dolughoff spat words at them. "It is the devil who keeps me from speaking. First it was the politicians and generals, and now it's the devil.... But I cut his heart out."

The infantry subaltern looked at Dolughoff with disgust. The fellow didn't belong to his unit, thank God! Some sort of a mongrel foreigner. And before the men. People that talked about their souls! When everyone knew we were like blasted ants scurrying about on a bit of mud. Why pretend that we were so damned important, then? But after all, the poor devil was obviously off his chump.

Dolughoff went on talking, talking, talking. They could see his mouth opening and closing.... But they could no longer hear him, for the barrage had once more dropped on them. It thundered down upon them, and to brace themselves all over again, after the interval of quiet, was to endure a subtle addition to their suffering.... Dolughoff crept out into no man's land with an unsheathed bayonet between his teeth, but only Alastair saw him go.... Alastair hesitated a moment, then crawled after him.

Dan braced his feet against the sides of the trench and, lying back, lit another cigarette ... and waited. Each explosion drew the nerves together into a cringing knot, and before that second passed in which you had begun to relax, the next monster charged in like an apocalyptic doom. The sheer din, coming after

the surcease of sound, was flattening; it hammered and disintegrated the personality into crazy fragments of thoughts, desires....

Someone was yelling into Dan's ears: the infantry subaltern.

Dan said: "What?" gathering himself together.

The infantry officer pointed.

The barrage had lifted and dropped behind them. The subaltern straightened himself as well as he could without showing
all of his head above the shell crater and threw away his cigarette.
"Well, lads, here they come!"

They came in little, uneven knots of men, lightly weighted
with equipment, but nonetheless stumbling and sliding down
into scummy shell holes, struggling through the mud that sucked
at the legs like glue. In driblets they came, but there were a lot of
them.... They withered to the chatter of rifles and Lewis guns
like a house of cards when you flip your finger. Their own barrage came down like a breaking comber and simply blotted them
from sight in smoke.

The infantry officer scurried past him, not bothering to
stoop any longer, and shouted over his shoulder. "They're in on
the left. Bring your bombs, gunner. Now's your chance!" Dan
got Loversedge and they scuttled down the shallow ditches that
were ditches no longer but a tossed up runnel of stinking mud
vaguely conforming to the trench line: as if a shaking finger had
been run through a bowl of porridge. Action lifted his spirit and
cleared his mind of the poisoning thoughts that formed like a
cesspool while you were waiting to be blown to fragments. As
he ran, he marvelled that anyone could have stayed alive in these
crazy ditches while the earth round about and beneath was being
pummelled into new shapes. The answer was that not many had;
all that remained of most of the defenders lay beneath him and
before him and had to be tripped over and trodden under as he
ran. But those few, those devoted few who were left alive, were
firing, cursing, or singing, or simply firing as coolly as if they
were at the butts.

A black object on a short stick came hurtling toward them end over end. It was not well aimed and exploded short. Coal-scuttle helmets were visible bobbing and weaving to the left. "While my bombs last," Dan thought. He threw at the helmets. Arms splayed out centrifugally above the rim of a shell crater. He heard groans. He felt neither fear, nor rage, nor pity, only the release of power.

A few minutes later, those of them who were still alive had crawled into the pillbox. They were a mere handful of gunners and infantry, including Dan and Loversedge, and Alastair and Dolughoff (both wounded). The pillbox reeked with the fumes of explosion, and the living shared it with the dead. A shell of large calibre had struck the entrance which faced the German lines, and the lintel had sagged drunkenly, partly blocking the opening. Under this girder, a broken Lewis gun projected, its muzzle drooping toward the ground like a dejected dog's tail.

"Where are you hit, Alastair?"

"Arm. It would be a good blighty if — not that I'll ever get there from here."

"Did you bring Dolly in?"

"Dragged him in from no man's land."

"Why? It was a hundred to one you'd both be killed."

"He was mad … and I mocked him," said Alastair soberly. "Keep a look out, Dan, and I'll see about Dolly."

Friend Jerry was coming on again, not looking as if he liked it much. Knots of plodding pilgrims, muddy, stooping, methodically ploughing knee deep in the muck, came on. They saw the crumped entrance to the pillbox, drew their conclusions, and passed by. That outraged Dan's professional instincts — they ought to have chucked in a bomb to make sure. Apparently, then, there were amateur soldiers among the Jerries, too: in it just for love, without any professional background.

Loversedge was beside him, smoking. His swarthy skin was covered with sweat, his face was filthy, and he lay with his hands behind his neck. He looked as if he were enjoying it — in a way. "Remember when we sat talking and drinking in the boat shacks in Wellington, Jobey?" — "I remember you farther back than that, sir." — "We talked a lot of rot about 'freedom,' I remember. Well, we got caught in something bigger than us, Jobey." — "No, sir. I'm still a free man. It's inside you, freedom is. Hard to find, easy to lose track of again."

Beside Dan and Loversedge sat an infantryman, unconcernedly oiling his rifle. Here today, gone tomorrow — well, maybe. But what he bloody well wished was that he bloody well hadn't ditched his fags by mistake when they were in the haversack with the army forms he was bloody well humping up to company headquarters two days ago. (Weighed down in the muck with cartridge pouches, water bottle, gas mask, entrenching tool and handle, bayonet in scabbard, rifle, overcoat and groundsheet, he had sensibly, and of course ethically, dumped the stationery into a shell hole and reported it destroyed by shell fire). How could he have forgot them blasted cigarettes in the bag? He didn't so much mind drinking tea drummed up from a tommy cooker, brewed with water from shell holes full of urine, like as not. As long as he had a fag…. Maybe if he asked the officer — He asked for and got a handful.

"Loversedge," said Dan, "keep a lookout. I want to see Mr. Dolughoff." He went over to where Alastair was kneeling beside Dolughoff.

"Slip me your flashlight, Granny," said Alastair. "Mine's napoo."

Dolughoff, who was in pain, wished to be let alone and said so; he added, gasping: "I have things to think about."

"You'll be all right. We'll get you back, presently."

The Russian was visibly trying to collect his energy. Presently, he whispered: "You think I'm done for, don't you?"

"You'll be all right," repeated Alastair.

"You tell me, Daniel Thatcher. Do *you* think I'm done for?"

After a moment's hesitation, Dan said: "You've got a bad one, old man, but —"

"Well, you're both mistaken," interrupted the Russian, painfully rising on his elbow. "I've a job to do. I shan't be killed until it's done.... I'll be back. You'll see."

Alastair could not resist murmuring: "Still thinking of the message, Dolly?"

But Dolughoff stared beyond him.

Loversedge was cutting off chunks of bully beef; the infantry private had his mouth full. "How about some food, sir? We have bully beef, bread, margarine, and jam with shell hole tea." They ate like starved men. To eat reassured one about the normalcy of the body.

Dan whispered to his brother: "Are you going to report his conduct?"

Alastair shook his head. "He's done for, Granny."

"You shouldn't have asked him that question, old man."

"About his blasted 'message'? I know. Caddish of me, under the circumstances. I shouldn't have mocked him either. It just popped into my head — the irony of it, you know." Alastair looked at Dan queerly. "You see, I was with him when he got the packet of steel.... Something fishy about it, Dan."

"What do you mean?"

But Alastair would not explain. "Let it go, Dan. He's done for. He was sort of a mixed-up blighter, wasn't he?"

The acrid fumes had cleared away a little. Now British guns were playing about the pillbox.

"Let's lie down and talk quietly, Al.... What are the chances?"

"Slim, I suppose. Still, if they got chased back quickly. Are we friends, Dan?"

"I hope so, old man."

"I played you a dirty trick, Dan."

"That's all done with.... I was always jealous of you, Al."

"I didn't know you were. I've always been jealous of you. You've got character. I'm like Uncle Charles's personality to burn, but everything by fits and starts."

"It was damn silly of us to be like that."

"Dan, you don't mind now about Cynthia?"

"Cynthia? Give her my love, old man. And do let bygones be bygones like a good fellow."

The infantry private said in a matter-of-fact tone: "Them Jerries are coming back, sir. Shall I draw bead on them?"

The subalterns looked through the firing slit. The coal-scuttle helmets were coming back in a hurry. They had not reached the second line and had gone to earth in shell holes. Now they were being cleaned out at bayonet point. They came back at the double, in a panic, like a flock of squattering chickens. They bobbled past the pillbox. Alastair exclaimed:

"We'll get out of here at the double!"

He poked his head and shoulders underneath the tilted girder and yelled to a Canadian subaltern who had his arm drawn back to throw a bomb. "Kamerad, brother! Just throw that damn thing in the other direction, will you?"

The subaltern arrested the sweep of his arm, and stood frozen with the Mills bomb, pin drawn, in his hand. Then he threw it away from him like a hot potato. It burst in the air. The officer cursed.

They started back to the battery. "Now, old man," said Dan, "off you go to the field dressing station to get your wound dressed. See you later. I'll go down to the casualty clearing station, if I can get off." They shook hands.

But on the way back, Alastair was hit again and severely wounded. When Dan arrived at the CCS, he found his brother unconscious.

# CHAPTER XI

i

Dan sat in the bottom of a muddy sap using his shrapnel helmet as a seat. Behind him, a signboard said: "Abandoned German mine. Careful." How exactly were you supposed to be careful of an abandoned German mine? Presumably, by keeping your mental balance continually poised for a swift ascent into the air. He thought of home.... Englishmen have a small country that is like a garden. Canadians can't say as Shakespeare did, *This other Eden, demi-paradise.... This precious stone set in the silver tea* — that sort of thing. Canada is like a great, sprawling, awkward lad who hasn't yet come into his strength. Sensitive of other people's opinion, looking up to his parents, and yet rebellious, too. (We don't like being called "colonials" in the tone of voice the English use.) No telling what we'll make of our manhood when we come into it. We are pioneers still, really, and that means materialists. But we won't always be. We ought to dream dreams. Maybe someday we, too, shall give the world something lasting just as the Greeks and the Jews, yes and the English, did.

But when you think of your country, you always have at the back of your mind your family and your friends who make it "yours." Your family is your other self waiting for you after the war; it doesn't change. Dan thought of the family sitting at this moment before the fire at Ardentinny, reading and talking just as they had always done in the evening.

But returning to the battery from that tour of duty at the OP, Dan found waiting for him a cable from Wellington. The curt message told him that his father, true to his principles, had faced a mob bent on mischief and that the shock of that experience had caused his death.

## ii

Letter from Beatrice Elton to Dan:

> Dear Dan,
> Though I know you won't want to talk about it, I must write you about your father. I have thought often and often of what a *mean, selfish, blind, little beast* I was to you before you went overseas. I realize now that the war has wounded you as badly as it has wounded me. I was really half crazy at the time, and I just wanted to hurt somebody. I'm a selfish person, Dan, and to me, I'm afraid the war just meant my fiancé at the front. I never could take a larger view of the war and I don't suppose I ever shall. I think most women are like me, deep down — we don't see beyond our own kith and kin. Anyway, you'll forgive me for what I said in those days, won't you? Probably, you've forgotten all about it.
> I will say this, Dan, though it will be cold comfort to you. I think your father was *right*. And remembering him as I do, his sense of duty and his honesty, I think he would be glad of what he did; that is, if there is any other life from

which you can look back on this life. He had
his loyalty, Dan, and he gave his life for it just as
truly as Matthew did for his.

I go about like a lame duck, not really car-
ing about anything, working as hard as I can to
keep from brooding (I'm what they call a VAD
here). If you come to London on leave, do look
me up for old time's sake.

Your sincere friend,

Beatrice Elton

P.S. They have insisted on sending Alastair
to Canada to convalesce, and they won't let
Cynthia go with him. Isn't that just like the war!

To this letter Dan replied:

Dear Beatrice,

Thanks for your decent letter. I suppose you
mean the white feather? Good Lord, I never
blamed you for that; I understood well enough
how you felt — and feel. Anyway, everyone is in
the same boat, and in some way or another, the
war is bound to get us all in the end.

I'd like you to know exactly what happened. Father died of heart failure; the crowd
of God-forgotten drunken fools who did for
him hadn't the least idea of what they were
about, they were simply irresponsible sheep
like nine-tenths of the human race. These men
were soldiers from up-country on their way to
Valcartier; none of them came from Wellington,
thank God! The only thing they knew about
my father was that he had refused to pay his
taxes to support the war (they had got hold of

that fact from some yellow gutter-sheet which had printed a wild attack on Father). When they came up against a man who had a sense of responsibility and a soul of his own, they didn't understand him (people never do!); I suppose it just made them angry to find someone who wouldn't go with the crowd. Of course, nobody in Wellington had a hand in it, and they are all sympathetic as hell — for what *sympathy* is worth.

Well, these men drank too much, got hold of that dirty rag, read it, and started out for Ardentinny. The family were asleep; they were wakened by a stone thrown through a bedroom window. Mother and Aunt Fanny tried to get Father to hide in the cellar because of his bad heart, but this he simply refused to do. He insisted that the door should be opened and that these men should be allowed to come in. His exact words were, "I will talk to them, Maud. Let's have dignity."

So Graham (he's the butler) let them in and they came scrambling up the stairs. I believe — I'd like to think — that some of the soberest among them were already a little ashamed of themselves. Fanny stood at the top of the stairs, and told them they ought to be! They said that they were not going to harm any woman, but that they had come to put something right. "We know who we want, isn't that right, boys? And we're not going to *hurt* anybody. We're just going to show a certain party there's a war on, see?" I don't think they had the least notion of what they intended to do. They pushed past

Fanny and started to kick at Joanna's door. Then
Father came out of his room and spoke to them
quietly, told them they were frightening women
and acting in a pretty cowardly way that dis-
graced their uniform. Somebody asked Father
who he thought he was to criticize soldiers.
Then he told them he had two sons in the army
and about Alastair being wounded. That made
some of them still more ashamed, but there were
one or two ugly, drunken louts there who did
not care what they did. One of these men staggered up to Pen and shouted: "Here's the man
who stabs the soldiers in the back," with a lot
of foul language. Then he drew his fist back and
knocked Father down.

At any rate, it's a consolation to think that
nearly all these men, though they were drunken,
irresponsible fools, were not *brutes*. They turned
on the coward who knocked Father down and
fairly threw him down the stairs.

Then the most amazing thing happened.
The parrot who hasn't spoken for years suddenly
screamed: "Down on your knees sinners!" All
the men began to laugh, and the whole atmosphere changed. After that somebody started to
apologize sheepishly to Mother, and presently,
they went away.

But Father never regained consciousness.
He wasn't strong, and I suppose, his heart gave
out. I like to remember that not for an instant
did he lose his courage. I suppose, really, that
is why I wanted to tell you exactly what happened. I think I have a right to be proud of him,
whatever people may say.

I am due for a leave soon, though I can't say
I care a great deal. Still, I shall take it, of course.
I shall certainly look you up.
>   Sincerely yours,
>   Daniel Thatcher

### iii

A long way from the war, across an ocean, Alastair Thatcher, wearing a blue wound brassard, was saying to Tessa Thatcher in a strained voice:

"It's ironical when you think of it, my being sent home to convalesce, away from Cynthia. It's so confoundedly typical of the war, that. Isn't it? ... I shouldn't be talking to you like this. It isn't the right thing. Decent reserve and all that sort of thing. But good Lord! Once in a while you have to boil over to someone.... You know it's hell being away from Cynthia. You see, we really love each other, and I need her. You've had experience of life, Tessa; you're not a child. You know what I mean.

"I'm a bit morbid, I expect. I never used to bother about things. There's no getting round it, *this* — (he shook his crutch) — has shaken me up a lot. I don't seem to know myself at all these days. Want to do the craziest things sometimes.... I'll wager you wouldn't have guessed from the calm way we've talked together before today that my nerves are shot to bits. Pitcher went down to the well once too often, you know. Maybe you have guessed, though. Women tumble to what's going on underneath the surface of a person's thoughts. Intuition, I suppose. You're old enough to know what people are like: yet it's odd, I never think of you as older than I...."

Alastair's voice, not his words, echoed in Tessa's nerves. *It is folly for us to talk in this way....* She looked at him. Thin, pinched, his eyes restless. "This is what it has done to Alastair, to him of all people.... Why shouldn't I mother him a little? Take Cynthia's place a little till she can come home? Why not? Why shouldn't I? ... What am I getting from life? It's all so barren and futile...."

But she knew she ought not to. With another sort of young man, yes, but not with Alastair.... Alastair was right. She had had experience of life, she was not a child, she understood what he meant.

# CHAPTER XII

i

At Folkestone Dan cabled to Joanna: *On leave for ten days.* Joanna and his mother had a right to their ten days' leave, too. He meant to enjoy his leave intensely.

But he soon found that even in London you could not get away from the war. He stayed at the Strand Palace Hotel, which was a rendezvous for Canadians on leave. He played billiards, went to the British Museum and Westminster Abbey (both sandbagged), played squash, went to revues (plays weren't fluffy enough), and even went to a ball given by a peeress, who was kind to "homeless colonials," where the maidens he danced with had subtly the air of performing a war job. Everywhere you went, you met the British Army on leave, and you could not forget that you were only here on sufferance, "out on rest," and that the very steward who served you a martini every night before dinner was probably wondering idly when you would go back to France and be seen no more.

One day he met Flint whom he had not seen since St. Horatius days. Flint's RFC cap was cocked at a jaunty angle, and the rather solemn lad Dan remembered had become a debonair youth with a roving eye for "little bits of fluff."

They had a drink. "Been out?" asked Dan.

Flint flicked his cigarette casually. "For two weeks. Copped one in the leg over Lens. An archie, you know. I'm going out again in a couple of days."

"Anyway, you lucky devil, you fly over. You don't have to take the leave train."

Flint shrugged. "I wish to hell I'd spent my last leave in the country."

"Why?"

"Oh, I don't know. London throws you off your stride, don't you think?"

"Well, it is different."

"It lets you down. Softens you. Just when I'd got my thyroid, or whatever it is, working at top speed."

"Still the objective man of science, Flint?"

"Goddamn it, let's have another drink.... We'll drink this to good straight shooting to kill, Dan. No bungling — either side."

They drank to no bungling.

Dan could not get into human relations with civilians; they seemed to him like puppets worked by strings that were pulled from the nineteenth century; they were walking in their sleep and they still talked as if the war were the First Crusade. After a stiff bombardment, you had a feeling of nervous relief, but that was physical. He wanted something more. What? Well, a moral holiday from himself; to be irresponsible for a short while. Charles said you could sometimes escape from yourself into what he called the *largior aether* — whatever that was. For Charles, it meant poetry. "The trouble with me is I can't get out of myself easily. Flint was right. I ought to have chucked people and gone out on the moors somewhere."

But he knew that his real enemy was time. He had four more days in England, and after that, a fifty percent chance of coming through the war if 1918 was anything like 1917. "Even in the artillery, I've had eleven close shaves, not counting that time up the line on the salient when, by any logical reckoning, I shouldn't have come through at all."

That day he met Quentin Thatcher by Nelson's Column in Trafalgar Square. A satirical voice behind him said: "Looking at Lord Nelson, I see. Do you know what one of Nelson's tars said when he saw that column? He said, 'Why, they have mastheaded the admiral!'"

They shook hands. Dan said: "I'm glad to see you. What are you doing in the king's uniform, old man? I thought —"

"On my way to France. So am I glad to see you; a damn sight more than you would ever realize." His eyes took hold of Dan's with that remembered look of challenging affection. "Would you have gone back without looking me up?"

"Probably.... I've been ashamed of that letter I wrote you from Canada. I was a silly young jingo full of bust and devil at the time. Sorry I let you down, Quentin. I wasn't such a hell of a good friend."

"No, you weren't. Who in blazes were you to refuse your friendship to me because of my opinions? Never mind that, though, I'm glad to see you."

"Nice of you," muttered Dan, irritated.... He thought that Quentin was bound to speak of his father — people always did — and he decided to forestall him. "You heard about Father?"

"Yes. Do you want to talk of it?"

"No!"

"Then I won't. Except to say that it was stupidly unnecessary. People don't think above their emotions. *I* don't."

"Is that why you are going back to France, Quentin?"

"Yes, partly. I can't really explain. I found I couldn't nourish an intellectual loyalty in an emotional vacuum — if that means anything to you. That will do for a reason as well as another.... I found I depended more upon people than I thought."

"You've done the right thing, Quentin."

Quentin jabbed with his swagger stick at one of the lions at the base of the column and his lips curled bitterly. "I did the wrong thing. Couldn't help it, though.... Too much for me," he muttered, "I couldn't stick being told I was a blasted hero sacrificing myself for the poor dumb driven sheep in France.... Yes, I guess that was it."

"The other day," said Dan, "they were changing guard at the palace. The king came out onto a balcony and you could feel everybody's backbone stiffening. It took me out of myself for a moment. That's in us; you couldn't escape from it even if you wanted to."

"Come on, Dan, let's walk.... I'll tell you the difference between you and me. You've never accepted death; in the war, for instance. I have. I joined up not expecting to come back. It's as if I'd died already — gone through the pangs of it. The consequence is your whole mind is spent on proving to yourself you're not afraid of it. You're like an ascetic always driving yourself to danger to prove your contempt of death. I've proved mine."

Dan did not like this; it was not the way he saw himself. "Rot. If I were that kind of a hellion I'd apply or transfer to the infantry or the air force, but the fact is I don't want to; I want to last out the war. Of course, I'm not a coward, either, and if I were in the infantry, I suppose I should stick it through as well as most. I think the best men, those naturally brave like you, went into the infantry. I'm just an average chap."

"You're always getting physical and moral courage mixed up."

"Well, I have physical courage, Quentin; I mean I'm brave enough when I get a military order to obey, or when I know a thing's a duty. But I think only the best chaps are brave on their own initiative; I mean, going out of their way to do brave things beyond the line of duty. Unless they've got to convince themselves that they're not afraid. I know a gunner subaltern who got shell-shocked, and instead of getting a cushy job at home, he applied for transfer to the light trench mortars — suicide club, you know."

"Well, when your nerves begin to go *phut*, don't you do that, Dan?" He added thoughtfully, "I never seem to understand other people's problems and they never understand mine.... There's only one thing I want desperately."

"What's that, old man?"

"Peace of mind. A mind that's not divided.... I shan't get it now."

They walked in silence.

## ii

"It's donkey's years," Dan reflected, "since I've talked to a decent girl of my own sort."

He grinned at himself derisively, and then he thought of Beatrice. She had asked him to look her up in London. Well, why not?

He had her address and telephone number: somewhere near Russell Square. He put two pennies into the telephone and thus bought and paid for fate. Presently, her voice came to him clear and fresh — just as he remembered it. Good to hear a friendly girl's voice.

"Dan? I'm so glad you called me. Of course I'd like to see you. Come here at three. I'll be off duty then. We'll go places and see things. How much longer have you?"

"Two days after today."

"Look here, I'll try to wangle a holiday and we'll play together. Shall we?"

"I should say so!" exclaimed Dan enthusiastically.

He went to the Russell Square address and was shown into the reception room; he wondered what she would be like. He remembered her as a lithe, dark-haired girl whose expression held you aloof with a sort of mocking affection.

While he was trying to recapture his image of her, she took him by surprise, standing in the doorway smiling at him.... The same, and yet different, though perhaps the change was in his own way of looking at her. She was not fluffily dressed. He saw at once that that would not have suited her best. She had the kind of personality that made you realize instantly that she was an individual as well as a woman. She was wearing a tailor-made suit which made sex less a matter of costume and more of personality. It was in her eyes looking at him and in her smile, which was frankly welcoming. She was feminine, all right.

Under his admiration, she blushed faintly but without the least awkwardness. One could not imagine her ungraceful.

"We've both changed since last we met, Dan. But let's pretend we have not changed a bit."

They ordered tea in a dim place with divans. She took off a glove and patted her hair, then she bent over the rite of tea. She saw that he was confused with pleasure and became instantly very self-possessed and sisterly.

She passed him a cup of tea; clever, small hands she had. It was delightful to watch her smiling calmly over the rim of a tea-cup, coolly mistress of herself. It was enough simply to listen to her clear voice. Nice to hear a girl's voice that sounded well-bred and young....

Beatrice put down her teacup and, opening her purse, took out a bright new penny. This she presented to Dan and smiled at him teasingly. "I've asked you a question twice, sir! And you simply sit looking at me like a cat before a jar of cream.... Now I've paid for your thoughts."

He pulled himself together. "I was thinking that one ought not to see too much beauty all at once after fasting. It goes to one's head."

Beatrice blushed. "You know, Dan, you aren't as easy to manage as you used to be. You take the bit in your teeth."

"First I'm a cat and now I'm a horse. I'm not as easy to manage because now I know what direction I want to go in."

They laughed.

"Seriously, though, Beatrice —"

"No, let's not be serious. We've got two days together, if you like —"

"If I like!"

"And for two days let's not be serious once. You can flirt a little, though, if you want to. What would you do if you had ten thousand pounds and the power of Harun al-Rashid to go anywhere in London and do anything you wanted?"

"Advertise in the agony column for Scheherazade, first of all. No, I wouldn't. You'd do. You be Scheherazade and tell me a story, and mind you amuse me or you'll lose your head…. Maybe I'll lose mine if you do."

"If I lose my head?"

"No, if you amuse me."

"You flirt nicely, I think. You know the rules."

"What are the rules?"

"To show that you know you are talking to a person who might be dangerous to you. To pretend you're risking that danger — but not really to risk it."

"Well, I am in great danger, and I'm trying to lead you into it."

They chattered nonsense and their spirits rose. It was fun discovering under the trite phrases of conversation what Beatrice was really like, and it was fun hinting what you were really like yourself without revealing too much too quickly.

"Now then, Beatrice, what shall we do?"

She stood up lithely and her eyes sparkled. "Let's just sally forth. We're sure to have an adventure."

They went for a ride on top of a bus; then walked aimlessly from Marble Arch to Regent Street, the Haymarket and Trafalgar Square. In front of the National Gallery, they stopped to look at some chalk drawing on the pavement over which knelt the artist, a shabby old man with a whimsical eye. He stood up and pointed to a highly coloured picture of a sailor on a battleship engaged in the most unsailorly act of waving his cap at a female ashore; her arms

were stretched out toward the ship. Caption: *Farewell, my true love.*
"That there," said the old man, "is my sheff doover. There ain't a
thing in the National Gallery that's got the feeling, as you might say,
that that there picture's got. Them pictures in there are all dressed
up for a party, like, if you know what I mean. But this 'ere picture is
the real thing. It's got the war in it, see? Worth a tanner to you, sir?"

"A shilling at least. Here you are. Did he come back to her
afterwards?"

"Sir?"

"The man and the girl…. Did he come through the war
all right?"

"Well, sir, that there *is* a question to be sure. Funny you should
ask that. I've often wondered myself, that I 'ave. 'Oo knows?
That's art for you, sir. You don't know and yet you know. See?"

"The answer," said Beatrice in a voice that had undertones,
"is much simpler than all that. He did not come through all right."

They walked on. For a moment or two Beatrice seemed
depressed, then she became gay again.

"Do you know," said Dan, "that I really feel extremely
friendly to everybody we pass by. And the funny thing is that this
morning, I almost hated people. You're good for me, Beatrice."

"You've been good for me, too. Now what shall we do?"

"Dinner. Then a show, if you feel like one."

"Where shall we go for dinner?"

"Some place in Soho? No! A plague on French cooking.
Let's go to the Criterion."

They went to that sumptuous restaurant, and Dan managed
to get a good table where they could see if they wanted to but
could talk without being overheard.

"Well, here we are, Beatrice, dining together, and I've known
you for a thousand years. When you've known a person that long
you can be serious."

She smiled to herself as if at some secret kept from him.
"What shall we be serious about, then?"

"About something really interesting. Let's not waste time."

Beatrice waved her hand flippantly: "Why not? Let's waste it. I hate it when you can't waste it."

"Then let's waste it nicely. Let's talk about you and me."

She smiled a little defensively. "Of course. But we have been."

"No, only about what we've been doing. First we talked about me, then you. Now let's talk about us both together." He lifted his wine glass. "To our being friends, Beatrice, and to being a little in love besides."

She hesitated, then drank. "Yes — just a little. Not too much. You'll be careful we aren't too much?"

"If you're not in love, the only thing left is to talk about being in love, don't you think?"

Beatrice became suddenly serious. "Dan, I've changed a lot since you knew me."

"You're more beautiful. But that's simply because I've changed, not you."

She sighed and an unbidden thought came to her: Why do I want to run my fingers through his hair? She said earnestly: "I really have changed. The war, of course. It cheated me and I'd like to cheat it back. I'm not at all the sort of person you think I am. I'm reckless and quite cynical."

"You, Beatrice? Not you!"

"Yes, I am." She bent over her plate. "What *are* we talking about? One would think we were really understanding each other!"

"We are…. What I used to like most about you was your downrightness. I used to think you've no nonsense about you. What a fool I was."

She said a little constrainedly: "And now I have nonsense about me?"

"Anyway, I like it!"

Their eyes met and she smiled. Then, suddenly, she grew grave. "Dan, promise me something."

"Anything you like."

"If you ever fall in love, don't wait till after the war."

"I won't."

"Because you'll regret it — or she will, if you do."

Dan nodded reflectively. "All the same, when I get married I mean it to be for keeps."

"Yes, of course, but —"

"Well, I mean this mess everybody is in is pretty beastly." Dan's expression had sobered, and for a moment he looked beyond her. "Sometimes under a strafe, you know … people screaming — that sort of thing…. Sorry, Beatrice, I won't talk about that. But sometimes you have a feeling that the whole world has turned putrid and you with it, and as if — it's hard to put it into words — as if the powers that be — if there are any — were laughing at you out of the mouth of a big gun. It does things to some people. It would be easy to go rotten and cynical. Well, I don't want to. I think falling in love should be a little sanity you could hang on to in the mess. I mean, you can say to yourself, 'Anyhow, there's love in the world; that's not rotten.' And that *would* be decent if you made it so. Not just animal, you see. It's to bring life…. Beatrice, I've hurt you!"

She bit her lip. "It's all right, Dan. It's just that what you said made things hurt again." Her eyes softened and became maternal. "Don't you suppose I've felt that, too?" She added in a low voice: "It *is* beastly. I, too, used to think love was to bring life. But war is to bring death, Dan. There's no time for life these days."

"I mean to get it somehow. And so must you."

But she simply shook her head. After a moment she said: "You've made me think, though … that there are some kinds of fool I won't be."

Though he urged her, she would not explain what she meant. Finally, she said: "Are you ever afraid of anything?"

"Of course. Aren't you?"

"Fear of death, Dan?" she asked gently.

"No. Except indirectly, perhaps. No more than anyone else. After all, that's something you can't help, so you don't have to think of it much. And besides, everyone is in the same boat."

"Of what, then?"

"Oh, of myself mostly."

"So am I, Dan."

"It's funny, isn't it, how easily you and I can tell each other things. I couldn't have said that to anyone else. I feel as if I really understand you."

"No, you don't really. You're sweet, though.... Dan, the champagne is wasted if we talk about things like these. Let's just enjoy life now. Let's be crazy and reckless and gay. Rome can do its silly old burning without us for two days."

They went to *Arlette* for a while and then to *Zig-Zag!* at the Hippodrome, which, though it wasn't very good, was gay and had an acceptable chorus who came down gangways into the pit carrying fishing poles with which they angled for unattached subalterns.

Then they went to a place where they could dance.

"Do you remember the last time we danced together, Beatrice?" She drew in a quick breath. Pain. Clumsy of him. "Yes. At college, at the Lotus Club. It was when I was first engaged. I remember telling you how settled and sure of my own self it made me feel."

Not knowing what to say, Dan ventured upon a platitude: "Life goes on, Beatrice."

"Does it? I don't feel that it does. I don't want it to.... May I ask you a question, Dan?"

"Of course."

"Do you still love Cynthia?"

He stiffened, then smiled slowly and shook his head. "Do you know I don't anymore, though I've only realized that — lately. That was springtime love. You're not really in love until you need a person."

"So you've found that out."

The room was dark except for a kaleidoscope whirling coloured gems over the uplifted faces of the dancers. The orchestra brooded and throbbed and swept over the curving wave of the waltz, making a languid shallop of rhythm which floated the couples onto a dim sea. *With her it is beautiful again. It is poetry again. Does she feel it too? But she must!*

They went home in Beatrice's car, which she kept parked in a public garage. She backed it out and got the fender caught. "Loud cheers," thought Dan, secretly pleased. In certain moods she seemed all too competent and sure of herself to prosper male vanity. They drove home humming a snatch from *Arlette*.

> *I love — her — emphatic'ly,*
> *But — quite — dip — lomatic'ly,*
> *That — is — the only way.*

But was it indeed? ... They put the car into a garage and walked to her house. Dan thought of walking back to his hotel alone; the thought revealed a disturbing and joyful fact to him. "I am in love with Beatrice," he thought.

He said: "Do you like saying good night? I loathe it."

She caught her breath, a little startled.

"I want to kiss you, Beatrice, instead."

She said nothing. He put his arms about her and kissed her lips. She shivered.

"Do you mind?"

"I meant you to from the first…. Goodbye, Dan."

He could not read her expression, but some secret reserve in her manner alarmed him. "Don't say 'goodbye.' Just 'good night.'"

But for some reason she would not say it.

"This isn't going to be enough, Beatrice. Something has happened to us."

Pain shadowed her face and, for an instant, she closed her eyes. "Dan, it *must* be enough.... Unless —"

"Unless what, Beatrice?"

"It must be enough. You and I mustn't fall in love."

Dan said anxiously: "I'm a clumsy fool, I'm afraid. It was just, thinking how lovely you look ... and that we've only got two days more. Never mind it, Beatrice. We'll talk about it tomorrow if you'd rather.... Let's kiss just once more."

She said "No!" passionately.

He went home charmed and uplifted, thinking what mysterious creatures women were. Full of unlooked-for reticence.

"I am in love with her, and I've got to go back to France.... Needn't think of that yet." He went through the dark streets, and the people who passed by him might as well have been ghosts; he did not see them. The sigh of London tortured by thousands of hidden passions passed unheeded. Wraiths fluttering past the subaltern on leave who was strolling slowly, hesitated, touched his sleeve, and breathed a question. He did not hear. He was dreaming of Beatrice.

### iii

Next morning there was a letter waiting for him.

> Dear Dan,
> I think we had better not meet again after all. I really mean it. You and I like each other too much without liking each other enough. I want to be honest with you, Dan. You see, you want just the things from a woman that I haven't got to give. I don't love you and I couldn't. I just like you awfully; but I might like someone else just as much — that way. I wouldn't be a sheet anchor.

I'd just be a broken reed. You deserve better than
that from a woman. I have been really in love
once and I know.

It isn't that I don't *want* to see you. The truth
is, you're making me irresponsible, and I don't
want to think just of myself. I won't be at home
tomorrow or the next day and you don't know
where my hospital is. Really, it is better that way,
Dan dear.

After reading this letter for the first time, Dan was
panic-stricken. Then he became angry. Then he felt that, unless
he found her, he was lost.

He set off to discover from the authorities whether a certain
VAD could be found. She was his sister, he said, and he had had
bad news from home. At last he discovered her hospital and sent
a telegram.

*I have just had bad news, need your help. Meet me at
four at the Crimson Dragon Tea Room, Oxford Street.*

He spent the rest of the morning pulling strings to get a special licence for Daniel Thatcher to marry Beatrice Elton without
publishing banns. Then he went to the hotel clerk and said:

"Have you a really nice room — A suite, rather. A large
room with a sitting room attached — and so on."

"Well, sir, we haven't much room at present."

The clerk had a silver disablement medal on his lapel.

Dan said casually: "You see, my wife is arriving from Scotland
this evening.... Do be a good chap!"

The ghost of a smile appeared and disappeared on the
clerk's official countenance. "Well, in that case. Yes, perhaps it
can be managed."

"Thanks. Decent of you."

"Would you like dinner or supper in your room?"

"Why not? Yes, by all means."

Dan ordered flowers to be sent to the hotel.... What other things might a woman want?

At four he went to the Crimson Dragon Tea Room. Beatrice entered almost at once, saw him, and came swiftly to him with her hand outstretched.

"Who is it, Dan? Is it your mother?" She put her other hand on his wrist.

"Tea first, Beatrice. Then I'll tell you."

They had tea and tried to talk about things that did not matter. Then she said:

"Now, Dan, tell me about it."

"About what?"

"Dan!"

"About the bad news? It was the note I got from you. I had to see you again."

Her eyes hardened and she studied him over the rim of her teacup with a pucker between her brows. Then she put down the cup and stood up.

"Will you please pay my bill, Dan! You had no right to do that."

"Please, sit down, Beatrice, and don't be angry.... You haven't been fair, either. You had no right to drop things like that. You know very well there was something special between us. You said so yourself."

"You want to marry me, Dan. Is that it?"

"You know that, Beatrice.... I've arranged everything. You are to come to the Strand Palace tonight as my wife. It's quite simple."

Her mouth drooped and she looked away from him.

"It *is* simple, Beatrice."

She looked at him again and shook her head slowly. "You see, Dan, I'm still in love with Matt."

After a moment Dan said shakenly: "Isn't it pretty hopeless just remembering that always? You've got to go on living, you know."

Her lip curled satirically: "Living? Yes, I suppose so. On my own terms, though." Then her look softened and she gave him a queer smile he could not understand. "There is something between us, Dan. I feel that, too. I'm so fond of you, and if only I could give you your heart's desire.... I'm empty, Dan. You want a whole heart. I haven't it to give."

"I'll risk it, if you will."

Her voice became agitated: "Why are you so — so — You make me feel so torn to bits! ... Listen, my dear. When you were in love with Cynthia, did you let yourself go absolutely? Did you, in your own mind, give everything you had to give?"

"No," said Dan thoughtfully, "I didn't. I didn't need her as I do you."

"And I needed Matt. He could have had all of me. Everything.... I wish we had!" she added passionately.

It hurt him amazingly to hear her say that. Not jealousy exactly; he loved her too much for that — but not being able, however much he loved her, to give her the happiness of first love completed.

"So you see, Dan, I couldn't give myself like that again. When Matt was killed he took me — all that with him.... And even if I could I'd be afraid to. It hurts too much when — if —" She stood up blindly, turning her head from him.

"There's just one question I must ask, Beatrice. Don't you want to be loved?"

"Yes ... you blind — *fool!*"

Dan exclaimed, bewildered, "I can't understand you a bit!"

"I know.... Sorry I called you a fool. You're sweet.... I'm restless, Dan. Let's go somewhere. Let's *do* something!"

They left the tea room and found themselves in a thick fog. Looking down you could not even see the sidewalk, and Beatrice stumbled off the edge of it and clutched his arm.

"This must be what they call a pea souper. It's the first I've seen."

He could not discern Beatrice's expression, but he could feel that her mood had altered abruptly. She snatched at an adventure.

"Isn't it fun! … Dan, let's get lost. We'll walk a lot and turn corners. Then, when we've got thoroughly mixed up, we'll go into the first house and find out where we are."

"Right you are! Why don't other people have ideas like that? Only, hang on to my arm. I want us to be lost together. I wonder what sort of a place we'll turn up in."

They walked for an hour and soon lost all sense of direction. People with things to do, in a hurry and irritated by the fog, bumped into them and were surprised by laughter from two phantoms — a man and a girl, evidently. It is not in that spirit that one takes life in a big city!

"Fifty steps more, then we'll turn to the right and see where we are. If it's a church, you'll have to marry me." Her clasp on his arm tightened and her fingers curled into it.

They turned to the right and bumped into an iron railing. Dan felt along it until they came to a gate. They went in and up a flight of steps and, presently, touched a doorknob.

"There's a knocker, Dan. And — wait — here's a brass plate with something written on it. Can you read it?"

Dan felt the letters on the plate with his finger tips and read aloud slowly: "T-E-T-I. *Teti Psychologist and Spiritual Life Reader.…* Here's an adventure for you! Fate might have sent us to a green-grocer or an undertaker, but out of all London, she sent us here."

"Shall we knock?"

"No, wait. Obviously, it's our destiny to get our fortunes told. We will pretend we are lovers. That won't be difficult for me to do. We are lovers and we want to know whether we ought to get married before I go to France. Our families don't approve of hasty war marriages. We're gullible and superstitious and we want to get the advice of the stars.… Come on, Beatrice."

"I don't know, it might be bad luck; laughing at something serious, you know."

"What harm can it do? You *are* superstitious. If an adventure like this pops up, you have to seize it."

The knocker felt like a man's face surmounted by some sort of headdress from which projected the out-thrust head of a serpent. Dan let it fall and knocked at the gate of destiny with an Egyptian uraeus.

The door opened, showing a hall dimly lit with gas. An impeccable butler confronted them. "That means at least three guineas," thought Dan.

"Good afternoon. We should like to see Mr. Teti."

"Come this way, please."

They followed him down the hall into a large room full of strange objects. A grate held red embers and gave the room its only light. Coloured casts of Egyptian bas-relief hung on the walls. A great figure that looked as if it had been carved in diorite sat, hands on knees, at one end of the room, more still than Buddha. The face was serene and noble, the lips parted lightly in an aloof smile. "Atmosphere," thought Dan, "at least five guineas."

"Have you an appointment with Teti, sir?"

"No. But we thought —"

"Perhaps we ought not to bother Mr. Teti," said Beatrice eagerly. "We thought —"

"Excuse me, Miss. If the savant felt that anyone in real need had been turned away, it would grieve him and interfere with his strange gift.... What is it you wish to know?"

Dan recited their story glibly and the butler condescended to nod sympathetically. "Under the circumstances, I think I may venture to disturb him." He moved out of the room ponderously.

Beatrice whispered: "I don't like it, Dan. This place makes me feel creepy."

"Rot, Beatrice. Don't be taken in by the hocus-pocus. The chap must have quite a technique to earn this." Dan waved toward the diorite statue. "Must be worth listening to."

The savant stepped into the dull glow from the embers. He wore none of the usual trappings of charlatans — no embroidered gown, no jewelled turban — yet he was far from a conventional figure. A white shirt with a Byronic collar opened beneath a massive but finely cut face. A white beard, carefully trimmed, might have been that of King Khafre himself; Mr. Teti's face, too, was as serene as that of the ancient Egyptian, and the expression of his eyes —

"The savant is no fool," thought Dan. "He's clever enough, really, to *like* people; they feel it instantly."

Once again Dan reeled off his story. Mr. Teti beamed at them benevolently. "What you tell me, my dear young people, may be quite true. To me you could say anything — *anything*, true or false, and most likely I should believe you. But the powers who speak through me see with the all-seeing eye of Osiris — *they* will read the true thoughts in your hearts — or in your liver, as the Egyptians put it." Mr. Teti allowed himself a smile. "I shall be glad on your behalf to prepare myself for spiritual messages.... Now you sit here and I shall sit over there. Do you like music?"

"Yes, but —"

"Tchaikovsky's Sixth Symphony, then, but very softly, *very softly*. Unless the mood, *your* mood, is right, I can do nothing. The Sixth is the symphony of love and of death. They go together, always together, always. Love, and behind it, lending it meaning, always the fear of ultimate extinction — as in your hearts you very well know.... You see, I am at least wise."

Mr. Teti, sitting in the shadows of King Khafre, was visible only as an indistinct figure, a second Khafre. Music softly throbbed and wailed, sang of love and of love's briefness.

A flute-like voice, tremulous but clear as the sound of ripples lapping on a beach, hovered over the statue of the Egyptian pharaoh.

"Hear the voice of King Unis. Death loose thy bandages. They are not bandages, they are the locks of Nephthys weeping over the body of her dead brother.... Behold, I have set my face toward the doors of the sky, to that tall sycamore east of the sky whereon the gods sit. Behold, I am come to the Lily-Lake and 'Look-Behind' the ferryman waits with his face turned from me in his boat of rushes. Whence hast thou come? He bringeth not his boat to me...."

Beatrice murmured: "He means death, doesn't he?"

"That's cribbed from the pyramid texts, I think," Dan whispered back. He gathered that a certain soul was at the door of the sky, wanting to get himself ferried across a sort of lake at the bourne of eternity, but in vain. Dan listened, spellbound, sceptical, but in another way, held by the power of a hypnotic voice and the just weighting of vowels and consonants by a born rhapsodist. Beatrice's hand crept into his. The flute-like voice flowed on, setting aflight again phrases from a far age.... *The barque of the millions of years.... None cometh from thence that he may tell us how they fare. Encourage thy heart to forget it, making it pleasant for thee to follow thy desire while thou livest....* Phrases spoken thousands of years ago, telling of man's everlasting revolt against death.

The music ceased. Mr. Teti stirred and came forth from the shadow, a man, pale and exhausted, but with the venerable air of one who has trenched on mystery. Art is a matter of well-placed reticence, and Mr. Teti was an artist in mystery. He waited for them to speak.

"An impressive performance," said Dan politely.

"Yes? I should be interested to know what they said."

"But surely you remember?"

"I? My dear young man, you must think of me as emptied, a mere vessel; for the time being, as empty of life as that statue of King Khafre. They come — these presences, these earthbound presences; they sigh, they whisper now this, now that. *I* cannot hear them; their message is not for me."

"Well, they were most poetic. 'Gather ye rosebuds while ye may' — that sort of thing. They quoted a lot from the pyramid texts, I think, with other stuff mixed in." (Mr. Teti winced and raised his eyebrows delicately at the word "stuff.") "The fact is we have an Egyptologist in our battery. The new army is a real university, you know."

Mr. Teti's air of confiding benevolence deepened. "Now that is really remarkable! No doubt the very emotions, the authentic human fears which produced those strange and touching hiero-glyphs in the pyramids of Pepi and Mernere twenty-six hundred years before Christ, have reproduced themselves — the atmosphere being favourable and somewhat analogous — through my humble mediumship, for your instruction.... However that may be, the message for you, my dear young people, is clear. We live — we die; and who knows what befalls us when we reach the door of heaven. Live then! ... And now, sir, the spirits give their wisdom free to those who have the wisdom to listen. But alas, I, their servant, must live. It always distresses me to mention sordid matters. The fee — to you, to two young people caught in the net of universal calamity — is five guineas. I will be frank. I am the vessel of super-natural powers, and though I am by nature extremely avaricious, I dare not, on their account, make more than a mere living from my mediumship." The beaming altruism in Mr. Teti's eye — who could doubt its sincerity? — repulsed the crude expression of scepticism. Mr. Teti did understand psychical forces very well, indeed.

iv

They rode home on the top of a bus. "This is our barque of the millions of years, Beatrice," said Dan with a grin. "That's what that fakir called it."

"It's a lonely phrase, Dan, isn't it? It fascinates me. You are in the boat, you cannot get out of it, and you are alone."

"Well, we are in it together now. But not for a million years. Just a bus ride together and a walk and then good night. Then another day together. Then farewell."

She caught her breath and shivered.

On the bench behind them sat an old man who had long outlived his family. He watched them with interest: a slim girl in a trim brown tailored suit, obviously a lady; a young fellow in love with her and quite oblivious to the landscape or to other fellow travellers on the bus. Lucky young people! To be in love was the greatest of all happiness. But he remembered dimly that it was often a trouble, too. He had no son to go to war and be killed. For a moment he almost wished he had. One more thing to cut an old man off from the world. Acting on impulse, he leaned forward and touched the youngster in uniform on the shoulder.

"On leave?"

Dan turned sideways and nodded. "One more day."

"Well, young man and you, mademoiselle — make the most of your time together and don't worry about the future. Youth is the time! When you're as old as I am you'll look back at your young days and wonder why you ever worried about things at all then."

Dan smiled a little shyly. "There's always an 'if' and a 'but,' sir."

"Slay them! Don't be a half-man and a half-woman. You can't get the most out of life if you are always trying to live it by grammatical logic. Mark my words, young people; take each day as it comes.... You're a nice looking couple."

They got off the bus at Southampton Row.

"What are you thinking of, Dan?"

"A lot of things. That after seeing you it's going to be harder to toughen up when I get back. I was thinking of that God-forsaken leave train at Victoria. It goes at 7:40 in the morning, so you have to get up in the dark.... Sorry, Beatrice, wash that out about Victoria. I shouldn't have minded it a bit if I hadn't had this time with you."

"Shall I see you off?"

"No. Better not to."

"Why not, Dan?"

"Too bittersweet. I'm restless. I'm better out of London. I think I'll go back tomorrow."

Her mouth drooped.

They passed the British Museum, where the problems of former men and women long since terminated, for good or ill, in dust, lingered on coldly and peacefully recorded in marble and print.

"Beatrice, the old man on the bus was right and so, in his way, was that fakir, Teti. We have two more streets to pass and then we'll have to say goodbye.... Have you thought — it's a long voyage to take alone. Matt was a fine fellow; he wouldn't want you to go through life as if it were a desert."

She put her clenched hands to her forehead. "I can't. I can't."

"All right. I understand how you feel about it, Beatrice. We'd better say goodbye now."

She did not want to say goodbye. There are some arguments you support against your will; only when *you* have won them do you realize how much you wanted to lose them. "What's the good of it," she thought, "this will make us both unhappy." She tucked his arm in hers and by looking at him in a certain way made it impossible for him to go. She said:

"Do you like me less now?"

"No. I think you are logical as blazes. Your head rules your heart. I'd no idea women were so cold blooded."

"That's not true! ... Supposing I'd said I would marry you and we had got married before you went back, would it have made a difference?"

"Beatrice, you've got a devil in you. I wish I weren't what I am. I'd take you somewhere and make you pay for asking me that."

"Don't be bitter. I have a reason for asking."

"Well, why do you want to twist the knife in the wound? Is it fun?"

"No, it isn't fun. I think people get like this when they want each other and don't.... Would it make a difference? Please tell me."

"You're not stupid, Beatrice. You know how it would. I could always think of you as if you belonged to me. We would be one flesh, you know."

"I think it might be worse, then. We wouldn't be together."

"It would be worse, but it would be better, too."

"Are you going to walk back to the hotel, Dan?"

He stared at Beatrice in amazement. "I suppose so. But that's a queer question. Why did you ask me that?"

"Oh, I don't know. Yes, I do. I want to think of what you're doing. When you leave London the day after tomorrow I won't know anymore, then it will be finished. Will you kiss me, Dan?"

"Yes. Then you step over the doorstep. I shan't pass the doorstep. That's the easiest way."

"No. You won't pass the doorstep, Dan. I understand that."

They kissed and Beatrice went past the doorstep. Strangely, her eyes were shining.

Dan groaned. "Oh, my God! I wish we hadn't."

"Goodbye, Dan."

"Goodbye."

He went without looking back. That was the best way. On the way back to the hotel, he did not notice people or things. They were simply shut off in another world.

He went to the desk for mail. There was a letter from Alastair.

The clerk smiled at him sleekly: "Mrs. Thatcher has just arrived, sir. Did you miss her at the station? She went up to your room."

Dan dropped Alastair's letter and fumbled, picking it up. The clerk looked sympathetic. He thought he understood the situation. "I told them you would be wanting dinner, sir. I knew you would be back immediately."

"Thanks," Dan mumbled.

He went upstairs. He knocked at the door and went in.

A table was set for two. Flowers on the table; a fire in the grate.... She was sitting in a Morris chair by the window. She stood up, looking at him tautly with wide, frightened eyes.

"Do you know what you're doing, Beatrice?"

"Dan, please, be nice to me."

With an effort he made his voice sound satirical. "There is one small thing about me you don't seem to have thought of, Beatrice. Forgive the heroics, but I'm supposed to be a gentleman."

She flinched as if he had struck her. "That's brutal, Dan! What does all that matter between you and me? Why should you have scruples if I haven't? It is not wrong. Who cares a rap about us, and whom could we hurt except ourselves? I'm lonely. I want to be loved. Let's just be happy and not *think*."

Dan walked to the window and looked out. You could hear the hum of the Strand below them. People going to theatres. He took out his cigarette case and put it back. Silly thing to do! He could see her satchel on the floor. When he knocked, she must have been looking for something in it — a box of cigarettes, perhaps. It lay open and he could see flimsy things inside it.... He did not want to look at her yet.

He said, trying to smooth agitation from his voice, "It isn't too late yet. Let's do this the right way, Beatrice. You're a nice girl and I'm not a cad.... We'd be sorry after the war if we didn't."

Beatrice turned from him and sat down, staring moodily into the fire. It was as if she realized she had lost. "There isn't any 'after the war.' Not for me anyway.... You want to make me into something I can't be. I've told you, Dan. I loved Matt and I've never got over it and I never will. That's why I won't marry you. I have a conscience, too. I'm not just being a loose woman."

Scourging himself to anger, he said harshly: "I'm to fall in love with you; we're to love each other — after a fashion. Then we are to say goodbye politely and think of something else. Is that it?"

She gasped and they stared at each other, each seeing a stranger. Why was he saying these things? He felt as if someone other than he was uttering his thoughts. But he could not check the words that poured forth bitterly.

"You are hugging a dream. It isn't natural for a living human being to go on crying over spilt milk for the rest of her life. It's morbid. Matt was a fine chap. Better than me, perhaps. But he is jolly well dead. And death's something you can't get over. After all these years, you don't still love him as you did. You only think you do…. And what's more, Beatrice, if you liked me well enough to become my mistress — well, that's the word for it, isn't it? — then you'd like me well enough to marry me."

Beatrice gazed at the luckless young man who had spoken his mind to a woman; she gazed at him with hate.

"That's enough! That's quite enough! Now you are being a cad!"

They were at cross purposes and at the mercy of one of those antagonisms that arise between a man and a woman when they desire each other and when the desire has not been fulfilled.

After a moment her hand fluttered into the crook of his elbow. "Hopeless, isn't it, Dan? I can't reach you. You've a right to feel like that if you want to. I can see that. Now we'd better really say goodbye…. No, don't come down with me. I want to say it here…. We'd better not kiss. You turn and look through the window and say goodbye, and I'll say it, too. Then, when you turn round again, I'll be gone."

"I'm sorry, Beatrice. I didn't mean to hurt you. I'm half-crazy, I think."

They said goodbye. From her voice he could tell she was crying. When he turned round, she was gone….

The telephone rang: "About your dinner, sir?" asked a smooth voice.

"You can eat it yourself if you like."

"I beg pardon, sir?"

Dan slammed the receiver on the hook…. The flowers on the table. He took them and hurled them into the fire. His face twisted and he groaned: "Goddamn it all! Goddamn it to hell!"

V

In the inner confessional of the mind, Dan fought obstinately to retain the comfort of bitterness against Beatrice. "What if I misunderstood her motives? ... Her motives? Quite cynical. She justified herself with a lot of balderdash about making *me* happy. Lot she cared about me! She loved Matt and she wanted an affair with me because she hadn't the pluck to go on facing the loss of him. She's a coward."

He was in a thoroughly evil mood.

"Damn women! You go along a London street and you pass a lot of them. You pass them and they look at you for an instant or not at all, and it makes the world seem pretty damned unreal.... What am I doing with myself, anyhow, these days? Nothing. I am simply standing still waiting for d—

"I won't say that! Father despised a man who pitied himself.

"Waiting for death to come along and pluck my sleeve. I ought to come to my senses. Sound phrase, that!"

He had a ticket for the Shaftesbury Theatre, but discontented, he left after the first act and decided to walk back to the hotel. Coventry Street was crowded with men in uniform from the four corners of the Empire and from the allied armies. A tentative butterfly touch on his arm and a voice breathed out of the darkness: "Are you lonely tonight?" He put his head down and ploughed on. A restaurant door, opening, poured light over passersby. He caught a glimpse of a small, dapper Chinese, in a grey felt hat and horn-rimmed glasses, looking like a pet mouse, talking with a prostitute. Darkness absorbed them, and from it, the woman's voice floated back to him: "Jesus! Did you see him looking at us?" and a reckless laugh. It seemed to his inflamed senses that everywhere sex confronted him.

He went back to the hotel and sat in the lounge watching people living their lives about him. He, sitting alone, shared his mood with too much drink. Without altering his mood, it made him reckless.

About midnight the sirens sounded a warning and gunfire began to the east and south. At first it was faint, but soon the anti-aircraft barrage swept over the sleeping roofs of London in swift onslaught. An air raid suited his mood. In the deserted streets, walking alone in a tempest of sound, lust would exhaust itself beneath the battering of impersonal violence.

He went through the swing door of the hotel, in spite of the commissionaire's protest, just as the last pedestrians came scurrying in from the street. Maroons were bursting red and green in the sky. Police whistles rose above the prolonged drumming of gunfire. Belated taxis were drawn up at the curb and deserted by their drivers. Spent shrapnel bullets pattered onto the sidewalk, and now and then the sharp explosion of a gun, fired from a roof somewhere nearby, cracked sharply above the drumming of the barrage. Shells burst high up and swirled momentarily in little whirligigs of light. Searchlights probed the sky with delicate fluttering fingers, intersecting, disengaging, sweeping from horizon to horizon. The flashes of guns firing danced over the city like flitting marsh lights; Dan could see them over the line of roofs and on the skyline at the end of the long corridor of the Strand.

Presently, he heard someone approaching. The sound was the staccato footfall of high heels: a woman, then. But she was not walking fast. At night, he ruminated, women usually walked *clip-clop*, *clip-clop*, at the speed of a quick heartbeat, as if they were afraid of being accosted. Somebody who was tired.... Her figure loomed before him: a woman bent forward with her eyes on the ground, walking as if in a daze. She did not see him.

Just as she came abreast of him, something mortal cleaved the air and close! — hurtling down with a vicious *yaup*. It smote the street and sent bits of cobblestone whirring through the air to whack against the walls of houses. Dan flinched and then laughed aloud. It was a dud shell. "I've gone soft after a fortnight's leave."

But the woman was terrified. She stumbled and Dan caught her as she fell. She struggled and fought him and began to sob and scream hysterically.

"Are you hit? Are you hit?"

He saw that she was not hurt; simply frightened out of her wits and hysterical. He shook her and said brutally: "Stop that! You're not hurt.… What are *you* doing out?" he asked her when she had become calmer.

After an instant she answered him, her voice was sullen, a little hoarse. "I've got to earn my livin' same as anyone else, mister."

"I see," said Dan.

The girl — a quality in her voice told him she was young — leaned her head back and relaxed her body against his. "I can't stand looking up with them things bursting up there. It seems like the whole sky is falling on you." The hysteria caught hold of her again.

"Stop it! Stop that, do you hear!"

It was no time for a woman, any woman, to be out, Dan thought. He could not blame her for being terrified, but somehow her craven fear, that shameless shrieking, had disgusted him.

She seemed to feel his disgust. "Yes, I was afraid. I can't stand them things coming down from the sky."

"You'll be right enough now; the shelling has died down a bit. Where do you live? I'd better see you home."

That struck her as amusing and she began to laugh. "Yes, you'd better, sweetheart. Someone might molest me.… I don't mind it with a roof over me head. It's when they come down out of the sky, naked, like. The sky's kind of big when it's dark with them things. It's kind of big. It's kind of big —"

"Now don't start that again."

"I won't. I'm all right."

She walked beside him, not offering to talk, and he for his part, though it was ridiculous not to be able to talk to her simply as if she were a human being, could think of nothing to say.

The touch of her body clinging to him with fright had whipped desire to life. He said politely, and his voice sounded unnatural in his own ears:

"The air raids must be hard on Londoners."

She gave him a quick, sidelong look.

"Oh, it isn't so bad. I was in Paris all summer and that was worse. They had air raids there, too. And it seems worse, somehow, when people are jabbering at you in French; makes you feel a stranger, like. So I packed me things and nipped back to London. I don't hold with the French, anyhow. Stingy beasts, that's what they are."

She stopped before a short flight of steps leading to a door with a polished brass doorknob — a respectable looking place, Dan thought — and began to fumble in her purse for a latchkey. She found it and opened the door into a dark hall. She turned her head over her shoulder and said in a different voice: "Well, here we are. Coming in?"

It was on the tip of his tongue to say: "No. Goodnight." But he waited too long and found himself inside, and the door closing behind them muffled down the barrage to a duller rumble.

"We're safe here. A roof makes all the difference, don't it? But my sister doesn't know that. She goes crazy when the guns start."

He followed her up a narrow flight of stairs into a room lit by gas. Naively, he expected the room to look sordid. It did not. It was simply a lower-middle-class room. On the wall was a lithograph of a little girl and a dog in garish colours. There was a chest of drawers with one of the knobs off and a walled-in mantelpiece whose sole function was to uphold a dish of wax fruit. A door led into another room.

"What's the matter, sweetheart? Don't you like my room? Sit on the bed. Ain't it soft?"

"It's all right. I was wondering what had become of the framed text, 'God bless our home.'"

"That's better. Now you're gay."

Madam Wanton, when he looked her full in the face, was not alluring. Her face was young, but the woman had fled from her eyes and she had a prostitute's mouth, raddled and set hard in the harlot's curve, as if disgust had been permanently etched upon it.

"'Ere. What's the matter with me? What's in your gentleman's mind, I'd like to know?" She gave him a look and began to laugh. "I thought you were a regular babe, at first. Well, don't mind me, officer. I'll like what you like and give you worse." Her look threw mud on their common humanity.

"What's your name?"

"Gipsy, they call me. But I ain't really a gipsy. Lily's my name. I don't hold no truck with gipsies. Dirty people without no home of their own."

She sat on the side of the bed murmuring a lewd song about Adam and Eve sitting on the grass. Her eyes invited him to defile the spirit shamefully — and like it.

He cried, "Shut up!" with a burst of sudden rage he could not account for.

"Now, then! Mr. Impatient!"

Then, not far away, there was a loud crash. He had completely forgotten the air raid which, suddenly, seemed to resent having been overlooked. There was another crash so near them that Dan could hear the whine and patter of falling debris. The windows rattled in their casements, and somewhere in the house, glass tinkled from a window broken by the blast. The sharp sound of a girl's voice shrieking with sudden fear came from the room beyond the closed door. Without explaining or turning to look back at him, Lily ran to the door, swung it open, and banged it shut behind her. Dan had time to see a bed on which sat a trembling girl who looked about twelve.

Her cries subsided almost at once to a whimpering, and he could hear Lily's voice in a soothing murmur. There was another salvo of crashes, far off this time. No further danger; they seldom dropped two in the same place.

After about ten minutes the girl quieted down, and presently, the door opened and Lily reappeared looking back through the door as she closed it.

"Who's that?" asked Dan.

"My sister. She's that frightened of air raids. Makes her sick at her stomick. She ain't strong." She put up her hand to her forehead and rubbed it as if to clear her mind. "Sometimes I really wonder what we are all coming to. Reely, I do. This war.... I'm sorry, sir, I 'aven't been givin' you much of a time, 'ave I?" Her tone, thought Dan, was positively that of an apologetic shopgirl. Visibly, she pulled herself together. "Jesus," she said, "let's have a drink!"

The expression of distress humanized her; it did not dignify her face, but it made her look miserable. So that Dan, who had steeled himself for anything, was genuinely shocked when, after having a drink, a lewd expression came into her eyes and she began to hum again in her hoarse voice the song about Adam and Eve.

"She's crying again," said Dan harshly.

"Daisy, keep quiet, can't you? That don't do no good. And you're bothering my gentleman, can't you see? ... I 'ave to go in, dearie. She's that nervous."

As soon as she was out of his sight, Dan snatched a banknote out of his pocketbook and put it on the table, then opened the door and fled downstairs.

"Women! God almighty, how I loathe them." He felt as though he had been dragged through ordure. Then he thought: "I was a swine to go with a tart after knowing Beatrice.... Whatever I want it's not a dirty mechanical adventure with someone who is more of an animal than a woman — not feminine anyway. The sort of thing that cad, Dolughoff —" What really shocked him was to have found a person when he had looked for a *thing*.... "When you think of it, it's damned odd: I and that tart and her scared sister, all under the same sky. The same stuff all of us, flesh, blood, and nerves."

At the hotel he found a cable from Alastair. *Mother died suddenly, early this evening.* The message was dated the previous day. This news steadied him but it was not a surprise. She had never got over his father's death; that had broken her heart, there was no other phrase for it.

He thought of his mother. "She hated 'messiness.' She liked the peaceful, decent things. She loved tea in the afternoon with pleasant, civilized talk and small compliments given and taken. And she liked to read a quiet book like Jane Austen: nice appraisals of social status, for instance — whether Fanny Price was 'out' or not; settled conventions that were never questioned and upon which crude violence never intruded. 'Poise,' that was what she liked."

## Brother Newt to Brother Fly

Mysterious the twisted ways of men,
    Dear Brother Fly,
    And now and then
I marvel at the way the creatures die.
They perish joyfully to prove their soul —
    I wonder why?
Now I, had I a soul, should eat the whole
    Affair on earth;
Not love and kill and die so terribly
    To prove its worth.

Lo, yonder by the shattered German trench,
    A case in point —
    *Ein kerker Mensch!* —
The face (it's buried) has a bluish squint,
    And half a lip.
That he was *man* remains one only hint —
    That leg and hip.
It sticks there like an exclamation point
    That booted tip.

Mysterious the twisted ways of men,
    Dear Brother Fly,
    I marvel when
I see the curious way the creatures die:
A shell strikes, he erects that airy foot
    And so affirms
His soul is saved — and Germany to boot;
    So, glad to die.
Thank God we have no souls to justify,
Let's dine on worms.

                (From Quentin's Notebook)

# PART IV

# WIND IN THE STUBBLE

# CHAPTER XIII

i

The winter of 1917-18 was a winter of exhaustion. Russia was out of the war and the British Army, overspent by Ypres, eyed the Germans, expecting them to rush in for the kill. "Have you seen the GHQ Summary of Intelligence?" remarked Lynch. "The Germans moved seventeen divisions from the east to our front in December alone. Draw your own conclusions, my lad."

"'Ripeness is all,'" quoted Charles cheerfully. How about pushing off to Amiens for a dinner at Godbert's?"

Late in February the Wellington Battery was moved out of the Canadian Corps and down to the Third Army front, south of Arras. "We're for it, my lads," said Jiffy Tripp, "they must know something or they wouldn't lift us out of our own crowd."

One day the officers of the artillery brigade were addressed by their colonel who, though he loathed the public exhibition of sentiment, felt vaguely that these men under his command were, after all, human beings risking their lives and — well, dash it all, a soldier wasn't a mere machine! Flushing, and a little fierce with them because, on their account, he had to commit his inarticulate soul to sentiment, he looked over their heads and uttered remarks obviously prepared in advance. Gentlemen — hm — Perkins, close that confounded window, will you? A man can't

hear himself speak with that infernal row (the troops were playing a quiet game of "house" offstage). Gentlemen, you are going
back to your batteries with the certainty that, within a few weeks,
the enemy will launch against you the greatest attack in history. I
have every confidence that the attack will be foiled, and that you
will acquit yourselves in a manner — er — in a manner — hm
— that you will prove yourselves worthy of the highest traditions
of the Royal Artillery. The regiment's highest traditions — yes.
Hm. Hm. Well, dash it all, gentlemen, we'll take all that sort of
thing for granted, what? What I really want to say to you is simply 'good luck to you all.'" ... The irrepressible Tripp murmured
to Dan, "'Once more into the breach, dear friends, once more!'
Nice old boy, the colonel."

Letter from Dan to Beatrice:

Dear Beatrice,
Sorry I showed such a mean streak in London.
I admit I had no right to say what I said. If you
were to put down my remarks to pure jealousy
you would not be far wrong. I do understand
how upset you are, and in a way, I sympathize
with your point of view, though I am absolutely
certain you are wrong! Of course, I ought never
to have forgotten even for an instant that you
are going through *dies irae* and can't be yourself.

If I take back what I said, will you do likewise? Or no, you needn't take it back. Very likely
it was true. But at any rate, let's be friends, and
do write me now and again. Write often! I happen to be in love with you, as you very well
know, so I think you might! I could say more
about that, but I won't till I hear from you.

All's well with me. Our small fraction of the
British Army in France is cultivating its garden

and waiting for whatever is to be. Nothing much I can tell about "ours." Oh, yes. You remember my speaking of Dolughoff, the crazy Russian? He is with the battery again, as egotistical, quarrelsome, suspicious, sanely mad or madly lucid (I don't know which) as ever. He took me aside and said: "I told you I'd be back, didn't I?" I had to admit that that was true. "Look here, Thatcher," said he, "I count on you to say nothing to the major about that episode in the salient. You know yourself that anyone, even as good a soldier as I, may do queer things under a strafe. You promise?"

My batman, the gipsy Jobey Loversedge, deserted. No, "deserted" isn't quite the word, as you shall see. One day he simply vanished — and so did one of the battery motorbikes. I told the major he'd be back. "I know Loversedge, sir. He wouldn't clear out without saying a word to me." Sure enough, after two or three days, Jobey rolled up drunk — in the ration lorry. Told us an amazing story which I didn't believe. Said he meant to desert, but got tight and decided to sleep it off in a lorry which turned out — amazing coincidence! — to be the battery ration lorry. So he was tumbled back willy-nilly. Of course, being Jobey, he would never admit that he hadn't a perfect right to desert. All he would say was, "I'm a gipsy, sir. They can't tie *me* to no gun wheel." Of course, he'll get blazes, but he's too stout a fellow to be charged with desertion.

Do write to Cynthia and tell her to give Al a good shock. He's making an idiot of himself with my flighty relative Tessa. It's no use

Cynthia's sitting back and just being proud,
I know my Al. She'll have to take him by the
scruff of the neck. He's a spoilt devil. You write
to Cynthia, and I'll give Alastair blazes.

    Yours affectionately (if you don't mind),
    Dan

He had to wait a long time for her reply.

Dear Dan,
I suppose I am to be grateful for your effort
to make an honest woman of me in your own
mind? It so happens that I am too fond of you
not to overlook the priggish side of your nature,
though I admit your utter nobility of character exasperates mere human me a good deal.
No doubt it will be good for my soul — or
whatever it is — to trail along in *friendly association* with you, picking up whatever crumbs
from your largior aether you choose to throw
me. That's that. You are a stick-in-the-mud and
a prig but somehow likeable. Am I really only
twenty? I feel at least fifteen years older than
you. I shall certainly write to you now and again,
and I hope you will write to me — if you want
to. What is the "more you could say about that"?
I can't imagine what you mean.

    I am more anxious about you than I ought to
be for my peace of mind. No! I won't be niggardly.
I *am* anxious about you. I can't think of anyone
else whose safety means a snap to me. I am going
to a base hospital "somewhere in France" next
week. Maybe — no, perhaps we'd better not see
each other again. Just letters. It wouldn't offend

me much if you explained what you meant by
the "more you could say about *that*."

Your affectionate (seems safe enough),

Beatrice

P.S. — I had a visit from your uncle Murdo on
his way to France. He is going as a surgeon, not
a chaplain. He said to me: "Since the church has
given up preaching peace, goodwill toward men,
it might as well shut up shop for the duration of
the war because soldiers won't buy there."

Spring came early. Soon the parti-coloured daisies that poets
write about were pushing up among the tumbled rubbish of
what had been villages. The March sun melted the dormant mustard gas in shell holes and one or two men were gassed. At times
one could not help feeling in a holiday mood; the spring air,
the quiet evenings and the longer twilight, the first flowers, the
feeling of expectancy. Not even the smells of war: the stench of
chloride of lime, the faint, sweet, nauseating, poison gas smell, the
odour of moist new-turned earth, the rank smell of explosives,
of decomposition, of wood and charcoal burning in the braziers
— not even these could spoil one's rejoicing at spring in the
making. Sometimes as many as twenty or thirty planes grappled
in a dogfight over the trenches, they seemed like midges in the
spring sky, while soldiers leaned back smoking and cheered them
as though they were a bank holiday spectacle. A speck dropped
from the swarms of whirling midges for a thousand feet like a
stone, with another midge swooping down on its trail. Suddenly,
an engulfing billow of black smoke curled about the lost plane
and a black mite jumped from it — the pilot. "A long way to
fall," Dan said to Charles, with a sinking feeling in the pit of his
stomach. "'From eve till morn he fell, from morn till dewy eve, a
summer's day,'" Charles quoted soberly.

The forward section of the battery clung to the side of a long valley at right angles to the trenches. In front flowed a little stream, in full flood now, spanned by a road bridge and a trestled railway bridge. Two sappers made their appearance and went to work laying a demolition charge under the bridges. Thereafter, they bivouacked beside the switches, night and day.

The bivvy where Dan slept, a rough erection of sandbags and corrugated iron, had been built into the side of the valley about eight hundred yards behind Dan's guns. Tripp and Charles Burnet shared it with him. The three of them were lying on chicken-wire bunks. Jiffy stood up, yawned, and stretched.

"I'm down for OP duty tonight. Better be on my way." He put on his trench coat and took down revolver and gasbag from a peg.

"Which OP, Jiffy?"

"Cascara." He grinned at them. Cascara observation post was in the front line.

The telephone buzzed and a calm voice from the exchange came over the wire. "Dispatch rider for you, sir."

"Send him in," said Charles.

The battery dispatch rider stooped and entered the bivvy, saluted, fumbled in his pocket, and handed a message to Charles.

"Had I better wait?" asked Tripp.

"What do *you* think, Jiffy?" asked Charles grimly.

"Same thing you do. I'll wait."

Charles opened the message, read it, and looked up at them in silence.

"Is it?" asked Dan.

Charles nodded, not looking at Tripp. "Listen. 'The enemy is expected to attack in the early morning of March twenty-first or March twenty-second. Acknowledge receipt of this message to brigade.'"

"Tomorrow or the day after," said Jiffy. "I like the adjutant's terse style. What price the trenches tomorrow morning at daybreak? Want my job? Well, cheerioh."

He lingered at the doorway. Without consciously reasoning why, both Charles and Dan stood up. "I say, skipper, give me a spot of your whisky for my flask, there's a good chap." Charles got the whisky. Tripp waved and turned to go out.

"Jiffy —" said Charles.

"Captain Burnet, sir, at your service."

"Er, Jiffy — well, good luck, old man!"

"It will have been nice to have known you," said Jiffy dryly. He hitched his shrapnel helmet on one side of his head, gave his haversack a tug, and disappeared into the dark — into the dark.

Charles said: "It's odd. I *knew* that message was coming tonight. Anyhow, that's that!" He gave his nephew an intimate look, affectionate and quizzical. "Well, Dan — 'Hast any philosophy in thee, shepherd'?"

"D'you know, Uncle Charles, in a way I believe you've actually enjoyed the war."

"No-o. *Enjoy* isn't the word, of course. But I am a bit of a mountebank. Play-acting is second nature with me. No, first nature. I get a kick out of playing the *beau rôle*. And I will say that the war has brought out my best.... I haven't exactly made a mess of life; I always meant to enjoy it and I have. I have always been myself, you know, though people never thought I amounted to much before the war. 'That charming, irresponsible fellow Charles Burnet, let's ask him to dinner. He's such fun!' That's what they used to say. Well, I don't regret a damn thing!"

"But for God's sake, Uncle Charles," exclaimed Dan, "you talk like — like the Ides of March."

"Just a feeling. Against my end, as the Scotch say. The Burnets are fey, didn't you know?"

During the night, at two hour intervals, the big howitzers had to awake to the business of searching and sweeping German back areas, and each time Dan had to get up and go down to the guns. They fired the last rounds of the night's program an hour before daybreak. The gun detachment relaid the gun on the SOS lines and faded back into the darkness to their bivvies.

The air was chilly and a light mist lay along the valley. There would be a mist! Dan strolled about the gun position and looked up the quiet valley toward the trenches.

He walked humming to himself the Habanera, though he did not know he was humming. He spurned the earth, he did not know it was there, and No. 041006, Gunner Harris, T., the gas guard, sole guardian of the night, scratched his anonymous head in whimsical surprise to see the officer bump into Moll Flanders who weighed several tons and was no lady, without even cursing, without seemin' to notice it 'ardly.

Dan went back to the hut. Charles was soundly asleep with a placid expression on his face. Dan put his holster and gasbag where he could easily reach them in a moment, and lay down fully dressed. He fell into an uneasy slumber.

He awakened to a fearful impression that, in the darkness, the walls were whirling about him and that the solid earth under his feet, as he jumped up, was solid no longer but tilting this way and that, drunkenly. The impression was not entirely wrong. The walls of the bivvy were actually shaking from the impact of shells along the valley, and through the soles of his boots, he could feel the vibration of the earth. Against the terrific din he distinguished an insistent note close at hand: the crazy buzzing of the field telephone. He took up the receiver. "Sir —" began a voice, then the line went dead. Cut somewhere. You had to gather yourself together; there were things to be done, quickly. He snatched his accoutrements and put them on … a match flared beside him. He had completely forgotten that he was not alone. Charles was on his feet, and the spurt of light illumined a face bent with absorbed intentness over the act of lighting a pipe. Charles said coolly: "Here we are. I'll take the rear section; you go up forward and see that they're started on the SOS. I'll be up later. Jump to it, Dan!"

Outside, the din swooped upon him with malignant opacity and made him stagger. He ran as fast as he could go, up the road toward the guns. As he ran, he faced the most terrible and beautiful sight he had ever seen. Off on the horizon, where the Day of Judgment had come to the poor devils in the trenches, the flashing of the German artillery was like the northern lights, and along the road and valley in front of him, he could see the flowering of a multitude of jets of fire wherever shells were falling. Over his head and round about him as he ran, he could hear the whine of splinters, flying and landing with a *thwack* in the bank alongside the road. He felt lonely and sick. Once he stumbled into a shell hole in the road and fell prone, cutting his face and filling his mouth with dirt; and in the act of falling, he heard a soul-shattering crash, and a shower of mud and pebbles spattered over him. For a moment terror took him by the throat. He was alone. About him were nothing but blind forces, without soul. "Must I go on? ... Mustn't think, mustn't think, mustn't think." He ran on, pounding out the phrase to a crazy rhythm — lurching from side to side. At last he reached the guns. He shouted, "Number One and Number Two — action!" and hoped the crews would come running. They did. Now he felt exultant, intoxicated with the power he felt over himself. "I can do anything!" ... Moll Flanders pushed her snout up through the net and spat out her first shell; it went screaming up, up, to be absorbed in the universal noise. Number Two gun fired almost in the same instant. Over their heads, they heard shells from the rear section boosting themselves into the sky. "That's the stuff to give 'em, sir," said Sergeant Critchley.

It was twenty minutes to five o'clock on the morning of the twenty-first of March, 1918, zero hour of the German army's Kaiserschlacht, their final and greatest bid for victory in the World War.

## ii

At zero hour minus one minute, twenty-one minutes to five on March the twenty-first, Jiffy Tripp stood in the trenches beside an infantry officer, looking over no man's land. It was still dark. At zero hour plus five seconds the shell bursts actually threw a sort of witch's kaleidoscope onto no man's land, and he was reaching for the SOS rockets. Red — green — red. Three hours later, as Jiffy was crawling through a thin stream of blood at the bottom of a saucer-shaped muck heap which had been a trench, a shell splinter knocked him scuttling. An infantry subaltern said to him: "Take it easy, old man, you'll be all right. Just lie low and keep your head down." But Jiffy was in great pain, and the pain made him angry. He said: "Goddamn it to hell, do you think I want to spend the rest of my life in a wheelchair! Just prop me up. I'd like to have a crack at the bitches." He tried to get up and collapsed. Then, with an air of pulling himself together, he began to make a joke about drawing his full rations. Then he began to cough, and after that, it was a serious business. He lay still. At zero plus five hours, the German infantry came over with "hurrahs" and found not a single soldier on his feet in that trench. At zero plus five hours and two minutes, a German private stepped on Jiffy Tripp. Jiffy raised himself on his elbow and saying, "Take that, anyway, you bastard," fired his revolver. Then sank back with a bayonet point in his throat and, presently, lay still for good.

At zero plus twelve hours, at an advanced dressing station, Captain Murdo Burnet of the Royal Army Medical Corps was busier than he had ever been before. Even after the hours of cutting and patching, the priest was not entirely submerged in the surgeon; behind the mangled bodies with which he had to deal lay mangled souls; with them, too, he was professionally concerned. "This man," ordered Murdo, "I'll take him next. Gunshot wound in the head. Ventricles traversed by the bullet. Fatal nine cases out of ten." ... The things I should have liked to tell these poor fellows.... No use telling all ranks that God loves them and will care for them even as he does for every sparrow. True, of course, but they don't believe it nowadays, and you can't blame them. They know that a shell can kill a lot of sparrows. It is the old theme of the debate between the body and the soul. Body tells us we are machines — and badly out of gear, too. Soul denies it desperately. That's the real problem of the war for human beings: "Is a spiritual view of life possible?" ...

"The things I could say," thought Murdo, "if only they would listen. Thoughts boiling in me, if only I could preach.... *Mustard gas in the eye. Conjunctivitis with corneal complications. Can't open his eyes and, of course, he thinks he is blind....* I would say to them something like this:'Hardly one of you but must in his heart have faced despair. Not one of you but has seen the body so mangled and tortured with pain that it seems to eclipse the spirit with all the spirit's better hopes, so that a man seems little but a raw wound crying out to God for mercy against his agony.' ... *Perforating wound in the abdomen. I've hot tea for him and only a quarter grain of morphine. Keep him warm!* ... 'Then it is the body's hour and the soul is hidden for a while and we seem to die not differently from the beasts of the field.' ... *This man is dead, Sergeant. Take him off the table....* Then I'd say:'But can we not believe that a loving God will disinter the spirit from the debris of the body even as we, we men, in anxious and loving fear, would dig clear the body of some comrade buried under the earth of a shell burst?' But they wouldn't believe *me*. Christianity is a *faith*; one must have faith.... Say to them:'It is my faith — perhaps it is yours, too — that when we are in great need, if we will but forget ourselves and look to others, God will give us help through them.' ... *Multiple gunshot wounds in the face. Eyes, nose, mandible. Shock and profound pain. Morphia one half grain, 1,500 units of anti-tetanus....* 'What comes after death? Life, I believe; my faith tells me so. But I cannot be certain; nor can anyone of us. That is in God's hands who made us; he will not be less just than the least of us made in his image would be in his place...."'

At zero plus twelve hours Lieutenant Dolughoff, sundered from his unit by forces beyond his control, namely, the retreat of two armies on a seventy-mile front, found himself among infantry holding a trench dug to the depth of a foot. At zero plus eleven hours and thirty minutes, he was still fighting. A soldier next to him was hit and fell to the bottom of the trench, holding in his intestines with his hands. Dolughoff looked down at the soldier and something snapped inside his mind. He threw down his rifle, climbed up on the parapet, shouting at the top of his voice, and put up the palms of his hands, one toward the Germans, one toward the British; the gesture was exactly that of a policeman halting traffic. He shouted: "Stop! In God's name, I tell you to stop." It never occurred to him that he would be hit. Nor did it seem to him that he was committing a folly. God, he thought, had at last revealed to him something that had to be done, and he was doing it. In that din no one could hear what he was shouting, but the infantry cheered at the sight of a brave man standing unarmed on the parapet. At zero plus eleven hours and thirty-two point five minutes, the British infantry swarmed out of the trench, past Dolughoff, to give Jerry a taste of cold steel. Dolughoff stared unbelievingly at the khaki backs, tense, bowed forward, cat-footing it step by step toward the uncertain enemy, hoping to stay alive, braced to kill.... "God gave me a message. He gave it to me, to me, Dolughoff! I have spoken and they would not listen. *Stop! I have a message. I have a message. I ...*" His voice ran down and he peered about him like a cornered rat. Mud. Shell holes. Dead men hanging with dangling arms over the rusty barbed wire. He looked up at the sky. It seemed indifferent and empty.

*Quick Quick! Before I see what it means. Before I see —*

Dolughoff snatched his revolver and put a bullet through his brains.

### iii

For hours under intermittent shell fire, the forward section of the Wellington Battery had fired on SOS lines. About nine o'clock there was a lull in the shelling, and Charles Burnet sauntered into the gun pit where Dan was standing.

"Any news, Skipper?"

"Only rumours. All the lines are cut, of course, and I've seen no runners from the front."

They were still firing on SOS lines, and behind them, and to their left and right, they could hear the sound of British artillery. But in front of them in the trenches, where a few moments ago there had been infernal noise as if from the crumpling of mountains, there was now a desolating stillness. Not even a rifle or a machine gun. What did that mean? Charles put Dan's thoughts into words. "If the Germans are through, we shall see them coming over the crest."

The battle rolled toward them, first in rumours, then in visible form. A battery of field guns came powdering down the road and over the road bridge, guns jouncing from side to side; some ambulances passed and a trickle of walking wounded grinning because they were out of it. Charles asked:

"Are they through?"

"I think so, sir. A man told us they were coming down Noreuil valley. We got our blighty at battalion headquarters." They hobbled on.

"I'm going to have a look at those bridges," said Charles. Dan watched him go down the slope in front of the guns to the stream. He stood talking to the two sappers for a moment, then he came back. "Are they ready to fire the fuses?" asked Dan.

"Yes. I was afraid of the charges being blown prematurely by an exploding shell, but there's no chance of that. The charge is well protected. The only way it could be blown would be by a straight shot fired from on top, directly downward."

"Supposing the fuse gets blown away?"

"It would be a pity!" said Charles dryly.

They went on firing.

"Look over there," exclaimed Charles suddenly. The lone figure of an exhausted man was staggering across the road bridge.

"It's Lynch," said Charles.

When Lynch got to the gun pit, he slumped down and lay on his back, staring dully up at the sky.

"You all right, Lynch?"

"Yes," said Lynch in a queer, flat tone.

"The signallers?"

"All done in."

Dan's eyes wandered down to his legs. "Man! You're hit! Quick, Skipper, give me your field dressing." From the shins down, Lynch's puttees and boots were oozing blood, saturated with it. With an effort he sat up and stared at them, an expression of horror in his eyes. "I'm not hit," he muttered. "It's not my blood." He began to gasp.

"Easy on," said Charles soothingly, and Lynch fell back again with his head pillowed on his arm. "You've no idea of it, Burnet. Never saw anything like it even in the salient. It's a shambles."

"Did you see anything of Tripp?"

"No. Brigade OP was in the support lines. Jiffy's was in the front line. You won't see him again."

"Have they broken through?"

Lynch nodded. "Clean through on the flanks. There's a strong point at Arlette OP and they left us alone, at first; pounded out the trenches each side of us and filtered past. Then they came for us."

"What about ours?"

"Mostly gone. About half a battalion left up in front. I came back to give you warning.... Well, there goes your blasted war. They'll take Bapaume today, Amiens tomorrow. Nothing to stop them."

"I don't believe it!" exclaimed Dan.

Lynch gave Dan a strange look, envious and ironic: "You're a silly young fellow. We are beaten to the wide. Napoo fini!" He hunched his shoulders and looked with a frown across the thousand yards of valley to the crest of the next hill.

Charles said curtly: "Rot, Lynch. What you need is a drink. Here.... Now, old man, get along to the rear section and warn them. Then go back to the billets.... Don't forget all of you that we rendezvous at the reserve section at Villers-le-Château."

But Lynch was rebellious. "No, you don't, Captain Burnet! I'll go back no farther."

"Lynch!"

"All right.... I'll go.... But I've been under a barrage for four hours and I haven't even seen a German to pot at yet."

He went off down the road with his head stooped. He seemed not to notice the shells that were still falling intermittently along the valley.

Dan started to say something, but Charles interrupted him. "Want some excitement?"

"What do you mean?"

"There they are. Look at the crest."

Sure enough, Germans were dribbling over the crest of the hill; at that distance they looked like slugs. In a minute machine gun bullets came zipping by somewhere in their neighbourhood. Charles said quite cheerfully, "We'll pop off one more round with reduced charge — just for the gesture of the thing. Then we'll take the breech blocks out." They did so.

"Time to go?"

"No, wait. We've got the Lewis guns, eh? If they would only blow those bridges, we could hold 'em up a bit."

Even as he spoke, the road bridge went up with a great roar. But the trestle bridge stirred not — nor did the sapper lying beside the switch. Shot. The other sapper started to run toward the switch in order to blow up the bridge — a little fellow, bent double like a gnome, running for dear life. Suddenly, he tumbled head over heels like a shot rabbit and lay twitching.

"Thatcher!" shouted Charles, "bury the breech blocks and work your Lewis guns. So long, Dan, old man." And Charles Burnet started to run toward the railway trestle, dragging his revolver from the holster.

"For God's sake, come back!" Dan yelled after him. "The fuse is shot away."

But Charles kept on running.

By a miracle he got there without being hit, took one look at the fuse and shook his head. Coolly, he drew his revolver and walked out on to the bridge. About halfway he stopped and sat down with his legs astride a tie. Then he started shooting at the charge.

"Christ!" breathed Dan, and it was a prayer.

The bridge went up in a cloud of dust and smoke from which fragments of ties went spinning in all directions. And Charles Burnet went up with it.

# CHAPTER XIV

i

Alastair and Tessa were dining together at a restaurant in Toronto. When he was worried, it was a temperamental impossibility for Alastair not to feel that other people, particularly Tessa, ought to be making a special effort to be cheerful.

"I'm not feeling 'specially gay tonight, Alastair.... I was awfully fond of Charles."

He said at once, with the ready sympathy that was one of the most charming things about him, "I know you were. So was I." His face clouded again. "Tessa, you know how desperately in love with you I am.... What are we going to do?"

She avoided his look and gazed moodily at the couples lingering at other tables over coffee and cigarettes. Everyone seemed, somehow, to be managing happiness — at least they looked happy. She said gently: "I know, Alastair. Let's not think of it tonight, though. I do feel blue."

Alastair said defiantly: "Perhaps we did wrong to fall in love, but the mischief's done now."

She shivered. "I suppose it is."

"Look here, I can get a fortnight's leave from the camp. We'll go away together, now — tonight — we'll let divorce and that sort of thing take care of itself.... This is our chance, Tessa," he pleaded earnestly, "if we don't do it now, the whole thing — circumstances will be too much for us."

"You're afraid to face Cynthia tomorrow and tell her that you no longer love her. Is that it?" asked Tessa remorselessly.

He twisted uneasily. "Yes, dammit all, I would be," he admitted.

"It's so beastly. Cynthia's my friend, you know. I can't bear to think of her coming home to you, not knowing —"

"Cynthia never cared for me — as she should have cared. She really loved Dan, I think. But we won't talk of that.... There's a right time for love. If we don't take it —"

Tessa looked at Alastair a little askance. How young he was! He understood her expression and it made him resentful. "If you really loved me, Alastair, if you loved me so much that nothing else mattered, then you would be brave enough to meet Cynthia and tell her yourself."

"What good would it do!" He crunched his cigarette savagely into the ashtray. "My idea of hell on earth would be to meet Cynthia and find she was in love with me, and explain in a nice, cool, reasonable, friendly way that I had to desert her because I loved someone else better. In fact, I don't think I could."

"We ought to have thought of that before, Alastair."

"Well, we didn't! At least I didn't.... Oh, Lord, I'm not in love with myself. I just happen to love you like the very devil, that's all. And if you ask me, I think you're pretty cold, Tessa!"

Anger flashed into Tessa's eyes. "You've no right to say that! For one thing it is only three days since we heard about Charles being killed. He was a sort of brother to me. It makes me want not to be selfish."

"Yes, I know. But we need each other. That's something we can't argue away."

"It wouldn't be fair to my husband."

Alastair exclaimed irritably: "He doesn't need you. He is really glad to be by himself in Washington. He just wants to be let alone. He's *old*, Tessa."

"Or to Cynthia."

"I know that.... Tessa, all I can think of is that I love you and life simply isn't worth looking forward to without you."

These words wrung her heart, as he knew they could. She closed her eyes and her lips trembled. "I wish you and I.... I wish we'd never.... It's all so sordid!"

"You can't really love me or you wouldn't say that. You're cold, Tessa," said Alastair gloomily. But she exclaimed passionately:

"Can't you *see*.... We're gentlefolk, Alastair. That ought to mean something.... Anyway, we can't just be cads about this.... I must think.... You must meet Cynthia, dear. Then, if you still want me — No, I won't promise, even then. And do not come again for a week, Alastair. Please. I must think of this by myself."

## ii

The train from New York got in early in the morning. Alastair drove down to meet it feeling very unhappy and more of a cad than he could remember ever before having felt. He was a young man who had always to think well of himself. Explaining to Cynthia was bound to be a miserable business; to think of it brought him face to face with a picture of himself that he did not want to see. It would have been much better, he reflected, and in fact kinder, when one looked at it realistically, for Tessa and he to have avoided all this by simply going off together. "When Cynthia and I meet it will seem as though we are almost strangers." An unpalatable thought!

The train came slowly to a stop. Alastair walked down the long line of Pullman cars, trying to steel his mind. The usual nondescript throng of civilians, one or two returning soldiers ... and there she was.

She, too, had caught sight of him at the same moment, and she flew toward him with hands outstretched and face alight with joy. He had forgotten how pretty Cynthia was; and when a pretty woman, whom you have not seen for months and who happens to be your wife, looks at you like that —

"You don't look a bit different. Yes, you do — you are prettier! ... I couldn't get away to meet you in New York." The lie brought him back sharply to his dilemma. *What a cad I am!*

"Orders, I suppose," murmured Cynthia, smiling at him. "You're thin, Alastair. You do look glad to see me. You *are*, aren't you? Am I not to be kissed?" he kissed her.

"You took me by surprise. You looked so pretty and glad to see me." ... It was easy for him to put off the unpleasant future. He smiled at her admiringly.

"You do look so peaked, poor dear. Alastair, you must have had a wretched time."

"Pretty beastly. My nerves went back on me a bit, you know. I haven't really been myself — in a way."

"Never mind, my dear! I'll make you forget all that. You'll see what a good wife I shall be." She tucked his arm in hers and squeezed it. "You know, I've grown up, Alastair. I'm not a child anymore.... But I shan't talk of that yet. You'll see, though.... The baggage man wants my trunk checks."

Alastair's elation lasted until they were in his motor leaving the station. Still bubbling with pleasure, she began to tell him how she had pulled strings to leave England. "The matron was against it. She pointed out that her son at the front could not come back to England rain or shine, life or death, for any reason at all except for a wound; why should it be any different for me? I said it was entirely different for a woman, that a woman's place was beside her husband. Then I went to General Simball. He said he supposed that one VAD more or less made no particular difference. He said (here Cynthia blushed) I could come home if I would promise to raise 'not the devil but a family.' — those were his exact words.... Why are you silent so, Alastair?"

Now surely, if ever, was the time to tell her. But he could not.

Cursing inwardly at his own cowardice and at the hell it opened for him, still he could not get it out. She was so pretty and trusting, and she seemed so fond of him.

She snuggled close to him. "Alastair, I want you to know that I do love you — deeply. Being alone so long and seeing Beatrice's trouble has made me understand myself better. You've been so patient with me. And when I think what a foolish, frightened little soul I must have seemed —" She smiled a little shyly, plucking his sleeve with her fingers. "I want us to have a baby. I'm not afraid anymore — not the least bit. And it will bring us so close to each other that nothing will ever again trouble us that way."

In that moment Alastair knew for certain that he could never tell her.... He would simply have to steal off with Tessa — like a coward.

"Where are we going?" asked Cynthia.

Alastair flushed and spoke a shade too fast. "To your father's, dear. You see, we rough it at the camp, there are no married quarters for officers."

Cynthia said, "Oh!" in a small, deserted tone.

"And you see," went on Alastair eagerly, "I'd feel mean having you stay at the hotel in the village — which is wretched! — by yourself when I could be with you so seldom. And, you see, I have to be at the camp by Retreat almost every night. And besides, it's only twenty miles from the camp to Wellington."

Constraint had risen between them — Cynthia did not know exactly why. They found very little to talk about during the remainder of the ride. They turned onto Galinée Street and came in sight of the Elton house. The car came to a stop with a discordant jerk.

They got out in silence.

Alastair's behaviour during the next week bewildered Cynthia and made her unhappy. The chief thing that troubled her was that he seemed so unlike himself. He would be almost pathetically glad to see her one moment, and the next he would be moping in the depths of dejection. He was only at ease when they were doing something in a crowd; dancing or going to the theatre. She told herself that Alastair had really been shell-shocked — and of course that accounted for everything.... But she was not convinced.

At last she sought out Fanny Burnet and asked her hesitantly if she saw anything strange about Alastair — not just the effect of his wound exactly, though of course, that would be enough to cause *any* moodiness. She explained to Fanny diffidently that she didn't want to worry Alastair by questions when perhaps his nervous condition —"

"Nervous condition, fiddlesticks! Wound, fiddlesticks!" exclaimed practical, downright Fanny. Without mincing words, she told Cynthia exactly what was the matter with Alastair.

"The point is," she added briskly, "are you going to take it lying down like a nice little nonentity, or do you want him back?"

Cynthia looked at Fanny sharply.

"He's only partly to blame. He was just — just weak and foolish. It was partly my fault."

"You do, I see. Well, you're married to him and that gives you one great advantage. Alastair hasn't the moral courage to toss away everything and think it well lost for a woman. He's too fond of thinking well of himself. And for another thing, you're beautiful and you are more than ten years younger than Tessa. That's conclusive.... Why don't you go and see Tessa? She has more character in her little finger than Alastair has in his whole make up. The trouble with Alastair is he is spoilt. Too handsome and charming for his own good. Gilded pup! As for Tessa. Well, the war is bad for women. They want to mix in it too much. I do myself."

Cynthia remembered with a start of surprise a note she had received from Tessa that morning. "She wrote asking me to have tea with her this afternoon. That's odd."

"What's odd about it? She is a lady, you know. Go, by all means."

### iii

"I'm so glad you've come, dear," said Tessa. "We used to be such good friends, and I want to talk to you. Daniel will be so glad to see you, too. He's here from Washington for the weekend, and of course, he simply *had* to go at once to his beloved garden and putter round. He'll be in shortly."

They sat down in the drawing room and the maid brought in tea. They chatted about things that did not matter.

"It's nice," said Tessa at last, "to find that we're still the same friends we were before you went to England. I often think — don't you? — that the war makes people live in an abnormal sort of atmosphere, even people like me who have nothing at stake."

Cynthia suddenly groped for Tessa's hands. "Oh, Tessa, I've been so unhappy!"

"I know, dear. So have I been…. But that's over now…. Yes, you must have been unhappy. Alastair has been, too. He has needed you terribly…. And now you are here, and it will be all right…. Child! Child! Don't. You twist my heart!"

Cynthia stood up and dabbed at her eyes with her handkerchief. She held out her hand. "I'm glad, too, that we are — friends."

Tessa said in an altered tone: "I am so sorry that Daniel and I can see so little of you. You see, I am going back to Washington with him on Monday…. Say goodbye to Alastair for me in case I don't see him before we go."

"But you will see him?"

"If he comes," said Tessa gravely.

"I think he will."

When Cynthia got home, she found Alastair there. She composed her voice and said: "Dear, Tessa wrote me a note; she's going to Washington with Daniel on Monday, and wondered if we would call sometime before she goes."

"To Washington!"

"Why, yes."

"Tessa is?"

"Why are you so strange? Please, let's go. I'm so fond of Tessa."

In the end, they went because Alastair, once having lacked the courage to tell Cynthia the whole truth, could think of no good reason for not going with her.

When they were near Tessa's, Cynthia complained of a sudden, blinding headache.

"Let's go home," said Alastair eagerly.

"I think it would be better," agreed Cynthia. "I simply am not fit to talk to anyone but you. But first, dear, you run into Tessa's and explain to her." He agreed readily. With an ironical expression, she watched him go.

When he found Tessa, she was knitting socks — for his own brother, she said. She bent her head over the task as she might have continued to do in the absence of any casual caller.

He sat down, laid his stick on the floor, and bending toward her, took the knitting from her. "Now, Tessa. Please. What does it mean?"

She folded her hands in her lap and met his look honestly, not pretending to misunderstand.

"It means, Alastair, that I am going back to Washington with Daniel — though he doesn't know it yet." Her lips twisted in the faint beginning of a bitter smile. "It means, my dear, that you and I are going act like decent folk. You will go back to Cynthia because she loves you and is your wife and because you have loved her and will again — presently."

It became easy for Alastair to grow indignant. "But that's just nonsense, Tessa! It doesn't make sense, at all. You talk as if we two were not in love with each other."

Tessa realized, with pain, that she would have to quarrel with him. "Well, have we been — really? I am very fond of you ... in a way. And I always shall be.... But there is something you ought to know, Alastair.... It is going to be difficult to tell you this.... I've been fond of you, and terribly sorry for you, too, but —"

WIND IN THE STUBBLE

"Have you gone mad?" muttered Alastair.

"I don't really love you; not enough, anyway.... I know this will wound you, but it must be said.... What I really want more than what you call love, is — I've wanted a child of my own.... That is the truth, Alastair." She looked at him with stricken eyes. "I have been thinking and thinking about it. My dear, I did not want to wound you, but I shall have to. We would be desperately unhappy together. I am not a child. I am ten years older than you.... Alastair, dear, you'll never forgive me for saying this, but just as I'm not enough of a woman to make us happy, so you are not enough of a man. You wouldn't be sturdy and loyal enough."

Alastair said: "Tessa, please look at me."

She turned to him; her eyes pleaded with him not to make it hard for them.

"Now tell me that what you have just said is true."

She breathed deeply, then said in a whisper: "It is true."

He fumbled for his stick and went away without speaking again. He did not look back, and she watched him go, feeling that he took her youth with him.

Alastair went back to the car, and for the first time in his life, his self-esteem was completely punctured; fury struggled with whipped vanity in his mind, and his feelings were in such a turmoil that he quite forgot to feel heartache. He had not yet reached the cleansing mood of disgust with himself.

He got into the car beside Cynthia and put in the clutch with a rasping of gears that made her shudder.

They drove in silence halfway to Wellington. Once, Cynthia said: "If you drive like that, Alastair, we'll kill someone for certain!" He did not seem to hear her, and she gave it up.

About twenty miles from Wellington, he stopped the car at the side of the road and turned to her. She met his look gravely and he saw that she knew.

"You and I, Cynthia," he said in a taut voice, "is it any use?"

"Do you want it to be, Alastair?"

He put his arm about her and drew her head to his shoulder. "God! What a cad I've been…. And what a blind fool! I do love you, Cynthia. And you are so sweet and good and understanding. I haven't really been myself since this wretched wound…. Yes. That's the truth of it. It made me desperate. And you were so far away."

She sighed. "I'm so weary of it all, Alastair. So very weary."

"I do love him!" she thought fiercely, "I do. I must! … But, dear God, if something could only wound him as he has wounded me!" At the back of her mind was a fear she would not admit to herself. *It should have been Dan.* But Alastair was hers. He needed her. She clung to that thought. And there was good in him. Perhaps in time — with life — there would be strength, too. "I won't look back! Alastair is mine."

He did not dream of what was passing through her mind.

## iv

It was getting too dark to see any longer, and with a sigh of regret, Daniel Thatcher put the garden tools into the wheelbarrow and trundled it into the toolshed underneath the veranda. Then he turned back again into the garden to stroll round it for a last look.

He felt at peace with the world. Tessa, too, he thought, seems to have made her peace with life. She has grown up — that's it.

Looking from her bedroom window, Tessa saw her husband dawdling in his beloved garden, and she smiled to herself a Gioconda smile…. Poor Daniel! He feels so *safe*. I haven't troubled him for so many years now. (And she did feel a little pity for him.)

She felt calm and sure of herself at last; for man, the enemy, is woman's to do what she will with, when finally she has discovered what she really wants. And that discovery Tessa had made. To create life had become a deep, mystical need of her passionate nature, no longer to be denied.

She opened the window and called to her husband: "Daniel, are you going anywhere this evening?"

"To the library for an hour or so. I want to look up a reference," came back his voice.

"When you get back, will you come up to my room for a moment, I've something to show you and tell you."

At ten o'clock she heard him coming upstairs. She slipped on her negligee and sat down, quietly waiting. He came in in high good humour. "I have found just the quotation I wanted. It's been knocking at the back of my mind for weeks. I shall use it with telling effect, with I really think *conclusive* effect, in the final paragraph of the book. The purport of the quotation is that the things which happen to you mean very little in themselves. But everything depends on what you *think* about what happens to you. It's to come in the chapter called 'Managing One's Attitude Toward Life.' ... What did you want to show me, Tessa?"

She paused for a moment to give him time to forget about the book. "I want to go back to Washington with you."

He looked at her in surprise, quite attentive now. "Why, of course, if you want to —"

She went on in the restrained, calm voice of one who has thought out everything that is to be said beforehand: "Daniel, I am at the end of my tether. We seem to mean so little to each other these days. I simply can't stand it any longer."

Her husband looked at her incredulously. The last chapter of his book on "Managing One's Attitude Toward Life" tumbled abruptly into the limbo of wishful thinking. When he had adjusted himself once again to the old, old trouble between them, he pleaded in a panic: "We have talked about that over and over so many times in the past. You know why it is impossible. You know, Tessa, that it would mean your death."

She stood up and said in the same restrained voice — with the calm of an imperturbable force certain of its aim: "Why should a woman be less willing to risk dying to give a life than a soldier is to take one?"

He stammered: "If you should — if — I would never forgive myself."

"It isn't you I'm thinking of this time, Daniel. I am thinking of myself. Why are you so cruel to me?"

"Cruel!"

"All you want of me is that I leave you alone! I can't stand it, I tell you. I don't want to grow old and useless, with no one — nothing."

Daniel remembered, the recollection was too fatally easy, that there was only one thing to do with Tessa when these moods attacked her — to leave her to herself. He turned and began to walk toward the door. But this time she did not allow him to go.

"Daniel, first I have something to show you.... Then you can go — if you wish to."

He turned again.

"Open the bureau drawer. The second. Put your hand underneath the linen.... What do you see? ... Please, bring it to me."

He could not move. The colour had fled from his face, and though he opened his lips, he could not speak at first.

He found his voice at last. "Promise me you will never again think of using — this." He dropped the revolver in his coat pocket.... She knew she had won.

"I promise.... Oh, my dear, I have been so lonely, so utterly miserable. Hold me in your arms, Daniel. Look at me as you used to."

# CHAPTER XV

During the summer of 1918 Dan Thatcher began to feel fatigued and restless. He no longer thought of the war as an adventure; on the contrary, it seemed to him that he had been detached from his roots and borne on to the waves of a very deep and dangerous sea. In the battery all was flux and the familiar faces changed from month to month; Dolughoff, Currie, Alastair, Tripp, and Charles were gone and new lads had come out to fill their places. Only when one looked at these French peasants within shell range, going about their business, just as they had always done, did one feel that, after all, there was something stable in life.

After the battle they had gone into the line again, though they had not yet rejoined the Canadian Corps. They dug gun pits in the midst of fields not yet churned up and fouled with the detritus of war, and near them were unsplintered trees that soon began to show the first green mist of spring foliage. Actually, they had their mess in a little village a stone's throw from the battery, a real village with a real skyline, inhabited by real human beings.

At times Dan again felt acutely that first horror of shedding blood, which a good soldier soon learned to repress since he must inflict with indifference on his fellow men injuries that he could not perform on the bodies of dogs and cats without repugnance. He still had perfect confidence in his physical courage. But something, he could not tell what, had shaken him morally and disturbed the single-mindedness of a soldierly point of view. He was at the guns relaying the order to fire from the battery commander's post. *Number One gun, fire!* came the command, and it suddenly flashed through Dan's mind how he was an instrument of fate. "I give the order to fire. If I give it now, the shell might do nothing. If I wait a second, sheer caprice, I might catch a German gun at the crossroads. I might kill a gunner and never know I'd done it." Possible consequences raying out in all directions occurred to his imagination in a split second of time. For instance, the shock of news of death to a wife causing a miscarriage and a deformed child, who, perhaps growing up unloved in some orphanage becomes a criminal and kills.... "Utterly damn silly train of thought! Unsoldierly! Not the way to look at it. I didn't start the war, and it's either me or X over on the German side of the line; one of us gets the other. I take the same chance as he does." ... As if in answer to his thoughts, a whiz-bang fulminated behind the battery, showering them with dollops of mud and sending a splinter that came whirring over their heads to strike one of the gun trunnions with a sharp *whang.* The men looked at him.

*Number One gun, fire!* A gunner pulled the lanyard and the gun leapt forward and spat, sending outraged air buffeting against their eardrums, then slid coyly back against its buffer. You could follow the flight of the shell through part of its trajectory, a hurtling speck in the clear sky going to do its job, whatever that job might be, at the crossroads.

"That's the stuff to give Old Jerry. Take that you old bastard!" said the sergeant.

Dan touched the splinter of steel lying beside the gun; it was as hot as a flatiron.

If only he did not feel so *tired* ... the tiredness was less in the evenings and he slept fairly well. "The trouble with me," he decided, "is that I have begun to think too much about myself. I can stick it."

ii

Letter from Murdo Burnet to Dan Thatcher:

> My dear Dan,
> You ask me, "as a medical man — not a priest," to tell you what I make of this officer, Dolughoff. I confess it is difficult for me to separate the two professions — they are more closely connected than you think. You tell me of a man who has no home but the inside of his own mind, who has none of the ordinary curbs to his desires, and who has delusions about a message he is divinely inspired to deliver — from what you say of him, I venture to think him insane. What sort of insanity? How can I tell when I have never met him? Paranoia, perhaps. Think of a very prideful man who cannot cope with his shortcomings, and yet one who in his soul cannot bear the burden of them. Such a man may erect some delusion which will account for his sins or, perhaps, merely his failures, which will account for them and relieve him of the responsibility for them. A systematic delusion and a very logical one, if you grant the premise on which it is built, and yet a kind of madness, Dan. A very real madness, poor chap.
>
> To answer your second question: No, I do not think the war made him insane. War does not *create* insanity, it simply brings out what was there before, so physicians believe. A terrible

force, the human soul, Dan. Great and terrible. Sometimes it is like a broken shutter banging in the wind. One cannot say that the soul exists only in the conscious mind. The devil, "evil" if you like, works deep down in us where it cannot be seen or heard. Happily, so does God, call him what you will.

Was Dolughoff a close friend of yours? Why are you so *passionately* concerned about him? After all, the poor fellow is dead. Are *you* all right, my dear boy? The tone of your letter worries me.

Your cousin, Quentin Thatcher, has written to me anxiously for news of you. He says he has not heard from you for many months. He seems extremely fond of you....

"I'm not like poor Dolly," thought Dan. "At any rate, I've never had delusions."

At this time there was a shortage of officers in the battery and the major decided to detail Dan to do all the forward observing over a period of several weeks. This meant that every other day Dan had a tour of duty lasting twenty-four hours as brigade forward observing officer. The Germans, fearing an attack, were jumpy; they pummelled the front line with repeated bursts of hurricane fire, and raided them frequently.

Dan was disgusted and alarmed to find how much he loathed the idea of going up; and each time he had to go to the OP, it became more difficult, as his feeling of tenseness increased. His condition became rapidly worse. His irritability increased and added to the formless anxiety from which he suffered constantly: the fear of revealing his state of mind to other people. This increased his fatigue. Heavy bombardment was rapidly becoming intolerable. "No man can stick it forever," he thought.

Once during a German strafe, he was buried up to the shoulders by a caving trench, and though he suffered no apparent ill effects from this, he noticed that afterwards, any sudden noise, as of a shell bursting made him jump, though without uncontrollable fear. He noticed, too, that the faculty of telling where a shell was going to fall had deserted him: it seemed as if all shells were coming straight upon him. He began to drink in order to keep control of himself. Night was now worse than day; for during the day he still held the whip hand over his thoughts, but at night when he lay down to sleep, processions of images trooped before him in the darkness — scenes of horror he had witnessed during the day: Sergeant Watt lying beheaded at Passchendaele, the infantry officer who liked fishing disembowelled before his eyes. He turned from side to side; the images followed.

Something had short-circuited his imagination, that faculty by which men are brave or cowardly. The war, which for a year and a half had treated him with the inscrutable aloofness of a croupier watching a beginner rake in his winnings, had at last taken notice of him. It had come too close, and he was waging a last ditch struggle from day to day to keep on terms with his self-respect.... Just as disease seems often to attack the strongest bodies, so a malady of the soul, a kind of spiritual exhaustion will often strike at the staunchest spirits, perhaps because they ride themselves hardest. Men with less self-respect will give a little at times and spring back the better for it.

Toward the end of Dan's tour of duty, the front quieted. He got a little normal sleep and felt better. "Not beaten yet," he thought. "When I get back to the battery, I shall be able to take things easy for a bit; then I shall be all right."

But when he got back in the early afternoon, Major D'Arcy met him apologetically. "Sorry, Thatcher, but you will have to go up with Imbrie and me tomorrow. We are to do an observed shoot on a strong point and I shall need you. Better turn in at once and get a good sleep." ... That, Dan felt, was the last straw. If he went up with the major and Imbrie, they would notice the funk he was in. Then it would be all up. The thought of going nauseated him and made him breathe fast. For the last week he had tried to believe that if only he could once conquer himself and endure the bout of duty at the OP, all would be well. Now, lest the horrors should return, he watched himself as a warder watches a prisoner who might kill himself. The horror was always lying in wait for him. Still there. Still to be fought everyday, every hour, every minute.

That afternoon Quentin Thatcher came into the battery and went to Dan's bivvy. He found Dan lying on his bunk with his hands behind his head. By the bed was a little heap of half-consumed cigarette butts, and the air was thick with smoke.

Quentin saluted and said, "Sir —" Dan jumped up and took him by the arm and made him sit on the bunk. "Quentin, how in blazes did you get here?"

"We are out of the line. I knew where you were.... Murdo told me you were blown up."

At the words "blown up," Dan blinked and made a grimace with a quick drawing back of the head (a *tic* which suggested starting back from something unpleasant). "Don't talk of that, Quentin. It makes me sweat."

Quentin's look bored into him. "Your man, Loversedge — he seems very fond of you — thinks you're in a bad way. You look damned ill to me. Why don't you —"

"If you're going to tell me to see the MO," interrupted Dan furiously, "you can damned well go to hell, Quentin!"

"All right, old man, take it easy."

"Need some sleep, that's all. I can't stand people staring at me!" His mind pounced on something to occupy it. "I've got to go up to the OP, but I have two or three hours first. Don't feel like sleeping.... Let's go for a walk, Quentin."

"I'm a private, you're an officer —" began Quentin.

"I don't give a damn what they think! You're my cousin and my best friend. Come on!"

They walked into the ravaged skeleton of a green copse which had been fought over that spring. A railway terminated suddenly; the ends of the rails had been tossed up and twisted. They picked their way over shell holes full of weeds and scummy water, and passed a cross marking the grave of an unknown British soldier with a steel helmet hanging by the chin strap from the arm of the cross. Dan was so absorbed in his thoughts that he seemed to have forgotten the friend he was walking beside. "Must get him to talk," thought Quentin. He spoke about trivial things: musical comedies in London, the place to go for a good meal in Abbeville, the chances of getting leave. Between fits of taciturnity, Dan talked rapidly, as though to outpace his thoughts…. Quentin stole a furtive glance at his friend. Dan's face was drawn, his forehead wrinkled as though from some chronic mental pain. All at once he knew that Dan was desperate. "I can't stick it!" was as plainly to be discerned in his expression as if he had spoken the words aloud. A phrase from the New Testament flashed into Quentin's mind: *Agony and bloody sweat.* The trivial talk with that undertone of strain became suddenly ghastly.

"Thank God I came," Quentin thought, "I've got to make him see the medical officer. But he's obstinate. A proud devil. Always shies off when you want to help him." *But I, Quentin Thatcher, am here beside the only friend in this world I care about, at the moment he most needs a friend. Call it by God's providence. I must help him through, somehow. I've got to!*

They had reached one of the small copses that abound in Picardy, and they pushed into the thick undergrowth clustering about the shattered holes. Presently, they stumbled upon a German soldier who had fallen and been forgotten, perhaps a month or two earlier, during the last counterattack. It was not a pretty sight. The face was swollen and discoloured and vandals had cut off a finger, perhaps in order to steal a ring. Quentin said musingly: "*He* is all right. I don't mind the thought of that. Going back to the earth from which we came. That's nature — simple and natural. No beastliness about it, really." One of Housman's verses came into his mind and he quoted it,

> When shall this slough of sense be cast,
> This dust of thoughts be laid at last,
> The man of flesh and soul be slain
> And the man of bone remain?

That's it!

"When we have lived too long and seen too much, we won't want the immortality of the soul, which can only mean struggle world, without end. We want peace for the soul." ... If he could get Dan to talk of the things that lie deep in the mind. But he would have to bring him round to it obliquely.

Quentin realized suddenly that Dan had not heard a single word. He stopped abruptly, and Dan, feeling the silence, smiled apologetically.

"Sorry, Quentin. I'm afraid I was wool gathering. Must be tired.... What did you say?"

"I was thinking of what poor old Flint used to say. That a man for all his pretensions is merely a machine. No more, no less. Sometimes I think so."

Dan grunted impatiently.

"The sort of half-baked idea a second year medical student would have! Just words! Just theories they get from cutting up frogs in laboratories. A man has a will. He can make himself do things. I mean.... A man might be ... a coward, but there is something in him that doesn't acquiesce in his cowardice."

"Yes," said Quentin, not daring to look at Dan, "but the will is human, isn't it? There comes a time when a man can't go further without help from something outside himself." Quentin hesitated. "From a friend, perhaps.... For instance, a man's body may trick him into — cowardice ... as you say. Only way out for such a man is to forget himself. He can only escape through being needed desperately by some friend." *Dear God, if he would only boil over and tell me. If he'd only talk! Can't he see I understand?*

Dan stiffened resentfully. *He thinks I've gone to pieces....* It was like Quentin to want a friend to come crawling for help. "You can't put your fear in another's hands," he thought. "A man's alone. Has to be. Quentin would be tender and womanish, weaken me." ... He said with sudden brusqueness:

"We're talking a lot of silly rot! Who started it?"

Never in his life had Quentin felt more baffled, more helpless, more futile. During the rest of their walk, they had little to say to each other.

That night at one o'clock, an hour when churchyards are supposed to yawn and a man is least himself, he set off for the front line OP, "all passion spent" for the moment.

The three officers got into the battery light car and drove toward the flares, down a road built first by Julius Caesar. The night was peaceful; not even a machine gun chattered. Dan watched his mind warily.

"If a shell comes.... Mustn't let him see. Damn him! Not that *he* would notice." A single shell addressed to a village far behind, boosted itself through the air above them. Dan, sitting beside the major, hunched himself involuntarily. Major D'Arcy gave him a sharp look. "Coming out of a peaceful night like this, eh? ... Drink?" He proffered his flask.

"No!" cried Dan furiously.... "No, sir. Thanks."

Presently, when they had reached the splintered remains of a small wood, they left the car to enter a communication trench.

"Quite a cheerful place, this," remarked Imbrie. "Trees, I mean to say — some of them still alive, too. I mean to say —"

This was the last sentence that Imbrie ever meant to say in this world.

They heard the boom of howitzers firing and the swelling roar of an express train rushing upon them, and they threw themselves flat at the moment of the shell's arrival. Three shells — *crack, crack, crack*. Spouts of earth rimmed them round and fell over them.

The major got up shakily.

Dazed, Dan saw, as at a long distance, Imbrie, unspeakably mutilated, scrabbling with his hands and trying to scream.

The light car driver came running from the car. Can't do nothing for him, sir. Mr. Imbrie has drawn his full rations."

"Mr. Thatcher! Get him out! For God's sake, man, be quick!"

A shell had disintegrated the earth under the pawn called Daniel Thatcher, and taking him in its blast, had tossed him into a shell hole and hurled dirt on top of him. Incapable of voluntary movement, he lay with dilated pupils, trembling and breathing shallowly. Frantically, they scooped away the dirt with their hands till they got him clear. His face was the colour of dirty paper, and his mouth was open and full of mud. Presently, he came to and began to retch. Still stuporous, he met their looks with frozen panic, unable to separate them from malignant nature.

They went to Imbrie.... But the light car driver was right. There was nothing they could do for him. In his eyes there was a look all soldiers know and remember: despair and dumb revolt. The spirit flickered out of them nakedly, then sank inward and went out.

The major's voice: "Hold up his head while I give him a drink.... How do you feel, lad?"

Dan opened his lips to speak, then gestured instead. At last he managed to speak; each word was a painful achievement. "I-am-all-right.... Am-I-hit?"

"No, no. Not a scratch! Just shaken up. A good rest — a week or two at Paris-Plage and you will be as good as ever."

Some uttermost power of endurance in him, some final resource of the mind foundered at these words and sank into the chaos of fear that pressed upon him from all directions. *Did I want to be wounded?*

"Must get on with the shoot," muttered the major.

Dan gasped for breath. Must act.... Mustn't think. He said, though he knew that the words mocked him: "All-right ... in-minute." To prove that he was, he stood up and tried his legs — he staggered a little but he walked. Then he was sick again.

"No, you don't, my lad!" exclaimed the major harshly. "You will go back to the battery in the car, I shall carry on. And in the morning you'll see the MO. No nonsense! That's an order, my boy. And if he says you are all right, you will go to Paris–Plage officers' rest camp for a bit."

With the driver's help, the major lifted the mortal remains of Imbrie into the backseat of the car.

"Get along as quickly as you can," said the major crisply. "Take Mr. Thatcher to his billet. Then telephone the MO to look him over."

"Very good, sir," said the driver, saluting smartly.

The car went back over the Roman road carrying one living driver, one dead subaltern, and one who, for the moment, was neither one nor the other.... But he was to have a rest, and after a time, he began to feel a little better.

But when he undressed in his billet alone, and lay down, he fainted: the delayed action of the subterranean machinery of terror. Whether he actually lost consciousness or not he could not be certain, but for a few moments the mind stream flowed so madly that he could remember nothing of what he had thought.

Next morning the MO stepped into his billet.

The MO had been friendly with Dan. He was friendly now, too, professionally so.... First he gave Dan a physical examination.

"Now my dear chap, let's have a drink. Take a cigarette and answer some questions. It's necessary for you to be frank."

"I'm all right," said Dan querulously.

"Dare say you are — so far. No doubt what you need, more than anything else, is a rest.... Have you started having nightmares?"

"Yes," said Dan in surprise.

"You wondered how I knew, didn't you? Of course, in the back of your mind you've been thinking you were the only chap in the British Army bothered this way. Thousands of 'em. Sixty percent are quite all right again after a week or two of rest in the casualty clearing station.... These dreams, were they about your duties as an officer?"

"At first, they were. I'd be trying to do some job. Laying a gun platform for instance; and I wouldn't be able to get it down in the right way."

"And then the dreams got — er — more military in character."

Readily enough Dan told him of a dream which came repeatedly now, about being helpless under a barrage. 'It's always about fighting. It isn't distorted like ordinary dreams. Always about real people I'm with in the daytime — and real events I've seen. But ... it's more terrible than those events really are."

"Steady, old man.... Anyway, in your dreams, you've always fought back."

"Yes.... Until the last day or two."

"Good. I've got you in plenty of time.... Did you lose consciousness?"

"No-o. Not exactly."

"Bad headache?"

"A little one behind the eyes — only this morning."

"Any worries — outside the war, I mean?"

"Who hasn't!"

"Quite. Quite. How long have you been out?"

"About a year and a half."

"The salient?"

"Yes."

"Married, Thatcher?"

"No!"

"Don't get shirty. About sex — we're all strange creatures, all of us! Animal after all, you know, only on two legs with — er — a soul, so they say."

"So I've heard," said Dan sarcastically.

"That's what makes the trouble. Never heard of a mule with an anxiety neurosis, did you? ... Got to ask these questions. I've asked lots of people. About sex, have you ever —"

"No, I haven't!" interrupted Dan savagely.

"On leave?"

"No."

The doctor drew a deep breath. "It's always the highly organized person with — er — ideals — the 'thoroughbred' so to speak. Well, lately now. Bother you? — That sort of thing, I mean?"

"No."

"No desire?"

"No. I wish to God you'd finish this."

"Quite normal that you shouldn't — under the circumstances.... Now, as a child, were you shy with people?"

"Not that I can remember."

"Weren't afraid of things like thunderstorms, high places, tunnels, or crowds — anything like that? Don't be upset — it's a stock question."

"No."

"You've a good resistance. Normal sort of chap. Good stuff for a soldier." Suddenly, he shot a question sideways at Dan. "Sorry for the Germans?"

"No — yes. I don't think of that."

"Quite.... Well, my dear fellow, you're lucky. You've got a light shell shock, as they call it. I'll be damned surprised if you aren't quite fit again after a good rest. A week in the hospital, two or three weeks at the rest camps. Come and see me for an examination when you get back. Without fail!"

Dan said, gasping: "It's so ... blasted ... mysterious. With a wound you would know where you're at."

"It's just a wound like any other — a wound of the mind. As a matter of fact, nearly every soldier has it — a little. It isn't a moral problem at all. You're living an abnormal life. Pumping hormones into the bloodstream at a great rate to meet unusual situations. Finally, get an overdose. Of course, it takes different people different ways. But millions of people are being doped that way. Ten million men are going to be restless as hell after the war. Probably won't realize what is wrong with them. There'll be hell to pay. You'll see! Things are going to be started after the war that will take a long time to finish.... You'll get over this very quickly. Completely."

# CHAPTER XVI

i

"Listen," said Lynch, "'The First Army has been ordered to press the enemy back toward the frontier without delay —' What do you think of that, Daniel, my lad? It's to be a hell of a big attack, and we've already won the war — on paper…. Then, here's the plan of operations." He flipped over the sheets of mimeographed orders. "We are supplying the forward observing officer for brigade. Over the top with the best of luck."

"Who is going, Lynch?"

Lynch gave Dan a quick, sidelong look. "Don't know, old man."

He does know, Dan thought. He won't tell me because he thinks I'm touchy.

Lynch and the others had not been at ease since his return to the battery a week ago. They were too cordial, and he could feel them watching him furtively, as if he were different from themselves; now they were the mess and he was "one of our chaps who went into a tailspin." There was a conspiracy, he felt, to keep him from taking his share of sticky jobs. They were waiting to see whether he was sure of himself.

He was not sure of himself. He could not be until he had been under shell fire again.

Each night, rounds of ammunition were dumped by the pits in readiness for the attack. Watches were synchronized by the Heavy Artillery Corps. Reams of information and instruction began to sift down through the various headquarters, gaining mass and momentum with each added series of mimeographed sheets bearing the inevitable phrase "passed on for your information and necessary action." This paper warfare was an earnest of better things to come.

Dan went to the major's billet. "May I see you for a moment, sir?"

"Of course. Smoke? Drink?"

"About the attack, sir. Have you decided what I'm to do?"

"Mmm, yes. As a matter of fact, I was coming to tell you tonight. You see, most of the subalterns are still pretty green. We shall need an experienced officer — er — one who knows the ropes —"

"Yes, sir?"

"To take charge of the rear section. If things go as well as we expect, the guns will be out of range in an hour or two. They will have to be moved up promptly."

Dan lit his pipe, bracing himself to say what, in one respect, he did not want to say. "May I ask you a frank question, sir?"

The major bent to reach for some papers, his face was thus turned away from Dan. "Yes, what is it, Thatcher?"

"Why don't you give me that FOO job, sir? There's no subaltern who has had my experience except Lynch, and he was FOO on March twenty-first. It's my turn, I think."

The major stood up. "Are you sure you are fit?"

"Never better, sir."

"One ought to wear into harness gradually, I think, after — er — after — fact is, the MO says —"

"He's an old woman, sir. Takes your blood pressure one minute, and pi-jaws you about your immortal soul the next!"

The major's look was a vain effort to probe the condition of Dan's nervous system. He said, at last: "Right. If you are sure you are fit. Likely to be a sticky job, you know. Couldn't risk sending a shell-sh — a man who wasn't absolutely fit.... Tell you what, Thatcher. You think it over tonight, and if you should decide that you need to wear into harness — er — more gradually —"

"I shan't change my mind, sir."

But next morning something happened which shook this fine resolution. Mail, which had somehow missed the battery for several days, came up with the ration lorry. On top of a pile of letters for Dan was one postmarked Abbeville, France, written in a strange hand. From curiosity he opened it first, and when he had read it, he no longer remembered the other letters.

> Lieutenant Thatcher, CGA
> Dear Mr. Thatcher,
> I am writing to you in the faint hope that you might be able to help my friend Beatrice Elton, who, like myself, was nursing as a VAD in this hospital. She has a very serious case of the Spanish influenza, and it is doubtful whether she will pull through. The doctors think that if she lives through Wednesday night, she may possibly recover.
>
> I am sending this note, against my better judgment, because Beatrice keeps asking for you. Frankly, though my opinion will mean nothing to you, I cannot help feeling that you have had something to do with her illness. I know nothing about her personal affairs (she is a very reserved girl), but I do know that she has worried herself into a state of mind intolerable for beast or human being over some man. The fact is she does not want to recover. If you can possibly get away, and if it means anything to

you to save a life, then come at once! Ask for me
at the base hospital here.

I am, sir, yours faithfully,
Mary McCreery

Dan had to read the letter twice before its meaning came home
to him. It had been written on Tuesday morning, and this was
Wednesday morning. Beatrice's critical time was tonight, and he
was to "go up the line" for the attack tomorrow. In civil life,
someone sent you a telegram saying, "Death near.... Come at
once," and you dropped everything and came; but there was a war
on, and in the army, they were likely to look at you with a steely
eye and say, "Too bad.... Can't be managed."

He went to Major D'Arcy. "I've just had a letter, sir, about
— my fiancée. She's a VAD in the base hospital at Abbeville. She's
desperately ill with influenza — may not pull through. May I go
there, sir?"

The major looked both relieved and disappointed. "My dear
chap, I'm frightfully sorry to hear it.... I'm afraid it can't be managed. Shorthanded, you know. And this show coming off.... Er
— on thinking over our talk today I've changed my mind. I think
you'd better take the rear section, after all. You're not quite ready
to pull your full weight to the h—"

"My God, sir, I'm not trying to get out of the FOO job. I'm
telling you the truth. And I give you my word of honour, I'll be
back by six o'clock Thursday."

"Right, Thatcher," said the major crisply. "It's my duty to
warn you, though, that if you are not here by six o'clock Thursday
I shall send you up for court martial."

Dan hurried to his billet and snatched his wallet and a haversack. Then he suddenly remembered that Murdo was somewhere
near Abbeville, taking a course of some sort. A stroke of luck.
Hurriedly, he looked up Murdo's address and drafted a telegram
to be sent to him at the first opportunity.

Dan was lucky in getting lorry lifts so that he reached Abbeville at dusk, and went at once to the base hospital. He found it maddeningly official. Here hundreds of people lay between life and death; what time was there for the private affairs of one insignificant individual?

He waylaid a medical officer and told him he wanted to see Beatrice Elton, a VAD in the hospital.

"Who is she?" said the officer beginning to move away. "Never heard of her. What do you want to see her for? "

"She's my fiancée," said Dan angrily. "She has Spanish influenza."

"Then she will not be here. And if she were, you certainly could not see her. Contagious disease."

"Where is she?"

"Can't say…. Sorry, I'm very busy. Ask over there in the office. They won't let you see her, though."

He went to the office. This time he gave his name and asked for Mary McCreery, Beatrice's friend. He sat in the office and waited what seemed an interminable time while typewriters clicked and orderlies came and went with brisk, inhuman efficiency.

Presently, a tall, raw-boned woman with untidy red lair and a masterful manner came into the room, picked him out with a single sharp glance, and strode over to him. "I'm Mary McCreery."

"I'm Daniel Thatcher…. Where is Beatrice, please."

"At the house of some French people where we were lodging. Sit down again; I want to talk to you." Her look appraised him shrewdly. "Now what are you going to do when you see her?"

"Is she conscious?"

"Yes — now."

"I'm going to marry her."

"Oh, you are, are you? … But, my good lad, unfortunately you can't do that. What about a licence? What about the French civil authorities? It's jolly difficult to get married in France."

"My uncle will be there. He's a clergyman, and he's the sort of man you can count on. The marriage may not be legal, but she'll think it is. We'll do it properly later on."

"How do I know whether you will?"

"Look here, I'm a decent chap — what's called a gentleman. That's what you are wondering about, isn't it?"

"Yes. I was.... Well — I daresay you are. Though you've managed to get Beatrice into the devil of a state of mind, my lad.... It might be a good thing." Hers was the easy superiority of dominating women without strong passions.

"Come along, then," she said. "I warn you, she's very weak and she doesn't know her own mind."

They went in a cab to Beatrice's house and there, in the hallway, they found Murdo Burnet waiting for them, impatiently slapping his stick against his puttees.

"Thanks for coming, sir. I knew you wouldn't fail me. You've seen her?"

Murdo nodded. "She's very weak, but she could pull through now, I think — if she wanted to.... What did you really get me here for?

"To marry us, sir."

"Eh! ... Wouldn't be legal for one thing."

"I took out a licence when I was on leave. Anyway, I can fix that up later."

"Well, you seem to know your own mind.... I daresay I am breaking the letter of the law. Still, under the circumstances, why not? Go up, then, and let me know when you want me."

"Excite her a little, young man," said the McCreery VAD, "but, mind you, not too much! She is very weak. And tie this handkerchief over your nose and mouth."

"No, thanks," exclaimed Dan.

"Do as you are told!" ordered Murdo curtly.

So he went up the stairs masked like a bandit, and quietly opened the door of Beatrice's room.

All he could see of her was a dark mass of hair on the pillow. A woman sitting by the window got up and went out. Beatrice turned her head toward him, and two feverish eyes bored into his. "Hello, Dan. I'm not much to look at.... Captain Burnet said you were coming." Her voice was a weak whisper.

He bent down to kiss her, but she would not let him. "It isn't safe. You can hold my hand, though.... I wanted to see you before — before I —"

He said brusquely, "It isn't a question of *that*, Beatrice. Murdo says you can pull through now, if you want to. And you must for my sake because I need you desperately.... Listen carefully to what I'm going to say; I can't talk to you for long because you are very weak. Murdo is downstairs. When I call to him, he will come up and marry us.... No, don't think about it, Beatrice, just trust me and *do* it."

She said nothing for a long time, then whispered: "Why, Dan? I'm not going to live."

"You must because you are needed." He told her about his shell shock and added: "It's hard to talk about it, Beatrice."

Her fingers tightened and she moved her head restlessly. "I am so tired, Dan."

"You must be plucky. People don't just give up and die these days.... You've got into a rut. You've had a dilemma you couldn't solve, and it has made you sick. I'm going to solve it for you."

She began to weep. "Don't bully me, Dan. I feel so weak. So very weak."

He said gently: "You are going to pull through."

She did not answer, but her eyes said no.

This time, instead of arguing, he said simply: "I'm to go over the top tomorrow. Let's get married first. I might not come through, either."

This statement roused her from thoughts of herself, as he had meant it to. She gathered energy to exclaim: "You must not think that, Dan."

"Then I won't think it if you won't."

"Will it make a difference if I live?"

"All the difference in the world, my very dear."

After a moment she whispered: "Dan, will it be difficult for you, going over the top?"

He hesitated, then said frankly: "It nauseates me a little even to think of it.... That's a secret between you and me and the Creator, Beatrice."

Her eyes softened and misted; it was as if some long held tension suddenly had melted there. "I've just been thinking of myself, haven't I? I've been such a coward."

"Everyone is a coward sometimes.... You and I have to help each other, dear. That's our job."

He stole to the head of the stairs and beckoned to Murdo. Murdo came up quietly, and with him came Beatrice's friend and the French woman and her husband. They sat down about the bed, each of them with handkerchiefs tied over their faces, as strange a congregation of human beings as ever defied death through wounds or sickness, by the life-giving ceremony of marriage.

Murdo stood up and, opening the prayer book, began the Form of Solemnization of Matrimony in a low, grave voice. *Dearly beloved, we are gathered together here in the sight of God and in the face of this congregation, to join together this man and this woman in holy matrimony....* The words of the prayer book swept in solemn procession into their hearts. *Not by any to be enterprised, nor taken in hand, unadvisedly, lightly, or wantonly.... First it was ordained for the procreation of children ... for a remedy against sin ... for the mutual society, help, and comfort that the one ought to have of the other, both in prosperity and adversity.*

When they were married, Dan said:

"Now my wife must rest for a bit. You must sleep, Beatrice. I'll be here when you wake up."

"You are so dear!" she whispered. "You will truly be here? You won't go away without waking me?"

"Word of honour, Beatrice."

She sighed and closed her eyes. Then opened them again. "Dan?"

"Yes, dear?"

She put out her hand for his. "Will it be all right? Us, I mean."

"It will be, my very dear. You are mine now, and I am yours. You will feel that more and more."

Beatrice did sleep, and Murdo, more pleased than Dan had ever before seen him, said several times in accession, "I've little doubt of her pulling through now. Hm, yes! All she needed was the will to live. The will to live."

She awoke shortly before dawn and, bewildered by the darkness, called out Dan's name.

"I'm here, dear." He took her hand.

"I feel better."

"You *are* better."

"Dan, when must you go?"

"When you are out of danger."

She was silent a moment, then she said: "Light the lamp, Dan. I want to see you.... Now, dear, you told me you had to go back today."

He groaned.

"Dan, you have helped me. And we are married, aren't we? No secrets. You must let me help you, too."

"The major thinks I'm afraid to go over the top.... And the damnable thing is I'm not sure he is wrong.... I'm not sure of myself, Beatrice. I can't tell for certain until I go."

"Then you must go, Dan. I will get better, I promise.... When, Dan?"

"If I leave now, I can just make the battery in time."

"Then hurry! Hurry! ... Dear Heart, I am wearing your ring. I love you. I'm not a coward any longer."

"Will you promise to have them send me a telegram about you everyday?"

"I promise.... You aren't going to be killed, Dan. I know it for sure. I can't tell you how I know but I do ... and I'm not going to die, either. We shall have a long life together, dear. And we'll make it count for something.... Take my hand and kiss me goodbye on it."

Murdo Burnet was waiting for him downstairs "Well, my boy, I suppose you must go now?"

Dan nodded.

"I don't think you need worry about Beatrice.... You know about the attack tomorrow?"

"Yes, I'm brigade FOO."

"I shall be in it, too. I am going up the line today. If you come through and I don't, remember this from your closest older relation — remember that those who come through the war have their lives loaned to them with a debt to pay. See that you pay it, Dan.... You have turned out better than I thought you would. You parents would be satisfied, I think."

"Thanks, sir.... I've got to hurry."

Dan got back to the battery by lorry. He had had no sleep that night and he would be lucky if he got any tonight. He had a feverish headache, and he realized that he was very tired. "Beatrice will be all right now, thank God!" he told himself over and over.

At the battery he went to his billet to get a little rest. "I feel rotten," he thought; "I wonder if I am getting the influenza?" ... He decided grimly that nothing on earth would induce him to report sick until after this show. "They'd never believe I wasn't scrimshanking."

On his bed lay the packet of letters which he had not opened thirty-six hours ago. The first of these was a cable from Wellington. He opened it with a sinking heart; a cable probably meant bad news. It was from Joanna.

*Tessa died today in childbirth. Please write to Uncle Daniel. The child may live.*

Dan thought of the time years ago in the drawing room at Ardentinny when he had accidentally overheard Tessa and his uncle. "She wanted a baby," he thought; "Daniel didn't. I wonder whether the war had a hand in this."

ii

Quentin Thatcher threw his pack beside Dan's bunk, took off his boots, and lay down hoisting his feet above his stomach and holding them against the plank wall to rest them, as recommended in "Infantry Training." He began to whistle under his breath, watching Dan, who was packing a haversack (Chaucer, a change of socks, a flask, a shirt, extra food) with quiet, satiric eyes.

"Are you going over, too, Dan?"

"I'm brigade forward observing officer."

"Truly? Then, perhaps, we shall meet up the line."

"Smoke?"

"No. But I'll have a drink. Got any?"

"Enough for about two spots. You may not believe me, but it's Napoleon brandy."

Quentin grinned. "It seems there are things in this life I still cling to. Bring it out and I'll be thinking of a good toast."

Dan rummaged in his Wolseley valise for a bottle. "Why are you so beastly cheerful, Quentin? There's still a war on, isn't there?"

"I shall be finished with it by this hour tomorrow, old man. I'm travelling light this time. I've finally chucked overboard a whole packful of useless illusions. I don't care a damn anymore."

"You're a queer chap, Quentin. I never get to the bottom of you. Thank God I'm not a poet."

"Listen, Dan. You know how an expression on a person's face or, perhaps, a fine view that you come on unexpectedly can make you unreasonably happy for time? I've pretty well lost that faculty since France. But today, coming up here, I passed a wheat field ready for harvest. There wasn't a soul about, not a single human being, thank God; and there was that field rustled by a light breeze under a blue sky, just being beautiful and not giving a damn whether anyone saw it or not."

"Yes, but —"

"That was the beauty of it, Dan — its supreme indifference to us. We might never have been — the whole human race — and yet it would still have gone on being beautiful. I got off my bicycle and lay down full-length among the stalks, smelling the earth smell. And it flashed into my mind that this was the first time in all my life — since childhood, anyway — that I'd seen beauty without wanting in some way to possess it and make it part of me.... But how in hell can I make even you understand what I felt? First thing I knew, an officer was shaking me and swearing at me. 'What the blankety-blank are you doing there, my man? Are you hurt or simply befuddled?' I said: 'Neither, sir, merely bemused.' Then he got angry and cursed me some more, and I went on my way rejoicing."

It irritated Dan that he could find no response to this. Quentin always affected him that way. Something intense and exacting about him that froze up one's friendliness. When Quentin said, "I have finally thrown away a lot of useless illusions," Dan felt resentfully that his friend was thrusting, in his ironic way, under Dan's guard. It was like Quentin to say that! His deepest remarks somehow always carried the suggestion that Dan had failed him as a friend. And besides, no one ought to reveal himself as nakedly as Quentin always wanted to. It wasn't decent to.

Dan uncorked the bottle and tilted it, remarking: "It's a shame to drink stuff like this out of a cheap teacup. I suppose that's a sort of symbol of the war.... There's enough for another drink after this."

"Then we'll save that for philosophy, Dan," said Quentin, lifting his cup. "First the personal sentiments, then philosophy. That's the right order, though I didn't find it out till too late.... I drink to your health, Dan. If you come through and I don't, enjoy life for me, will you, old man?"

"Here's to yours, Quentin. And" — Dan stammered slightly, avoiding his friend's eyes — "one can't tell what's going to happen tomorrow ... thanks for being my friend. I'd say more if I knew how to. I can't talk properly about those things."

Quentin answered soberly: "We each gave — what we had in us to give, Dan.... I've been a queer, crabbed, disappointing sort of beggar in the human relations, haven't I? And very exacting; that is what has spoilt things between you and me. Of course, you could always get on with me at times when no one else could. And you could always have got on without me, too."

Dan thought: "There's a hard streak in Quentin. He won't forgive me for not being what he wants me to be. Well, what he says is true, and I can't lie to him about it. And I won't.... Anyway, he would know I was lying."

Quentin said reflectively: "Do you know what first made me want you for a friend?"

"I can hardly remember a time when we weren't friends. I suppose I have taken it too much for granted."

"It was when I realized about Joanna; that you had sickness in your family, as I had in mine, and that you were taking it as I did. I thought in the vague way a boy does: 'We're alike. We'll be friends.'"

"I knew your mother was an invalid. I never quite ventured to ask you about it."

"Do you know about Mary Lamb, the sister of the essayist?"

"Yes."

"My mother was like her.... A thing like that may fix a man's destiny, I think. It stirs him up and gives him a sense of responsibility — young."

"I know.... Hand over your cup, Quentin, there's another drink for each of us."

"Well, this time we'll drink to the finalities."

"Are there any? What are they?"

"Death, old man. And immortality or the lack of it — that sort of thing.... Do you remember once when we were walking together on the campus in Toronto? We passed two freshmen coming from a philosophy lecture; one of them said to the other, 'Do you believe in God?' and the other replied, 'Hell, no!'"

"Yes, I remember. You winked at me and said: 'So that's settled.'"

"I know.... Well, *do* you?"

"Yes, of course."

"There isn't any, 'of course,' about it."

"Yes, I do, then. Do you?"

"And do you believe that Christ died to save men?"

"I don't know. I think I may understand that when I'm wiser."

"I might have been loyal to Christ as a person if I had thought of it — soon enough. Then I wouldn't have been beaten looking for perfection in a mere human being. I know very well that a man has to love someone flesh and blood, not merely an *idea* like God; if he can't, he becomes sick in his mind. Trouble is I can only love those whose souls I see. Mostly, I only see their bodies; I only see that they seem to be all body and nothing much else. I suppose Christ, being closer to God and yet a man, too, like us, always saw a man's soul: what it was and what it might be."

"What about a future life, Quentin?"

"I'm only twenty-two, Dan, but I'm tired. I've seen too much and thought too much and struggled too much. I've seen a lot of horror — yes, and done it, too.... I can't forget.... If I took my personality to another life I'd have to take that, too."

"Why did you come back to France, Quentin?"

"Because I lost my drive."

"But *they* didn't make you?"

"No. It was what was inside me. The machine in us is too strong. Look at you and me, for instance, killing fellow human beings from a sense of duty, like good dependable reaping machines."

"I don't think that's quite the way it is, Quentin."

"You're not like me, though, Dan. You were always obstinately normal."

"I wasn't — after I got blown up."

"Are you all right now, old man?"

"Right enough, I hope. Can't tell for sure until tomorrow.... Nobody is quite the same — do you think? — when he has once looked into himself."

"True enough. So you, too, have seen the clockwork inside you.... What is your idea of the Last Judgment, Dan? Mine is that there will be a machine to sort out souls; large sizes in the heaven-basket on the right, small sizes into the hell-basket on the left. No. It'll be like the army, all smothered in red tape. Your theological credentials will have to be precisely in order; then they'll send you from one understrapper to the next, as they do when you go to find out something in the War Office, all little men dealing with you by rule of thumb.... What's your idea of it, Dan? The scales of Osiris to weigh your soul in the balance against truth?"

Dan thought of Mr. Teti and his mythological hocus-pocus and said, violently: "No! You remember the epitaph to Martin Elginbrod:

'Here lie I, Martin Elginbrod:
Hae mercy o' my soul, Lord God;
As I wad do, were I Lord God,
And ye were Martin Elginbrod.'"

"Yes," said Quentin, frowning at his teacup. "If there were a sort of celestial court martial, it would be interesting to know what has happened there to all those chaps we knew. Jiffy Tripp and Charles Burnet; yes, and the bad hats, too.

"Mind you, Dan. I'm not afraid of death. Not a bit. Being wiped out — *phut*." — Quentin spread his arms in an explosive gesture to indicate a man hit by a shell and disintegrating into nothing — "Being wiped out is the ultimate reality, very likely. Suits me. Only thing I'm afraid of — and hate — is this damned unreality we live in here and now: not knowing what we are, or what we are here for; desiring — and not knowing why we have to; wanting life, more and more life, and getting death; wanting some *law* behind it all of form and style and beauty, and always bumping up in the end against the God-forgotten *machine*." Now Quentin spoke with passion. "Who was it that wrote, 'I see passing on the wall as it were vague shadows and I am afraid'? Don't you feel that? Don't you feel the unreality?"

"No, all of it is too real, Quentin."

Quentin put down his empty cup. "When do you go up the line?"

"I leave the battery at one."

Quentin stood up and worked the straps of his pack over his head. He said to Dan abruptly: "Got to get back to the battalion. Cheeroh, Dan. Perhaps we'll meet again."

Dan put his equipment ready beside his bed and lay down in his clothes for a few hours of sleep. He was over-tired and feverishly wakeful. "If I sleep tonight, I shall dream," he thought with a sinking heart. From "up in front" came the rumble of a trench mortar strafe. Already columns of infantry were marching past the battery toward the assembly line. It nearly always rained before a British attack, and he could hear the rhythmical *slosh-slosh-slosh* of feet through the mud. The marching men did not talk or whistle or sing. Dan's mind, between sleeping and waking, detached itself from the fetters of the five senses and wandered among the potsherds of his soul's experiences. Fevered fatigue and the troubled premonitions of coming battle seemed to lend the scenes and faces and fragments of forgotten conversations, which raised in his mind a significance that just eluded him.

He slept.

To the east the guns swelled suddenly into hysterical volume: merely an episode of the night; some trench raid, perhaps. The threatening sound reverberated through his dreams like the roar of the surf thunder-crashing on wreck-strewn rocks.

# CHAPTER XVII

Trafalgar Square. Distorted. Apocalyptic....

A tall, granite column with stone lions at its base thrusts upward into twilight. Around it a phantasmal throng seethes, and its clamour is the shocking burthen of primal pain. From the base of the column, the lions smite the evening with peal after brazen peal in murderous rhythm like the crashing of the surf against the wreck-strewn rocks.

He, who awake, calls himself Daniel Thatcher, looks because he must and goes closer. At his side walks a figure dim but known: Quentin, his cousin and friend.

The multitude swarms from every quarter; those in the distance move sluggishly, but as they are sucked into the whirling centre of commotion, they race faster and faster until at last they seem fairly to fly. Some fling up their arms in a gesture of horror; some appear and disappear in an instant's flicker with no cry, no gesture; many are in khaki, bearing rifles at the port; some are borne on stretchers; some are blown to bits before his eyes; but all approach and disappear with set faces and urgent eyes that see some inevitable goal to which they speed.

To be alone in this mortal chaos is to know panic. He is beside Quentin, but his friend does not see him and Daniel Thatcher is bereft of speech. He is being rushed against his will toward some dreadful discovery which he is not ready to make ... not ready.

Quentin, too, he can tell, is panic struck. Words tumble without coherence from his lips. "These shadows … like shadows on the wall … and I, too —"

Quentin seizes the arm of one of those drifting past them. The phantasm — shade or man — struggles like a beast and babbles crazily. *Let me go. Let me go. Let me go.*

"Where are we going?"

*Let me go! I must go!*

The phantasm tears itself away and Quentin, glancing down in unbelieving horror, sees himself holding a hand and arm. He throws it from him; it goes flying after the body. He and Daniel run faster and faster down a nightmare street until something bursts inside their minds and they stumble and fall flat.… There is a ringing silence.

They get to their feet in the middle of a street as empty as a rifled tomb.

A distant rumble, as of gunfire, changes into the music of the spheres. A vast erection of clockwork rises before them and ticks somberly. Planets dance about it in ordered rise and fall. With each revolution of the second hand, the planets complete their orbit; and with each revolution an unseen choir chants a metrical foot.… The ticking stops abruptly, the voices cease in mid-beat, the planets are arrested in their orbits. The clock rusts and, presently, disintegrates into debris; the planets dissolve into space.

Quentin, buried beneath the wreckage of life's illusion, struggles to be free. "*Still my terror. Fill the fearful vacancy into which I pour my restless, idle acts, my dead habits, and my unworthy desires.… Give me one true friend. Teach me to win, to bind him to me.…* I would have loved him, but he would not listen. I would have helped him when he needed me, but he repulsed me. If I should call him now, he would not hear me.… Dan!"

Daniel: "Look toward me, Quentin. I am beside you."

Quentin does not hear him.

Heavy footsteps clump toward them. Quentin lifts his head from his hands and eagerly summons the approaching night-hidden figure. "I summon you by the need of one soul for another in no man's land. Speak to me!"

A gigantic form looms up. On his shoulder he carries a rifle. He stops before Quentin and orders arms with a smart rap on the pavement, waiting to be addressed.

Quentin: "Let us be friends. I am Quentin Pilgrim Thatcher. I am lost … and you?"

"I am Zero."

Quentin, suddenly terrified, gabbles: "It seems to me, sir, we might have much in common. Yes. I confess I am not much good at friendship, but considering the unusual circumstances —Yes, a friendship cemented by the unusual circumstances in which we find ourselves —"

"Indeed? … It seems to me, chum, that your wireless sending set is out of order. I get nothing from you but static. You must really excuse me. In a great hurry. Duty to perform … you understand?"

"A duty?"

"I have to kill a Bavarian Jäger in Desire trench, X22d4–I, at precisely —" he looks at his wristwatch "— at precisely twenty hours, four minutes, and point nought one seconds."

"A family man?"

"Can't say I'm sure…. And now with your permission…? These engagements are very exactly timed. One must calculate the effect of the atmospheric pressure on the bullet to a fraction of a second."

"Mr. Zero, who are you? Where are we going?"

"Sorry, I cannot explain. Sorry, I cannot wait. Good day, chum. Good day."

The two cousins slowly climb a flight of steps leading to a colonnaded building, darkly isolated, menacing in its obscure solidity: the War Office. They are not alone. Motor ambulances drive up and stop; blanket-covered stretchers are lifted out from which protrude heavy, nail-studded boots. The stretchers are carried up the stairs and through the door, to disappear into a murky corridor. Quentin hesitates in front of the door. No one pays the least attention to him. He murmurs: "This must be the place. But what am I here for? Whom am I to see? What is it I want to find out? Perhaps it would come to me if I began to write a request on one of their army forms.... Supposing I did not enter ... supposing I went back to the city...." He turns uncertainly. Instantly, the street and the dim buildings on each side of the War Office are swallowed by a void. He turns about again, buttons the collar of his greatcoat as if suddenly chilled, and marches through the entrance. Daniel Thatcher follows.

Inside the door a warrant officer sits at a small desk with stacks of printed forms before him. Soldiers and civilians step up to the desk, fill in the forms, and are led away by messengers into the dark, musty mazes of the building. There is a babel of talk: explanation, confused remonstrance, objurgation. "If this isn't just like the War Office! It chokes you to death with red tape. Last time I was here —" Quentin halts in front of the desk.

The warrant officer, with the air of a patient automaton, hands him a printed form. "Fill in this chit. State the nature of your business as briefly as possible." Over Quentin's shoulder, Dan can read the first few lines. *Army Form XY094/030. Name — Rank — Religious Affiliation —*

Quentin stares at it helplessly.

"Get on with it, my lad!" says the warrant officer briskly. "You are keeping the others waiting."

"But I don't know how to answer it."

"Give me the chit. Now ... name?"

"Quentin Pilgrim Thatcher."

"Rank?"

"Private.... Formerly lieutenant."

"Court-martialled. I see.... Age?"

WIND IN THE STUBBLE

"Twenty-two."

"Twenty-two, what?"

"Twenty-two — sir."

"That's better.... Religion?"

"Don't know, sir."

"No religion," repeats the warrant officer scornfully, writing.

"Oh, no, sir, I shouldn't like to say that. You see —"

"Make up your mind. You either have or you haven't! ... Next question — dead?"

Quentin looks at him uncertainly. "What's the alternative, sir?"

His look is met with a cold, parade stare. "Dead," says the warrant officer in a voice that repulses all argument, and he writes *dead* on the form. "Nature of your business?"

"Well, sir, I hoped *you* would tell me that."

The warrant officer smacks his fist on the table. 'You're wasting my time!" He scans the army form superciliously. "'No religion'; humph! ... Look behind you and you'll see three thousand soldiers of all ranks — field officers some of 'em — civilians, too — waiting their turn. And every one of them knows what he wants and where he belongs. It may not have occurred to you that there's a war on.... And you have the — the sanctified audacity to come *here*! Without knowing where you belong or what you want. Get on with it quickly — or get *out*!"

"I don't belong anywhere, and I don't know where 'out' is. But I want — I want —"

The warrant officer (with ominous patience): "Tell me, then, that is if you know anything at all, *whom* you are looking for."

"That I can answer, sir. Myself."

(Voices from behind. "*Nah then, nah then, sergeant-major!*" ... "*Do we bloody well have to muck arahnd all the muckin' night while this here muckin' ex-orfcer makes up his muckin' mind abaht sweet Fanny Adam?*")

The warrant officer bends over his papers, and Quentin Thatcher, shadowed by Daniel, his friend, fades into the background, slips past the desk, and turns down the first dim corridor that presents itself. "If he can't tell me *that*, then he jolly well doesn't know his job. 'Irregular and improper!' How like the army. Muddle through on red tape, I suppose."

They go down one dim corridor after another, meeting no one. Quentin meditates audibly upon his life. What is he? What does he, the homunculus Quentin Pilgrim Thatcher, "amount to"? Theories of damnation flit across his mind only to be rejected. No hell, he reflects, could be more degrading than that state of ignorance in which, throughout life, we pursue or are pursued by our fates. What has he learnt? And what has he done? He has learnt the futility of mere ideas, which are, he suspects, a mechanical form of cerebral activity fitfully disturbing nature's quiet and empty vacuum merely while heat lasts, presently to be absorbed in the forgetfulness of eternity. And what has he done? He has, with some courage, devoted himself to an idea — but not unto death. Emotion, disturber of reason, which is God's geometry, has thrown him off his course. Failure.... He, Quentin Thatcher, signifies nothing.

"And these three thousand standing in line who 'know their own minds,' what of them? Were they loyal to their theories? Not by a damn sight! Compromisers, every one of them. Lived simply for the sake of being alive.... Why didn't I? Puritan, I suppose. Missed life by trying for it too hard. It would all have been so much simpler without the everlasting 'why'?

"They live in their emotions, every one of them. Talk about love. *Luv!* Sentimental twaddle. Let's have some realism. Love is one-sided. *Un qui baise et un qui tend la joue.* A yearning and a bafflement, whether it's for God or man. I always wanted to be above man's condition. Be myself. *Myself....* Must look into this further."

Quentin, followed by Daniel, comes to the end of a corridor. Two doors face him. Over them is a placard reading: *Quartermaster-General's Department. Service of Love.* On one door is inscribed the word *sacred*, on the other the word *profane*.

Quentin tries the door marked *sacred*. It is locked. He touches the handle of the door marked *profane*, and it flies open. He enters. Daniel follows. On the floor is a rag carpet, threadbare and very dirty. At one side of the room is a four-poster bed with brocaded valances and a counterpane. Louis Quinze chairs are piled on top of the counterpane. From a rat hole, two red eyes peer out at Quentin. He draws his revolver and shoots; the rat scurries away. He touches the counterpane. It is covered with dust. "That seems a pity," Quentin remarks thoughtfully.

Hanging on the wall opposite the open door is a portrait in oils of a woman in eighteenth century costume, and Quentin exclaims: "Why, that is the portrait of Dan's great-great-grandmother, the gipsy queen with the faraway look.... Pray, madam, do not look beyond me. Though, to be sure, I am not your flesh and blood, I have looked at you so often in Daniel's company at Ardentinny in the old days that I almost feel as if I belonged to your family. I should like to ask you a question."

The eyes of the gipsy lady do not alter their remote, intent focus.

"Tell me, madam, what you are gazing at.... Have you escaped?"

She does not speak, but (is it the illusion one has when gazing at a portrait?) her mouth seems to move with the ghost of a mocking smile.

"Perhaps if I, too, look where she is looking I may see what she sees."

He turns his back to the portrait and gazes. He sees nothing but the imperturbable darkness in the corridor beyond the open door.

Quentin leaves the room with a heavy sigh. As he leaves it, he murmurs: "Daniel, if you had been either more of a friend or less, I shouldn't have lost myself."

Daniel speaks: "I did not understand, Quentin." But Quentin does not hear him.

They come to a large blackboard ruled in columns. At the top, written in chalk, are the words: "*The First Army has been ordered to press the enemy back toward the frontier. Zero hour, six o'clock tomorrow.* The following of all ranks will be casualties and will report to this building immediately on death, bringing with them their crime sheets." A long list of names follows, so long and so finely printed that it is difficult to make them out. Paralleling the list are two columns headed: *Died a brave man. Died a coward.* An attendant is making entries on these columns. There are many *braves*, few *cowards*.

Quentin stands before the board and ponders, "Shall I look? No. I shall know by tomorrow ... or perhaps I shan't." Then with a sudden burst of fury: "If *he* knows all this beforehand, why does he permit it? I want to know! ... My eyes are opened. I used to fear emotion, thinking Deity was reason and law. But I was wrong. Life is short and it is valueless. As the generation of leaves, so is the generation of man. Imperturbable darkness closes round our footsteps...."

Two professors in cap and gown pass, arguing. "Nonsense! Man is simply a physico-chemical machine, actuated by the duct-less glands. Bravery, cowardice, faith, despair — these are simply meters to measure chemical secretions in the body." ... "My dear fellow, I do not agree. Man does not merely *suffer* the doom of existing. He masters it by accepting it and by creating within himself an existence which stands against destiny and apart from it by being conscious of it. 'God' is man's co-operation with his destiny." ... "My poor colleague, I am afraid you are merely an unscientific philosopher." ... "And you, my dear fellow, are an unphilosophic scientist."

Quentin: "Drunk with words! Scuttering round in libraries like rats in an oxygen tank! What do *they* know?"

They pass many shut doors from which issue muffled groans and words. Quentin mutters: "This is like a madhouse." ... His step is suddenly frozen to dead stop. "That voice! It is Dan's sister."

Joanna's voice, high, urgent, cuts its way to them, through a shut door. "*Mother, come quickly! Come quickly!*"

Daniel Thatcher and Quentin, his friend, rush to the door, vainly shoulder it, and pound the panels with their fists. "Let me in! Let me in! Let me in!" Beyond the door there is silence.

Quentin mutters in a strained voice: "Must find a way to break into these locked rooms."

An abstracted, gloomy figure passes them, whispering to himself. "The Commander-in-Chief has a message for me. An important message. I can't find him. It was an important message. A message ..." his voice trails off.

Quentin: "I, too, want to see this Commander-in-Chief."

They approach a door, inscribed: *Private Secretary to the Commander-in-Chief. Do not disturb.*

"For twenty-two years I've wanted to see this magnifico." Quentin hurls himself against the door and bursts it open.

Inside the room there is a telephone switchboard. On the switchboard is a printed notice: "Out for lunch. Calls plugged through to warrant officer at the front entrance." On the wall is a photograph of Satan loaded with chains. This figure stirs and comes to life; he addresses Quentin.

"Why have you starved me? I exist. I, too, was created. Do you think I was created simply to be starved!" He strains suddenly against his fetters, shrieking: "Out fiends! Cry war! There is no God."

Quentin: "Someone has got to be responsible for this rotten mess. I am going to see that flunky at the entrance."

Followed by Daniel, he strides purposefully through the murky corridors. The warrant officer looks up impatiently from his printed forms.

"You, again?"

"Yes. Give me that chit." He writes: *To see the Commander-in-Chief concerning certain defects in the cosmos.*

"Well, why didn't you say so before? The C-in-C won't have time for you, but I shall send you to someone who will deal with you.... You realize, young man, what you are in for?"

"You mean — court martial? Hell and all the rest of it?"

"Perhaps."

Some fleeting thought rising from Quentin's soul twists his face with emotion and he tries vainly to speak. At length he says, "They cannot do more than brush me from the face of the world as if I had never existed. Do you think I should mind that?"

Rummaging amongst his papers, the warrant officer brings out a red slip. "It is usual to fill in this report on the Seven Deadly Sins. Pride, envy, gluttony, lechery, avarice, wrath, sloth. They have invented some new sins, but we haven't the forms for them yet.... Which of these —"

"Pride," Quentin interrupts brusquely.

"Pride," the warrant officer repeats, dipping his pen in the inkwell. "Any others? Lechery, for instance?"

Quentin shakes his head. "It is my friend Daniel Thatcher whom you have in mind. Though a gentleman, he is strongly sexed. I should be obliged, sir, if you would give him a hand when he comes this way. He does not understand himself very well."

The warrant officer hands the slip of paper to Quentin. "Take the first turning, then straight on until you find what you are looking for."

They turn into a corridor so dark that they cannot see its walls. Other footsteps, hurrying or dragging back reluctantly, reverberate about them. Daniel hears the sound of his friend's tread; he no longer sees him.

Then Quentin's face becomes suddenly visible, caught in a beam of sunlight streaming through a window. Quentin goes to the window and looks out; Daniel looks over his shoulder. A field of yellow wheat ripe for reaping lies under a blue sky. A breeze winnows it gently and blows clean earth smells to them. Quentin speaks: "The way the breeze runs its fingers over the bending grain as though it were one with it. It is as if I had never really seen it before. I used to lie level with the stalks of wheat and imagine that they were part of me and I of them, and that their sap and mine came from the same hidden root. I did not mind being alone then…. I should like to remember this. Why do we see this when we are children and then forget? Why do we see it and care nothing for it, taking it for granted that it is ours? Why do we leave it and never see it again?"

He breathes deeply, then steeling himself, turns from the window. Once again darkness and the hurrying footsteps receive the two wanderers. They come to a door at the end of the corridor. It swings open before them. They enter.

Seated at one end of a vast room, Daniel Thatcher looks about him; his friend Quentin is no longer beside him. Two sounds break the silence: the noise of hammering and the murmur of subdued talk. There is one bright light from a shaded lamp set on a judge's bench in the middle of the room. A military figure dressed in a uniform with scarlet tabs and the rank ornaments of a major-general sits behind the desk, ruffling papers with his fingers and talking to another officer beside him. Beyond this centre of light, gloom gradually fills in; the corners of the room are in complete darkness. Along three walls there are tiers of pews. Upon these pews lie coffins.

The cause of the hammering now becomes clear to Daniel. Two wheeler-corporals are prising the lids off the coffins. They remove the lids, lift out the bodies, and seat them upright and rigid on the benches. Next to Daniel sits a staring row of these figures with wax-like, expressionless faces. They are all dead.

Horror-stricken, he jerks himself to his feet and stumbles to an empty pew nearer to the light. There, he can overhear the officers seated at the desk. The general speaks….

"Have you the crime sheets there, sergeant? Had one or two unusual cases today. Some rebels, colonel. This man, now…. It's odd how they all want to be *shown*, these days. There used to be a phrase in my youth. Faith is the — the — how does it go?"

Colonel: "'… is the evidence of things not seen,' is what you have in mind, sir. Trouble is, nowadays, most of them have too much evidence of things seen."

"Yes. A great deal of fear in the world, nowadays."

Colonel: "Now, sir, one more matter before we begin.… Er — knowing your opinions, I hesitate to mention it. But coming from the trenches today, I met Satan and he is very upset. He complains that hell is practically empty these days, and he protests about the quality of those war-damned souls who are sent to him. He claims that they are so blasé he can do nothing with them.… I took the liberty of bringing a battalion of demons. They are standing easy outside the courtroom. Also, prison vans and a lorry-load of fetters."

"Is it really necessary?"

"No one has been sent to hell for a long time, sir. Isn't it time we made an example? A little old-fashioned discipline —"

"It's against modern ideas to bully a man into the good life through fear. And besides, there are so few cases of downright, conscious, robust, unmitigated sin, these days. Modern psychological research has shown —"

"Souls are much as they have always been."

"Well, have your demons stand by where they won't be seen.… I think I know a better way. Sergeant, who is first?"

"A civilian, sir. We didn't want to let him in. He insisted he had a right to see you."

The sergeant (in official singsong): "Penuel Thatcher! Penuel Thatcher!"

An old man, stooped, uncertain of his walk, enters, supported by two RAMC orderlies. With eyes downcast, he totters to the bench; there, he straightens himself and, without waiting to be addressed, asks a question. Aged though he has become, his voice rings true in Daniel's memory, and he recognizes his father.

"Are you, sir — Deity?"

The general: "No. God forbid! Mortal like yourself. Created by you in your deepest mind."

"I wish to be judged."

"I do not judge people. I help them to judge themselves."

"Then I demand to be sent to a higher court."

The general glances at his papers. "But you do not believe there is a higher court."

In Pen's expression, profound despair struggles with intellectual triumph. "Then there is no higher court!'

"That is not for me to say.... And now, sir. Who are you? What do you want?"

"I am Penuel Thatcher. I am of puritan stock. I am an upright man who eschewed evil. I want to know —"

"Ah, yes — I remember. You have thought of yourself as the modern Job. You are not without vanity — almost pride. You lack, however, one quality which Job possessed. You do not believe in God and yet you have led an upright life. Exactly. But why?"

"Because it was in me so to do."

"You do not believe in God and yet you wish to be judged. Why?"

"I want an answer to tragedy.... I am an upright man. I have followed the spirit in me. That has not given me happiness. Sir, because of that I have destroyed my family; my wife I gave over to despair and death; my memory is a shame to my children. Did I do well? I demand judgment."

The general, moved, turns to the officer at his right hand. "And you, colonel. What do *you* say?"

The colonel: "He is an upright man — one cannot send him to hell, but — Sir, you have quoted the Book of Job.... Will you, then, curse God?"

From the shadow in the corner of the room, Maud's voice rings out suddenly. "Do not listen to him Penuel.... Sirs, this is my husband whom I understand strangers cannot know his heart, but I know it. He is an upright man. Where he goes I will go. If he is damned, I, too, will be damned."

Penuel: "Though I were perfect, yet would I not know my soul. I would despise my life. This is one thing, therefore I said it. He destroyeth the perfect and the wicked.... If I be wicked, why then labour I in vain? Shew me wherefore thou contendest with me."

The general: "Penuel Thatcher, you have read the signpost and chosen your road. Go down it. For one like you, doubt is a prodding spear ever at your back. Do you regret what it has driven you to? Are you ashamed of what you have done?"

"No, sir."

"You are one who needs a goad to find his task. There is much for you to do. Go in doubt yet a little while."

Like a shadow, Penuel vanishes, without seeing Daniel, without looking back.

The colonel: "I cannot understand a man like that. I prefer old-fashioned saints and old-fashioned sinners. One knows how to deal with them.... I distrust change."

The general: "So do I, unless I plan it."

"At any rate the next man is an old-fashioned sinner. Clearly a case for Satan."

"Who is he?"

"A Russian by the name of Dolughoff. A hater of his fellows, an unrepentant lecher — and worse."

"Send him in, sergeant.... Order there! Who is this? Where are your sentries, sergeant!"

At this moment, the door of the room bursts open with a bang. Through the doorway hurtle two figures in violent motion. The first of these, scarcely more than a boy, is a German soldier; following him — pursuing him with bayonet drawn back to strike, cursing, eyes blazing with bloodlust, is Geoffrey Tripp. "One more shot at the bastards! Christ, let me go!" Through the open door reverberates the distant *rush-wrack-ak* of drumfire.

"Halt!"

The syllable from the general cuts the atmosphere like the crack of a whip. "Seize him, sergeant. Bring him here."

Trip is dragged, shouting and struggling, before the general. The German private, a dropped heap of clothes, cowers with twitching limbs. Tripp's struggles grows less, a sane light comes into his eyes, he relaxes, stands to attention.

"Name?"

"Geoffrey Tripp, sir."

"Well, Tripp. What did you want to kill him for?"

Tripp looks unbelievingly at the huddled human heap. "I — I don't know, sir."

"Look at him more closely, Tripp."

Tripp looks. A circle of dirty red widens out from a tear in the back of the faded, blue-grey tunic.

"Why do you want to kill him twice, Tripp? Do you hate him, then?"

Tripp (in a low voice): "No, sir. Never saw him before today."

"Stand at attention, Tripp! Brace up, man.... Now make your report."

"I died fighting, sir! I am brave — but I was afraid, too."

"Any harm in you, Tripp?"

"Lustful, sir. I can't help it. I love life too much, I suppose. I usually act on impulse. I've stuck to my code, though — I've never let down a friend, violated a virgin, or forgiven an enemy. I treat tarts decently."

The general turns to the colonel. "Put him down in that column. He belongs to the great majority; something likeable about him.... I think you will admit, Tripp, that you are pretty raw stuff."

"Yes, sir."

"A throwback to the beast. We do not blame a tiger for *liking* to kill, or even a dog. But you are a man."

"Yes, sir."

"Give him a little imagination next time, colonel. Give him as much as he can stand at this stage.... Get on with it, Tripp. Don't let me see you in this condition again."

"Very good, sir."

"Sergeant."

"Sir?"

"Send in Dolughoff next."

Dolughoff enters, shuffling with fettered legs. He stands before the general, head thrown back, eyeing him as an equal.

"I've been looking for you everywhere. Kindly tell these stupid fools that you've a message for me. I don't like chains!"

The general looks at him broodingly. "You are charged in the first place with lechery, shameless, degrading, committed with deliberate intent to defile, and without regard for human integrity, either your own or others'.... Step forward, Dolughoff."

The fetters clank. Dolughoff looks round him; the door is closed, armed men surround him, there is no escape. He composes his face to an air of specious frankness, though his eyes slide shiftily from one to the other of the two judges, searching their faces for a hint. "Not guilty. Oh, in the stupid technical sense — yes. But these laws cannot apply to me."

"Here people tell the truth; you know that."

"Sir, I am a proud man. Is it my fault if I was born with fifty scourging devils in my blood? If I was made that way, it was for a purpose."

"You fought these devils?"

"I am a proud man and a man of dignity. Could I bear to be beaten everyday of my life.... I made them mine."

"You are charged with hating people."

"They hated me.... I put them out of my mind. I have had the courage to do what I liked and I have lived like a god; no one has ever had power to touch me.

"You lie, Dolughoff. You are charged with a crime that disproves what you have said. You are charged with a crime known to the Greeks as *lipotaxia*: desertion of one's post in battle. At a moment when your fellow men, in mortal need, were depending on you, you were seen by a fellow officer, one Alastair Thatcher, attempting to shoot your brains out — and prevented. All your life you have been a miserable coward fleeing from yourself, trying to think that you lived like a god and could do whatever you liked, glorying in having no soul — so you thought! — hating people, and yet, in your hidden heart, wanting them to love you. And when at last your true self caught you and you had to face the maggot lying behind the likeness of a man, you tried to escape again — to death, like the coward you are, thinking that by killing the body you could cheat the soul."

Dolughoff's white face works. "I was sick of myself. I wanted to die. I was sick of myself. Sick!"

The general (softly): "Supposing you were told to take up your body and struggle with it."

It is as if the words strike him a physical blow. For a moment he sags and drags down the arms holding him; then he begins to struggle against his fetters, against those holding him, with such despairing agony that Daniel Thatcher, watching, suffers with him.... Shaking one of his arms free, he snatches a revolver from the guard's holster, raises it to his forehead, and fires.

The general's expression does not change, he does not move. "Let go of his arms men.... Ah, yes, Dolughoff, you always thought you could kill your soul with a revolver.... Well, colonel?"

The colonel: "Let Satan have him. He is no use to God or to man."

"That is hardly for us to say. Nor can we, who are mortal, say how much or how little he, an insane man, fought to save his soul.... Remanded for judgment to a higher court. Let him go by himself, men."

Fettered, the irons making a dismal clanking, Dolughoff stumbles blindly toward the door alone. The door opens for him. Gasping and muttering incoherently, he pitches headlong through the opening into the darkness of the unlit firmament.

For a moment no one speaks. Daniel Thatcher, strength drained from him, covers his face with his hands.... The colonel's voice breaks the silence, cloaking his feelings, his fear, with a tone bitterly ironical. "General, let us have someone who is more of a credit to the so-called human race."

"Sergeant, bring in Charles Burnet."

Charles strolls in, looking a little frightened, but determined to put a good face on the inevitable. With courteous dignity: "I trust I am not intruding, sir. I could come some other time."

"Captain Charles Burnet," says the general, referring to his papers. "Rather brave, rather gay, rather kindly, well-meaning, poetic temperament without being creative. Everything about you, sir, seems to be 'rather.' What are you doing here, anyway? No particular complexities to you that I can see. Why did you come to this court?"

"The fact is, I rather thought — well, isn't there usually a judgment, er — a ceremony of some sort? ... Of course, I'm guilty, I expect. I've never been a serious-minded person. Still, I've always been myself, and rather a cheerful soul, too, if I may say so. No real harm in me, I think."

"And a great deal of good, I dare say. It's not my job to judge you, captain. You are a routine case. You should have been handled downstairs. Why did you come here?"

"Well — call it intellectual curiosity, sir."

"You do not yet know enough to have it satisfied. Just how *real* are you, Captain Burnet? Oh, I admit you have a charming presence on the stage, but you are always acting the *beau rôle*, aren't you? And doing it well, too — and that's a good thing, in its way.... In the war you got a trifle more than you bargained for. You got a bit rattled, hurried your lines, and for an instant the audience went blank before you. Then you had an inkling — that is why you are here."

"Perhaps," Charles assents. "You must admit, sir, that I stuck it."

The general agrees politely. "Nothing in life so well became you as your taking off. You have a good sense of exit.... Captain Burnet, you have always had sufficient money, passions that were not tyrannous, and superb health, haven't you?"

"Yes, general, that's true," Charles admits thoughtfully.

"Then, sir, why in the name of common sense — Forgive me for being short with you, but you should not be wasting my time and you know it! But bless my soul, I can't be harsh with you, you are such a charming fellow. And well loved, too, I believe.... Next, sergeant!"

The colonel (reflectively): "It is a strange thing, sir, that all those whom we have seen have come here through fear or because they want something."

The general: "The love of Maud Thatcher for her husband?"

"Unselfish? Perhaps, or was it habit? Who knows? But do none of these moderns love something quite outside themselves?"

The general: "They have five good senses. The sixth is rudimentary, as yet. It is easy to love a human being, or perhaps even an idea; it is difficult to love a spirit.... Is there anyone else, sergeant?"

"A man who wants to be damned, sir."

"An unusual wish, certainly. It suggests an unusual character. Bring him in."

Quentin Pilgrim Thatcher enters, naked. His glance wanders over the officers without surprise or interest. His attitude indicates that there can be no thought or experience which he has not anticipated in his own mind.

"You are Quentin Pilgrim Thatcher?"

"I was, before I discarded all identity."

"Your age?"

"Twenty-two — in years."

"And you wished to be damned? Why?"

"Because I am nothing. Because to be damned is to pass into the nullity of the universe. Whilst we live we must contemplate our futility. That is hell. When we die, mercifully, we cease to be."

The general (ironically): "All this has a very familiar ring.... Thatcher, why do you say you are nothing?

"Seeing clearly the greater loyalty. I turned my back upon it and chose the lesser. I knew that a man such as I was had to fight against the war, not simply because it brought suffering to the world but because it destroyed men's love of life and faith in it. And by putting despair in its place, destroyed their spirits.... I did not persevere unto the end."

"Other men believing as you believed have faltered, and have not been damned for it."

"Mine was not the treachery of Peter but of Judas. Peter was a simple man, a follower, and he knew it; when he denied Christ, he could turn again and plod back over the bitter path. But Judas was a leader, a man of ten talents. He saw the truth and understood it. Judas hanged himself."

"Why did you betray your belief?"

"I stood alone."

"But you were not the only conscientious objector. You were imprisoned with others who thought as you did."

"They were different from me. They had not fought in France. They were not my friends. My friends were in France."

"Go on, Thatcher."

"I could not find in myself the strength to stand alone. I lost my faith in life or in God — call it what you will. This bloodiness and filth and cruelty that I went to, lived in, and left only to think of the more — how could there be a plan working through it? How *can* there be? I tried to pray; I have always thought of prayer as the elevation of the soul to God. I have read of patriarchs in the old days beseeching God for a sign, and in their despair beating their fists against a wall till the blood flowed. I never thought that I, a cold modern, an intellectual, could come to that.... But I did."

The general (gently): "If a man tries to believe and cannot — do you think he is to blame?"

"Yes! Those things which we put into the mind's well we must take out. In the pride of intellect one occupies the mind with doubts about the trivial points of dogma that do not matter. One dwells wilfully in materialism. Through lazy sluggishness one does not lift the soul, and presently, that other world grows dim and fades beyond recall. We *make* our thoughts, and the seeds we plant bear fruit a thousand fold.... *I know....* For Peter this would not bring damnation. But I was gifted."

The general meditates, his hand shading his eyes. Presently, he stirs and is about to speak, but as if dissatisfied with his thought, says nothing. Daniel Thatcher, a spellbound atom full of fear, present at the baring of a soul, attempts to read the thoughts of those sitting behind the bench. Not once before this moment has the general hesitated or changed his expression. Before those others, he has listened as if to old stories, which he knows by heart, that break off in the middle, and to which he can, if he wishes, add a sequel. But now, so it seems to Daniel, the general, too, is suffering with Quentin Thatcher, and in agony he is searching his heart for some pretext to be lenient, to be merciful.

The general (wearily): "What was this lesser loyalty to which you gave yourself?"

"I had cut myself off from those I respected. They were men with whom I had faced death. I went back to them."

The general breathes a deep sigh. Is it of relief? "At least you have not betrayed your loyalty for thirty pieces of silver.... Will any of these friends speak for you?"

There is a long moment of silence, then Quentin answers: "None."

Daniel Thatcher, bereft of strength by his friend's denial of him, pulls himself to his feet and advances, every step a struggle through quicksand, toward the circle of light. There he flings out his arms to bar the path against the guards who are leading away Quentin.

"Wait! You cannot damn my friend unless you damn me, too. He did it for me. How can you damn one of us unless you damn all? He is my friend. He is part of me."

He tries to take Quentin's arm. "Together we will go, my friend and I." With outstretched hands, he clasps, but cannot seize. Like drifting smoke, the phantoms pass over him and beyond him. The general's voice, unheedful of him, swells into prophetic volume.

"Contemplate your failure for a time but not forever. We are instruments of a will; that is our destiny. Out of eternal flux comes everlasting creation. Our reward is to share God's joy in creating. There is no other joy...."

Daniel gazes inward into the deeps of his own being. There, on the inner retina of his mind, he sees an island surrounded by a fathomless sea: a sea unchangeable, continuous, vast, still, and empty as primal chaos.

On the island there is life. Looking down upon it from a great height, it seems no larger than a fragment of floating wreckage, but still, he can make out dark, little manlike creatures, scurrying about with bent backs, casting no shadow. As he hurdles like a star nearer and nearer, the islet becomes larger, and after a time he, too, is standing upon earth amid the hastening figures.

The island is surrounded by a wall made of fresh masonry here, of old and crumbling stones there. Now he can understand why the little men are hurrying so and why they never pause nor look up. They are engaged in a desperate struggle to build a dike against time and the great sea. Whilst they labour, some sing, some pray, and some curse. At times as they work, they crowd one another, for the island is small. Then, raising a spade or a trowel, one will strike another, and in the resulting confusion, the dike begins to crumble; thereupon, they go hastily to their labour again.

Each figure is bound to another. What seems like a cord, bright and transparent as light, stretches from each man to another and from the other to another, still, until all are joined so that they look like insects struggling in a dewy cobweb glistening in the sun. Looking down at himself, Daniel perceives that he, too, has a cord of light which stretches from him to the bent back of a toiling figure.

A group of men throw down their tools and, with their bare hands, begin to struggle one with another, forgetful of the dike.

Water seeps quietly through the wall and trickles onto the dry land. The men still fight, unmindful of their danger. The wall crumbles, the trickle becomes a flood, and that part of the island breaks away and sinks into the void, carrying with it the contending figures. It falls out of sight and out of remembrance except for the quivering cord from the last of the lost men to the nearest of the saved, which spins out like a cobweb stretched by a dropping spider's weight. He to whom the cord is attached does not feel its tug at first, but presently, he turns from his work, sees, and gestures to his comrades who come running to him. Some of them set to work to build a new dike against the flood, but he and those nearest him mount the wall near the breach and peer over it fearfully. They hesitate for a moment, then jump out from the wall and plunge downward. Time passes. A new dike has checked the flood and the builders have long since gone elsewhere. Then at last a ripple glides over the still sea, the ripple become a swell, and the swell a tidal wave that breasts the island wall and hurls its flotsam onto dry land. There they lie, the lost men; and those who have brought them back bend over them as Daniel has seen soldiers stoop over men who have been hit. Beaten, weary, bedraggled, sorely wounded, they have all been cast back by the sea.

Time passes. Everywhere the dike has been made stronger and higher, though many men must still guard it and constantly repair it. But at first singly, and then in greater numbers, men turn from their toil to take leisure. They gather in groups, conversing and arguing. "What shall we create that we may know joy? What is most beautiful? ... Something growing. A fine field of wheat, yellow for reaping, with the sun shining on it and a light breeze winnowing the ears so that they bend and whisper amongst themselves of fruition. And we will make new souls to live and work in that beauty, better men than we are, but part of us."

All this is done and well done. And that mortal among mortals, Daniel Thatcher, bears a part in it.

The inexpressible joy is his of a union secretly desired with longing, though never hoped for, yet strangely inevitable, at long last: this, my hidden despair all these years — that we come to vain dust. The union is the whisper of the truth, not thought but felt, in a flash of conviction as certain as light. What I do unto my friend I do unto myself; for he is myself. The walls of the prison burst asunder and the individual called "Daniel Thatcher" ceases to be, freed and absorbed in spirit which first made the body.

But the heavy inertia that weighs upon his soul rends him from the moment of joy too great for a mortal who has not put on immortality. Horrified, he sees that once again the dike is breached and that a flood sweeps through it onto the field. The cord pulls him to the edge of the wall and he peers over it and sees the white, upturned face of his friend, Quentin, falling from him. Forward or back he must go; he cannot stand still. He leaps forward into the void like a pilot from a burning plane. Downward through revolving circles of space he falls, the emptiness beating about him till he closes his eyes and his mind. Like Satan, he falls from his immortal kinship and becomes Daniel Thatcher, a broken splinter of the one in many. The roar of space drums in his ears and a single word rises to him again and again out of the formless abysm. *Time. Time. Time. It is time.*

"Time. Time to go, sir. It's time, sir."

Dan, half awake, stared blankly at the face of Jobey Loversedge.... This was his billet. He thought: "My God, what a dream —" He had thrown off his blanket, and in his sleep, the collar of his shirt, which he had forgotten to button, had become twisted about his neck like a cord.

"You was muttering and tossing in your sleep, sir. I had a hard time waking you."

Dan shivered. "It's cold. I feel damned ill. Coffee, Jobey!"

"Here, sir. Strong and piping hot.... The signallers are waiting at the cookhouse, sir."

Dan threw his legs over the side of the bunk and took he cup. He rubbed his face with his other hand to bring the blood to the dry skin and considered. The world of the flesh, with its familiar prison walls, closed round him. Through the door of his bivvy he could see the howitzers as dark masses, six great toads, squatting under their camouflage; the limber gunners were removing the breech and muzzle covers while the rest of the gun detachments were busy fusing shells. There was a steady rumbling to the east like shot rolling in a vault. The attack. *I've got to go up.*

What did I dream? Something about Quentin being dead. But there was something that made me happy, too.... It has gone from me. But I can remember the feeling of happiness. Like dreaming your mother was alive, then waking up. A lot of people, I knew: Father, Charles — yes, and Dolughoff. There was a kind of crazy logic to it. Something important, if I could only remember.... They were all dead, I think. It's probably better not to remember. If I recalled it, it would all seem nonsense most likely.... Something that made me happy.

"What time is it, Loversedge?"

"One o'clock, sir. The signallers are waiting at the cookhouse."

"Right. What's it like out?"

"Bit of a do, sir," said Jobey with a wide gesture toward the gun flashes on the horizon. "Our SOS just went up. Jerry's nervous. Thinks something's up, sir. This is the second raid tonight. Looks like we won't catch him with his pants down this time.... Ten minutes ago, sir," he added rhetorically, "it was as silent as a tomb."

Dan stood up, slapped water on his face from a canvas bucket, and put on his equipment: gasbag, Sam Browne with revolver, field glasses, haversack, and helmet. Having thus given himself over to action, he felt better instantly. *There was something about a judgment.... No, they judged themselves. God! What a dream.*

From the doorway he said over his shoulder: "Mind you have a hot bath ready for me when I get back, Jobey."

"That's arranged for, sir. Sir?" "What's on your mind, Jobey?"

"I'm going up with you, sir."

"Why in the devil should you?"

"It's been sort of dull lately for a gipsy lad, sir, and I thought —"

"Out with it, Loversedge! What's your real reason? Been stealing the battery rum ration again?"

"Oh, no, sir. I'm as sober as a dud pipsqueak. It's nothing serious. I needed some nice new boots and it seems I took some as was earmarked for the sergeant-major. 'Major' is popping mad, sir — like a bandolier of cartridges in a bonfire. He's going to have a kit inspection."

"Did you steal them from his kit?"

"No, sir! It was honest scrounging. They was still in the quartermaster stores."

"Oh, all right. Come on, then."

"I got a nice pair for you, too, sir. Shall I put both them pairs in your kit?"

Dan began to laugh. Jobey made him feel decidedly better. "Get the signallers, Jobey."

Coats buttoned up to the throat, bodies thrown forward and swinging to the mind-lulling rhythm of the long trudge over the muddy road, they became five shadows in a swollen river of shadows marching eastward to the line. Searchlights fingered the sky and gun lightnings briefly flashed. Gun teams passed at the trot, lorries slithered by like playful saurian, dispatch riders on motorcycles thrust arrogantly through the spattering mud, leaving a ripple of curses in their wake.

Out of darkness they tramped into the lurid light of a burning cartridge dump at the roadside; darkness waited for them again a few paces farther on. Within the momentary tableau, figures scurried purposefully, too many of them to be taken in as individuals by the inner eye. A detached figure slouched against a pile of lumber, smoking, looking on with a sardonic eye. A field gun, hit, was posed in final disintegration with its snout crazily resting upon a broken wheel.... The men swarming like maggots, the aloof gunner, the broken gun, etched themselves unforgettably on the hovering night. Dan and his men marched on, darkness received them again, and the vignette from a netherworld of fire became what, on waking, one calls a dream. The broken gun? The scurrying men? They are gone; they have no more than an instant's life; passing this place tomorrow, one would not know it, *or* them.

What was it I dreamt? Why did it make me so absurdly happy? Gone from me, all but the feeling.

"Well, Jobey. Are you still a free man?"

"Still free, sir. Oh, I ain't sayin' I don't get scared now and again. But I've got a charmed life. Shells, they won't never touch me. I could sit down and go to sleep in the middle of a barrage, see? And I would not be hit. No, if ever a shell was made with my number on it, it was them shells that was fired at me when I was led up to the limber doing field punishment number one. I won't be hit."

"The time you deserted, Jobey, and then came back."

"Yes, sir. I owed that to my pride. I'm a Romany, see? You can't bind a Romany by tying him to no gun wheel. An' if I'd a wanted to stay away they'd a never caught me."

"Then why did you come back?"

"You know why, sir.... Sir, you've got book learning. You must know about them things. Why do the men stick it, sir? Most of 'em don't like it. Lot's of 'em think it ain't right, even, though that never bothered me."

"I daresay you know why as well as I do."

"I dessay I do, sir.... It ain't that they're afraid of being shot by a firing squad, except one or two, maybe. Everyone's got a chum ... or else he's got someone he looks up to, like. You know what I mean."

"I think I do."

"Funny about you and me, sir. Me a Romany, you a nob. In peace times we wouldn't be walking together in a month o' Sundays. You wouldn't want to and I wouldn't want to. But we meet in peace times, see? An' that's strange enough. Then we land in the same battery again — that ain't chance, sir. Seems like that was meant to be, don't it? It's a funny thing that, when you think into it."

"What about after the war, Jobey?"

"Oh, that! I don't think ahead much, sir. That ain't a gipsy's way. That's where we have it over the *gorgio*; we don't have no dealings with time. Not that the war ain't made a different man of me, though.... O'course, I'll come through. There won't be no shell get me. Nor no bullet neither. I'm nigh sure o' that, too."

They left the road and slithered and floundered down a track. A battery of field guns flashed just behind them *paang-paang-paang* followed by the *wish-wish-wish* of boosted shells. Somewhere in the upright world there was a sound like rending cotton, followed by the twang of a splinter ricocheting against steel. Then *CRASH — CRASH — CRASH.* The intermittent intensity of battle sound, ebbing and then rising like a man's passions, sucked the night silence into a whirling avalanche of sound that beat and burrowed and needled its way into hard-forgotten, swift-remembered crannies of the mind: *Zeeurzeeurzeeur — crashcrashcrash. Zeeurzeeur-crashcrash. Zeercrash, zeercrash, zeercrash, zeercrash.*

"We're for it, now!" he thought; and in the backward of his mind: "O CHRIST ALMIGHTY, let me stick it. Christ let me stick it. Christ —"

Aloud he said: "Keep together, men. Keep in touch."

# CHAPTER XVIII

Thatcher?" inquired the infantry colonel, looking Dan over with a senior officer stare. Good. This is Billings. He'll tell you anything you want to know."

Dan lit his pipe and followed Billings out of battalion headquarters. A watery dawn was thrusting under the night. Mist fumes swirled about dark figures, upright, or still wrapped in groundsheets and jackknifed into cubbyholes dug under the parapets. The guns had gone to sleep again.

"If the mist will only hold for an hour, Thatcher, and give us the luck of the weather for once. This is Desire Avenue. Silly name! I wonder who named it. Down here to the front line. There was a bit of stink last night. The Boche has the wind up. He came over up in front about one o'clock to look us over." "Up in front" had now narrowed down to the front line not more than a hundred yards or so ahead. "They bombed along a sap, but they only got in in one place.... Got in, but didn't get back again," he added grimly.

"Casualties?"

"Sixteen — theirs and ours. There are ours." He nodded toward a recess in the trench where a row of still figures lay on stretchers.

Just ahead of them, Desire Avenue ended in the front line, which was at an angle to it. As they approached, they heard talk from invisible men. "The way the captain talks," said a cheerful voice, "you'd think we was going to have a cakewalk over no man's land. We're to stroll over, see? And we are to have breakfast in that village of Stinkvillers. It's a bad sign, boys, when the captain gets cheerful. Mark my words, we'll breakfast in hell." Another voice whispered, "Eyes front — officer!" and the talk ceased abruptly.

Billings winked at Dan and muttered: "Grousing, grousing, grousing, always bloody well grousing, grousing in the morning, and grousing through the night.... It's a good sign." They went to a Vickers gun emplacement. "Want to look over no man's land? You can't see much in this mist."

No man's land sloped away in front of them down to the dried course of a stream, which was blocked from view by the wall of mist that clung tenaciously to the valley bottom. A thicket of barbed wire floated like wreckage in the mist. "That clump of trees, see it? That's where we are going. On a bit from that there is clean country without trenches — so they say. You go over with the second wave, don't you?"

"Yes."

"I suppose," suggested Billings satirically, "you unroll rabbit wire and hitch your telephone to it and phone through battalion headquarters to the artillery. I understand they practise it ump-teen miles behind the line and it's a great success."

"No, my good chap, we don't, not with such a barrage as we're going to put down for your mob. The line would be cut to ribbons in no time.... We'll signal with Lucas lamps. Runners, too, maybe."

Dan put away his field glasses and let his eyes fall to the fore-ground of no man's land. A familiar sight. Pockmarked, weedy, wire-sown, with here and there a bloated figure, swollen and black, staring with opened mouth and empty eyes — at nothing in particular. Just going back to nature. For seasoned soldiers there was no longer any horror in the sight; it had become simply an accepted part of one's environment, like insanity, slums, and pros-titution in civil life.

"In forty minutes I shall be going over there," thought Dan, and the thought made his heart beat faster. "Once you stand upright for anyone to shoot at, and keep going, you are either free or you are done for," he reflected. The thought of picking one's way through the wire — not too fast, nor too slow, but in orderly fashion — with crumps dropping their seeds and rowing in an instant into black flowers with a heart of fire, and with bullets whipping the stalks of the weeds made him feel naked.

Jobey Loversedge asked: "How soon, sir? ... It's quiet. You wouldn't think we was brewing hell, would you?"

The men had begun to realize the quickening of time toward zero hour and their nerves were tightening. But the cold hand screwing up the nerves in the pit of the stomach changed them outwardly very little; some were apathetic, some made a rapid fire of jokes at which men laughed too easily, some fussed minutely over their equipment. They smoked, worked their rifle bolts to make sure they were not clogged, and drew closer to comradeship, leaping out of fear with the thought that they were all at one — familiar faces, meeting their fate together.... The mist was lifting, the German trench system revealed itself, a loosely interwoven girdle of scars in the weedy landscape, putting forth filaments here and there to touch the British trenches, which not long before had been inside the German front line. On the horizon a dream city appeared with an unshelled church spire and toy fuses: the promised land.

A runner came along the trench distributing watches which had been synchronized at Desire Avenue.

*Thirty minutes.*

Time was a strange thing. "Thirty minutes to go ... *twenty-nine* now." It worked out into seconds; each second flowed separately over the nervous system instead of through the mind where one wanted it to flow.... It seemed to Dan that there ought to be a lot of questions one should finally settle in the last fifteen minutes. "For instance, about that dream — I wish I could remember. I haven't come to terms with my life yet." ... But instead of thinking of things like that, one simply waited, it seemed, and let time flow over one. *Twenty-five minutes.*

Someone was whistling through his teeth a revue song:

> *Après la guerre,*
> *There'll be a good time everywhere....*

"I wonder? I doubt it. We'll never be nearer death, and never so much alive as we are now. People will forget why men were willing to die. They'll think our chaps went West for nothing. It will be a sour, cynical world; take heroes of a different sort to live in it decently, very likely. Not my pigeon, anyhow. Probably won't matter to us ... *twenty minutes....* If I do come through — if I come back to the battlefield in ten years and if I should meet their ghosts outside some caved-in dugout, I'd have become a man they wouldn't recognize. I'd have forgotten how they felt; very likely I shouldn't even understand their talk.... Uncle Charles, now —" The sound of Charles Burnet's ringing voice, with laughter in it ready to well up joyously at any fun. "There's a good joint in Amiens: passable wine, music, sole in truffle sauce. Garçon, lead me to it!" The voice fades.... "We'd never again enjoy binges as we do coming out of the line." *Seventeen minutes.*

"Know what you've got to do, corporal?"

"Yes, sir. I know. Think them Lucas lamps will show through the smoke? There ain't much wind."

*Sixteen....* Barrage in twelve minutes.

Now he felt caught up by the stream of fate and time; a comforting feeling. Why worry? If a shell had your number on it, it got you, the men liked to say, otherwise it didn't.... He felt quite sure of himself. "Maybe Murdo is right; maybe time doesn't change, perhaps it is only we who change, and time is the bank of the stream we flow past. That's a thought that would amuse Quentin. Wonder where he is now?"

Billings came along the trench, grinning at his men, who obviously liked him.

"Billings!"

"Hello. You ready?"

"You don't happen to have a man with the same name as mine in your battalion, do you? I suppose it's hardly likely —"

"Thatcher? That's odd. Yes, he's in my company, too — or was. Any relation?"

"Quentin Thatcher?"

"That's the fellow. Brother?"

"Cousin…. Wounded?"

"Sorry, old man. Killed instantly in the raid last night…. You passed him coming down." Looking at Dan keenly, Billings waved his stick over his shoulder toward the row of stretchers in Desire Avenue. "Want to see him? We've just time to make it, if you do…. he had a notebook of some sort. If you are his cousin, you might take charge of it. You know how it is; one doesn't like to send those things to the next of kin uncensored."

They turned back to Desire Avenue.

"How did it happen, Billings?"

"Are you his friend as well as a cousin?"

"Best friend he had, and he was my best friend…. But you can say what you were going to say. I want to know how it really happened."

"All right, I will. He was a queer chap, was Thatcher. I'd no idea he'd have a best friend, though, of course, that's absurd of me: he was the sort of fellow who kept to himself…. Well, the Jerries bombed into our trench and the first two Germans that turned up were a couple of boys who didn't look more than sixteen — pin feathers on pink chins. The Germans are sending in the children now, you know. They were carrying egg bombs as if they weren't quite sure how to use them, and they looked more like frightened rabbits than soldiers. They came round the traverse upon Thatcher, and of course, he should have shot or bayoneted them forthwith; it would have been easy enough. But instead he yelled at them, 'Hoch die hände' or 'Geben Sie Sich auf' or whatever it is you say in their lingo for 'surrender.' They were much too frightened to understand, and one of the kids threw his bomb and managed to smash Thatcher and himself, too. Then the others came in and there was hell to pay for a couple of minutes."

"That was like Thatcher," said Dan musingly, "he was bayonet shy. He simply couldn't use it, couldn't work his nerves up to the pitch. He had a bellyful during the Somme, you know. He had run out of bombs and had to bayonet a squad of Germans as they filed out of a dugout."

"Well, it was damn bad soldiering, if you ask me. I had nothing against Thatcher before that. He was brave and a good soldier and quite responsible. But if he hadn't been so blasted soft-hearted, I shouldn't have lost him and my platoon sergeant, as well. I think charity ought to begin at home — for soldiers."

Dan said nothing. What was there to say?

"There they are," said Billings nodding toward the squad of stretchers aligned in a neat row in the mud. Groundsheets had been laid over the faces and quiet figures. In death they were still military, stiffly in rows and all exactly alike, even to the pairs of steel-studded ammunition boots projecting from under the rubber sheets. Those boots — without much effort of the imagination one could think of them springing upright and clicking to attention, say, on Judgment Day.

"Shall I take off the sheet?" asked Billings.

"No, let's get on."

Billings slipped his hand under the sheet and drew forth a black notebook from a tunic pocket. "Here it is." Billings looked at his watch. "Ten minutes to go. We'd better be getting back." They left the still row lying "at attention": the only soldiers whom the battle no longer concerned.

Nine minutes to wait. Back in the battery the guns would be loaded by now and laid on their initial targets, and the battery officer would be glancing now and then at his wristwatch. Dan took out Quentin's notebook and opened it idly. It was filled with diary jottings and with verse, some of it finished, some abortive, scrawled in indelible pencil. He turned over the pages. The last entry was dated that very morning, and it broke off in the middle of a word. "Quentin," thought Dan, "must have been writing this when the raid came." He lifted the notebook and peered at the rain-blurred writing.

"*Idea for a sonnet,*" Quentin had written. "*Call it 'The Unwilling Slave.'* The war shows what men once were like — beasts delighting to deal pain and shed blood. But it shows, too, how far we have come, that in peace times we can largely control those primal instincts and push them under at all costs. The devil is still alive, of course, and when he gets loose there's a war. Suggest, then, that 'God' chained that devil in us. No, 'chained' isn't the word. God was in us from the beginning and so was the devil. God is the 'mind' in human nature (conscious and superconscious) that knows where we are going, the devil is the energy, the brute instinct he uses, like a slave, to carry the soul on its shoulders —"

Jobey's voice interrupting. "Now then, pal! Go easy on that stuff! I said, 'take a mouthful,' not, 'take the bleedin' lot.'" Jobey had "half-inched" some rum from the quartermaster-sergeant, which he was sharing with a chance-met infantryman.

"The devil," Dan read on, "shakes the soul loose from his shoulders for a time, but the demon cannot see without the soul to guide him — and knows it. And in the end he always stoops again with his forehead in the dust for the soul to mount him again."

Billings interrupted Dan's reading. The infantry captain, upon reflection, was a little ashamed of his bitterness about one of his own men (after all, the chap was dead); he tried to justify himself to Dan. "It *was* damned bad soldiering, you know. After all, if soldiers started mothering the Boche, where would we be?" There seemed no answer to this question, and Dan made none.

Quentin had written a few more lines. "Try and work in my theory about the Golden Rule in the sestette of the sonnet. Be careful, though; people shy away from religiosity: too softening. I want to hint that if people thought of their neighbours as really part of themselves — same flesh and blood, same sap in them from the same roots — perhaps they would pay some attention to the Golden Rule. End on the theme that all men are *really* broth —"

The sentence broke off abruptly. "That's poor old Quentin to a T. Intense, humourless, soul-splitting puritan — and my very dear friend.… It's odd he should have thought that. There was something about it in my dream. And he must have been writing that down at the very time I was dreaming. I wonder if our thoughts crossed?"

*Six minutes.*

Jobey was humming a hymn tune under his breath. The words, however, which everyone knew very well, were not sacred.

> John Wesley had a little dog,
> He was so very thin,
> He took him to the Gates of Hell
> And threw the bastard in.

Billings leaned against the clay wall of the trench, wristwatch held before his eyes, mentally ticking off the seconds up to the bombardment.

"Here she comes!" he shouted suddenly. "Four minutes, short and sharp, and over we go."

A big gun fired behind them, and in an instant, rushing and roaring sound battened upon the terrain, and the German trenches blossomed in smoke and tumbling dirt. As far north and south as they could see, columns of white and brown and greenish smoke spouted, curled, intertwined into a fluctuating wall through which scarlet fangs of flame darted where shells burst.

The German artillery answered the challenge. Back of the British front line and in front of it, on the parapet, on the parados, coronets of earth shot up and curled over, spattering steel helmets.

The bark of guns, the cough of howitzers, merged into a full-throated, throbbing roar that split the sky in two and held it open. And yet still the sound mounted to a climax. The chaos of noise, the twining of taut nerves, brought nausea to many of the waiting men, the nausea changed to insufferable rage and battle lust, straining to be slaked by the release of power held in tension.

Jobey's voice shouting in his ear: "Makes up for the salient, sir ... blasted shells ... can't get me!"

Quentin.... He liked to quote Homer. "Antilochus, wail thou for me rather than for the dead — for me who live." ... Damn glad I'm alive, though. "*Three minutes.* Here's Quentin thrown on the dustheap for his principles and who's the better for it? ... Maybe not, though.... *Two minutes.* Mustn't guard my groin. What's coming is coming.... If I come through I'll try to see men's souls. *Forty seconds.* God Almighty and Jesus Christ forgive me if I take a life, I'm a different sort of man from Quentin.

*Twenty seconds.* "Fix bayonets! First wave — over we go, men. Keep up close to the barrage." Boots, in toeholds on the front side of the trench, scrambled and hoisted an irregular line of men over the parapet. They went up, over, and disappeared to eyes below the parapet level.... Behind the flickering, rocking line of shell bursts seventy yards in front of them, the line of men advanced, then knelt to wait for the barrage to jump forward, then broke up as men darted into trenches and shell holes to clear out the Germans at bayonet point, then sped on again to the line of the barrage.

"Now us," shouted Dan. "Come on Loversedge, let's see if you're really immortal."

The copse of trees toward which they moved seemed quite near — yet far away. Machine guns chattered steadily through the barrage and the bullets zipped and cracked through the air, making the still weeds at their feet jump suddenly. Shells, bursting round them in such numbers, confused Dan's shell sense. They advanced in short bounds, taking whatever cover there was to take between rushes. A last rush swept them into the wood, bayonets levelled to kill, teeth set and bared, breath whistling, nerves taut and burning with blood lust.

In the wood there were live Germans, some still with fight in them; field grey figures grappling with men in khaki. A wounded German cowered behind a tree, too frightened to put up his hands. Two others knelt with their hands high above their blanched faces. In the melee the wounded German who had not made up his mind got bayoneted. So did the two kneeling figures, since in a scrap where Death was dancing about among panting figures thrusting a bayonet — *in, out* — there was neither time nor inclination for fine distinction of conduct.... The fight was sharp and soon ended.

Gasping for breath, Dan relaxed and glanced about him. His fury died down. He was in a narrow trench just within the boundary of the wood. British infantry were about him. Of his own men, two had fallen somewhere. Jobey stood beside him.

"Well, Loversedge, here we are."

"What did I tell you, sir? Shells never do me no harm."

Lying on the trench bottom a few yards from them is a wounded Bavarian of the Leibregiment who had fallen with a stick bomb clenched in his hand. Stealthily, this man raised himself with one hand; then, holding the bomb under his armpit, he pulled the cord and tossed it at them, willing that they should all go to heaven together. The handle struck Jobey's chest, the bomb bounced back into the mud and stuck there, handle down, sizzling. Moved by some impulse — Dan never knew for certain what it was — Jobey threw himself upon the bomb and covered it with his body.

The bomb exploded with a sharp crack. The German slumped down with a bullet through his brain. The war was over for Jobey Leversedge…. Dan stooped over him. *You won't need your new boots now, Jobey…. You saved my life and lost yours…. You had no dealings with time, Jobey…. All my life I have believed in death, but you saved my life and lost yours. Why did you? Why?*

The Germans had given up the copse and now they turned their guns on it. Dan climbed out of the trench. "Must see about the Lucas lamp." Shells were crashing into the trees, sending splinters of wood and steel flying. A sudden conviction flashed upon him: "I'm going to be hit, Beatrice…."

A splinter needled through the foliage with a whine that dropped half a note in the scale as it came. He heard the whine. Then the splinter hurtled against his helmet; he fell and knew no more of that battle.

Hours later, long after the battle had rolled east, two stretcher bearers found him.

"No use carting him back, corp'ral. He's done for. He's copped a packet. Look at that tin hat."

They removed Dan's shrapnel helmet.

"Done for, my eye! He's copped a nice blighty one, that's what he's copped. That's what them tin hats are for. Here, put him on the stretcher. He'll be all right."

"Listen to him muttering. Something about a pair o' new boots…. I could do with them German field glasses. I know an off'cer who'd give thirty francs for 'em."

"Let him be. It ain't as if he was a stiffie."

"He won't need 'em in blighty. He's out of the war, the lucky lad. Besides, he's one of them muckin' artillery blokes."

"Don't argue the toss with me, my lad! You let him be. I don't hold with that kind of scrounging.

"What about the stiffs?"

"Them? Put them in a line in front o' the parapet. They'll take them back later."

"Hi, corporal! Here's that gipsy I seen this morning while we was waiting to go over. That's a funny thing. He says no shell is ever going to get him, see? ... Look at him now!"

"By the looks of him, no shell did. Looks like he sat down on a bomb.... It's blown off his identification disk."

"Well, if he ain't got a cold meat ticket, they'll bury him Church of England."

"That won't matter to him. Gipsies have no religion.... What's his name, chum? Write it on a bit of paper and stick it in his pocket for the next of kin."

"He didn't tell me. He had some rum, see? And he mucked in with it. Then he told me he was a gipsy and had a charm against shells."

"Name or no name, Church of England or muckin' atheist, it don't matter to him now. Come on, catch ahold here. Up over the parapet. *Heave!*"

## To a Poet Fifty Years Hence

Poet unborn, who ponder bitter rhymes
And turn a frayed and ancient calendar
To curse our shabby modes and worn out times
(Because we sowed the seed of what you are),
We suffered once, like you, and once we wondered,
We looked upon the misshaped Past, and wept;
Then to the Future set our will — and blundered:
We laughed like you and dined in state, then slept.

Think well, the quickening air of every breath
You breathe today is from our sunny sky,
We, too, for glorious moments jeered at death
In self-oblivion for some passerby,
Like you. The way that you must tread, we go —
Uphill and down, I and my living peers,
We, earthy remnants of battered bones, laid low
In green forgetful graves these many years.

*Poet, do you as all men must,*
*Close up the book as I these passions do —*
*These roses, red for blood, that pricked once to the bone,*
*Long since borne down with days and dropping dust:*
*The singing has not made me less alone*
*Nor will it you.*

(From Quentin's Notebook)

# APPENDIX I

"The Pessimistic Novel: Re-Discover the Normal Man"
By Philip Child

*The Canadian Author*
Vol. XV, No. 1
September 1937
Pages 22–23

Philip A. Child, in a paper modestly called "Some Remarks on the Pessimistic Novel," said:

> I shall not rashly attempt to "dispose of" the pessimistic novel, since obviously the sway between the optimistic and the pessimistic mood is too characteristic of the flux of experience not to be the very heart-beat of the novel. According to our temperaments we may view as greatest those writers who feel that life is essentially tragic yet strangely mingled with good, or vice versa. But sheer optimism in a book, or undiluted pessimism we should find strangely flat.

For my part I simply suggest a distinction — not in the least original — between the pessimism that is bracing and fruitful and that, on the other hand, of the spoilt ego-maniac full of gall who "can't take it," as we say, and who gets his revenge on the public.... Purposely I have stated the extreme case.

Since the war, for reasons obvious to us all, the novel has grown more pessimistic. The Edwardian novel was critical, the post-war novel is inclined to be not only critical but skeptical. The change is only partly due to the war. Other elements which everyone is aware of have entered into the picture: the "discovery of the subconscious," the crowding into cities and the rootlessness and instability of city life, universal education and consequent mediocrity of ideals — to name a few. Property is no longer the axiomatic fundamental of society. Virginia Woolf expresses this change with intentional exaggeration. "About December 1910," she writes, "human character changed.... All human relations have shifted — those between masters and servants, husbands and wives, parents and children. And when human relations change there is at the same time a change in religion, conduct, politics and literature."

### Exploring Consciousness

Now I venture to believe it is not human character that has changed, but our view of the significance of human character. Even the proud certainty of science has descended to a theory called "relativity"; and it has been suggested that our doubt of the nature of knowledge itself is more serious than the loss of faith in the supernatural, which marked the nineteenth century.

It is not surprising in these circumstances to find the writer turning from what is known to that which knows — to the individual consciousness; to find him turning inward in his pursuit of reality to explore consciousness with his own mind as the main object as well as the measure of experiment.

That this turning inward has been fruitful, that it has perma-nently enlarged the scope of the novel no sensible person will deny. But the movement has had the defects of its qualities. Too narrow a light, however strong, has been thrown on the single individual atom of humanity. The movement has led too often to the pessimism of myopia. Since the war we have had from gifted persons strange and exciting jungle growths of personality, twisted, titanic Marlowesque — but exotic. Where are the char-acters, Tom, Dick, and Harry, whom we agree to like or dislike at their face value and who make us feel at home in a novel as they do in life?

### Life Under a Microscope

The total impression is somehow distorted. Why? Is it not because here we are seeing life not with normal eyes, but under a micro-scope? And life is not lived with the eye glued to a microscope. As every psychologist knows, the best mental cure for a conscious-ness locked up in introspective pessimism is a turning outward of the eyes of the mind.

Those powerful but star-crossed novels about the war pose in an acute form this pessimistic question (and it is our ques-tion!): "In a world where men hate one another, and where the gods seem to laugh at our puny idealisms out of the mouths of big guns — is a spiritual view of life possible?" That is the ques-tion of the war and in a less acute form of peace time too. These war books pose the question, but with a few exceptions they do not attempt, however desperate the effort, to answer it. To cope with the question, to attempt an answer, however inadequate, has become the social responsibility of the writer.

For many years now it has been a fashionable theory that the novelist's job is to describe life without attempting more than a tacit interpretation of it. Now, I venture to assert that more and more the novelist must become a philosopher: yet always with the proviso that he must somehow or other manage to translate philosophy into fictional terms. And I do not need to remind you that that is the most difficult technical feat of all....

## Find the Normal Man

The modern novelist must rediscover the normal man in the modern world. Who is he? He is the man who manages somehow in spite of everything to live creditably, to preserve his sanity, his humour, and his sense of proportion. He is the good husband and the good father, and he is the man who makes the world go round. He is Mr. Chips (a little sentimentalized: and why not?) and in grimmer mode, he is the hero of Hans Fallada's book *Little Man, What Now?* (there he is the good and normal man under misfortune). And (for of course he belongs to both sexes) he is Mrs. Dalloway in Virginia Woolf's fine novel. He is not the heroes of D. H. Lawrence's novels, who are sex-ridden egotists. Nor is he the hero of Joyce's *Ulysses*, a man whose egotistical pride grows like a cancer on his soul.

For my part, I find one great lack in our contemporary pessimists. What I would suggest is that authors and perhaps the public whom they represent are far too serious about their own little, individual selves, and too little serious about that larger self, of which to be sure we are a part, and which is called humanity.

## Sad Lack of Humour

It is alarming that the most significant modern novels, those which delve deepest, have too little of humour in the broad human sense that Chaucer and Shakespeare and Fielding and Dickens had it.

Now humour is doubtless many things, but whatever else it may be it is a way of looking at life. It contains an element of humility, in the true and not the degrading sense of the word, combined with a sudden flash of understanding that the burden of the universe is not after all on one's own shoulders.

Satire there is in plenty, but, as I see it, satire is wit of the mind, not of the heart. The urge behind satire is dislike of humanity (think of Swift), the urge behind humour is love for one's fellows.

Dickens, the great Victorian humorist, could be angry at a social abuse (and in those days Dickens' anger was a powerful weapon for good), yet at the same time he could laugh at Charles Dickens the individual. The character of David Copperfield, as you all know, is drawn from Dickens himself. And with what gentle humour does Dickens smile at the youthful mistakes, tragedies even, of David. Dickens seems always to be saying: "Yes, as a man, I too have suffered the common lot, — but everything I or you suffer, dear reader, is worth the paying merely to be alive. Around me, after all, is that grand, full, salty world of men and women, in which merely to live, move, and have our being is enough."

I ought not to end on too solemn a note. Let me then repeat a story once told by Sir Gilbert Murray to illustrate the fact that an artist ought to view with a certain objectivity not only his creations but also himself.

The story concerns on the one hand a celebrated teacher of art in a London school who was a witty Frenchman; and on the other, a very young lady who was his pupil and would not do what she was told. In vain did he attempt to drill her in the fundamentals of drawing, she persisted in following her own aberrant notions of what a work of art should be. Finally, in desperation, he told her that unless she obeyed his instructions he would teach her no longer. "But," she objected, "my mother wanted me to draw so that I could express my personality." Her instructor shrugged as only a Frenchman can shrug. "Mademoiselle's personality interests only her mamma."

# APPENDIX II

Philip Child wrote the following war poems in 1924 while he was a lecturer at Trinity College, University of Toronto. These are some of the earliest examples of Child's war writing, and though both were unpublished, Child included them in a handwritten collection of his poems he presented to his parents for Christmas in 1927, titled *Heaven in Hell's Despite: Verses by Philip Child*. This manuscript contains eighteen poems, including "Brother Newt to Brother Fly" and "The Apple," which both appear in *God's Sparrows*.

## Battle Scene

Yonder by broken wire and twisted tree, a
frozen face
Lies quiet as the sleeping stars, and wan
As the scant moon it gazes on.
The hand of night upon the marble brow is
        sweet and cool
And flowing seas of silence steal upon the
spellbound place
The whole world lies, as it were dead within
        an ice-filmed pool.

Here slumber those who rest from torment, and
wake to sorrow;
Sweet rest!  the utter peace unmans the soul.
But now the moon stoops down and bears the
spell away:
Upon the rack another day is bound; -another
day!
Whose turn to lie forever in peace of moon and
stars tomorrow?

(1924)

## An Eight-Inch Howitzer

"Old dodder-shanks, you've reached a sorry pass,
Squat on your muddy haunches, brooding still,
A baleful snout yet poised to hurl a mass
Of hissing iron, at your master's will.
What now old spitting toad, had you a voice
You could unfold of men and war a story choice."

"Be quiet, friend, respect an aged soul
Who lately served you and your kindred well
E'er war, receding, left him in this hold,
Who fired many a round of goodly shell
E'er time, remorseless, trod him under heel,
Rusted his age bore, and stooped his creaking wheel.

"Good friend, respect in me the works of man;
Despise me not, I was his paragon,
The very acme of the sculptor's plan,
Worthy to place beside the Parthenon.
They made cantatas for their souls to sing,
Then forged my thunder — knowing that a worthier thing.

"I helped their 'Evolution,' too, of course,
Destroyed the fit, to let the weak survive;
I was their greatest joke, their *tour de force*,
I served to keep their irony alive.
Some power, too, I had beyond man's will —
By God, my breezy friend, you should have seen me kill."

(1924)

www.ingramcontent.com/pod-product-compliance
Lightning Source LLC
Chambersburg PA
CBHW020421030726
47495CB00006B/1615